BURNING PARADISE

**ROBERT
CHARLES
WILSON**

® TOR

A TOM DOHERTY ASSOCIATES BOOK
NEW YORK

This is a work of fiction. All of the characters, organizations, and events portrayed in this novel are either products of the author's imagination or are used fictitiously.

BURNING PARADISE

Copyright © 2013 by Robert Charles Wilson

Edited by Teresa Nielsen Hayden

A Tor Book
Published by Tom Doherty Associates, LLC
175 Fifth Avenue
New York, NY 10010

www.tor-forge.com

Tor® is a registered trademark of Tom Doherty Associates, LLC.

ISBN 978-0-7653-6917-8

Tor books may be purchased for educational, business, or promotional use. For information on bulk purchases, please contact Macmillan Corporate and Premium Sales Department at 1-800-221-7945, extension 5442, or write specialmarkets@macmillan.com.

First Edition: November 2013
First Mass Market Edition: September 2014

Printed in the United States of America

0 9 8 7 6 5 4 3 2 1

It is natural for the mind to believe and for the will to love; so that, for want of true objects, they must attach themselves to false.

—Blaise Pascal

PART ONE

UNSPEAKABLE TRUTH

Nature is mindless, but it has mastered the art of deception.

—Ethan Iverson,
The Fisherman and the Spider

1

BUFFALO, NEW YORK

Everything that followed might have happened differently—or might not have happened at all—had Cassie been able to sleep that night.

She had tried to sleep, had *wanted* to sleep, had dutifully gone to bed at 11:30, but now it was three hours and some minutes past midnight and her thoughts were running like hamsters in an exercise wheel. She stood up, switched on the light, dressed herself in gray sweat pants and a yellow flannel shirt, and padded barefoot down the chilly parquet floor of the hallway to the kitchen.

Unusually, she was alone in the apartment. Except for Thomas, of course. Thomas was her little brother, twelve years old and soundly asleep in the second bedroom, a negligible presence. Cassie and Thomas lived with their aunt Nerissa, and Cassie still thought of this as Aunt Ris's apartment although it had been her home for almost seven years now. Usually her aunt would have been asleep on the fold-out sofa in the living room, but tonight Aunt Ris was on a date, which meant she might not be back until Saturday afternoon.

Cassie had welcomed the chance to spend some time alone. She was eighteen years old, had graduated from high school last spring, worked days at Lassiter's Department Store three blocks away, and was legally and functionally an adult, but her aunt's protectiveness remained a force to be reckoned with. Aunt Ris had made a completely unnecessary fuss about going out: *You'll be all right?* Yes. *Are you sure?* Of course. *You'll keep a close eye on Thomas?* Yes! Go! Have a good time! Don't worry about us!

The evening had passed quickly and pleasantly. There was no television in the apartment, but she had played records after dinner. Bach's *Well-Tempered Clavier* had the useful effect of making Thomas drowsy even as it rang in Cassie's head like the tolling of a divine bell, echoing even after Thomas was in bed and the house was eerily quiet. Then she had turned off most of the lights except for the lamp on the living-room end table and had huddled on the sofa with a bowl of popcorn and a book until she was tired enough to turn in.

So why was she prowling around now like a nervous cat? Cassie opened the refrigerator door. Nothing inside seemed appetizing. The linoleum floor was cold under her feet. She should have put on slippers.

She scooted a kitchen chair next to the window and sat down, resting her elbows on the dusty sill. The corpses of six summer flies lay interred behind the sash-tied cotton blind. "Disgusting," Cassie said quietly. November had been windy and cold, and wisps of late-autumn air slipped through the single-pane window like probing fingers.

The window overlooked Liberty Street. Aunt Ris's apartment occupied the floor above a store that sold and repaired secondhand furniture, in a two-story brick building like every other building on the block. The next-door neighbors were a Chinese restaurant on the north side and a grubby antique shop on the south. From where she sat Cassie could see the wide glass display windows of the Groceteria and a half dozen other businesses on the north side of Liberty, all the way to Pippin Street and Antioch Avenue. Not much traffic this time of night, but the after-hours clubs in the entertainment district were just closing. On other sleepless Fridays—Cassie was a restless sleeper at the best of times—she had watched cars rolling through red lights in drunken oblivion, had heard drivers gunning their engines in mad displays of masculine enthusiasm. But just now the street was silent and empty. Of pedestrians there were none.

Or, she corrected herself, no. There was *one* pedestrian: a man standing alone in the mouth of the narrow alley that separated the Groceteria from Tuck's Used Books.

Cassie hadn't seen him at first because of the Armistice Day banners strapped to the high standards of the streetlights. The city had put up the banners a couple of days ago. There was a parade every year to mark the 1914 Armistice, but this year the city (the state, the nation, the world in general) was making a big deal out of the centenary: one hundred years of peace. Relative peace. Approximate peace.

Cassie had always loved Armistice Day. Next to Christmas, it was her favorite holiday. She still remembered her parents taking her to watch the parade back in Boston—remembered the sidewalk vendors who sold roasted chestnuts in twists of paper, the Floats of the Nations populated by schoolchildren in implausibly colorful ethnic dress, the battling cacophonies of high-school marching bands. The violent death of her mother and father had taught Cassie things about the world that would never be acknowledged in any Armistice Day parade, but she still felt the bittersweet tug of those times.

The Centennial banner flapped in a brisk wind, alternately revealing and concealing the man in the shadows. Now that Cassie had seen him she couldn't look away. He was a drab man, an ordinary man, probably a businessman, dressed for the season in a gray coat down to his knees and with a fedora on his head, but what unsettled Cassie was the impression that *he had been looking up at her*—that he had turned his head away the moment she had seen him.

Well, but why not? At this hour, hers might be the only lighted window on the block. Why shouldn't it catch his eye? It was only deeply ingrained habit that made her suspicious. Aunt Ris and the other local survivors of the Correspondence Society had trained

Cassie in their secret protocols, of which the first rule was the simplest: *Beware the attention of strangers.*

The solitary stranger was no longer looking at her window, but his attention still seemed fixed on the building where she lived. His gaze was flat and unwavering and on closer inspection subtly lunatic. Cassie felt a knot tighten in her stomach. This *would* happen on a night when Aunt Ris was out. Not that anything had really *happened,* but it would have been nice to have a second opinion to call on. Should she really be worried about a lone man standing in the windy street after midnight? It was a calculation difficult to make when she was too conscious of the empty rooms around her and the shadows they contained.

These thoughts were so absorbing that she was startled when the wind lifted the Armistice Day banner once more and she saw that the man had moved. He had taken a few steps out of the alley and across the sidewalk; he was standing at the edge of Liberty Street now, the toes of his brown shoes poised where the curb met the gutter. His face was upturned once again, and although Cassie couldn't see his eyes she imagined she felt the pressure of their attention as he scanned the building. She ducked away from the window, crossed the kitchen floor and switched off the overhead light. Now *she* could watch *him* from the shadows.

During the time it took her to return to her chair by the window he had moved only slightly, one foot on the sidewalk, one foot in the street. What next? Was he armed? Would he cross the street, come inside the building, knock on the door of the apartment, try to break it down if she refused to let him in? If so, Cassie knew what to do: grab Thomas and leave by the fire escape. Once she was sure she wasn't being followed she would hurry to the home of the nearest Society member . . . even though the nearest Society member was the disagreeable Leo Beck, who lived in a cheap apartment five blocks closer to the lake.

But the man seemed to hesitate again. Would a killer hesitate? Of course, she had no real reason to believe he was a murderer or a simulacrum. There had been no violence since the flurry of killings seven years ago. Probably the man was just a drunk disappointed by a luckless night at the bars, or maybe an insomniac with a mind as restless as her own. His interest in the building where she lived might be only an optical illusion; he could have been staring at his own sad reflection in the window of Pike Brothers Furniture Restoration and Sales.

He took another step into the street just as a car turned the corner from Pippin onto Liberty. The car was a dark-colored sedan, blue or black, she couldn't tell which under the uncertain light of the streetlamps. The driver gunned the engine crazily and the car fishtailed as it took the corner. Cassie supposed the driver must be drunk.

But the solitary stranger didn't seem to notice. He began to stride across the street as if he had suddenly made up his mind, while the car sped on heedlessly. Cassie looked from the vehicle to the pedestrian, calculating the obvious trajectory but not quite believing it. Surely the car would swerve at the last minute? Or the stranger would turn and leap out of the way?

But neither of these things happened.

The Armistice Day banner flapped twice in the November wind. Cassie pressed her forehead against the chill glass of the window. Her hands gripped the fly-littered sill, and she watched with sick anticipation as the collision evolved from possibility to inevitability to sickening fact.

The car's fender took the pedestrian at knee level. He dropped and rolled under the grille as if he had been inhaled by it. For one awful moment he simply vanished. All Cassie could see—resisting an almost overpowering urge to close her eyes—was the double bounce of the car's suspension as its wheels passed over him. She heard the shrilling of the brakes. The car swerved sidelong before it came to a stop. White smoke billowed from the exhaust pipe and swirled away in the wind. The driver turned off the engine, and silence was briefly restored to Liberty Street.

The pedestrian wasn't just hurt—he was dying, was probably already dead. Cassie forced herself to look. His neck was broken, his head skewed so that he seemed to be staring at his own left shoulder. His chest had been crushed and split. Only his legs seemed completely intact—a perfectly good pair of legs, Cassie thought madly.

The car door swung open and the driver lurched out. The driver was a young man in a disheveled suit. His collar was open and he wore no tie. He leaned on the hood of the car to steady himself. He shook his head twice. He looked at the remains of the pedestrian, then looked away as if from a blinding light. The Armistice banner (CELEBRATING A CENTURY OF PEACE) flapped above him with a popping sound that made Cassie think of gunfire. The driver opened his mouth as if to speak. Then he doubled over and delivered the contents of his stomach onto the asphalt of Liberty Street.

The dead man had made a far bigger mess. There was a lot of blood. Blood everywhere. But not *just* blood. Something else had come out of him—a syrupy green fluid that steamed in the night air.

Cassie stood silent and rigid, the events she had witnessed doubling in her mind with a memory of other deaths, far away, years ago.

Because she had to be sure—because there must be no mistake this time—she threw a jacket over her flannel shirt and hurried down the stairs that led from Aunt Ris's apartment to the small tiled lobby and the street door.

She opened the door just a crack. She dared not leave the building while Thomas was asleep. She just needed to be sure she had seen what she thought she had seen.

Cold air rushed past her. The popping of the Armistice banner was angry and random. The driver sat on the hood of his car, sobbing. Lights had begun to wink on in upper-story apartments all along the street. Faces like pale or occulted moons appeared at windows. The police would be here before long, Cassie supposed.

She put her head out far enough to get a good look at the corpse of the pedestrian.

One of the last monographs circulated by the Correspondence Society—it had been written after the killings—had been *Notes on the Physical Anatomy of a Simulacrum*. The author was Werner Beck, the wealthy father of Leo Beck. Of course Cassie hadn't read it at the time, but last winter she had found a copy among Aunt Ris's keepsakes and had studied it carefully. She could recite parts of it from memory. *The lungs, heart, and digestive system, along with the skeleton and musculature, comprise the simulacrum's only identifiable internal organs. Those organs are contained in an amorphous green matrix, covered in turn by layers of adipose tissue and human skin. The rudimentary circulatory system produces less bleeding with traumatic injury, and it is not obvious that even massive blood loss would be immediately fatal to a simulacrum. The undifferentiated green matter suffuses much of the chest and abdominal cavity as well as most of the interior of the skull. It evaporates on exposure to air, leaving a pliant green film of desiccated cells.*

Werner Beck had written that, and he would know: he had wounded one of the things in his home with a shotgun, then had retained the presence of mind to attempt a dissection.

The mess in the street was consistent with his description, and Cassie tried to look at it with the same soldierly dispassion. Blood, but not as much as you might expect. Yellowish fatty tissue. And the green "matrix," which was everywhere. Cassie could smell it. She had a fleeting memory of her mother, who had cultivated roses every summer and occasionally recruited Cassie in her garden work. At the age of eight Cassie had spent one endless afternoon pinching aphids and thrips from the leaves and stems of Alba roses, until her hands were coated with an aromatic grime of chlorophyll, garden loam, leafy matter and insect parts. The smell had lingered on her hands for hours even after she washed them with soap and water.

That was what the dead pedestrian smelled like.

Mrs. Theodorus, who lived over a shoe store on the opposite side of the street, emerged onto the sidewalk wearing a pink nighty and fuzzy white slippers. She seemed about to scold the weeping driver for disturbing her sleep, but stopped when she came within sight of the corpse. She stared at it for a long moment. Then she put her hand to her mouth, stifling a scream.

Above all these sounds—Mrs. Theodorus's scream, the driver's sobs, the popping banner—Cassie heard the distant howl of a police siren, louder by the second.

Time to leave, she thought. She was surprisingly calm. It was a mechanical calm, as exact as algebra, beneath which Cassie felt panic gliding like a shark in a sunny estuary. But she couldn't afford the luxury of panic. Her life was at stake. Hers, and Thomas's.

In a crisis always assume the worst, Aunt Ris had taught her, and Cassie tried to do that, which meant she had to believe that another general attack was underway. And this time no one associated with the Society would be spared. If not for a fortunate accident, the simulacrum who was currently spread across Liberty Street like a sloppy green-and-red compote would have come to the apartment and killed Cassie and Thomas. Aunt Ris might already be dead, a possibility Cassie refused to dwell on for more than a moment. At best, Aunt Ris would come home to an empty apartment and the discovery that her life had changed yet again, irrevocably and for the worse.

I could wait for her, Cassie reasoned. A Friday night date meant her aunt probably wouldn't be back before Saturday noon, but she might show up sooner than that. And it *might* be safe to wait, given that the sim who had come for her was dead. A few hours wouldn't make much difference, would it?

Maybe not . . . but Cassie had been trained for this moment since the death of her parents, not least by Aunt Ris herself, and she couldn't bring herself to break protocol. *Pack, warn and run,* that was the rule. Packing was simple. Like her aunt, like her little brother, Cassie kept a fully-loaded suitcase in her bedroom at all times. She hurried there now and yanked the suitcase from under the bed. It had been inspected and repacked just last month, to make sure she hadn't outgrown any of the clothes in it. Cassie put the case on the bed and quickly dressed herself, keeping in mind that it was cold outside and winter was coming. She double-layered two shirts and covered them with an old woolen sweater. She caught a glimpse of herself in the vanity mirror—pale, lumpy and terrified, but who cared how she looked?

Aunt Ris had left a number where she could be reached in an emergency—and this was surely an emergency—but Cassie didn't even consider calling it. That was another rule: *no telephone calls.* Under the circumstances, anything important had to be said face-to-face or not at all. Even an innocuous call from this number would be a red flag to the entity they called the hypercolony. Out there in the darkness, mindless but meticulously attentive, it would hear. And it would act.

She could leave a note, of course, but even then she would have to be careful what she said.

She took her knapsack from the closet in the hallway and filled it with simple food from the kitchen cupboard: a half-dozen trail-mix bars, apple juice in single-serving boxes, a foil bag of mixed nuts and raisins. On impulse she grabbed a book from the shelf in the hallway and tucked it into a side pocket. It was a book her uncle had written: *The Fisherman and the Spider,* a tattered paperback edition Cassie had read twice before.

Time was passing. She strapped her watch to her wrist and saw that almost twenty minutes had slipped by since the death of the sim. The police were in the street now. Whirling red lights blinked through the window blinds. She guessed the police officers would be bewildered by the corpse of the victim—as much of it as hadn't already evaporated into the night air. And the city coroner, tasked with analyzing the remains, might end up questioning his own sanity. But no report would be published in the morning papers. The sobbing, drunken driver would never come to trial. That was a foregone conclusion.

Cassie took a pen and a sheet of paper into the kitchen and controlled the trembling of her hand long enough to write,

> *Aunt Ris,*
> *Gotta run—you know why.*
> *Just wanted to say thanks (for everything).*
> *I will take good care of Thomas.*
> *Love to you always,*
> *Cassie*

It would have been dangerous to say more, and her aunt would understand the shorthand—"gotta run" was their personal Code Red. But it wasn't enough, it wasn't *nearly* enough. How could it be? For seven years Aunt Ris had looked after Cassie and Thomas with kindness, patience and—well, if not love, at least something *like* love. It was Aunt Ris who had calmed Cassie's night terrors after the death of her parents, Aunt Ris who had gently introduced her to the truth about the Correspondence Society. And if she had been a little more protective than Cassie would have liked, Aunt Ris had also helped her strike a balance between the world as it appeared and the world as it really was—between the world as Cassie had loved it and the world she had come to dread.

"Thanks" was hardly adequate. She hesitated, wanting to say more. But if she tried to do so she would have to fight back tears, and that wasn't helpful right now. So she taped the note, unaltered and inelegant as it was, to the refrigerator door, and forced her attention to the necessities of the moment.

Finally, she tiptoed into Thomas's room and woke him with a hand on his shoulder.

She envied her younger brother's aptitude for sleep. Thomas slept deeply, silently and reliably. His small bedroom was tidy at the moment. Thomas's toys sat neatly on a wooden shelf, his clothes hung freshly-laundered in the closet. Thomas himself lay on his back with the comforter up to his chin, as if he hadn't moved since Cassie tucked him in a few hours ago. Maybe he hadn't. Twelve years old, but his face had kept its childhood roundness; his blond hair, even in disarray, made him look like a fat angel in yellow jammies. He woke as if he were returning to his body after a long absence. "Cassie," he croaked, blinking at her. "What's wrong?"

She told him to get dressed and get his suitcase from under the bed. They had to leave, she said. Now.

Dazed as he was, the implication wasn't lost on him. "Aunt Ris—" he began.

"She's not home. We have to leave without her."

She hated the anxiety that surged from his eyes and felt reproached by it. She wanted to say, *It's not my fault! Don't blame me—I don't have a choice!*

Worse, perhaps, was the look of frightened resignation that followed. Thomas was too young to remember much about the murder of their parents. But what he did remember, he remembered with his body as much as his mind. He sat up and steadied himself with a hand on the edge of the mattress. "Where are we going?"

"To see Leo Beck. After that—we'll figure it out. Now get dressed. Hurry! You know the drill. And dress warm, okay?"

He nodded and stood up straight, like a soldier at reveille. The sight of him made her want to cry.

* * *

The high window at the end of the hallway opened onto a wooden fire escape bolted to the building's sooty brickwork. The stairs descended into the alley behind the building, which meant that Cassie and Thomas, climbing down, would be invisible to the police, who in any case were probably too busy sorting out the events on Liberty Street to worry about what was happening in a vacant back lane.

As she raised the window Cassie caught a reflection of herself in the dusty glass. A young woman, dowdy in an oversized sweater, wary eyes peering out from under a black woolen watch cap—mouth too big, eyebrows too darkly generous, unattractive in what Cassie considered the *best* sense: she would never be stared at for her looks, which suited her fine.

In high school she had been considered not just odd-looking but personally odd. She had heard boys calling her "dead fish" behind her back. And it was true that she had become expert at concealing her feelings. That was part of what it meant to be a Society kid. There were truths you could never acknowledge, feelings that had to stay hidden. So it was okay to be a dead fish, to stand outside the hallway alliances and weekend social circles, to be looked at sidelong as you walked from class to class. Even to be sneered at, if you couldn't avoid it. Her slightly geeky looks were helpful in that respect, a useful barrier between herself and others. She knew how to fly under the radar: never volunteer an answer, never expect or demand real friendship, do your work well but not conspicuously well.

In the presence of other Society offspring she could let her hair down a little. But she had never really enjoyed the company of that crowd, either. Society brats tended to be gnarly, cliquish, complexly screwed-up. Herself most certainly included.

She bit her lip and took a deep breath. Then she clambered over the low sill onto the wooden stairs, lifted out her suitcase and Thomas's, and helped Thomas climb out behind her. The weather-worn wooden platform lurched under their combined weight. The alley below was a brick-lined asphalt corridor, empty of everything but a solitary Dumpster and the fitful November wind. That suited her, too.

She tried not to think about what she was leaving behind. When they reached ground level she gripped Thomas's hand in hers (*"Ow,"* he said) and led him through the alley to the corner where it opened onto Pippin Street. Then she turned left, heading for the home of the disagreeable Leo Beck and a future she was afraid even to imagine.

2

Early in the morning, not long after the first sunlight touched the barren branches of the maple trees and began to burn the skin of frost out of the shadows, a man approached Ethan Iverson's farmhouse. The man was alone and walked slowly, which meant Ethan had plenty of warning.

Ethan watched the stranger's progress on a video screen in the attic room in which he kept his typewriter, his Correspondence Society files and a small arsenal of firearms. He had been in the kitchen when the alarm sounded, preparing his standard breakfast of eggs and ham fried in an iron skillet. Now the meal was going cold on the stovetop downstairs, the eggs congealing in grease.

Ethan had lived alone in the farmhouse for seven years—seven years and three months now. Entire weeks passed when he spoke to no one but the checkout girl at Kierson's Grocery and the counter clerk at Back Pages Books, his two inevitable stops whenever he drove into Jacobstown for supplies. One useful device by which a solitary man could keep touch with sanity, he had discovered, was a regular schedule, strictly obeyed. Every night he set his alarm clock for seven o'clock, every morning he showered and dressed and finished breakfast by eight, regardless of the day of the week or the season of the year. Just as meticulously, he was careful to maintain and keep in good repair the array of motion detectors and video cameras he had installed on the property not long after he moved in.

For seven years, that system had registered nothing but a few stray hunters and mushroom pickers, a religious pamphleteer who believed God had granted him an exemption from the many and conspicuous NO TRESPASSING signs on the property, one determined census taker, and on two occasions a member of the family of black bears that lived beyond the western boundary of Ethan's property. Every time the alarm sounded Ethan had hurried up to this attic room, where he could see the intruder on his video monitor and evaluate the possible threat. Every time— until now—the intruder had proved to be essentially harmless.

He switched the monitor to a new camera as the man walked up the unpaved access road toward the house at a steady pace. The man Ethan saw on the monitor seemed surpassingly ordinary, though a little out of place. He was probably not older than twenty-five, overweight, dressed like a city dweller in a drab overcoat and black shoes that had surrendered their shine to the moist clay of the road. From his looks he could have been a real-estate agent, come to ask whether Ethan had considered putting the property up for sale. But Ethan was fairly sure the guy wasn't even human.

Of course, the man's physical appearance meant nothing. (Unless the very blandness of him could be construed as a strategic choice.) What tipped Ethan off—what was, perhaps, *meant* to tip Ethan off—was the way the stranger gazed at each camera lens as he passed it, as if he knew he was being observed and didn't care, as if he wanted Ethan to know he was coming.

As the man approached the thousand-yard mark, Ethan considered his choice of weapons.

He kept a small armory up here. Mostly hunting rifles, since those could be acquired easily and legally, but including a couple of military-style handguns. In the rack by the window he kept a fully-loaded Remington moose rifle with a German scope, and he had trained himself in its use well enough that he could easily pick off the invader at this distance with a single shot from the attic's small window. The peculiar anatomy of the simulacra made them less susceptible to injury than human beings, of course, but they were far from invulnerable. A well-placed head shot would do the trick.

Ethan thought about that. It would be the simplest way to handle the situation. Pick off the invader, then pack a bag and leave. Because if the hypercolony had located him, it would be suicidal to stay. If he killed one sim, more would come.

. . . *if he was sure this man was a sim.* Was he sure?

Well, his instinct was pretty strong. If he had to bet, he'd have put money on it. But he couldn't trust a man's life to instinct.

He eyed the long gun wistfully but let it be. Instead he picked out a shotgun and a device that looked like a stocky pistol but was built to deliver 300 kilovolts from a pair of copper prongs. His research had led him to believe the latter would be an effective short-range weapon against a simulacrum but probably not lethal to a human being. He had not, however, tested this theory.

He watched the monitor a moment longer, trying to shake off his fear. He had known this day might come. He had planned for it; it had played out in his imagination a thousand times. So why were his hands shaking? But the answer was so obvious he didn't have to frame it. His hands were shaking because, despite all the precautions he had taken, despite his superior firepower and his carefully calculated avenues of escape, what was approaching the house might be one of the creatures who had already taken the lives of too many of Ethan's friends and family— a thing neither human nor self-aware, as casually lethal as a bolt of lightning.

He tucked the shock pistol into his belt and made

sure the shotgun was loaded. He put a pair of extra shells in his shirt pocket. He felt a sudden urge to empty his bladder, but there wasn't time.

Death came up the creaking porch stair and politely rang the doorbell. Ethan went down to answer.

The green-on-the-inside men (and women: Ethan reminded himself that some of them were women) had already cost him his marriage and his career. They had achieved that remarkable feat over the course of a single day in 2007.

On that day Ethan had been a tenured professor at the University of Massachusetts Amherst campus, author of several well-received journal papers and a couple of reasonably successful popular-science books, an asset to his department and an active researcher who could command a cadre of undergraduate students. His specialty was entomology but lately his research had taken him into the field of paleobotany, the study of ancient plant life; he had joined a team of researchers who were isolating airborne spores from ten-thousand-year-old Antarctic ice cores. He was also engaged in a more clandestine sort of research—the kind that interested the Correspondence Society.

The members of the Correspondence Society were scientists and scholars, but they never published their findings in peer-reviewed journals. The Society was known only to itself, and its members were sworn to secrecy. As a grad student Ethan had been introduced to the Society by his mentor at MIT, a man whose mind and ethics Ethan had admired without reserve. Even so, Ethan had been skeptical at first. The Society had sounded like something eccentric and deeply old-fashioned, a survival of some Edwardian dons' club that had once flourished in the cloisters of Oxford or Cambridge. He would have dismissed it as a joke—a frankly *preposterous* joke—if not for the names associated with it. Mathematicians, physicists, anthropologists, many with impressive pedigrees, and the roster of the dead was even more impressive, if true: Dirac, von Neumann, Fermi . . .

He had been warned of the risks he would be running if he agreed to ally himself with the group. The rules were stringent. Members could communicate about Society business only by mail or face-to-face. People who spoke about the Society too publically faced reprisals, not from the Society itself but from sources unknown. If he said the wrong thing to the wrong person Ethan might begin to find his research proposals rejected without cause, might fall out of favor with academic and peer review committees, might lose tenure. He understood these risks, and once he joined the Society he had been scrupulously careful. But no one had warned him that he might be killed. That his family might be put at risk of their lives.

Ethan had survived the massacre of June 2007 purely by accident. He had been recruited as a last-minute delegate to the annual ESA Conference, and he was at Logan Airport waiting for a flight to Phoenix when the first reports flashed across the TV in the boarding-area lounge. His attention was drawn by the photographs alternating on the screen—chillingly, all of them people he knew. Benson at Yale, Kammerov at Cornell, Neiderman at Edinburgh, Linde at Saint Petersburg. And more, a dozen in all. The caption under the newscast said UNIVER-SITY MURDERS. Ethan moved closer to the screen, already sick with dread; the volume was turned low, but he heard enough of the newscaster's murmuring to confirm his fears. *There is no conclusive evidence linking the various murders which took place on three continents this Wednesday, but it seems more than coincidental that so many well-known academics and scholars should die violently in such a short period of time . . . Local authorities are cooperating with the police arm of the League of Nations to determine whether the deaths are part of a larger pattern . . .*

The news must just have made the wire services. The Asian and European killings had happened overnight; the American murders were only hours old. And Ethan didn't need the help of the League of Nations to recognize "a larger pattern." All of the named victims had been members of the Correspondence Society.

He found a pay phone and placed a call to his office in Amherst. The Society had taught him to distrust telephones—even local calls were routinely bounced through the radiosphere, part of the global telecom radio-relay system—but he hoped a quick call wouldn't attract undue attention. The business-class boarding announcement for his Phoenix flight came while he was dialing; he ignored it.

Amy Winslow, Ethan's office assistant, answered after three rings. "Professor Iverson! Are you okay?"

He kept his voice carefully neutral and told her he was fine. Before he could say anything more, she asked whether he was in Phoenix yet or whether he could come right back to the office. It was terrible, she said. Tommy Chopra had been shot! Shot and killed! A janitor found him dead! The police were everywhere, talking to people, collecting evidence!

Ethan couldn't disguise his shock. Tommy Chopra was one of his grad students. Tommy was an early riser and a compulsive perfectionist; Ethan had given him a key to his office and Tommy was often there before sunrise, compiling data while the rest of the campus was just flickering to life. According to Amy, he had been shot and killed sometime before seven this morning. No one had seen his assailant.

But it wasn't Tommy they meant to kill. It was me.

"Can you come back and talk to the police?"

"Of course. In the meantime, call the conference and tell them I had to cancel. The number's in the literature on my desk. I'll be right in."

It was a deliberate lie. Ethan didn't mean to go anywhere near his office, not that day or ever again.

Instead he drove for two hours directly to the South Amherst apartment where Nerissa had been staying during their "trial separation," as she liked to call their rehearsal for divorce. He had agreed not to drop in unannounced, but circumstances overruled that polite agreement. He understood very little about what happened to the Society, but his next move was obvious. He needed to tell her what had happened, why this might be the last time she would see him, and what she had to do next.

The green-on-the-inside man stood patiently on the porch. Ethan, inside, watched the man's image on a monitor mounted above the door and connected to the video camera hidden in the porch rafters. He tried not to wince when, again, the man looked directly into the camera lens.

If this *was* a simulacrum, it was running some new kind of strategy, since it didn't appear to be armed and hadn't tried to disguise its approach. Ethan figured that made it more dangerous, not less.

The camera hookup included a microphone and speaker. *Never engage a sim in conversation* was one of the rules Ethan had written for himself, based on his and Werner Beck's theories about the way the hypercolony functioned. But what was the alternative? Throw open the door and put a load of buckshot into the face of someone who might, just *might*, be an innocent civilian?

He keyed the microphone and said, "Whatever you're selling, I'm not interested. This is private property. Please leave."

"Hello, Dr. Iverson." The sim's voice was calm and reedy, with an upstate New York accent. "I know who you are, and you know what I am. But I'm not here to hurt you. We have a common interest. May I explain?"

There was no mind in back of those words, Ethan reminded himself. Nothing but a series of highly-evolved algorithms aimed at achieving a strategic result. Engaging in dialogue with such a creature was no more useful than trying to fend off a scorpion by quoting Voltaire. Still, Ethan was curious in spite of himself. "Are you carrying a weapon?"

The simulacrum gave the camera an ingratiating smile. "No, sir, I am not."

"You care to prove that? You can start by taking off your hat and coat."

The simulacrum nodded and removed its hat. The sim had brown hair and a bald spot at the crown of its head. It shrugged off its jacket, folded it and placed it alongside the hat on a sun-faded Adirondack chair.

"Now your shirt and pants," Ethan said.

"Really, Dr. Iverson?"

He didn't answer. The silence lengthened, until the simulacrum began unbuttoning its shirt. Shirt and pants joined hat and coat, revealing the sim's pale, potbellied, impeccably human-seeming body. "Shoes and socks, too," Ethan said.

"It's chilly out here, Professor."

But the creature cooperated. Which left it standing in nothing but a pair of white briefs. *A monster in its underwear,* Ethan thought.

"Now may I come in and speak to you?"

Ethan threw open the door, leaving only the wire screen between himself and the green-on-the-inside man. Ethan leveled his short-barrel shotgun at the creature's chest. The sim focused its attention on the gun. "Please don't shoot me," it said.

"What do you want?"

"A few minutes of your time. I want to explain something."

"How about you give me the short version right now?"

"You and some other members of the Correspondence Society are in real and immediate danger. That's not a threat. I'm not your enemy. We have mutual interests."

"Why should I believe any of that?"

"I can explain. Whether you believe me is up to you. May I come in?"

Ethan kept the gun leveled and pulled open the screen door with one hand. "Move slowly."

The simulacrum stepped across the threshold. "Are you going to keep that shotgun on me?"

"I guess not." Ethan shifted the shotgun to his left hand and let the barrel droop.

"Thank you."

"This'll do fine," Ethan said, taking the shock pistol from where he had tucked it into his belt and forcing the prongs into the sim's flabby belly as he pulled the trigger.

Three hundred kilovolts. The green-on-the-inside man dropped like a felled tree.

3

BUFFALO, NEW YORK

The walk to the low-rise apartment building where Leo Beck lived kept Cassie warm in the face of the wind, but her little brother was beginning to show symptoms of anxiety. He had her left hand in a grip she was afraid would leave her bruised, though Thomas hadn't held hands with his sister since he was six years old. "Sun'll be up soon," she said, trying to distract him. They passed a ponderous slow-moving machine that sent torrents of soapy water into the sewer grates. "Street sweepers already at work, see?" Thomas shrugged.

Buffalo was a prosperous city, but that prosperity had bypassed these old South Side buildings. Leo's low-rise squatted on its corner lot like a tired troll, tattooed by coal smoke that had drifted in from the mills and refineries of West Seneca and Lackawanna in the decades before the EPA mandates. She had to be careful here, in case the simulacra had come or were coming for Leo. She tugged open the sheet-metal outer door and stepped into the foyer of the building. The air inside was warm but smelled like cabbage and sour milk. She examined the bank of electrical bells—a row of buttons with the names of tenants printed beside them. One of the buttons had come loose and dangled from its socket like a poked-out eye. Just below it was the button marked BECK, LEO.

"Is it safe here?" Thomas asked, echoing Cassie's own thought.

During their walk she had told Thomas about the sim who had been killed by a car on Liberty Street. What it meant was that she and Thomas had to get away even if Aunt Ris couldn't join them. *So where are we going?* Thomas had asked, but Cassie didn't have an answer. *It depends.*

I have to go to school.

Not anymore. We're sort of on vacation.

But Thomas was too perceptive to be easily consoled. And no, it wasn't safe here; she couldn't honestly say so. Leo Beck might be dead on the floor of his single-bedroom apartment for all Cassie knew. But it was her duty as a Society survivor to warn the nearest potential victim, if that was possible. She kept an eye on the stairs beyond the foyer's inner door, ready to run at the first sight of a suspicious stranger. She pushed the buzzer again.

After a moment Leo answered, and he wasn't pleased. "Whoever the fuck you are, push that buzzer one more time and I'll be down there kicking your sorry ass."

Thomas went owl-eyed. "It's Cassie Iverson," Cassie said hastily. "I need to come in, Leo."

Silence. After a long pause the electronic lock on the inner door clicked open. Cassie hustled Thomas up the stairwell to a second-floor corridor lined with peeling floral wallpaper. Leo's apartment was 206. She knocked lightly, not wanting to wake the neighbors.

But it wasn't Leo who opened the door—it was Beth Vance.

Cassie supposed she shouldn't have been surprised. She had seen Leo and Beth together at the last survivors' meeting, acting more than friendly toward each other. Beth was the daughter of John Vance, whose wife Alice had been a tenured professor at NYU and a member of the Correspondence Society. Alice Vance had been one of the victims of the 2007 attacks.

Beth was only a year older than Cassie, though she tried to appear vastly more sophisticated (and usually succeeded, Cassie had to admit). Beth was tall, dramatically skinny, and she wore her straw-yellow hair fashionably short. This morning she was dressed in jeans and a flannel shirt that looked as if she had just thrown them on. The shirt might have been one of Leo's. She gave Cassie a condescending glare.

"I need to talk to Leo," Cassie said.

Beth rolled her eyes but called out, "Yeah, it's the Iverson girl. And her little brother."

Leo's voice came from elsewhere in the apartment: *"Her what?"*

"Little brother!"

As if Beth didn't know Thomas's name.

Cassie pushed past Beth and tugged Thomas inside. Leo came out of the bedroom barefoot, wearing black denim pants and a sleeveless undershirt. He was twenty-one years old and a little over six feet tall. Conventionally good-looking but there was something odd about his eyes, Cassie had often thought: the way they turned down at the corners, as if they had been installed upside-down. It made him look smug.

But he wasn't actually smug and he certainly wasn't stupid. He looked at Cassie, at Thomas, read their expressions, then took a breath and said, "Oh, fuck. It's happening again, isn't it?"

Cassie managed to nod. "Again."

"And you came here first?"

"Aunt Ris is out. Yeah. We haven't talked to anyone else."

She told him the story of what she had seen from the kitchen window, sparing no details even though Thomas grew visibly more frightened as she spoke.

"Okay," Leo said, frowning massively. "Thank you, Cassie." He turned to Beth. "Anything you want to keep," Leo told her, "get it quick and throw it in the car."

"The car?"

"We're leaving."

* * *

Thomas sat next to her on Leo's grubby sofa while Leo and Beth finished dressing.

She wondered how much he understood. Aunt Ris hadn't neglected Thomas's education. He knew about the 2007 massacre, at least in general terms. He knew he shouldn't discuss certain subjects, like the death of his parents, outside of the family. He knew the suitcase under his bed had been put there for a purpose. That burdensome knowledge had made him more reserved and cautious than most twelve-year-olds. Thomas seldom talked about any of this, but he occasionally came to Cassie with questions that troubled him: *Is it true the radiosphere is alive?* Or, *How does the hypercolony hear us when we talk on the phone?* Or, *Why does it want to kill people?* Cassie had always tried to answer as honestly as she knew how. Which meant Thomas had to be satisfied with a whole lot of I-don't-know.

Beth remained skeptical, and Leo Beck came out of the bedroom still talking down her objections. "Cassie wouldn't lie about something like this," Leo said, gratifyingly. "It's code-fucking-red." He jammed a few items of canned food into a sports bag along with his spare clothes. "We knew this could happen." He added, "At least we're together," which Cassie guessed was meant to mollify Beth, though she gave him nothing in return but a queasy stare. The process of packing up was brief and efficient. Leo didn't seem to own much, from what Cassie could see of his apartment, apart from a couple of shelves of books. All Beth had was her overnight bag, which Cassie suspected amounted to little more than a makeup kit, emergency tampons and a couple of condoms.

"So where's the car?" Beth asked.

"Parked a couple of blocks away. Anything else you think we need?"

Beth looked around unhappily, then shook her head.

"Okay. Let's go."

"What about *them*?" Beth asked—rudely, but Cassie had been wondering the same thing.

"Can't leave 'em here. Is that all right, Cassie? Do what you like, but you're probably better off with us than out in the street."

"Yes," Thomas said before Cassie could answer. Cassie just nodded. Leo knew the drill as well as anyone; whatever else he might be, he was the son of Werner Beck, the most influential man in the Society. They would be safer together.

They left the building. Outside, the first light of morning raked the street. A few workers had begun to trickle out of these old residential buildings, burly men and a few women, most of them bound for the Lackawanna and West Seneca production lines. Once, driving through this part of the city with Aunt Ris, Cassie had wondered aloud whether the men then trudging home really believed the world was as prosperous and forward-moving as her high-school civics classes had made it sound. "Probably not," Aunt Ris had said. "They don't look terribly inspired, do they? They're not rich by a long stretch. But they have jobs. The mills and machine shops pay a living wage plus benefits. A lot of these men could probably afford to live somewhere better if not for liquor or alimony or bad luck. Their lives might improve in the long run. And if they need help, they can get it." In other words, the civics classes had been mostly right.

Aunt Ris had always been scrupulous about giving the devil his due.

Leo's car was an old Ford, its brown paint bubbled with rust. It was probably older than Thomas, but it was the best transportation Leo could afford on the money he made at the restaurant where he worked nights. His father, though famously wealthy, hadn't set him up with a fancy income. But as of now, Cassie thought, Leo had spent his last day bussing tables at Julio's. She heaved her suitcase and Thomas's into the empty trunk of the car, next to Beth and Leo's few things, then slid into the backseat with Thomas.

"So where are we going?" Beth asked.

It was a good question. Cassie waited to hear the answer. Sooner or later she would have to ask herself the same thing.

"First stop, your place. See if your father's okay. What we do then depends on what we find."

* * *

Ten Society families had fled to Buffalo after the massacre. Most had been associated with (or had lost loved ones associated with) Harvard, the Massachusetts Institute of Technology, or UMass. Aunt Ris had known them all socially, and it was she who had organized the exodus.

All those families had sustained attacks. All were grieving for lost husbands or fathers, mothers or wives. Wisely, they had been unwilling to go on living in the homes where their loved ones had been killed. They may not have been in immediate danger—the attacks had been narrowly targeted at active members of the Society—but they had been made exquisitely aware of their vulnerability. The last generally-distributed Society document (a letter to survivors from Werner Beck) had been laced with dire warnings and tips on preserving anonymity.

There were other such enclaves of survivors around the country and elsewhere in the world. Only a shadow of the old Correspondence Society still existed, but the emotional and occasional financial support it provided had been invaluable. Survivor gatherings were the only occasions when grief and anger that had to remain hidden from strangers could be openly expressed and understood.

But the need for secrecy was always corrosive, especially for the children of such families. Cassie and Thomas fell into that category. So did Leo and Beth.

School, for instance. Cassie had attended Millard Fillmore Secondary School until her graduation last spring, and every day had brought some sharp reminder that she was an outsider only passing for normal, a refugee from a different and darker country. History classes had been a particular torment. Before the massacres of 2007, she had been allowed by her parents to believe the narrative of technological and social progress the textbooks loved to portray: the discovery of the radio-propagative layer above the Earth's atmosphere (the so-called radiosphere) in the 1890s, the Great War and its aftermath, the abolition of segregation in the U.S. in the 1930s, the European and Eurasian peace pacts, the gender liberation of the 1950s . . . above all, the comforting near-certainty that the world was every day a little wealthier and a little more just. It was only after the death of her parents that Cassie had been introduced to the real truth: that there was an invisible hand at work in human history, indifferent despite its apparent benevolence, often cruel, occasionally murderous.

That knowledge had set her apart from her classmates. Her few friendships were really just temporary alliances with other social outsiders—with Annie Jessup, for instance, who wore a stainless-steel leg brace; with Patrice Kossuth, who stuttered uncontrollably on the rare occasions when she attempted to speak. And what good was friendship when Cassie was obliged to conceal so much about herself? The only people of Cassie's age to whom she could truly unburden herself were the children of the Society,

who all had stories like hers and whose sympathy
was therefore generic and often insincere.

Despite all that, she had methodically planned a
future for herself. Since she left high school she had
been working as a counter clerk at a Main Street department store called Lassiter's, saving tuition and
book fees for a semester at NYU. Her ambition had
been to take a biology major that would ultimately
allow her to focus on the study of invertebrates: her
uncle's career and his books on entomology had
been an obvious inspiration. She would get a post-
graduate degree, maybe end up teaching at some regional college; she would lead a quiet but useful life
and make a modest contribution to the sum of human knowledge. She had imagined herself living in a
book-lined room on a tree-lined campus, with a window through which she could watch the seasons
change. She would be alone, perhaps, but she would
also be contented, useful, *safe*.

It was a stupid delusion, and she blushed at the
thought of it. Because now the green-on-the-inside
men had come back, and there would be no sheltered
room, no window from which to watch the winter
snow. The events of the last few hours meant she
would lead the rest of her life in strict anonymity, perhaps under an assumed name, taking the sort of jobs
that required no experience or documentation, probably living in a sequence of rented apartments in a
sequence of obscure towns. And the same, she realized with belated anguish, would be true of Thomas.

Thomas put his head against her shoulder and closed his eyes. The motion of the car and the emotional overload of the morning had made him sleepy. That was a blessing, Cassie thought. She stroked his hair and let him doze.

Leo drove with an eye on the rearview mirror, making sure they weren't being followed. The route to Beth's place took them across town through thickening traffic. Cassie spared a thought for Beth, sitting pale and silent in the passenger seat up front. Cassie had always felt a cordial dislike for Beth, richly reciprocated, but they were in the same boat now.

"If my father—I mean," Beth said, "if he's not home—if we can't find him—where do we go after this?"

"Depends," Leo said.

"Because even if he *is* home, I don't want to stay with him. We had this discussion once, what to do if the sims come back. He has fake ID for both of us and he says he has enough cash to keep us in some little place, maybe Florida—but I don't want to live in fucking Florida! I don't want to live with him *anywhere*."

"Okay," Leo said gently. "It's up to you. Whatever happens. But if he's home, we need to warn him."

"So where are *you* going?"

"West."

"Where west?"

"To where my own father lives."

Leo's father: Werner Beck, patron of the Correspondence Society and the closest thing to a leader the fractious and disorganized Society had ever had. Famously intelligent, famously well-organized, and famously difficult to deal with. Cassie had once heard Aunt Ris describe Werner Beck as "a smart man, but a classic authoritarian."

They left the parkway for a neighborhood of tall apartment buildings much nicer than Leo's low-rise. Cassie caught a glimpse of Beth's face in the rearview mirror, now a mask of silent apprehension.

The Society kids in Cassie's circle had given each other nicknames. Cassie was "Raccoon," probably for the way her eyes looked after a typical sleepless night. Beth when she was younger had been "Angel," but lately she had been called meaner and more explicit names. She had gone out with a lot of guys in school, mostly of the leather-jacket-and-flick-knife persuasion. Leo himself had credentials with that crowd . . . though, by Beth's standards, Leo constituted a step toward respectability. Cassie had tried to ignore all that talk.

No angel could have looked as terrified as Beth did now. At the first sight of flashing red lights a few blocks away she went rigid.

And so did Cassie. Cassie had been harboring an unexpressed hope that they would find Beth's father safe at home, that the death of the sim on Liberty

Street had been a weird anomaly, that Aunt Ris was therefore also safe, that a semblance of sanity or at least *continuity* would be restored to her life. . . .

But the ambulance in front of Beth's building was flanked by police cars, and as Leo drove past she saw two paramedics come through the lobby door with a blanket-covered body on a wheeled gurney.

"Stop," Beth whispered.

"I can't."

"Leo, for fuck's sake!"

"I can't stop, Beth. We shouldn't even be this close."

"Jesus!"

He sped up, though he was careful not to attract the attention of the police. Beth pounded her fist on the dash and started to cry—choked sobs, not loud enough to wake Thomas. At the corner Leo turned left and headed back to the parkway.

After a fill-up at a National Oil station in Cheektowaga Leo merged onto the Interstate, following the long curve of Lake Erie toward Cleveland. Thomas dozed fitfully, his head on Cassie's shoulder as she watched exit signs announce the names of pleasant-sounding small towns: Mount Vernon, Wanakah, Pinehurst. Bars of November sunlight angled across Cassie's eyes. From time to time Leo cracked the driver's-side window, admitting gusts of chilly air. The four-lane highway glinted with mica flecks and sun mirages.

Cassie respected Beth's grief with her silence. Leo had already said everything that could be said, including that the body on the gurney cart might not have belonged to Beth's father. Beth had retreated into a sullen, steely indifference. "I don't want to talk about it." So no one talked.

Once they crossed the state border Leo left the Interstate for secondary roads where, he said, they were less likely to be followed. Outside Medina, Ohio, he stopped at another gas station so they could top off the tank and use the toilets. Cassie and Beth took turns at the ladies' room, wordlessly. Back at the car Thomas complained that he was hungry. Cassie went into the convenience store and bought him a chocolate bar (Hershey's with almonds) plus one for herself and a bottle of orange juice to share, along with an activity book she imagined might keep him busy. Puzzles, mazes, connect-the-dots. He looked at it with disdain. "Are we going home now?"

"No. You *know* that."

"So where do we sleep?"

"We'll stop at a motel, I guess. Soon."

As the sun drifted toward the horizon Leo switched on the vehicle's anemic heater. Lodi, Mount Gilead, Cardington: *All these little towns,* Cassie thought. Here a main street, a hardware store, a Chinese restaurant announcing itself with a neon dragon. Here a neatly whitewashed church with a wooden steeple. Here the last of the season's dry leaves, wind-delivered to curbs and windowsills.

Small houses leaked yellow light from curtained windows. These were the homes of people who had never seen past the skin of the world and never would. Once, Cassie thought, she had been one of them. This was the world from which she had been banished: warm as a winter blanket, seen and abandoned in the same moment. She loved it with an exile's love. It ran past the car in fading colors. She was tempted to wave good-bye.

4

Once the sim was incapacitated—the 300-kV shock pistol was spectacularly effective—Ethan dragged the creature down to the cellar of the farmhouse.

Whatever he did here, he would have to do quickly. The sim had come unarmed and begging for a conversation, and it might be important to find out why. But he couldn't waste time. Obviously, the hypercolony knew where to find him. Which meant his sabbatical at the farmhouse had come to an end, and every second he lingered here put him at risk.

In the meantime his cameras and trip wires and automatic alarms continued to survey the property for intruders. Ethan bound the unconscious simulacrum to a heavy chair with duct tape, then went upstairs to consider his options.

He retrieved the sim's jacket and shirt from the front porch and examined them. Both items bore midprice store-brand labels and could have been purchased anywhere in the country. There was a wallet in the sim's jacket pocket—that was unusual.

The assassins of 2007 hadn't carried identification, which was part of the reason local and federal investigations had failed to learn anything useful about them. (The fact that the few sims who were killed in the attacks had left radically unconventional corpses might also have had something to do with it.) Ethan opened the wallet cautiously.

He pulled out a hundred and fifty dollars in tens and twenties and a raft of cards, including two major credit cards, a Social Security card and a driver's license. The documents had all been issued in the name of Winston C. Bayliss. The address on the driver's license was 22 Major Street, Montmorency, Pennsylvania, and the laminated photograph resembled the face on the thing in the cellar.

Interesting. The simulacra were in most ways a mystery. None of the surviving members of the Correspondence Society had been able to determine how they faked their human appearance or to what extent they had infiltrated conventional human society. So how did an artificially-created monstrosity come to possess a Social Security number? Had it stolen the identity of a real (presumably now deceased) Winston Bayliss? Or were the cards simply forgeries?

How was he supposed to picture this? An inhuman monster living a quiet life in a small Pennsylvania town, waiting for the right moment to strike? Or, even more absurdly, an inhuman monster churning out fake ID on a clandestine printing press? And why had Bayliss (*call him that for now*) carried these documents to the farmhouse, knowing they might fall into Ethan's hands?

But those were only footnotes to the larger question: Why had Bayliss shown up, unarmed and apparently defenseless?

It's chilly out here, the creature had said. *May I come in and speak to you?*

And it had said something else:

You know what I am.

"Yeah, I know what you are." Living alone had given Ethan the habit of thinking out loud. His voice bounced between the walls of the farmhouse kitchen. "And I know it's no use listening to you."

No use at all, because—if Ethan's research and the conjectures of the Correspondence Society were correct—it wouldn't be "Winston Bayliss" who did the talking. It would be the hypercolony itself, using Winston as its puppet. And the hypercolony would lie. More precisely, it would say whatever advanced its interests. The distinction between truth and falsehood was irrelevant to the hypercolony, perhaps even imperceptible to it. It generated human language solely for the purpose of manipulating human behavior.

Would Ethan discover anything useful by listening to it talk?

He guessed there was only one way to find out.

* * *

"What are you doing with that pistol, Professor Iverson?" the simulacrum asked.

It was awake again. The creature was still securely bound to the chair, wearing nothing but its underwear and taut ribbons of duct tape. Its head was immobilized, but it managed to dart sidelong glances at Ethan and at the revolver Ethan wanted it to see. The creature looked convincingly like a frightened, slightly pudgy Caucasian man shivering in the cool air of the cellar.

Ethan didn't answer its question. His first order of business was to make absolutely sure that what he had here was one of the green-on-the-inside men, not some misguided or demented human being. He aimed the pistol at a point between the knee and the ankle of the creature's left leg.

"Wait," Bayliss said. "You don't need to do that."

Ethan pulled the trigger. The detonation was painfully loud in the enclosed space of the cellar. The bullet passed through Bayliss's leg and cratered into the floor beneath him. Ethan ignored the ringing in his ears and assessed the results. Bright red blood gushed from the wound, along with a slower pulse of green viscous material. A sliver of bone showed through the damaged tissue, pale and moist.

After the gunshot, Bayliss's expression became impassive and thoughtful. Ethan knelt and wrapped the wound with more duct tape to staunch the bleeding, wrinkling his nose at the rotting-flower stink of the green matter.

"That wasn't necessary," Bayliss said.

On the contrary. Now Ethan knew for sure what he was dealing with. "You said you wanted to tell me something."

The simulacrum hesitated as if considering its answer, but Ethan put that down as theater: these creatures lied with gestures as easily as with words. "We have a common interest, Professor Iverson. It's complicated—"

Ethan put the barrel of the pistol to the creature's head. "Just speak."

"You know what I am. I'm the same sort of thing that killed so many of your colleagues seven years ago. But I represent a different interest."

"That makes no sense."

"Most of what the Correspondence Society conjectured is true. The radio-reflective layer around the Earth is an active, living entity—that was a clever deduction and a correct one. It constitutes the body of what you call the hypercolony. The hypercolony is a living thing, another correct conjecture. But like any living thing, the hypercolony is mortal. It's also subject to infection and predation. I represent an autonomous parasitical network that has infected the hypercolony and is struggling to control it. My interests are inimical to the hypercolony's interests. I believe you're capable of understanding that. That's why I came to you unarmed and alone."

The sim had simply reiterated what the Society had already inferred, with the addition of that claim about a "parasitical network." Ethan would consider the plausibility of it some other time. "What exactly do you want?"

"I want your help. I can explain, but I'll need more time."

"Why would I help you do anything?"

"It would prevent a humanitarian catastrophe. And it might save the life of your niece."

Startled, Ethan tightened his finger on the trigger of the pistol.

"That wasn't a threat," Bayliss said.

"What do you know about my niece?"

"It's not safe here. It's not safe for either of us. Take me away, and I'll explain."

Of the many humiliating aspects of Ethan's life since the events of 2007, perhaps the most demeaning was the veneer of craziness he had been obliged to assume. He refused to own a telephone, a television or a radio; he lived inside a lunatic's cordon of security devices; he maintained an arsenal of handguns and rifles in his attic; and now there was a captive in his cellar, bound with duct tape and shot through the leg. How would that look to an outsider? Nothing short of rabidly, dangerously, self-evidently psychopathic.

It had been years since he had socialized with anyone who shared his ideas. Most of his old friends and colleagues were dead or isolated. Should he need to defend his sanity, he could call no living witnesses. He still had his letters, his Society papers, his unpublished research. But those would have looked about as crazy as he appeared to be.

His ex-wife Nerissa would have understood all this, as would any of the surviving families of Correspondence Society insiders, and in his loneliness he had been sorely tempted to talk to her—but there was no way Ethan could get in touch without putting her at risk. He had remained in contact with the Society's financial and intellectual leader, Werner Beck, but only by mail . . . and Beck was, if anything, more complexly paranoid than Ethan himself.

The sim calling itself Winston Bayliss had implied that the life of Ethan's niece, Cassie, was somehow at risk. Like everything else the creature said, that might be a lie. Sickeningly, however, it might equally well be true. Ethan hadn't seen his sister-in-law's daughter for seven years now. He remembered Cassie as a quiet child, moody but thoughtful and easy to like. She would have turned eighteen this year.

What did the hypercolony want with Cassie Iverson?

The question was probably unanswerable, a distraction. Coming up from the cellar to the kitchen, he glanced at the clock. An hour had passed since the sim's arrival. Too long. He pictured himself dousing the floor of the farmhouse with kerosene—he kept jerricans of it in the barn where his car was parked—and setting it on fire. Burn the farmhouse, burn the barn, burn Winston Bayliss. Get behind the wheel of his old Ford and drive away. The charred bones and skull in the cellar, if they were discovered, would raise questions, but by then Ethan would be long gone . . . and he doubted any merely *human* agency could track him down.

But if the best he could hope for was to live out the rest of his life in some new and even more hermetic state of solitude, he might as well burn himself along with the building.

I want your help, Winston Bayliss had said. *It might save the life of your niece.*

But the thing in the cellar couldn't be trusted. That was the bottom line.

He cradled the pistol in his hand. Killing the sim might be a tactical error, but it was the closest thing to revenge he would ever be able to take.

He was headed for the cellar when the alarm sounded a second time.

5

Leo, whose father made sure he received every year a generous selection of fake ID and matching credit cards, rented a room in a roadside motel. The motel—pine forest on three sides, an empty pool behind a chain-link fence—was shabby but quiet in the off-season. Leo and Beth had signed in as a couple, so Cassie had to hurry from the car to the room with Thomas on one hand and her suitcase in the other in order not to be seen from the lobby. Sunset was fading from a cloudless sky, and although Cassie took only a cursory interest in astronomy she guessed the bright star on the horizon was the planet Venus. She caught a glimpse of it as the door closed behind her. One clear, cold eye.

The air of the room carried an undernote of mildew and Lysol. There was a small TV on the pitted and ring-stained dresser, and Thomas gazed at it with undisguised longing. Aunt Ris had not owned a TV set, on principle. Cassie had occasionally attempted to raise counter-arguments—even if television broadcasts were subtly deceptive, you could watch them as long as you kept that in mind, couldn't you?—but her aunt's ban had been non-negotiable.

Cassie guessed she understood. All radio and television signals were bounced through the radiosphere. That had been true since the days of Marconi and Edison. She remembered a photograph from her high-school history text, of Marconi and a crew of assistants at an experimental antenna station in Newfoundland, demonstrating what they called "resonant contact" with a sister station in the French town of Saint-Malo. Marconi's feeble signals had been amplified by the radiosphere and accurately recorded by his counterparts in France. Of course, no one in those days had called it the radiosphere. "Radiosphere" was a term devised in the 1920s: a high-altitude boundary layer that had the surprisingly useful effect of propagating radio signals around the circumference of the Earth, depending on signal strength and frequency. What this layer was made of and how it worked remained open theoretical questions (in fact research was subtly discouraged), but broadcast engineers had rushed to exploit it. Global radio broadcasts had begun after the Great War, in 1921. Primitive black-and-white television broadcasting followed in 1935. Cassie had seen one of those vintage receivers for sale in a dusty antique shop: a comically small glass screen in a comically large wooden case; the proprietor had claimed it still worked.

So all radio and television was modulated by the radiosphere, as everyone knew. What everyone *didn't* know was that the radiosphere was the distributed body of a living entity, and that the signals passing through it didn't necessarily pass unaltered.

Three years ago Cassie had discovered a box of Correspondence Society monographs buried in the hallway cupboard where Aunt Ris kept the things she couldn't bear to throw away but never looked at. The papers had belonged to Cassie's parents; perhaps they had come to Aunt Ris after the murders, as a macabre heirloom, much like Cassie herself. Therefore she had had no compunction about rooting through the box and reading anything that captured her attention.

Most of the monographs had been incomprehensible to her, with titles like "Intracellular Signaling in Isolated Etheric Cell Cultures," and these she quickly set aside. But one of the papers concerned TV broadcasting, and she had understood almost every word of it. The author, a television engineer, had compared studio recordings of nightly news programs with his own recordings of the same programs as they appeared after they had been broadcast. (Cassie imagined him poring over the footage frame by frame, with the sort of fanatical attention Thomas brought to the puzzles in his puzzle books—*find five differences between these pictures*.) In each case, the changes he discovered were numerous but dauntingly subtle. The most blatant example was a glitch (a momentary blackout) that obscured the spoken word "hatred" in a report about ethnic tension in Uganda. The least obvious were countless small but measurable modifications of the image and voice of the news hosts and reporters. What these subtle alterations of expression and inflection were meant to achieve the author couldn't say, though he noted "a general softening of emotional affect." It was really just one more data point in what Cassie had come to think of as the mysteries of the hypercolony (which was what Society documents called the collection of tiny living cells that comprised the radiosphere), but it helped explain her aunt's distrust of television and radio. What emerged from the speaker or appeared on the screen was tainted, poisonous, a subtle and insidious lie.

Cassie understood and agreed, but Aunt Ris's absolutism had still annoyed her. TV couldn't be trusted, but did that mean it shouldn't be watched? The shows people talked about at school sounded interesting, and Cassie was treated as slightly dim for not having seen them. Thomas's exposure to television had been the same: it was a rare treat, forbidden for reasons he didn't entirely understand and often resented.

Thomas looked at the motel-room TV, then at Cassie. Cassie sighed. "Go ahead," she said. "Turn it on." (It wasn't as if *it* watched *you*.) Moments later Thomas was sitting cross-legged on the bed, smiling at the dumb jokes on *Piggy's Island,* a sitcom about a group of shipwrecked British schoolboys.

On the dresser next to the TV was a telephone, white plastic gone the color of old bone. It was another device less useful to Cassie than to ordinary people. An ordinary person could pick up the receiver and make a call without a second thought, not caring that all calls, even local ones, were routinely routed through the radiosphere. If she were an ordinary person Cassie could have tried to call Aunt Ris. But such a call would be insanely risky, endangering both parties. Better not to think about Aunt Ris at all, if she could help it.

Leo and Beth retreated to the back of the room, talking in tones too low for Cassie to hear. Beth shot periodic aggrieved glances at Cassie, while Leo spoke slowly and showed her the palms of his big hands. Cassie ignored them.

Eventually Leo grabbed his jacket. "Beth and I are going out to pick up some food. Anything you guys need while we're out?"

Not really. Cassie's emergency suitcase was well and wisely packed. "Let me chip in," she said, going for her purse.

"Tonight's on me. Save your money. We might need to pool our resources later."

Moments later Cassie was alone with her little brother. She forced herself to pay attention to *Piggy's Island*. The two protagonists, Piggy and Ralph, had discovered a parachutist stuck in a treetop. Their attempts to get him down somehow involved pelting him with coconuts. Thomas watched somberly and laughed only once, a sound Cassie found startling in the wintry silence.

After an hour of television Thomas started to look drowsy, but the sound of voices as Beth and Leo came in—not to mention the smell of the pizza— brought him back to ready alertness. He grabbed two slices from the box and settled back in front of the TV.

Beth ate a little, then announced she wanted a shower. As soon as she had locked herself into the bathroom, Leo asked Cassie to step outside. Cassie was surprised and immediately apprehensive. Bad news, she suspected. Maybe Beth convinced Leo to dump her and Thomas at the nearest bus depot. And if so, she thought, so be it. She left Thomas to his pizza and joined Leo in the darkness just beyond the door, her woolen jacket draped over her shoulders. She waited stoically for the dismissal.

Leo took a cigarette from the pack in his pocket. He lit it, shook out the match, gazed at the pine tops silhouetted against a moon-blue sky. "Don't mind Beth," he said, breathing smoke into the November air. "She's dealing with what happened to her father. What *might* have happened to him. No love lost there, but . . . you know."

"I guess," Cassie said.

For most of her adolescence Cassie had been aware of Leo and Beth. They had been part of the older contingent of Society offspring, not quite in her circle. The Society survivors who had come to Buffalo were like family: quarrelsome, not always close, bound by shared secrets. Leo usually ignored her at the periodic gatherings, but she had made a careful study of him.

His tobacco habit, for instance. He smoked, Cassie suspected, for the same reason he carried around paperback editions of bohemian novels, for the same reason he affected an interest in the music played in downtown clubs and coffeehouses: it defined him as *other* in a way that required no explanation. It made his otherness seem like a choice.

But at least for tonight he had dropped the act. He coughed and said, "It's pretty obvious Beth isn't happy about you and Thomas coming along for the ride."

"Uh-huh."

"I just wanted to say, you shouldn't blame her. She can't see past her own unhappiness. She'll calm down sooner or later. So don't take it personally." He took more smoke into his lungs and let it seep from his nostrils. A truck rumbled past on the highway. "Do what you want, Cassie, but I think we ought to stick together at least until we get to Illinois."

Which was slightly surprising. "Until we see your father, you mean."

"Right. Because it's different this time. If the sims are going after people like your aunt, they must be going after everybody who knows anything at all about the Society. You, me, Beth—even Thomas. Do you have a plan to deal with that?"

"I have two sets of ID and I'm of legal age. I have enough cash to get by for now. I can find work somewhere and just . . . blend in."

"Blend in," Leo repeated, with a smile Cassie found irksome. "Are you sure the ID hasn't been compromised?"

She shrugged. "Can't be sure of anything."

"Which is why I think we're better off watching each other's back. At least until Illinois."

"I guess. Okay, so what happens in Illinois? What do you expect to find when you knock on your father's door?"

Leo dropped the cigarette and ground it under his heel, then parked his hands in his jacket pockets. "You know my father's reputation."

"Just that he has deep pockets. And some strong ideas."

"Of all the people who lived through '07, he was the only one who wanted to do something more than turn tail and hide. He told me once, the sims wouldn't have come for us if they weren't afraid of us. And if they're afraid of us that means we must have the power to hurt them. Hurt *it*." He turned his face to the sky. "That *thing*. Wouldn't you like to hurt it, Cassie?"

"If I thought we could. Sure. But—"

"What?"

"Well, I have Thomas to look after. Also, no offense,

but I'm not sure you know what you're talking about."

Leo's sharp look morphed into a smile. "You're right about your little brother. But stick with us, Cassie. I mean it. Stick with us at least until we're sure we're not being followed. Maybe until you get a chance to talk to my father, if . . ."

"If he's alive."

"If he's alive. After that you can find yourself a job in one of these dumb little towns. If that's really what you want." He opened the door to the room and held it for Cassie as she stepped back inside.

They're not dumb little towns, she thought. If saying so made Leo feel superior to the people who lived in them, so be it. But he was wrong. And at the root of the wrongness was envy.

All those little towns out there in the dark, she thought, and all those cities, too, all the people behind their yellow windows taking for granted the sanity and predictability of things in general. It would be easy and satisfying simply to hate them. But Cassie remembered too well the time when her own life had been like that, when she had been unambiguously proud to stand up on Armistice Day and salute the flags of the United States and the League of Nations and everything they seemed to represent: the century of peace, the inexorable advance of freedom and prosperity. Things she still wanted to believe in.

Thomas sat slumped on the bed, his eyes drifting closed though they were still fixed on the television screen. A news broadcast had come on, a woman in a neat blue suit talking about crop failures in Tanzania. Massive shipments from the International Grain Reserve had arrived at the port of Dar es Salaam. The newscaster's expression conveyed her sympathy. But that could have been an adjustment performed by the hypercolony, a subtle enhancement, what movie people called a special effect.

Beth came out of the bathroom wrapped in a towel, water dripping from her hair to her shoulders. "Turn that shit off," she told Cassie. "And get your brother off the fucking bed. I need some sleep."

RURAL VERMONT

Ethan grabbed his pistol—fully loaded apart from the round he had already fired into the leg of the creature in the cellar—and hurried to the door. He was in time to see a grimy blue Ford Elektra bumping down the unpaved access road. It pulled up nearly at his doorstep, the rear end fishtailing in a cloud of dust. The driver's-side door flew open and a woman stepped out. A shock of recognition left Ethan blinking.

Nerissa.

Seven years since he had last seen her. Even then, in the months before the murders, they had been living separately, only technically husband and wife. And even now, the sight of her provoked an upwelling of nostalgia and longing that was hard to suppress. He lowered the pistol and stepped onto the porch.

Her taste in clothing hadn't changed, though she'd obviously dressed in a hurry. She wore blue jeans, a plaid cotton shirt, and a wide orange scarf that dangled to her hips. A pair of glasses—those were new; she used to favor contacts—amplified her already large eyes. She was older now, of course, but apart from a few trivial lines she looked pretty much the way she had when he first met her at a faculty party in Amherst.

She walked steadily toward him as his initial rush of pleasure soured into dread. She came up the steps onto the porch. Then she was inches from him and he had no choice but to take her in his arms.

"Jesus," he whispered. "Ris, Ris—it's not safe here!"

She accepted the embrace, then stepped back from it. "I came for a reason, Ethan."

"You don't understand. You have to leave. The sooner the better. *I'm* leaving."

"Then we'll leave together. This is about Cassie."

Not the first time today his niece's name had come up. He tried to meet her eyes and couldn't. "You'd better come in," he said.

Her name had been Nerissa Stewart the day he met her, and by the end of the faculty mixer he realized he had fallen in love—if not with *her*, exactly, since he hardly knew her, then with her quick curiosity and the way she squinted at him as if he were a puzzle she wanted to solve. She was an English instructor specializing in William Blake, an English poet whose work Ethan had not read since a high-school encounter with Blake's *Tyger*, and Ethan's work in entomology had been equally bewildering to her. Later he would say he could find no truth in poetry and she could discover no poetry in invertebrates. But that was a packaged answer for people who asked about their separation. In fact, during the few years they were together, they had shared more than a few poetic truths.

And in the seven years since the last time he had spoken to her Ethan had rehearsed their reunion countless times. It was a fantasy he found shameful but couldn't resist, especially when he was locked in by winter snow and helpless before the momentum of his own thoughts. Sometimes these fantasies were erotic: the sex had always been good, a foundation stone in the otherwise flimsy architecture of their marriage, and it was difficult not to replay those scenes when the wind came butting against the walls of the farmhouse like an angry bull. On easier days he might imagine apologizing to her, forgiving her, being forgiven by her, laughing with her or listening to her laugh. But none of that mattered now. There was urgent business between them. The old business, the inevitable business.

"Cassie's gone," she said. "I mean, *missing*. I can explain, but . . . do you have coffee? I haven't had a coffee since yesterday. I drove here without sleep. Could use a bathroom break, too."

He apologized for the condition of the bathroom, and while she was in it he tried to organize his whirling thoughts. Cassie was missing. Which meant

Ethan wasn't the only one who had received a visit. The terror had started again. That fucking thing in the cellar! He had let it live—that had been a mistake, one he would soon correct. But he needed to talk to Nerissa first: listen to her, offer what advice he could, help her get away safely. And *quickly*.

She came back to the kitchen table and accepted a cup of lukewarm coffee without looking at it. Before he could assemble his thoughts she said, "I know you weren't expecting me. I could hardly warn you. I wasn't even sure you'd still be here. You gave me this address a long time ago. I was afraid you'd moved on. It's strange for me, too, being here, seeing you. But I came because of Cassie. Let me tell you what happened, what was it, my God, just two days ago. Then we can decide what to do about it."

"Time is an issue here."

"Then just let me talk."

Nerissa told him she had been away from her apartment the night a simulacrum came to Liberty Street. The next morning—arriving home to find the apartment empty and a dire note from Cassie taped to the refrigerator door—she had canvassed the neighbors and reconstructed what had happened. In the early hours of the morning and well before dawn, a man had been killed in a traffic accident directly outside the apartment. The neighbors' halting "you won't believe this" descriptions made it clear that the dead man had been a simulacrum.

Cassie, always a light sleeper, must have witnessed the event. And Cassie—like all the children of survivor families—had been trained to react instantly to the appearance of a sim.

"She would have assumed it was coming to kill her. And maybe it was. So she took Thomas and her suitcase and went to the nearest Society contact to warn him. Unfortunately, the nearest contact was Leo Beck."

"Werner's son?"

"Leo's twenty-one years old now, and he's as much a contrarian as his father. Society people were all the family he ever really had, but I think he hated us as much as he loved us. He was popular with Cassie's cohort, though. I guess he seemed less, I don't know, *passive* than the rest of us."

Werner Beck, Leo's father, had taken a similar position. Werner believed the hypercolony might be vulnerable to human attack, that the Correspondence Society's accumulated knowledge constituted a weapon that could be used against it. And it was an attractive idea, Ethan thought. At least until you began to calculate the potential cost in human lives.

"When Cassie told him about the sim, Leo must have assumed we were all under attack—that sims had been sent to wipe out every last remnant of the Society."

"Are you sure that's not true?"

"Of course I'm not sure. Everyone's terrified. The

protocol we set up for this situation was, if you come under attack and survive, you warn one person, then you disappear. I'm guessing the sim who died on Liberty Street was meant for me. So I talked to Edie Forsythe, who convinced me to stay with her until she talked to Sue Nakamura, who talked to—well, it went around the circle. And as far as we can tell, only two sims ever showed up. One was killed outside my apartment; the other was shot in the head by John Vance when it knocked at his door, asking for a *conversation,* if you can believe that. The sim John shot was unarmed, by the way. The one who was run down, I don't know. All very strange. But Leo bolted, and he took John's daughter, Beth, and Cassie along with him."

A simulacrum, unarmed and asking for a conversation . . . "Still, Ris. You shouldn't have come here."

"I'm not finished. The thing is, Leo idolizes his father. They've stayed in close contact. Everyone who knows Leo figures he's on the way to join Werner, maybe help Werner conduct whatever paranoid project he has in mind."

"Maybe so, but—"

"Just listen. Apart from his son, Werner Beck keeps his distance from survivor families. He writes occasionally, he sends money, he supplies us with fake ID on a regular basis, but none of that comes with a return address. But you're a full-fledged Society insider and you were always one of his favorites—you *must* know how to contact him. And if you *do* know, you have to tell me where he is, because we have to go there. We have to go there, Ethan. We have to go there and get Cassie and take her home."

She sat back in her chair and swiped her hair away from her eyes with a flick of her left hand, a gesture he had forgotten but which was instantly familiar.

"Ris . . . the situation is more complicated than you might think."

She looked at him impatiently.

"I had a visitor, too," he said.

It was the survivors of '07 who had coined the word "simulacrum" to describe their attackers. In his monographs Werner Beck sometimes called them "myrmidons." The reference was to Ovid's *Metamorphosis*, a passage in which Zeus turns ants into human beings in order to repopulate the country of Aegina. Ethan appreciated the insect reference, and as a literary scholar Nerissa would have recognized the allusion— but no one else did; *simulacrum* (or *sim*) had become the accepted word.

He told Nerissa as concisely as possible about the sim in the cellar, how it had shown up on his doorstep and what it had asked for and what it had offered him in return. She listened with careful attention and seemed surprised but not shocked until he got to the part about shooting it in the leg: "You really did that?"

"I had to be sure it wasn't human. Is that hard to understand?"

"No, it's just—I remember how you always hated guns."

He still did. To Ethan, holding a firearm felt like assuming a responsibility no sane human being should want to accept. But after moving into the farmhouse he had signed up for a target and safety course at a shooting range outside of Jacobstown, where he discovered he had a modest talent for marksmanship. He had grown accustomed to the heft of the pistol in his hand in the same way he had grown inured to the shooting-range stink of raw plywood and scorched steel. Hunting deer with a long gun had been a more difficult act to stomach. The act of killing sickened him. But he had hardened himself to that, too. "It's been a few years. I learned some things."

"I'm sorry. Go on. What did the sim say?"

"It mentioned Cassie—"

"What—it knew her *name*? My God, why didn't you tell me this?"

"I am telling you."

"Jesus, Ethan!" She stood up, nearly knocking over her chair. "And the thing is still alive?"

"Yeah, but—"

"I need to talk to it."

"Ris, it can't tell the truth—it can't distinguish between truth and lies. You know that. It uses words to manipulate people."

"Yes, that was your theory, wasn't it? Yours and Werner Beck's."

"It's how the hypercolony works."

"But it *might* be telling the truth."

"If we try to interrogate it, we're only giving it an opportunity to manipulate us."

"So why haven't you killed it?"

Good question. *Because it has a human-seeming face? Because I'm as easy to manipulate as anyone else?* "I was about to do that when you drove up."

"I still want to talk to it."

"Ris—"

"Now! We can't afford to waste time."

Of course they could not. He led her to the windowless cellar.

7

That first night, Leo dictated where everyone would sleep. He insisted that Cassie and Beth share the double bed, which they did, though Beth was ungracious about it. The cheap sofa pushed against the wall of the motel room was big enough for Thomas, who curled up with a spare sweater for a pillow and Cassie's winter coat for a blanket. He fell asleep instantly. Leo insisted on sleeping on the floor. It was a silly gallantry—there was room in the bed for three—but Cassie guessed it was a well-intended gesture.

The next two days were slow repetitions of their first day on the road. Leo bought a Rand-McNally road map and calculated a route he called "indirect," a drunkard's walk on two-lane blacktop, meant to confuse anyone who might have followed them from Buffalo. And it was Leo who did most of the driving, though Cassie took the wheel for an hour or two each day and Beth did the same. They ate at roadside diners or small-town restaurants. It seemed to Cassie that they passed through dozens of identical towns, a town where every river met a creek, and in each one she was tempted to get out of the car, take Thomas to the nearest bus station and buy a ticket for some destination she could barely envision—Terre Haute, Cincinnati, Wheeling: a place where she could be nobody in particular, a place where she would never have to think of the Correspondence Society.

But that was a fantasy, and Cassie was quick to dismiss it. After a day on the road, and a second, and a third, bitter reality set in. Beth and Leo were both dealing with the possibility that they had been orphaned: Beth had seen the stretcher being carried from her father's building, and Leo was driving toward what might well turn out to be a murder scene. Cassie was already an orphan (a word she despised), but now she might have lost Aunt Ris and should probably assume she had. On the second day of their road trip Leo stopped at a diner that sold newspapers from across the country, *The New York Times*, the Cleveland *Plain Dealer*, the *Buffalo News*. Cassie picked up the *News* and scanned it, but there was nothing about any murders; the Liberty Street accident had gone unreported and she found no familiar names in the obituary columns. But that proved nothing. Nothing at all.

All we have, she thought, *is each other.* Leo and Beth, Cassie and Thomas. What bound them together was uncertainty and dread. And guilt—especially after the third day, the day they bloodied their hands.

It started with Leo's paranoia and a confession from Beth.

Cassie failed to notice anything amiss until they pulled out of the parking lot of the motel where they had spent the night. She had slept badly and so had Thomas. During her wakeful moments, which seemed to arrive every half hour or so, she had seen her little brother tossing restlessly or lying passively awake, his eyes scanning the moonlit borders of the room. So far Thomas had been almost inhumanly patient, seldom complaining even when he was hungry or tired. But maybe that wasn't a good thing. It might be a symptom of emotional shock. This morning his eyes were red and bruised-looking, and he refused breakfast—a granola bar and a bottle of orange juice—when she offered it to him. Today would be different, she told him. Today, Leo had said, they were going to get back on the Interstate and head directly for the place where Werner Beck lived. No more meandering back roads. But Thomas only shrugged.

Leo was almost as quiet as he drove from the motel lot onto the two-lane county road. From where she sat all Cassie could see of him was the back of his head and his reflection in the rearview mirror. He kept glancing at the mirror and at Beth beside him as the road unreeled under trees with branches like outstretched fingers and a sky as flat as tinted glass.

After a while he broke the silence: "Any of you notice a guy in a dark suit, big glasses, old-fashioned hat?"

"Notice him where?" Cassie asked.

"Anywhere we stopped—restaurants, motels?"

Cassie hadn't noticed anyone like that. Beth shook her head. Thomas ignored the question and gazed indifferently out the side window.

"Because he was in the lobby when I was checking out," Leo said. "And he looked kind of familiar. I thought maybe . . . I don't know. Maybe it doesn't matter."

"You think we might have been followed?"

Leo frowned. Cassie had come to appreciate that frown, the way it bracketed his mouth. Back in Buffalo, among survivors, she had seen him escalate trivial arguments to the point of shouting, a quality she hated in him. But out here on the road Leo had shown a more thoughtful side. The frown signaled a mood more quizzical than angry. "It's possible," he said. "We have to be careful, right?"

"Yeah," she said. "Always. Of course." But she honestly didn't remember a guy with big glasses and a hat.

Twenty minutes later Leo glanced at the mirror and cursed. Cassie craned her head to check the road: there was a car behind them, far enough away that it disappeared when the road curved and reappeared when it straightened. A midnight-blue car, high-tailed and salted with road dust. It looked like it might be a few years old, though Cassie didn't know about cars and couldn't name the make or model. "Same as yesterday," Leo muttered.

"You've seen that car before?"

"Or one just like it. Fuck!"

"So pull over," Beth suggested. "Pull over and let it pass."

Leo waited until they reached a gas station, a little two-pump depot where he could idle inconspicuously for a couple of minutes. Cassie and Thomas hunkered down, but Cassie kept her head high enough to see the car as it went by. It didn't slow. It didn't speed up. It just whooshed past, neatly centered in the right lane. There was a single driver at the wheel: a middle-aged man wearing oversized eyeglasses and a dowdy, old-fashioned hat.

They sat for ten more minutes before Leo pulled out of the gas station, grit crackling under the tires as he steered back onto the road. He said, "It's possible we've been discovered. So don't take offense, but I have to ask: did either of you—or Thomas—maybe try to call home, find out what happened back in Buffalo?"

In truth, Cassie had been tempted. In every room they stayed in, every restaurant where they ate, there had been a telephone in plain sight. She was always

just one call away from knowing whether Aunt Ris
had lived or died. So yeah, it was a constant irrational temptation, like putting poisoned food on a plate
in front of a hungry person. But she wasn't stupid
enough to dig in. "No," she said.

"Thomas? How about you?"

The question seemed to startle him. "What?"

"Call anybody on the phone lately?"

"No! Not since we left."

"Are you sure about that? It's okay to tell me. I'm
not pissed or anything. I just need to know, right?"

"Right," Thomas said uncertainly.

"So did you call somebody, talk to somebody?"

"No. But *she* did."

She—Beth.

"Fucking little liar!" Beth said promptly.

"I saw her."

"Nobody cares what you think you saw!"

Leo took his right hand off the wheel and put it on
Beth's thigh, to reassure her or to keep her quiet,
Cassie couldn't tell which. "When was this?"

Thomas gave Cassie a questioning look.

"Go on," she said quietly. "Tell him. It's okay."

"At the motel. Two nights ago."

"In the room?"

"After dinner. Outside. She was at a phone booth."

"I was having a *smoke*," Beth said. "Come on, Leo,
this is bullshit!"

"You saw her use the phone?"

Thomas hesitated before he spoke. "I don't know.

I thought so. I was looking through the window. It was kind of dark. But it looked like she picked up the phone."

"I was in the *phone booth*," Beth said, "having a *fucking smoke*, all *right*?"

The car rolled on, silent apart from the growl of the engine and the asthmatic murmur of the heater. "I'm not passing judgment on anybody," Leo said. "I just need to know. I mean, it wasn't snowing or raining—you needed to go into a phone booth to have a smoke?"

After a longer and even weightier silence Beth said, "I never actually talked to anybody!"

"Okay, I guess I understand that. But you called?"

"I just thought . . . I'm talking about my father . . . if he picked up, at least I'd know he wasn't dead."

"Okay. And . . . did he?"

"Did he *what*?"

"Answer."

"Oh. Well—no."

"Uh-huh."

Beth bit her lip and stared out the window. "*I'm sorry*. It was stupid. I know that. It won't happen again."

"Yeah, good." Leo took his hand off her leg. "See that it doesn't."

The road curved through hilly, wooded land toward the Interstate. A few weeks ago, Cassie thought, the hills would have been gaudy with autumn colors, but November had stripped all the trees and burned the meadows brown.

Leo pulled off at a roadside stop, a gravel parking lot and a pair of cinderblock restrooms overlooking a broad valley. Away and below, a river stitched a quilt of forested allotments and freehold farms. The river must have a name, Cassie thought, but she didn't know what it was. A pair of turkey buzzards drew circles in the cloudless sky.

Cassie and Thomas left the car, ostensibly to look at the view, really to let Leo and Beth talk in private.

Cassie had never been close to Beth but she felt sorry for her now. For more than a year, at gatherings of survivor families, Cassie had watched Beth deliberately and systematically ingratiate herself with Leo, repeating his opinions as if she had always shared them, smiling when he smiled and sneering at whatever he disliked. Her hostility toward her father, her impatience with the timid and cloistered survivor world, even her raggedy-cuff Levi's and thrift-shop costume jewelry, all had been calculated to capture Leo's sympathy. And Leo had happily bought the act, much to Cassie's disgust.

But a few days on the road had fractured Beth's pretensions. Maybe Beth had resented her father, but she had cared enough about him to risk a phone call. And as stupid as that act may have been, Cassie understood it and sympathized with it.

"I wish we could just go home." Thomas tossed a

pebble and listened as it bounced down the slope toward the valley. He leaned over the plastic mesh fence meant to keep tourists from falling and hurting themselves. Not that there were any tourists this time of year.

"Yeah, I know," Cassie said. "So do I."

"So when do you think we'll actually live somewhere?"

"It might take time. Try to be patient, okay?"

Thomas nodded. Of course, he had already been heroically patient. "I think Beth hates us."

"She acts like it. But really she's just scared."

"So? I'm scared too. That doesn't mean I have to behave like an asshole."

Cassie laughed. "You have a point there."

Was she underestimating Thomas, treating him too much like a child? When Cassie was Thomas's age she had dreamed of joining the Youth Corps, the branch of the League that sent young people to monitor elections in remote countries where new parliaments were being formed. She had pictured herself defending ballot boxes from marauding bandits (which of course Corps volunteers never really did). The murder of her parents had driven all such thoughts from her mind. Was it possible Thomas harbored some similar ambition? *Could* he, after all that had happened?

She was tempted to ask him. But before she could speak Thomas turned up his face, frowning and attentive. "Car coming," he said.

Cassie heard it a second later. She turned apprehensively, spooked by everything Leo had said. To her dismay, the car pulled into the scenic overlook and parked in a spot next to the restrooms. It was the car Leo said had been following them, or a close match. The driver's-side door opened. A middle-aged man got out, stretching and massaging the small of his back. He wore big glasses and an old-fashioned hat.

The man who may or may not have been following them walked into the men's restroom. Cassie and Thomas scrambled back to the car. Leo and Beth got out, and Leo opened the trunk and began rummaging for something in one of his bags. He was tense and his arms moved jerkily. When he stood away from the bumper Cassie saw that he had found what he was looking for, a handgun.

That Leo carried a pistol was no surprise. His father would have encouraged him to keep one, might even have helped him acquire it, legally or illegally. But she was dismayed to see him holding it. It suggested possibilities she didn't care to think about. Even Leo seemed intimidated by it. The weapon trembled in his hand.

He meant to confront the man, Cassie realized, and she could tell by his expression that there would be no arguing about it. Wisely or not, Leo would do this. She could only watch. Or help.

If he had a plan he didn't stop to discuss it. Cassie, Thomas and Beth crouched behind the car while Leo posted himself outside the restroom door and made a shushing gesture, finger to lips. Cassie looked at Thomas, who had gone so bug-eyed she was afraid he might panic, but he held his body motionless and kept his mouth firmly closed. Was there some way to protect him? The man with the big glasses might be armed, too, if he was a sim. But there was nowhere better to hide than here, unless she wanted to tumble down the slope of the hill or run across the road to a stand of trees. Minutes passed, and Cassie became acutely aware of the cold air, the sun on her shoulders, the oily smell of the car and the beating of her heart. At last the crude wooden door of the restroom swung open and the man with the hat stepped out, blinking in the afternoon light. Belatedly, he registered the presence of Leo and offered a squinty, quizzical smile.

Leo came at him and shoved him against the cinderblock wall, showing him the pistol. "You've been following us," he said, and Cassie heard a thrum in his voice that might have been anger but more likely was fear. Now that the confrontation had started Beth stood up boldly and went to stand behind Leo; Cassie took a few steps in that direction as if drawn by some poorly understood duty, though she told Thomas to keep out of sight.

"You're a fucking sim," Beth said, "aren't you?"

The man's eyes, watery behind the lenses of his

glasses, blinked frantically. "I'm—what?" He looked at Leo, at the pistol. "What do you want? You want money?" He reached for his wallet.

"Keep your hands down," Leo said. "We know you've been following us."

"Following you?" The man seemed about to deny it; then he said, "But it's not—I mean, yeah, I heard you asking directions to the Interstate in the lobby at the motel. That's where I'm going. I mean, I'm shitty at following directions. So I thought if I kept your car in sight . . . ? That's all it was, really. So I wouldn't get lost! Is that a problem? I apologize. Like I said, if you want money—"

"*Fuck* your money!" Beth said. She stood next to Leo. "He's lying. He's a sim."

"Maybe," Leo said, "but—"

"But what? You need to take care of it!"

"Shoot him?"

"*Yes! Fuck! Shoot him! Now, while there's nobody around!*"

The wind blew and the trees on the hillside rattled their leafless limbs. Cassie felt a hand on her arm. Thomas. She bent down and whispered, "Go to the car. Get in the backseat. Get down. Close your eyes. Do it!"

The man with the hat and eyeglasses was beginning to look desperate. He held his hands out, palms up, and his face was as pale as the haze hanging over the river valley. "Come on," he said. "Hey."

Leo aimed the pistol at the center of the man's

body. Leo's face became a mask of concentration. His eyes narrowed. He was going to shoot, Cassie realized. He had seen the man following them, he had passed a verdict, and he was going to shoot.

"If you have to shoot him," Cassie said, "shoot him in the leg."

Leo's hand wavered. Cassie couldn't look away from the gun, Leo's knuckles pale and pink against the anodized metal.

"If he's a sim," she said, "we'll know. If not . . . maybe it won't kill him."

Leo nodded and lowered the pistol, but the sound of the gunshot when it came was so loud it made her gasp. It seemed to surprise Leo, too. He stumbled back a step, looking at the weapon as if it had burned his hand. A flock of starlings erupted from a distant tree like sudden smoke.

The man with the big glasses and the old-fashioned hat dropped to the ground. His mouth was open but no sound came out, and one hand groped at the cinderblock wall of the restroom before it reached for his leg. His right leg was shattered below the knee and Cassie was shocked to see the glint of an exposed bone. Blood pulsed from the wound in frantic gouts.

There was nothing green inside him.

Cassie's stomach clenched. She forced herself to stand and watch, furiously scrubbing her watering eyes. Leo was immobilized, staring. Beth had backed away and stood with her spine against the wall of the restroom.

Cassie spared a glance for the road—still empty.

The man on the ground clutched his leg at the thigh with both hands. His eyes had rolled up, showing the whites. "*Guh,*" he said—some senseless grunt.

"Oh, he's not," Leo whispered, "he's not . . ."

Not a sim. Cassie felt a weightless sense of clarity, as if the world had grown simple and brightly lit. "Okay, *we have to stop the bleeding.*"

"How?"

She had taken a first-aid course at school but it hadn't covered gunshot wounds. "Tourniquet," she guessed. "Make a tourniquet."

Leo nodded and took off his belt and bent down to wrap it around the wounded man's leg. The man didn't resist. He was barely moving now. His big glasses were askew on his face and his hat had rolled to the verge of the slope.

Cassie remembered what she had said to Leo (*shoot him in the leg*) and felt sick all over again. She had never seen a person shot at close range. She had imagined a neat hole, not this wholesale butchery. But if she hadn't said anything it would have been worse, wouldn't it?

Leo lifted the wounded leg and doubled his belt around the man's blood-soaked pants, but his hands shook and he couldn't find a notch for the buckle. "Here, let me," Cassie said. Where had this absurd *calmness* come from? She bent down, cinched the belt tight. The rhythmic pulse of blood from the wound began to slow. But the damage was awful. An artery must have been cut. The man needed medical help, urgently.

There was a payphone just inside the restroom entrance: Cassie could see it from where she knelt. "Beth," she said. "Call the police."

"What?"

"He needs an ambulance! Call the police!"

Beth looked at the payphone but didn't move. "I don't think we should do that. Won't we get arrested? We'll get arrested!"

"Beth, he's *dying*." The man's head was tilted back, his mouth was open, he was breathing in gasps, like snores, and although his eyes were open they weren't looking at anything. Cassie put a finger against his throat to feel his pulse. His skin was cool but slick with sweat. The beat she felt was erratic.

"Okay, wait," Leo said. "Cassie . . . I didn't mean to hurt him so bad."

"I know."

"He *was* following us. He admitted it."

"I know! He needs *help*."

"We could . . . maybe we could call from somewhere down the road."

And get away cleanly, he meant. Yes, but: "There's no time. Look at him, Leo!"

"There's nothing we can do for him."

"Of course not! He needs a doctor!" Then she understood: "You want to drive away and *leave* him here?"

"I don't *want* to do it. I don't think we have a choice."

"No! We shot him and we have to help him! Now! Now! Right away!"

"Cassie, listen to me . . . what about Thomas?"

She looked around guiltily. Her brother was standing back by the car. Not close enough to see the man's injury in any detail, but close enough that he must have witnessed the shooting. (*The killing,* she corrected herself: that's what it would be if they abandoned the man here.) But yes, it was true, if the police came, if they were arrested, who would look after Thomas? How could she protect him?

The man on the ground took a gurgling breath and fell silent. His hands ceased moving and his eyes looked blankly at the sky. Cassie registered the sudden slackness of his body. Her head filled with the sound of the wind in the leafless trees.

"Is he dead?" Beth asked.

Cassie felt for a pulse again, pointlessly. She stood up and backed away.

"We have to hide him," Leo said. "He'll be found sooner or later. Better for us if it's later."

"Hide him?" Beth asked.

Leo nodded at a place where the plastic safety barrier had been bent to the ground by weather or reckless tourists. "Help me," he said. "Beth?"

Beth swallowed hard but nodded.

Cassie watched in disbelief as they took the man's

arms and began to drag him toward the slope. The man's shoes left an irregular trail of blood. Cassie scuffed gravel over the pond of blood where the man had been shot, concealing the evidence. Soon her own shoes were spattered with blood. Were they forgetting something?

"His hat," she said.

Beth came back for the man's hat and tossed it toward the distant valley. It sailed on the wind and then dropped out of sight.

"Now roll him down," Leo said.

"We should go through his pockets first."

Cassie turned away. She couldn't bear to watch Leo turning the corpse on its side so Beth could extract the dead man's wallet. She walked back to the car, to Thomas, trying not to hear the sound (though she could hardly ignore it) of the man's body tumbling downhill through clumps of wild sumac and brittle brown grass. The noise dwindled and finally stopped. Somewhere in the woods a crow called out.

Later—after dark, the road unwinding under a shimmer of stars—Beth summoned the courage to look at what she had taken from the dead man's pockets and stuck into her purse: A leather billfold. A couple of hundred dollars in cash. And a prescription bottle of a drug called Bisoprolol. "It's a heart drug," Leo said. "He must have had a condition."

Leo dumped the billfold and the pills (all identifying labels removed) into a trash bin outside a post office in a nameless little town where all the stores were closed for the night. Later, at a twenty-four-hour gas station convenience shop off the Interstate, Beth used some of the dead man's cash to buy a selection of fresh and dry food, which she secured in the trunk of Leo's car.

Cassie sat in the backseat with Thomas as they drove on. During the night Thomas asked her whether the man with big glasses was really dead. "Yes," she told him. No point in lying. Thomas could be protected from many things, but not from this obvious truth.

Since then her brother hadn't said a word. He sat slumped with his head against Cassie's shoulder, eyes closed, not asleep but not entirely awake, hiding in his own somnolent body as the car rolled on. He was the only innocent one among them, Cassie thought. She hadn't been able to protect him from what they had done. But at least she had kept his hands clean.

RURAL VERMONT

Of all the nightmarish events of the last three days, Nerissa thought, this had to be the most grotesquely surreal: descending step by step into the cellar of her ex-husband's farmhouse, where something both more and less than human was waiting to be interrogated.

She was physically and emotionally exhausted. Coming home to find Cassie and Thomas missing from the apartment had revived every fear she had so carefully repressed since the slaughter of '07. During the drive from Buffalo she had been reluctant even to stop for gas, and when she did eventually stop she found herself wondering whether the station attendant (some acned teenager) was *one of them*. It was the kind of reflexive paranoia that might have protected Thomas and Cassie, had she practiced it consistently. But after seven quiet years she had relaxed her vigilance. A night out, she had thought, was a small thing to ask. A well-earned reward, in fact, after everything she had done (and done without complaint) for her sister's children. She *deserved* it, no?

The empty apartment, the packed bag absent from its place under Cassie's bed, the ransacked kitchen: that was her answer.

But she would find Cassie and Thomas, she promised herself. She would protect them. Bring them home. And to hell with Werner Beck and the Correspondence Society's rules of conduct. The Correspondence Society was dead. The only thing left was family. The only thing that mattered.

Ethan walked ahead of her down the wooden stairs. He was still talking about the sim, how it couldn't be trusted, but his words were only an ambient buzz. Nerissa didn't care. She just wanted to see the monster. To force some kind of truth from its stupid, lying mouth.

Of course she knew Ethan was right: the simulacrum—that is to say, the hypercolony of which it was a part—couldn't be trusted. It wasn't a human being. It wasn't even an animal. Ethan and Werner Beck had proved that.

Ethan had told Nerissa about the Society shortly after they were engaged to be married. He had confessed his membership as if it were an embarrassing truth she needed to know about him, like a minor case of herpes. At first she had thought of the Society as something trivial—Masonry for mathematicians, an academic boys' club with the pretense of a conspiracy as its binding secret. The ideas he had blushingly put forward seemed hardly credible. The radio-reflective layer (itself only an engineer's abstraction as far as Nerissa was concerned) as a *living thing*? Exercising subtle control over human history? Even if she had *wanted* to believe it, how could she?

She hadn't taken it at all seriously until he escorted her to his lab and showed her his cell cultures. He had been working with samples recovered from Antarctic ice cores, ostensibly studying airborne pollen deposited by ancient snowfalls. (All Society research needed a legitimizing pretext, he said. Research that cut too close to certain subjects had a way of losing funding or getting derailed during peer review. Careers had been devastated, back in the days before Society members learned to be discreet. But the names he cited were only vaguely familiar to her: who was Alan Turing, for instance?) The pollen was present in the ice cores, and Ethan had dutifully categorized the samples by species, teasing out the implications for the ecology of pollinating insects; his findings had eventually appeared in *Ecological Entomology*. What he didn't report were the tiny granules he had also isolated from the ice: microscopic spherules of what appeared to be carbonaceous chondrite, enclosing trace amounts of complex organic matter.

The spherules were few in absolute number and easily overlooked, hardly distinguishable from dust, but consistently present in a thousand years of deposited ice. The Society's hypothesis was that they had sifted down through the atmosphere from the radio-reflective layer, the radiosphere—that the radiosphere itself was an orbital cloud of trillions of such granules, evenly distributed around the Earth. The cloud was too diffuse to block more than a fraction of incoming sunlight or to detect with the naked eye, but the distributed mass of it, Ethan had calculated, must be immense.

Without its enclosing membrane of rock, the fraction of organic matter preserved in the spherules decayed on exposure to air. But Ethan had been able to accumulate measurable amounts of it in chambers bathed in inert gases and maintained at temperatures and radiation levels commensurate with the vacuum of space. Add a few molecules of carbon and ice, and the substance would bind to them. Give it a sufficient substrate of raw material and it self-assembled new rocky granules, and the new granules revealed more complexity than the degraded ones isolated from the ice cores: complex crystallizations, venous lacings of carbon and silicon . . .

By the time of their marriage—an unspectacular civil ceremony followed by a catered dinner at a country-club function room—Ethan had shared samples of his cultures with Werner Beck and with a few of what he called "the digital computation people" for further study. And although Nerissa tried to wall herself off from the implications of her husband's work, she had to admit it was a momentous and disturbing idea—that some ancient and actually *cosmic* force was screwing around with human communications. But what did that really mean, in practical terms? If the relative prosperity and tranquility of the twentieth century was a product of that intervention (which the Society had long believed), was it sensible to inquire too closely? Humanity's earlier track record was hardly inspiring: endless cycles of war, famine, superstition, pestilence . . .

But these ideas were remote and conjectural and ultimately easy to set aside. Nerissa had managed to go about the business of her life—her teaching position at UMass, a book in progress, her newly-minted marriage—without giving more than a moment's occasional thought to the nature of the fucking radiosphere.

It had seemed like a reasonable accommodation, in the years before the bloodshed began.

Ethan told her the monster in his cellar called itself Winston Bayliss. Nerissa wondered how it had come by the name. Had there been a real Winston Bayliss, perhaps killed and replaced by the sim? Or had the monster invented its name out of a statistical analysis of human nomenclature?

No way of knowing. And it didn't matter.

The monster wore a pair of white briefs, its pale belly drooping over the elastic waistband. Its torso, arms and legs were duct-taped to a heavy wooden chair, effectively immobilizing it. The monster lifted its head as she approached. It wore the bland face of a well-fed white male, not unhealthy but soft around the edges. Of course, its appearance meant nothing. The weary expression on its face meant nothing. Its beseeching eyes meant nothing. The creature's body was simply a display surface, a signaling mechanism. In a human being the look it gave her might have meant, *I've been through a lot. I'm all tired out.* But from the monster all it signified was an attempt to arouse and exploit her sympathy.

Promptly—as if the monster had read her mind, though really it was just interpreting her body language—the pudgy face turned smooth and indifferent. As if to say: *You know what I am, and I won't try to fool you.* And that was also a lie, albeit a subtler one.

Or not *even* a lie. If Ethan and Werner Beck were right, the monster operated by hive logic. Its verbalizations were neither knowingly true nor knowingly false. Ethan had explained this to her long ago. Hive insects—ants, for instance—operated according to a few simple rules, written on their genetics by evolution over the course of millions of years. They did amazing things: built cities in the soil, scavenged for food with startling efficiency. But no ant ever "decided" to do any of these things. Ants didn't plot strategy, and there was no board of directors in the hive. There was no conscious mind at work—there was *no mind at all,* only chemistry and environmental triggers. A cascade of such interactions produced complex behavior. But only the behavior was complex. The rules themselves, and the beings that enacted them, were relatively simple.

It was the same way with the hypercolony. It was a sort of nest or hive that had enveloped the entire planet. Its smallest component parts were the spherules of rock and organic matter Ethan had learned to cultivate. As small as they were, the spherules were capable of generating and receiving impulses over a broad band of radio frequencies. They were also capable, Ethan said, of performing enormously elaborate calculations. (Correspondence Society people talked about "binary code" and "quantum-scale computation," but Nerissa understood none of that; the only computers she had ever dealt with were the ponderous card-reading machines the utility companies used to generate her monthly bills; she took Ethan's claim at face value.)

The spherules weren't, in any plausible sense, individually intelligent. Like ants, they followed rules but didn't write them. Like ants, they exchanged signals and responded in programmed ways to environmental cues. What made the hypercolony remarkable was its collective power to manipulate electronic signals and mimic human beings. Mindless as it was, it could somehow generate a sim like Winston Bayliss and pass it off as human. But when Bayliss said the word "I," it was a noise that meant nothing. There was no "I" inside the monster. There was no one home. There was only the operation of a relentless, empty arithmetic.

She took a step closer to the chair. She could see where Ethan had shot the monster in the leg. He had bandaged the wound, either to keep the mess off the floor or to keep the creature from dying of blood loss. The bandage, improvised from a hand towel and a strip of duct tape, leaked viscous beads of red and green matter. The rotting-hay smell of it hovered cloyingly in the still air of the cellar.

She realized she was avoiding eye contact with the thing. That was cowardly, and the simulacrum would probably sense her fear and try to manipulate it. She refused to offer it even that slender advantage. She steeled herself and stared it in the face. Its eyes were brown and moist, its eyelashes almost femininely long. It returned her gaze unblinkingly. "Hello, Mrs. Iverson," it said.

She was shocked despite her expectations. She swallowed her nausea and said, "How do you know me?" Not because she expected a truthful answer but because she wanted to hear what the monster would say.

"The hypercolony knows you. I share some of that knowledge."

Its voice was a mild, reedy tenor. In itself, that

wasn't surprising. The parts of the monster that produced speech were all authentically human—throat, lungs, vocal cords.

"You *are* the hypercolony, isn't that correct?"

"I understand why you believe that, but no. That's what I came here to explain."

She shrugged. "Say what you want to say." Ethan stood beside her with the pistol in his hand. The simulacrum licked its lips.

"Most of what the Correspondence Society deduced about the hypercolony is true. It's a living thing. Its origins are ancient and incompletely remembered, but it has spread over vast distances, star to star. Its cycle of life is very long. It identifies and engulfs biologically active planets on which tool-making cultures might emerge. If such a culture does emerge, the hypercolony then exploits it for its own ends. Under ideal circumstances the relationship is beneficial to both parties."

"Is it?"

"Once such a culture begins to generate electronic communication, the hypercolony intervenes to foster certain outcomes. Peace as opposed to war, for example. In that way the relationship becomes fully symbiotic. The adopted species is freed from the consequences of its own bellicosity, while prosperity becomes generalized and formerly hostile tribes or nations grow mutually interdependent. Useful technologies then arise naturally and efficiently, and the hypercolony exploits these technologies."

"Exploits them for what purpose?"

"Reproducing itself," the monster said.

Symbiosis, she thought. In this context, the word was an obscenity. She had seen how that alleged mutual benefit actually worked.

It was Nerissa who had discovered the bodies of her sister and brother-in-law back in June of '07. She remembered the front door of their small Forest Park home standing ajar. She remembered the bullet holes in the floral living-room wallpaper Evelyn had loved (and Nerissa had hated: they had conducted countless amiable arguments over it). She remembered the sour, coppery smell of blood, thick enough to taste, and she remembered the blood spattered on her sister's collection of Hummel figurines, the porcelain milk maids and shepherd boys smiling through crimson masks.

Evelyn, whom Nerissa had always called Evie, had been shot twice through the torso and once through the head. She hadn't had time to get up from the sofa. Her husband Bob lay on the floor a few feet in front of her. He had also been shot through the body and had received a final killing shot to the head. Both their faces had been unspeakably distorted by their wounds.

It was a Wednesday afternoon, just past four o'clock. Nerissa had been trying to get in touch with her younger sister since noon and had finally decided to drive to Forest Park in hopes of catching her at home. She wanted to tell Evie about the disturbing telephone call she had received from Ethan, about a wave of killings running through the Correspondence Society, a wild claim but one which the TV news seemed to confirm. Bob Stoddart, Nerissa's brother-in-law, was a longtime Society member and a friend of Ethan's. It was Ethan and Nerissa who had introduced Bob to Evie. As she averted her eyes from their bodies Nerissa found her thoughts drifting back to the time some fifteen years earlier when she had been engaged to Ethan and Evie had been dating Bob . . . how she and Evie had laughed about these unlikely beaus they had somehow acquired, an entomologist and a mathematician (of all things), smart and funny but so often helpless about clothes or manners. Evie could no longer laugh, however, because a bullet had passed through her upper lip on its way through her skull. So Nerissa willed her attention back to the Hummel figurines, piebald with blood. She knew she ought to call the police, and she tried to focus on that task. She would call them from the kitchen telephone, she decided, because the phone on the end table next to the sofa, although it was closer, was clotted with Evie's brain matter. She would do that as soon as she could get her legs to work properly. Until then she leaned against the wall and gazed at Evie's Hummels. Evie had worked in advertising, and something about these figurines had appealed to her, not in spite of but because of their kitschiness: the Merry Wanderer, now lapped by a lake of blood; the Apple Tree Boy, the same color as his apples . . .

She almost screamed when she heard footsteps at the door. *They've come back* was her first panicked thought. But no. It wasn't the killers. A small voice called out, "Hello?"

Cassie.

Oh, God. *Cassie.*

Nerissa found her legs and turned. Of course, Cassie had come home. And Thomas . . . Thomas must be upstairs napping, must have slept through the murders or fallen asleep after the gunshots, or was he (no, this was unthinkable) also dead? But Cassie at eleven was old enough to walk the several blocks from Forest Park Elementary by herself. Cassie was an orphan but didn't know it yet. And she must not be allowed to find out, not *this* way, not by discovering her parents lying in the antic postures of their awful deaths. *Hurry,* Nerissa thought, *keep her away, push her out the door if necessary*—but the girl had already come too far. She was standing in the tiled hall just outside the living room. She had dropped her book bag on the floor. She squinted into the darkened room as if it had filled with a searing light. Her mouth hung open, anticipating a scream that somehow never began.

It had taken all of Nerissa's strength to pull the girl away, to kneel and to turn Cassie's head against her own shoulder, to accept the weight of her tears.

That's your fucking symbiosis, she thought, staring at the human-shaped thing in Ethan's cellar.

"**W**hy are you admitting this?"

"I'm not admitting anything," the monster said. "I'm not the entity that committed the murders of 2007, if that's what you're thinking. Mrs. Iverson, when you look at the night sky, does it seem lifeless to you? It isn't. Every star is an oasis in a desert—a warm place, rich with nutrients and complex chemistry. Many organisms compete for access to those riches. Their struggles are ethereal, protracted, and largely invisible to beings such as yourself. But the battles are as relentless and deadly as anything that happens in a forest or under the sea."

"Even if that's true, so what?"

The simulacrum glanced at Ethan, who was shifting his feet impatiently. "The organism of which I am a part has infected the hypercolony and taken control of its reproductive mechanisms."

"What, like a virus or some kind of parasite?"

"Approximately. But the process isn't finished. The hypercolony is still trying to reclaim itself. A struggle is underway."

"We're wasting time," Ethan said.

Nerissa was inclined to agree. All this cosmic Manichaeism wasn't getting them anywhere. "You said something about my niece, is that correct?"

"Before long the outcome of the struggle will be

decided. One side would like to exploit what remains of the Correspondence Society as a weapon against the other. Your niece is being manipulated. And she's not the only one."

Nerissa leaned toward the sim and let her hatred show. "What, *specifically,* do you know about Cassie?"

"I can help you protect her."

"If you have anything to say—" Nerissa felt Ethan's hand on her shoulder. "*What?* And what's that god-awful noise?"

"The alarm," Ethan said. "Someone's on the property."

"Cut me loose," the monster said.

Ethan told the monster to go to hell. But he didn't kill it, Nerissa noticed. He kept his pistol at his side and hurried up the stairs.

ON THE ROAD

Cassie took the last shift behind the wheel and drove until she spotted a Designated State Campground marker where a side road cut into the piney wilderness north of Decatur, Illinois. There was a chain across the road and a wooden sign hanging from it—FACILITIES CLOSED SEPT 20 TO MAY 30—but Leo kept a bolt cutter in the trunk, so that wasn't a problem.

The campground was a clearing in the forest dotted with stone-lined fire pits. The night was too chilly for open-air camping, but Beth spotted a cabin set back among the pines, and the padlock on the door yielded to a second application of Leo's bolt cutter. The cabin barely qualified as shelter—inside, they found a yellow mattress askew on an ancient box spring, a sofa pocked with cigarette burns, and patches of black mold like Rorschach blots on the bare board walls—but it kept out the wind.

Cassie's first order of business was getting Thomas settled. She was increasingly worried about her brother. He had slept in the car, he was groggy now, and he closed his eyes as soon as she tucked him into his sleeping bag. His face was moist, his thatch of blond hair tangled and greasy—he needed a bath, badly, but there was no running water.

Beth surprised Cassie by fetching a spare pillow from the car. "Here, use this," she said. "He'll be quieter if he's comfortable." As if she needed an excuse for an act of kindness. (And not even a *plausible* excuse: Thomas had been nothing but quiet for hours now.) Cassie thanked her and arranged the pillow under Thomas's head. He opened his eyes once, blinked, then sighed back to sleep.

But it wasn't just a pillow Beth had fetched. She was also carrying a bottle of vodka, a picture of a bearded man in a fur hat on the label. "Where'd that come from?" Leo asked as she unscrewed the cap.

"Bought it when we picked up supplies. Why not, right? Don't tell me you aren't interested." She offered him the bottle.

He didn't take it. "Did the guy at the store card you? Because that's not such a good idea, showing ID if you don't have to."

"No, he didn't fucking *card* me. You want some or not?"

"This isn't a good time."

"No? Really?" She shrugged. "More for me, then."

Beth used an empty thermos to mix the vodka with the contents of a can of Coke. She sipped and grimaced, sipped and grimaced. Stupid waste of money,

Cassie thought, but if it put Beth to sleep it might be worth it. But twenty minutes later Beth was pacing maniacally in the space between the mattress and the sofa, the floorboards creaking with every pass. When Leo suggested (with what Cassie thought was admirable restraint) that Beth might want to sit down and "give it a rest," Beth whirled to face him, staggered and aimed a finger at his chest. "Stop pretending you feel bad about what happened!"

"Beth . . . come on. Seriously. Don't do this."

"So *sad* and everything. All *how could I have killed that guy?* Get over it, Leo. You shot him in the leg so you *wouldn't* kill him. If he had some kind of medical condition, how were you supposed to know?"

"Beth, stop."

"Maybe you should have asked *me* to shoot him, if you didn't want to do it yourself. You're the one always telling us how dangerous everything is, how we can't take any chances, don't call home, don't get carded at the grocery store, watch out for strangers—"

"You'll wake up Thomas."

"I doubt it. He looks like he's fucking comatose. Seriously," turning to Cassie, "is your brother retarded or something? He barely talks."

"He's scared," Cassie said. *But not as scared as you are,* she wanted to add. "I think we all need to get some sleep."

"Fine. Go ahead."

"You're not making it very easy."

"If you're so fucking delicate, go sleep in the car."

"Maybe that's what *you* should do," Leo told her. "Take your sleeping bag out to the car, get as pissed as you want, and in the morning we'll drive the rest of the way to my father's place. Your hangover is your own business."

"What, are you tired of me now? You feel like fucking Cassie tonight? Is that it?"

Cassie had seen Beth drunk before. Every survivor of '07 in Cassie's circle had a way of lifting a middle finger to the world, and Beth's had been her nasty style of drinking—drinking as if to punish herself and everyone around her. But now, even drunk, Beth seemed to realize she had overstepped a boundary. Before Leo could answer she squared her shoulders and said, "Fine, maybe I *want* to be alone." She reached for her jacket and bundled her sleeping bag under her arm, muttering to herself.

Cassie watched from the cabin door as Leo followed Beth out to the car—ostensibly to make sure she was safe, more likely to see that she didn't damage anything. She harangued him from the enclosed space of the backseat while he put his key in the ignition and turned on the radio, maybe thinking a little music would distract her.

But the radio wasn't playing music, it was announcing the local news. Cassie caught orphaned words and fractions of sentences. *Body discovered,* she heard. *Wooded hillside.* She stepped out into the chill of the night, pine duff crackling under her feet. "Turn that," Beth demanded loudly, but she never got to *off,* because Leo whirled and told her to shut the hell up. Drunk as she was, Beth fell into a startled silence.

Cassie walked to the car as the newscaster finished the story: *State police say they will be conducting an exhaustive investigation of this, Wattmount County's first homicide in almost fifteen years.* Then the broadcast moved on to an item about a sawmill fire in some town Cassie had never heard of. Leo switched the radio off, scowling.

I'm a criminal, Cassie thought. An accessory to murder, if not a murderer herself. *We're all criminals.* At any moment the somnolent woods might fill with searchlights and bloodhounds. "Fuck!" Leo said.

"What do we do?"

He shrugged angrily. "Somebody might have seen the car, we have to make that assumption, but I doubt they'll have a description of us. So . . . I guess we ditch the car in the morning and hike someplace where we can catch a bus."

"You still think your father can help us?"

"If anyone can," Leo said.

Cassie sat on the plank sill of the cabin door while Leo covered Beth with a sleeping bag and a couple of spare blankets. The night was cold but not cold enough to be dangerous, as long as she had some protection from the wind, and if Beth woke up achy and shivering come dawn, whose fault was that? Thomas was still asleep inside, but Cassie was too frightened even to think about bed. Eventually Leo came and sat beside her, dragging on a cigarette while she exhaled the tenuous fog of her own breath. A full moon had risen but it cast no light into the body of the forest around them.

Leo stared solemnly at the cigarette in his hand.

"That's a nasty habit," Cassie said. "It's bad for you, you know."

He gave her an incredulous stare . . . then they both began to laugh, quietly but helplessly.

When the laughter subsided she said, "I hope it's true your father can help. My uncle Ethan was pretty close to him back before '07, you know."

"I know. In one of his letters, my father said Ethan Iverson was one of the few who wasn't totally castrated by the attacks." He gave Cassie a sidelong look. "His words, not mine. That's actually pretty high praise, coming from him."

"I like how you're still in contact with him." By mail, of course. The only medium of long-distance communication that wasn't hostage to the hypercolony, and God bless Ben Franklin and the U.S. Postal Service.

"You don't hear from your uncle?"

"Aunt Ris didn't think it would be a good idea. Any kind of contact with anyone who was personally targeted back in 2007 is risky, she said. But I read his books . . . you know he wrote two books?"

"Mm. About bugs, right?"

"Insects. He's an entomologist. But in a way the books are about the hypercolony, a way of talking about it without actually mentioning it, because it works by insect logic—hive logic. Like how you can get really sophisticated behavior without any kind of consciousness or self-knowledge . . ."

"I learned some of that from my father's letters," Leo said. "It's true, he said, but the Society made the mistake of treating it like a philosophical question."

"As opposed to?"

"Military intelligence. Know your enemy. Discover its weaknesses."

That fit with what Aunt Ris had said about Werner Beck, that he was obsessed with the idea of waging war against the hypercolony. Which was stupid, she used to say, even on its own terms. Part of waging war is knowing when you're outgunned. And as far as Aunt Ris could tell, humanity had been outgunned since Taft was president—probably for centuries before. Cassie said the idea of war seemed kind of unrealistic.

"Not necessarily. You have to ask yourself, what did the hypercolony take away from us? One answer is, the will to fight and the weapons to fight with. Every day they tell us how terrible war is, how lucky we are that the League of Nations is out there managing conflict, all that bullshit. So only a few of us are willing to make a fight of it. But even a few people can make a difference, if they have the right weapon."

"How do you fight something like the hypercolony? A cloud of dust, basically. You can't bomb it. You can't take it prisoner."

"I don't know. I don't have an answer to that. Maybe my father does. But if we weren't dangerous, they wouldn't be hunting us."

"Who—*us*? One guy, two girls, and a twelve-year-old? Yeah, we're pretty dangerous, all right. Dangerous to middle-aged men with heart conditions."

As soon as she said it, she wished she could take it back. She could see from Leo's pinched expression that she had hurt him.

"That was an accident."

"No, you're right, I know . . ."

"I never meant for it to happen. But even if it is our fault—my fault—he wouldn't be dead if the sims hadn't come after us. You think the sims feel guilty about it?"

"They don't feel anything at all. That's how we're different from them."

"You lost your parents, right?"

"Yes," Cassie said, and of course Leo knew that; all the survivors of '07 had heard each other's horror stories at least once.

"You ever get angry about it?"

"Sure I do."

"I mean really angry? Angry enough to want to do something about it? Or do you just try not to think about it?"

She shrugged, embarrassed.

"It's nothing to be ashamed of. Anger, I mean."
Leo stood and crushed his cigarette under the heel of
his shoe. A spark escaped into the wind and winked
out in the darkness. "You don't have to be nice all
the time. Get angry once in a while. You're entitled."

She knew better than to believe that the hypercolony
had extinguished the human capacity for violence
and hatred. Violence happened every day, everywhere in the world. Wattmount County hadn't seen
a homicide in fifteen years, according to the newscast, but Cassie was willing to bet it still generated its
share of bar fights and domestic arguments, maybe
even a few racial set-tos. And internationally: no major
wars, but there were enough violent rebellions and
lethal border skirmishes to keep up the body count.
It was only that these dangerous tendencies had been
ameliorated or tamped down.

The relative peace since 1900 could be measured
only statistically. Still, the numbers told a convincing
story: a dramatic decline in violent conflict and all
the consequences of war: famine, plague, economic
collapse. Cassie's high-school Poli-Sci text had cred-
ited material and moral progress for the change. And
maybe that was true. But it wasn't the whole story. If
you inquired into the details of history—as countless Correspondence Society researchers had done—
some obvious anomalies emerged. The crises averted,
the battles won or lost, the ceasefires that were even-

tually negotiated, all seemed to turn on pivotal acts of communication or miscommunication. Radiograms vanished in transmission or were subtly altered. Bellicose ultimatums failed to reach their intended audience. Unbreakable codes were broken, battleships were dispatched to the wrong coordinates, artillery emplacements shelled empty trenches. All this was mediated through the radiosphere. And in the aftermath of the Great War, in the age of mass communication, public sentiment was swayed by cues far too subtle and clever to be called propaganda.

But why? For what ultimate purpose?

The Correspondence Society had offered only speculative answers. Maybe they had been closing in on the truth in the decade before '07, when Ethan Iverson and Werner Beck produced conclusive evidence that the radiosphere was alive, a hypercolony (as Cassie's uncle had called it) of microscopic living things. But that explained nothing. Did the hypercolony mean to keep humanity pacified as it pursued its own purposes? Or did it have some more *specific* use for the human species?

In any case, Cassie thought, though it had made human civilization more peaceful, the hypercolony itself was hardly nonviolent. *You lost your parents,* Leo had reminded her, not that she needed any reminding, and as she sagged toward sleep she had to suppress the memory of how her mother and father had looked when she had last seen them, their faces shattered and the contents of their heads splashed

over the furniture where they had been sitting. Whatever else that atrocity might be or mean, it was not
the work of a *peaceful* entity.

She woke to the sound of rain on the cabin roof, of
rain trickling down the crude cabin walls, of a pounding at the cabin door.

She sat up and saw Leo struggling out of his own
sleeping bag. Feeble daylight penetrated the single
window. Her dreams were still heavy in her head and
she wondered whether this was one of them, until
the door flew open and she saw the silhouette of
a man in a yellow slicker and rain hat, his face obscure but his scowl unmistakable. "Park Service,"
the man bellowed, giving Cassie a contemptuous
glance but saving a fiercer glare for Leo, "and if you
think you can come in here, cut these locks, have a
little pot party or whatever you kids do, well, I got
news for you."

Cassie began scrambling out of her sleeping bag,
which had become an entanglement, a cocoon she
couldn't shed. Leo managed to stand up, empty-
handed and impotently angry. Cassie felt she could
see it all through the stranger's eyes: the Park Service
man running some routine off-season patrol, discovering the severed chain at the road entrance, the unfamiliar car parked in the pine glade, the broken
hasp on the cabin's padlock, his temper not improved
by the rain seething over everything . . . She stared

through the open doorway. *"Look,"* she managed to say.

"No, *you* look! You damage State property, you pay for it—that's the law, young lady."

But what she meant was, *Look behind you.* Past him, Cassie could see the open space between the cabin and the pines. She could see the Park Service man's white pickup truck, mud-spattered to the midline. She could see Leo's car next to it, the windows fogged and wet. She saw the car door opening, and she saw Beth climbing out, holding Leo's bolt cutter in her right hand, her hair slicked to her scalp. She saw Beth running toward the cabin through the vast wet rush of the storm. She saw Beth swing the bolt cutter by its handle. *Look,* she thought. *Look!*

But the Park Service man didn't look.

He toppled over in the doorway, his body half in and half out of the cabin. His head began bleeding immediately.

The force of the blow had knocked the bolt cutter out of Beth's hand, and she stooped to pluck it out of the mud. Her mouth twisted in some combination of a grin and a frown.

"Beth!" Leo said.

"He was going to arrest us," Beth said. "Or something."

"Yes, but—oh, *Christ!* All right—okay, we need to get our shit together—Cassie, get Thomas up. We need to get away from here, *now*. Make sure you don't leave anything behind. Beth, put the bolt cutter in the trunk and bring me a roll of duct tape."

Leo used the tape to bind the hands and feet of the Park Service man so he wouldn't be able to follow them when he woke up. *If* he woke up. He probably had a concussion, Cassie thought. At least. Or worse. Though by the way he had begun to moan, he wouldn't be unconscious for long.

Cassie couldn't help staring. "Roll up your sleeping bag," Leo told her curtly. "I mean it. And do something about your brother."

Thomas was sitting up in a tangle of blankets, crying. Cassie put her arm around him until he began to relax, then opened his small suitcase and helped him dress. Thomas wouldn't meet her eyes, but he held up his arms while she pulled his last clean T-shirt over his head. A bubble of snot dribbled over his upper lip. Go on, cry, Cassie thought. Some things were worth crying over.

Leo took a key ring from the belt of the moaning Park Service man and carried it out to the white pickup truck. He came back with a laminated map of the local conservation area. He looked it over quickly while Cassie loaded her suitcase and Thomas's into the trunk of Leo's car. She helped Thomas into the backseat, wishing she had set aside a dry towel: the rain had doused them and they would be wet for the rest of the day, damp even under their jackets.

Leo gave Beth the key to the Park Service man's pickup and told her to start it up and to follow the car. There was a road through the forest that would take them to a connecting county route and a town called East Cut near the federal turnpike. "What about him?" Cassie asked—the Park Service man, who was writhing on the floor—but Leo shrugged and said, "You and Thomas ride in the car with me."

Cassie forced herself not to look back.

A couple of miles down the road Leo stopped the car. Beth came over from the pickup and slid into the front passenger seat while Leo put the Park Service vehicle into neutral and pushed it over an embankment into a bushy declivity where some nameless creek ran brown and fast. The pickup wouldn't be especially well-hidden—even a cursory search would turn it up—but it would be out of sight at least until someone came looking for it. Or so Leo said.

Cassie thought about the Park Service man back at the cabin. Sooner or later he would wiggle out of his restraints. Without his truck he would have to walk to the public road, flag down a passing car, get a ride to the hospital or the nearest police station. All of that would buy them a little time. (Or, Cassie thought, the man might be too weak to set himself free; he might die of exposure on the filthy cabin floor, and they would be guilty of another murder . . . that was possible, too.)

Leo climbed back behind the wheel of the car, smelling of mud and pine needles, and drove wordlessly through the forest. The rain was a relentless obscuring wash against the windshield. Thomas, no longer sniffling, seemed comforted by the rhythmic noise of the windshield wipers. Cassie understood that. Since the death of her parents she had learned to value all the wordless consolations of the world—wind and rain, sunlight and moonlight, noonday shadows and darkened rooms—everything reliably felt and not treacherously unpredictable.

They reached the turnpike, and a mile outside the town of East Cut Leo parked the car behind the ruin of a failed and abandoned gas station. The rain had stopped, and they were able to hike through a gathering ground fog to the East Cut bus depot. A largely empty afternoon bus carried them to Kewanee, where they caught an express to Galesburg and from Galesburg a late-evening local that stopped in a town called Jordan Landing. On the outskirts of Jordan Landing was the house where Leo's father lived.

Leo didn't want to risk another payment on the credit card he had been using, so Cassie paid for the motel room where they spent the night. Come morning they set out on foot to find the address Leo had memorized.

The town of Jordan Landing had grown up around a Mississippi River wharf, a John Deere branch plant, and a brickworks. They stopped for breakfast at a Main Street diner with calendars from local businesses

tacked to the wall behind the counter. Leo picked a
booth by the restaurant's big window, where they
could see a shopkeeper rolling out his awning and a
grocer stacking boxes of lettuce on the mica-flecked
sidewalk. Today, Cassie realized belatedly, was Armistice Day. Banners had been strung between the
lampposts, just like back home.

The waitress who brought their breakfasts ruffled
Thomas's hair and asked whether they were visiting
or just passing through.

"Passing through," Leo said.

"Too bad. We're having a nice show in the park
tonight. Fireworks and all. Though I expect you've
seen better—you look like city people to me, am I
right?"

"Detroit," Leo lied.

I could live here, Cassie thought. It would be easy
to fall in love with this sunny street and all the sunny
streets surrounding it. She pictured herself in a room-
ing house with a pillared porch. Shade-dappled summer days, snug winter nights. And if a mindless and
conscienceless entity rolled through the sky like an
insect god, a blind guarantor of human progress,
maybe she could have lived with that knowledge . . .
could have, if she hadn't seen the blood.

They paid the waitress for their eggs and bacon
and whole-wheat toast dabbed with butter, for their
coffee and cream and for Thomas's mug of hot chocolate. The restaurant had begun to fill up with locals,
and Leo was looking fretful and impatient. Time to

get on with business. They all knew there was a real
possibility that Leo's father had been targeted in the
latest round of attacks. Werner Beck was famously
wealthy and well-defended, but even Werner Beck
was mortal.

The house where Leo's father lived was located
farther from the center of town than it had seemed
on the map, and as they walked Cassie could see the
tension rising in Leo's body, the way he hitched his
shoulders and glanced compulsively behind him.
Twice she asked him to slow down so Thomas could
keep up. The air was cool but the sunlight and the
brisk pace raised a sweat on her face. Jordan Landing
was a hilly town, and the Mississippi was occasionally
visible to the west, brown and busy with shipping.

She was surprised, though she shouldn't have been,
when they finally came within sight of the house:
it was modest and unremarkable, which was probably why Werner Beck had chosen it. Beck could have
afforded a Manhattan penthouse had he wanted
one, but prudence had led him to choose this perfectly ordinary house in this perfectly ordinary town.
It was the last home on a street that curved gently
eastward from the Mississippi embankment. Cassie
guessed most of these small houses belonged to workers at the brickworks or the John Deere plant. The
houses backed on unimproved lots, each divided
from its neighbor by a hedgerow or a picket fence.
Some of the houses had elaborate gardens, now bed-
ded in for winter; in one of these gardens an elderly

woman looked up from her work—laying canvas sheets over rosebushes—and waved tentatively. Cassie waved back as if she belonged here. It was better not to look furtive.

Leo followed the patio-block pathway to his father's door. Cassie saw with dismay that a few days' worth of newspapers had been delivered to the porch but never picked up. Leo had brought his pistol, tucked into his waistband under his shirt and jacket, and he took it out now, keeping it concealed in front of him. He knocked at the door, waited, rang the bell, rang it again. There was no answer. And when he turned the knob the door swung open, unlocked.

"Stay here," he said tersely.

Cassie felt Thomas grab her hand. Maybe it was reckless to have brought Thomas along, but leaving him at the motel had seemed equally risky. And she had not imagined that the sims, even if they had come to Werner Beck's house, would still be here—why would they? But she backed a few paces away just in case, and she leaned and whispered to Thomas, "If you have to run, *run*. Don't worry about me." Which frightened him, but it couldn't be helped.

Leo disappeared into the shadow of the house while Beth sulked on the porch. Minutes passed. Cassie heard the distant tolling of a church bell, muted by the morning air. It was if the day had been encased in cool blue glass.

Then Leo reappeared in the doorway, looking stricken, and waved them all inside.

* * *

There was no evidence that Leo's father had been killed. No blood, no upturned furniture or broken glass, no bullet holes in the walls. But Werner Beck was gone, had apparently been gone for some days, and seemed to have left in haste. An uneaten meal sat on the kitchen table: roast beef congealed in its own gravy and a slice of buttered bread from which a few threads of mold had sprouted. A copy of the *Jordan Landing Advertiser* lay unfolded beside the plate.

Cassie followed Leo upstairs, to a room that must have been Beck's study. An oaken desk shared the space with bookcases and filing cabinets. The filing cabinets had been rifled; the drawers were open, some pulled from their cabinets and dumped on the floor. "What happened here?" Beth asked.

Leo shrugged. "Somebody was looking for something, obviously."

"You think they found it?"

"Couldn't say. But I know a place they probably didn't look."

Downstairs to the small living room, which Werner Beck had furnished in a spare, almost offhand style: a plain sofa, a simple coffee table, no TV set or radio. Leo shoved the coffee table against the wall and pulled up the cloth rug, exposing the planked flooring. He examined the bare floor for a moment, then put his finger in a knothole and yanked.

A square chunk of flooring three planks wide

came up in his hand. It had been set so finely that the
seams hadn't shown. Underneath, in the space between the floorboards and the concrete foundation,
was a small steel safe, the dial of its combination
lock facing upward. "He told me he put this here,"
Leo said. "In case something happened to him."

"So what's inside?" Beth asked.

"What I would need. That's all he ever said. He told
me where to look for it and he told me to memorize
the combination. Nothing else."

He turned the dial, muttering the numbers to himself. Cassie crouched behind him next to Beth, peering over his shoulder as he opened the door on its
oiled hinges. He reached inside and pulled out a fat
manila envelope.

Leo emptied the contents of the envelope onto the
coffee table. Not much there, Cassie thought won-
deringly:

A map.

A handwritten list of what appeared to be towns
or cities.

A few typed pages, stapled at the corner.

And a key.

10

Ethan took Nerissa to the farmhouse attic and checked his surveillance feeds. Two sims were approaching from the direction of the main road. The afternoon light was fading but he could clearly see the automatic rifles the creatures held at a ready angle. Only members of the armed forces were legally permitted to carry such weapons, but these two men, roughly the same apparent age as the creature in the cellar, seemed not to be soldiers. One wore a business suit, the other wore blue jeans and a corduroy shirt. They moved in parallel on opposite sides of the access road, keeping to the shadows of the trees.

That was the front of the house. Out back, the surveillance cameras had apparently shut down, leaving Ethan entirely blind in that direction. But he could only address one problem at a time. He took one of the three hunting rifles he kept in a rack on the wall and carried it to the west-facing window. He had replaced the original window and frame with a sheet of double-thick birchwood ply into which he had cut an embrasure large enough to allow him to sight along the barrel of the rifle.

The first target would be the easiest. He waited until the sim in the business suit reached the clearing in front of the house. There was no way to approach the house without crossing that empty space. The sim left the cover of the trees, running. Ethan's first shot split the sim's skull, spilling a cascade of green matter threaded with blood.

The next shot wouldn't be as easy. The second sim, the one in blue jeans, broke from the woods before his companion had finished falling. He veered away from the front of the house, attempting to get out of Ethan's range. The narrow embrasure in the plywood afforded Ethan some protection, but it also restricted his field of fire. He brought the rifle hard up against the wood and squeezed the trigger.

He hit the target, but he hit it low. Ethan guessed he had clipped the simulacrum's spine, because the creature fell and couldn't stand up again. After a moment it abandoned the struggle and used its arms to drag itself toward the house. Ethan managed to put a second bullet in the sim's neck. Gouts of blood and green matter spewed from the wound and the creature stopped moving.

But Ethan still didn't know what was happening out back, where the cameras had been destroyed or deactivated. He ran to the east-facing window and leveled his rifle, pulling away in time to avoid a hail of bullets from a third sim's automatic weapon.

Plywood splinters peppered his face and a flurry of dust and debris showered down from the attic ceiling. He glanced back to make sure Nerissa hadn't been hit. She was still standing, unhurt but obviously terrified. He told her to get down on the floor.

The sim who fired on him had been crossing the open space in back of the house and was out of sight now, but Ethan didn't have to wonder where it had gone: he heard the sound of the back door being kicked in. The creature had entered the house.

Everything Ethan knew about the anatomy of the simulacra he had learned from Werner Beck. Werner Beck had not only survived the attempt on his life in 2007, he had managed to wound and disarm both of his attackers. And in the days that followed Werner Beck had taken his captive sims apart—piece by piece, making notes.

He had distributed a monograph on the subject to all the survivors loyal or reckless enough to stay in touch with him. Ethan had a copy in his files. *Anatomical Details of the Artificial Human Beings,* with diagrams and photographs. The photographs had been particularly disturbing: two sims, still alive, mounted on dissection boards and opened from the chest down. The skin of their torsos had been peeled back and pinned in place like the pages of a book, ribs and bloody musculature fully exposed, several small but functional human organs partially removed.

Ethan had forced himself to memorize the details. Sacs of green matter, essentially identical to the contents of the cells Ethan had cultured from Antarctic ice cores, occupied most of the gut and extended into the extremities including the skull. The skull sac was surrounded by a web of nervous tissue that presumably performed some of the functions of a human brain. The scaffolding of bone was indistinguishable from a human skeleton. In the abdominal and chest cavities, dwarfish human organs (a heart hardly bigger than a golf ball, a liver that might have been taken from a newborn infant) served the shell of flesh that gave the sims their human appearance. Cut a sim and it would bleed. Cut deeply and it would bleed green.

The green material was complex but amorphous, the same no matter where in the body it was located. That meant the sims were less vulnerable to some kinds of physical damage than human beings were. Attacking one with a knife would be nearly suicidal. A bullet through the soft parts would only slow it down, while a bullet through the spine would drop it in its tracks without killing it. A shot to the head was the best bet, Werner Beck had written, since the skein of nervous tissue under the skull was an essential interface, allowing the simulacrum to control its body.

Even then, death might not be instantaneous. Beck's captive sims had survived for days as he systematically cut and flayed them—they had pretended pain at first, and when the pretense failed they lapsed into an observant silence. Loss of blood eventually killed one of them: its small heart simply stopped beating; the other sim died when Beck experimentally fired a bullet into its skull.

Ethan traded his rifle for a pistol, then took a second one from its rack and offered it to Nerissa. "You know how to use that?" She nodded: like many other survivors she had taken a course after the 2007 massacre. Her hands shook, but she checked the pistol to ensure that it was loaded, then clicked off the safety.

"Stay here. Wait for me." *And shoot anything that comes up in my place,* he didn't have to add. Then he opened the attic door and moved down the narrow stairs to the farmhouse's second story, a hallway with more stairs at the far end. Daylight was fading and the hall was dim. Ethan paused every few paces, listening for sounds from below but hearing little more than the pounding of his own pulse.

If he had any advantage it was his intimate knowledge of the farmhouse, its angles, its shadows, its exposed places and its high ground. He hugged the left-hand wall until he reached the landing of the stairway, then leaned into the emptiness beyond the railing with his pistol sighted toward the front door. Nothing. But there was a rattle that might have come from the kitchen.

Ethan's respect for his opponent was complete. He thought again of Werner Beck dissecting the captured sims, an act that seemed both cruel and vengeful until you realized it was neither—the sims felt no pain and were indifferent to indignity. They weren't even individuals, in the human sense. They even were less autonomous than ants or termites, mere extensions of the superorganism that had created them: massive, complex, far-traveled, ancient. Not even remotely human, and above all, not to be underestimated.

Ethan hurried down the stairs, mindful that he was exposed to fire from the sim's automatic rifle. From the bottom of the stairs he could see most of the farmhouse's main room, which was empty. Which left the kitchen. The door to the kitchen was closed. He couldn't remember if he had closed it himself. He had no choice but to announce his presence by throwing it open, pistol ready, thinking with some fraction of his mind of Nerissa: she was armed but terrified, and if he died here—

But the kitchen too was empty. The back door was askew in its frame, hanging by one hinge where the sim had kicked it in. A trail of muddy boot prints led from the broken door to the entrance to the cellar. Ethan looked at the stairwell with dismay. He could only conclude that the sim was down there with Winston Bayliss.

Move, he told himself. He had no choice but to attempt the cellar stairs.

He was halfway down when he saw the sim at the foot of the stairs with its back to him, looking utterly human with its upturned collar, its sagging blue jeans, the nascent bald spot at the crown of its head. The automatic rifle was raised, but not in Ethan's direction. The sim began to turn as Ethan's foot hit a creaking riser. But it was no faster than a mortal man. Ethan had been granted that rare gift, an easy target. He squeezed the trigger of the pistol.

Simultaneously, the sim began firing into the darkness of the cellar. In this enclosed space the sound was deafening. Ethan flinched, but not before his bullet took the simulacrum at the base of its skull. The sim's automatic rifle sprayed a few more bullets, then fell silent. The sim toppled over, inert.

Ethan stood over the body and put a finishing shot into its head. Green matter gushed out, emitting a rank chemical-fertilizer stink.

Then he looked around the cellar, realizing what it was the sim had done: incredibly, it had shot Winston Bayliss.

The creature that called itself Winston Bayliss was still strapped to the chair where Ethan had left it, held in place by coils of duct tape, but its upper body slumped at a nasty angle: the invading sim's rifle fire had nearly bisected it at the hip. Bayliss was leaking blood and green liquid at a furious rate.

It raised its head and looked at Ethan steadily. "Please," it said faintly. "Please, will you bandage the wound? We still need to talk."

Ethan could only stare.

"As quickly as possible," Winston Bayliss said. "Please."

* * *

The idea of staying here even an hour longer had become absurd. It was past time to leave, and everything would have to be burned. His notes, his video gear, the attic arsenal—the farmhouse from its foundation to the peak of its mossy roof. Ethan had been preparing for this contingency since his first days here. He had stored a dozen canisters of kerosene in the main floor closet, and every morning he put a fresh book of matches in his hip pocket.

He came up the stairs to the attic and found Nerissa waiting, her pistol aimed at his chest. She lowered the weapon instantly, to Ethan's relief. The way her hands were shaking, one awkward twitch might have killed him. "Is it dead?" she asked.

He managed to nod. Though for all he knew there might be more on the way.

She relaxed so suddenly that he thought she might lose her footing. She put a hand on a shelf to steady herself.

All this must have been unimaginably hard on her. Ethan had loved this woman once and maybe still did, though the gap of doubt and blame between them had grown vast and was probably unbridgeable. He couldn't look at her without seeing the Nerissa he had once known: Nerissa across a table in the faculty cafeteria, quoting writers he hadn't read and whose names he barely recognized, her long hair threatening to interfere with a plate of French fries—her liveliness and her ready smile, then so available, now so completely erased. She looked unspeakably tired. Night was falling and he wished he had a comfortable bed to offer her, but there was much to be done and no time to hesitate. *Miles to go,* in the words of one of those poems she had liked to recite. *Miles to go before we sleep.*

He took the first of his dozen jerricans of kerosene into the cellar, where he poured the contents over the corpse of the dead sim and along the floorboards. Nerissa emptied another canister over the firewood stacked under the single window, which he had boarded over, and as she worked Winston Bayliss began to plead with her. "Bind my wounds," it said. "Take me with you."

The sim had bled out massively from its human parts, and now it was leaking its greener contents onto the cellar floor. A reeking mess, Ethan thought. But the fire would cleanse all that.

"He's practically cut in half," Nerissa said. "The one who broke in did that?"

"Yes."

"Why?"

"I don't know."

"What this thing said, about there being two kinds of sims, do you think that's possible?"

"I don't know. Half of what these things do is theater."

"I can explain," Winston Bayliss said. "If you bind my wounds. If you take me with you."

"Maybe we should," Nerissa said.

Startled, Ethan looked up from the trail of kerosene he had laid. "Are you serious?"

"I mean if it knows something about Cassie and Thomas."

"Cut off my legs," Winston Bayliss said. "They're useless. Tourniquets above the stumps will keep me alive for a time, if you do it quickly."

Madness, Ethan thought. But Nerissa turned to him and asked in a voice gone steely and indifferent, a voice he barely recognized, "What about it, Ethan? Do you have an axe down here? A hatchet?"

"*Jesus*, Ris!"

"Because if we burn it we'll never know why those others wanted it dead."

"What *exactly* are you suggesting? That we hack off its legs and, what, put it in the trunk of the car?"

"Well, it would fit," she said. "If we did that."

He hoped it was a macabre joke. Or maybe the kerosene fumes were getting to her. But no. He had always known when she was serious. "Ris . . . even if what you're suggesting might be useful, and I'm not admitting such a thing even for a second, we'd be taking a crazy risk. We don't know for sure what's looking out through that thing's eyes, but whatever it is, I don't want it watching us."

"That needn't be a problem," the sim said.

Ethan and Nerissa looked at it. The wounded sim had worked its right hand loose from its bonds—the flow of blood had slicked and softened the coils of duct tape. It raised its free hand to its face (its slightly pudgy face, now pale and unearthly in its bloodlessness), curled the thumb into a hook and thrust it into the socket of first one and then the other of its eyes.

Once the burning began they couldn't linger. In the dark, the fire would be visible for miles.

Everything Ethan had wanted to keep—fake ID, a supply of cash and traveler's checks, a fresh pistol—he had packed into a single cardboard filing box, which he slid it into the backseat of Nerissa's car. His own car, the secondhand Chrysler he drove into town on weekends, was parked in an outbuilding separate from the house. But it would be smarter to take Nerissa's car: no one had seen it here and there was nothing to associate it with Ethan or his farmhouse. He doused the wooden walls of the outbuilding with kerosene and tossed a match behind him. The tindery structure began to burn hastily, and by that time the farmhouse was already well along, flames creeping up from the foundation and licking out of the first-floor windows. Ethan hurried to the car: he wanted to be gone before the ammunition in the attic began to cook off.

He offered to drive and Nerissa nodded gratefully. She buckled herself into the passenger seat and allowed her head to slump against the headrest. Her breathing deepened into gentle snores as he drove away from the farmhouse. The fitful light of the fire reflected from the windshield, the dashboard, her face. Asleep, she looked exactly like the woman he remembered, but bent, Ethan thought, almost to the point of breaking: bent to the limit of her endurance.

He pulled over where the laneway met the county road. Nerissa opened her eyes and mumbled a word that might have been, "*What?*"

"Shh," he said, reaching through the driver's-side window. "Just picking up the mail."

One last time. He lifted the hinged door of the rural delivery box, withdrew a single letter and switched on the car's overhead light long enough to glance at it. The return address was illegible and probably meant to be, but he recognized the handwriting at once. The letter was from Werner Beck.

He tucked it into his shirt pocket.

Half an hour later he was on the federal turnpike, cold air from an open window flushing out the stink of kerosene and worse things. He hadn't thought about a destination. He drove west in a river of red taillights, Nerissa asleep beside him, headed nowhere but away.

PART TWO

THE FISHERMAN AND THE SPIDER

Consider a fisherman—let's say, a young man who owns a small boat and weaves his own nets.

One sunny morning the fisherman sails out from the harbor and casts his net into the ocean. By the end of the day he has accumulated a fine catch of succulent fish. Back ashore, he sets aside a share of the bounty for his evening meal. He guts and cleans the fish and roasts them over an open fire on the beach. Perhaps he calls down his wife from their seaside cottage; perhaps the couple dine alfresco as the sun sets, gazing into each other's eyes; perhaps, nine months later and as an indirect result of their activities on that happy evening, the fisherman's wife bears a healthy child . . . but these plausible sequelae are not pertinent to our story.

Now imagine another biological organism, in this case a spider: a common orb-weaver spider, of which there are some three thousand species worldwide and probably one or two in your own garden or backyard. Like the fisherman, the spider weaves a net (of sticky silk) and uses it to capture another species (a moth) as food. Like the fisherman, the spider prepares its meal before it consumes it—it pumps digestive enzymes into the body of the captive insect, sucks out the liquefied matter, and discards the empty husk, much as the fisherman discarded the inedible bones and organs of his fish. Perhaps the spider follows his meal by finding a mate, impregnating her, and offering his body to be devoured; perhaps the female then produces a pendulous, silk-encased sac of fertilized eggs . . . but all this, like the fisherman's amorous evening, is incidental to our story.

The fisherman's tale is pleasant, even heartwarming. The spider's tale is viscerally disgusting. But from an objective point of view, nothing distinguishes one from the other but the details. A net is a net, whether it's made of nylon or spider silk. A meal is a meal.

The important difference lies in the realm of subjective experience. The fisherman's day is richly felt and easily imagined. The spider's is not. It is extremely unlikely that the simple fused ganglia of an arachnid generate much if anything in the way of psychological complexity. And an anthill—although it is also a functional biological entity, capable of its own equivalent of net-casting and food-gathering—has no centralized brain at all and no perceived experience of any kind.

The rich inner experience of the world is central to human life and our appreciation of it. But the preponderance of life on Earth gets along perfectly well without it. In this respect, human beings are a distinct minority. The fishermen of the world are greatly outnumbered by the spiders.

—Ethan Iverson,
The Fisherman and the Spider

11

"I'm not what she said I am," Thomas insisted. "I'm not useless."

Sitting across from him at a table in the diner, Cassie was inclined to believe it. Not for the first time, Thomas had surprised her.

"Well, look who's back for supper," the waitress had said when they came in. "We close at seven," she added, "so don't dawdle. Fireworks start at eight—I guess you decided to stay for the fireworks?"

"Yes, ma'am," Cassie said. Maybe it had been a mistake to come back to the same restaurant where they had bought breakfast. Being recognized was never good. But most of Jordan Landing's restaurants had already closed for Armistice Day, and the other exception, a Chinese restaurant called Lucky Paradise, didn't appeal to Thomas.

The waitress brought meatloaf for Cassie and a hamburger and French fries for Thomas. Thomas tucked in eagerly. His appetite seemed to have come back, despite the trauma of the last few days. It was almost as if Beth's insult had invigorated him.

Once they had retrieved the papers and the key from Werner Beck's hidden safe, they left the house by the rear door, hiked through a wooded allotment to another quiet residential street, then circled past the commercial section of town to the motel. Back in their room, Leo insisted on reading the papers his father had left him before he would discuss the contents. When he finished, he looked up and said, "We have to think about what happens next."

"You could start," Beth suggested, "by telling us what's in those pages."

"Well . . . *lots*," Leo said. "It's sort of a plan."

"A plan for what?"

"My father wrote this and left it where I could find it in case there was another attack on the Society. Over the last few years he learned some things he didn't share, things about the hypercolony. Ways we might be able to affect it. Hurt it."

"Like?"

Leo shook his head: "I need to go through it again. But what I can tell you is, if we do what my father wants us to do, it's going to be dangerous. You might not want to get involved."

Beth rolled her eyes. "Fuck, Leo—I *am* involved."

"I know, and you're right, but we're talking about

a whole other level of commitment. I need a decision from you, too," addressing this to Cassie, "you and Thomas both. And even if you want to join in . . . I'm going to have to think about whether it's a good idea to let you do that."

Cassie felt a twinge of foreboding. Something about the expression on Leo's face, the pinched V of his brows: whatever was in those papers had frightened him, but it had also filled him with a kind of grim hope.

Beth remained sourly suspicious. "Are you even considering taking *them* along? Why? If this is so fucking dangerous. I mean, no offense," a brief and insincere glance at Cassie, "but they're baggage. *She* hasn't done anything more useful than pay for a few meals, and as for Thomas, he's a kid—he's useless."

Cassie flushed at the injustice of it (as if *Beth* had performed some invaluable service!), but before she could answer Thomas piped up: "I'm *not* useless."

"No?" A glimmer of cruelty in Beth's voice. "What have you done except sleep? Sleep and occasionally cry?"

"Nothing—"

"Right."

"Nothing except what you guys asked me to do. I don't try to have things my own way. I don't complain." He added, his eyes fixed on Beth: "And I didn't try to phone anybody."

Beth reddened and lunged forward—Cassie stepped

in front of her brother—but Leo put a hand on Beth's shoulder to hold her back. "Come on," he said. "Let's talk about this."

Meaning he wanted to talk to Beth alone. So Cassie grabbed her jacket and Thomas's and left the room with Thomas in tow. She said she'd find dinner and be back by nine.

After the meal—the waitress hurried them out so she could close up "before the fun starts"—Cassie took her brother by the hand and walked with him to the park at the center of town.

Henry Wallace Park, named for the former president, extended from the town hall on the north to the central post office on the south, and it was already filling with people. The park was pretty, Cassie thought, in a modest way—though probably at its best in summer, when the chinkapin oaks would be in full leaf and the air rich with the scent of mown grass. Tonight the skeletal limbs of the tree and the fading sunset created an atmosphere more somber than the mood of the crowd. But that wasn't surprising. Armistice Day, ever since it had subsumed Thanksgiving as the nation's end-of-November holiday, had always been about defying the first chill of winter, even here in relatively balmy southern Illinois. Colored lanterns had been strung around the bandbox. Behind a cluster of picnic tables, cheerful men in flannel shirts and gaudy aprons dispensed hot dogs from a smoking grill. A banner over the bandstand announced 1914—ARMISTICE—2014, and a group of children in school uniforms waved laurelwreath flags.

Since 2007 Cassie had felt ambivalent about Armistice Day. Her high-school history classes had seemed overlaid with an invisible (and literally unspeakable) irony. Of course, the "century of peace and progress" hadn't been as peaceful as everyone liked to pretend. It was true that the Great War with all its horrors had served as midwife to the Benelux Pact, the European Coal and Steel Alliance, the Treaty of Rome—all those dull but worthy defenses against war, along with generations of European statesmen whose names Cassie would forever associate with the smell of chalk dust and pencil shavings: Lord Lansdowne, René Plevin, Benedetto Croce. But there had been the Russian civil war, which had simmered hot and cold for almost a decade before the Smallholders Party finally unseated that nation's creaking, brutal monarchy. There had been the countless border disputes that always threatened to erupt into something worse—Trieste, the Saarland, the Sudetenland. The ethnic "cleansings" that had persisted even after the European Accord on Human Rights. And even as the nations of Europe settled into the detente of the 1930s and 1940s, their reluctant retreat from empire had sparked countless Asian and African rebellions. It had been the Century of Peace only by contrast with what had gone before.

But under all that was the unmentionable truth about the hypercolony. In her last year of school Cassie had written an essay about the social and political movements of pre-Armistice Europe, and she had been impressed by the arrogance with which certain famous men (Hegel, Marx, Treitschke) had claimed the mandate of history—a word they often capitalized, as if history were a physical force, as predictable and as irresistible as the tides. The twentieth century knew better. At least that was what the textbooks said. The twentieth century had discarded the naïve idea that history had a built-in *destination*.

But history was exactly what the hypercolony had hijacked. It had grasped the raw and bloody meat of human history and shaped it to its own ends. Whatever those ends might be.

The park was getting too crowded for Cassie's comfort. She led Thomas across the street to the post-office grounds, a broad swale of grass where they could sit unobserved and watch the fireworks. The sky was dark now, the first stars beginning to glimmer. Thomas shivered and leaned into Cassie's shoulder. "What do you think?" she asked, her own thoughts still wandering. "Do you trust him?"

"Trust who?"

"Leo."

Thomas pondered the question. Cassie liked this about her brother, that he was seldom quick to answer. Her own impulsiveness had gained her a reputation for being bright, while Thomas's reticence

made some people think he was slow—but neither
impression was really correct. Sometimes Cassie spoke
without thinking. And her brother, she suspected,
often thought without speaking.

"Depends," Thomas said at last. "He's not mean.
He thinks ahead. But that doesn't mean he's always
right. Like when . . . you know."

"When he shot that man," Cassie supplied.

"Uh-huh."

"Yeah, well . . . I'm sorry you had to see that."

"Why shouldn't I see it?"

*Because knowing the truth doesn't always make
you stronger.* "Because you're twelve years old, for
God's sake."

"But I need to get used to it."

"Used to what? People being killed? That's a horrifying thought!"

Thomas gave her a hard look. "You don't think
it'll happen again? I know Leo thought the guy was
a sim. He never meant to kill a real person. But the
Park Service man? Beth could have cracked his skull.
Maybe that's what she *meant* to do. He could have
died. Maybe he died anyway—we don't know."

"We can't let ourselves get caught. If that happens,
we lose, nobody wins."

"I didn't say it was *wrong*. All I'm saying is, it
could happen again. That or something like it. Probably *will* happen again, if we do whatever it is Leo
wants us to do."

"Well . . ." She couldn't honestly deny it. "Maybe."

"Back in Buffalo, back when all I had to do was get up in the morning and go to school, maybe it mattered that I'm twelve years old. But it doesn't matter to the sims. It doesn't matter to the hypercolony. I don't want to be protected, Cassie. I want to fight."

Thomas was a pudgy child and about as belligerent as a Quaker. He tended to cringe in the face of an argument. But the expression on his face was fierce now, almost steely. He *did* want to fight.

He said, "I guess this is what it was like when—"

The fireworks interrupted him. A rocket sizzled up from the park and burst into a brocade of silver stars. The noise echoed from the quarried stone of the post-office building, a sound as hard as a fist.

"What it was like when people went off to war," Thomas finished. "The big war, I mean."

Cassie had seen pictures in textbooks, of ranks of men in brown uniforms with rifles slung over their shoulders: the Allied Expeditionary Force, off to join the battered Brits and French. And pictures of the muddy European trenches: Ypres, Passchendaele, the Marne, where countless young men had been slaughtered by other young men as bewildered and obedient as themselves.

"Leo's not perfect," Thomas said. "But who is? His father knows a lot, and his father trusts him. So yes. I guess I trust him. Do *you* trust him?"

On what terms? To make a decision and follow it

to the necessary conclusion? To embrace even violence, if violence was necessary? To *go to war*?

Cassie surprised herself by nodding. "I do," she said.

And in the end, what choice did she have? As recently as a few days ago she might have considered accepting the burden and promise of anonymity, might have been willing to settle for a circumspect, hidden life.

But she was a criminal now, an accessory to murder. The authorities knew of at least one death. If the Park Service man had died, he would be the second victim . . . and if he *hadn't* died he would almost certainly have given the police a description of Leo, Cassie and Thomas. Local and regional police routinely shared reports by radio and fax, which meant those descriptions would have been available to the hypercolony, which meant it wasn't only the authorities who might be paying attention. "Anonymity" was no longer an option.

The fireworks display began to build toward a climax, to the loud approval of the crowd in the park. Thomas watched gravely. *The rocket's red glare,* Cassie thought. Rockets: a war technology, drafted into the service of celebrating peace. Some members of the Correspondence Society had once believed that larger and more powerful rockets could be used

to send scientific instruments (or even human beings!) into orbit around the Earth—or farther, as in
the science fiction novels she occasionally liked to
read. But the building of rockets bigger than toys
had been prohibited in the disarmament protocols
that followed the signing of the Armistice. And maybe
that, too, was the work of the hypercolony: the hive
defending its high-altitude territory.

The air grew sulfurous with the reek of burning
black powder. Mindful of the time, Cassie stood and
brushed brown grass off her jeans as the band in the
park struck up "God Bless America." She led Thomas
away from the park, approaching the motel from the
treed north side of the street, and she was glad she
had taken that precaution: a cycling blue glow visible
from a block away turned out to be the emergency
lights of two police cars, parked outside the wing of
the motel where she had left Beth and Leo a few
hours earlier.

Thomas had steadfastly refused to hold her hand
on the walk back, but he reached for her hand now,
and Cassie tugged him into the shadow of the trees
where she was fairly certain they couldn't be seen.
The presence of the police could only mean that their
descriptions had already been broadcast and that
someone—the waitress at the restaurant, maybe, or
the desk clerk at the motel—had recognized them
and alerted the authorities. And if Leo and Beth had
already been arrested—

But a voice called her name, startling her, and she

turned to find Leo and Beth sharing the darkness of this stand of oaks.

"We saw the cops pull into the lot," Leo said. "We left by the fire door. I have the stuff my father left me. But most of our luggage is still in there. Some of our ID. And most of our cash, except for whatever you're carrying."

Cassie felt a caustic weightlessness in her stomach. She felt the way she imagined a cornered animal must feel. "So what do we do?"

"I guess we start," Leo said, "by stealing a car."

12

ON THE ROAD

In the middle of our life—no, that wasn't right.

In the middle of the journey of our life (yes) *I came to myself in a wood* (but not just a wood; what was it?) *a dark wood, a dark wood where the straight way was lost* . . .

Nerissa came to herself in an unfamiliar bed in a small room with the shades drawn. Ethan's sleeping body was beside her for the first time in seven years, which was perhaps why lines from *The Divine Comedy* were running through her mind as she fumbled toward awareness, drawn out of sleep by daylight scything past the margins of the window blinds . . . reciting poetry to herself as if she were still chasing her degree, lost in memories more pleasant than yesterday's. *Oh god,* she thought. *Yesterday.* The sickening weight of what they had seen and done.

When they first arrived here (a generic Motel 6 off the turnpike) Ethan had been exhausted and driving erratically. He had barely been able to strip to his underwear before he tumbled into bed and fell fast asleep. Nerissa had been equally exhausted but she had forced herself to stand under a hot shower before she followed him to bed, needing to wash off the stink, real or imagined, of kerosene and soot and blood and crushed green leaves.

And today might not be any better than yesterday. *Face that fact*, she instructed herself. Yesterday the simulacrum had blinded itself and she had cut off both its legs and tied crude tourniquets around its stumps and dumped its surviving fraction into the trunk of the car. Today she would attempt to interrogate it. Or bury it. Or both. Probably both.

What was almost as hard to bear as the physical horror of yesterday's events was the look Ethan had given her, not once but several times, an expression of disbelief bordering on distaste. As if her actions had passed beyond the bounds of decency . . . and maybe they had, but that was a line she had stopped trying to draw.

Finding a place to interrogate Winston Bayliss was the morning's pressing problem. This rented room wouldn't do. So she paid the bill at the motel desk and they drove west, mostly in silence, and left the turnpike where Ethan's map showed a nature reserve. It was a cold day, the wind tumbling blunt gray clouds from the western to the eastern horizon. They parked on the margin of the road in a stand of sugar maples and yellow birch. Nerissa opened the trunk of the car, and Ethan helped her carry Winston Bayliss into the shadow of the woods.

She had bound the stumps of the sim's legs and wrapped a makeshift bandage over the clotted sockets where its eyes had been. She had covered the bullet wounds in its body with strips of flannel (from an old shirt of Ethan's) and duct tape. She had wrapped what remained of its lower body in a plastic trash bag, to keep the mess inside, and that was how they carried it, Nerissa grasping its arms, Ethan supporting the bagged torso, stepping through drifts of brittle leaves and over fallen tree trunks colonized by yellow shelf fungus, until they were safely distant from the road. Then they propped Winston Bayliss more or less upright against an outcrop of mossy granite.

Inevitably, the sim was dying. What was surprising was that it had not yet died. The smell coming from it was obscene, the same odor Nerissa had tried and failed to purge from herself the night before, a stench so ponderous she imagined weighing it on a scale. She was careful to stand upwind.

The simulacrum's voice was a moist, gurgling rasp. It began by asking for water. Nerissa put a plastic water bottle within its reach and watched as the simulacrum groped for it in the dry leaves. The creature looked oddly natural in this setting, she thought—as if it had grown from the detritus of the forest floor, mushroom-pale and streaked with autumn colors.

"Better just let it talk," Ethan suggested. "Let it

say what it wants to say." Because that was all it would ever say. It would say what it wanted them to hear. Nothing more. Nothing less. It was beyond any power of coercion.

The simulacrum repeated some of what it had told them yesterday, about the hypercolony being part of a vast ecology that stretched across light-years of space. It addressed most of these remarks to Ethan, who listened without expression. It insisted once again that it was part of a parasitical system that had recently infected the hypercolony in order to commandeer its apparatus of reproduction.

Reproduction, Nerissa thought: Ethan had once called it the blade of evolution. There was no intelligence in evolution, only the cutting-board logic of selective reproduction. She envisioned the work of evolution as a kind of blind, inarticulate poetry. What was it Charles Darwin had said? *From so simple a beginning endless forms most beautiful and most wonderful have been, and are being, evolved . . . There is grandeur in this view of life.*

Grandeur or horror. The idea that all the kaleidoscopic strangeness of biological systems could unfold without guidance or motivation was almost too unsettling to accept.

Ethan had written in one of his books that "nature knows without knowing," and in his Society papers he had compared the hypercolony to an anthill or a termite nest. The anthill knows how to build itself, how to breed workers, how to feed and cosset its queen. But in fact the anthill knew nothing: what looked like knowledge was only a set of procedural rules, a chemical template constructed by a complex environment. And thus the hypercolony. It appeared to know far more than human beings—it even knew how to *manipulate* human beings. But it knew these things the way an anthill knows. It exploited language but it didn't understand language. It excreted words the way a worker bee excretes royal jelly.

In its bed of leaves, the dying sim excreted words into the autumn air.

By human standards, it said, *the hypercolony's life cycle is immensely long. But it is finite. It begins and ends in a brief, intense pulse of reproductive activity, a kind of swarming, in which it broadcasts its progeny to distant stars. On Earth, that pulse began almost ten years ago.*

For ten years the hypercolony has been using borrowed human technology and unwitting human collaboration to construct its means of reproduction on the surface of the Earth. This is the culmination of the hypercolony's reproductive strategy. Any threat to the reproductive mechanism it has constructed is an existential threat to the hypercolony itself. That's why the Correspondence Society was targeted seven years ago—to protect the hypercolony's means of re-

production, which would have been threatened by premature disclosure.

It was a sinfully bloodless way to describe serial acts of murder, Nerissa thought. But, of course, the sim had long since ceased appealing for sympathy. And it claimed not to be the responsible party.

Snow began to fall from the cloud-heavy sky, gusting through the leafless branches of the trees. A few small flakes collected on the sim's face and melted into droplets, pink with dried blood. The creature's voice was hoarse. It paused to drink once more from the water bottle.

When it spoke again, Nerissa had to lean closer to hear it.

The hypercolony evolved to live in the vacuum of space, but so did many other organisms. The hypercolony was already infected with a parasite when it arrived in this solar system, or became infected soon thereafter. The parasite lay dormant and undetected for centuries. Once the process of reproduction began, the parasite was activated.

The parasite is analogous to a virus: it can reproduce itself only by commandeering the reproductive mechanism of another organism. For more than a year now it has been exploiting the hypercolony's resources for its own purposes. The mechanism by which the hypercolony reproduces itself has been hijacked. The facility that was meant to deliver the hypercolony's seed organisms to nearby stars has been doing something very different—creating and launching new viral packets to follow and infect the hypercolony's vulnerable offspring.

In one of Ethan's books there was a similar story, which Nerissa had found horrifying. Carpenter ants in Thailand were susceptible to infection by a certain fungus. The fungal threads germinated and grew in the ant's body, and as they infiltrated the infected ant's brain it would begin to climb obsessively—*madly*—to the highest leaf on the highest limb it could reach. There it died, creating for the fungal growth now sprouting from the ant's corpse a launching pad from which its spores would be distributed over as broad an area as possible. Some few of those spores might then germinate inside another carpenter ant, which in its fatal madness would climb to the highest leaf on the highest limb it could reach . . .

But the hypercolony isn't dead, nor is it entirely defenseless. Its final strategy is to destroy the reproductive mechanism it created, in order to deny its use to the parasitic entity and to protect its own potential offspring. And it wants to manipulate what remains

*of the Correspondence Society into collaborating
with it in that effort.*

Well, why not? From the human point of view, the
"reproductive mechanism" (if such a thing actually
existed) was little more than a debilitating tumor. It
deserved to be destroyed, no matter which side of
this celestial feeding frenzy it served.

The dying sim shivered. Its shiver became something like a convulsion. The water bottle dropped
from its right hand, while its left clenched empty air.
It coughed a spray of red and ochre phlegm into the
nearby leaves and freshly fallen snow.

"Excuse me," it said.

*E*xcuse me. *If you have any questions, you should
ask them while there's time.*

Nerissa had only one question—was Cassie one of
those people supposedly being exploited by the
hypercolony?—but Ethan stepped in front of her,
bending on one knee to address the sim. He looked
like he was praying to it, Nerissa thought. Or pro-
posing marriage. "The mechanism that manipulates
radio signals, does the hypercolony control that or
do you?"

You meaning the parasite, the virus.

"I do," the sim whispered.

(But there is no *I*, Nerissa reminded herself. No mind. Just process.)

"So the hypercolony can't use that tool anymore. But both entities are able to produce and control simulacra?"

"Yes."

"How are they created? How were *you* created?"

"I was born to a human mother."

No, Nerissa thought. *That can't be right.*

"The reproductive mechanism, will you tell us where it is?"

"No."

"Because you want to protect it?"

"Yes."

"And you're implying *we* should want to protect it."

"Yes."

"Why would we do that?"

"Its destruction would be disastrous for humanity. Not just because of the temporary loss of global communication, though that would be catastrophic in itself. The boundaries that have been placed on human behavior would be breached. Conflicts could escalate out of control. You know what warfare meant a hundred years ago. Consider what it would mean now, if it were allowed to happen again."

"I find that unconvincing," Ethan said.

"I don't expect to convince you. But I hope you'll

at least consider what's at stake. More specifically, it's entirely likely that people you care about will be killed unless you intervene."

"What people?"

The eyeless simulacrum turned its head toward Nerissa. "Cassie. And Thomas. And many others."

"Do you mean what they're doing is dangerous? Or do you mean you'll kill them if you have the chance?"

"Both."

"Then why in God's name should we help you?"

"I'm not asking you to help me. If you choose to protect your civilization in general or your loved ones in particular, my interests will also be served."

"Then tell us where Thomas and Cassie are—can you do that?"

"I don't know where they are, but I believe they're looking for Werner Beck."

Nerissa couldn't restrain herself any longer. "*How* do you know that? What do you know about Cassie and Thomas, and what do you know about Werner Beck?"

But that was a question the sim refused to answer.

It died as they watched.

Its human parts died first. Nerissa supposed the creature's heart simply stopped beating, exhausted by fever and infection. It exhaled for the last time, its stinking breath a cloud of moisture quickly carried away by the breeze. Then the internal parts of it lost all cohesion. The body went slack and began to leak green fluid from its many wounds.

Nerissa helped Ethan cover the remains of the simulacrum with a blanket of fallen leaves—not to protect the creature, and much less out of any misplaced *respect* for it, but because it would be an unpleasant and dangerous discovery for any hiker or local child who happened to stumble across it.

Animals would get at the remains, no doubt. The bones would be scattered. By winter's end only ants and beetles would have any interest in what was left. The sim's corpse might help feed a few insect colonies deep in the pine duff and rotting logs of the forest, an irony Nerissa found unamusing. *There is grandeur in this view of life*. Well, no, she thought. Not much.

"So we have to find Werner Beck," she said when they were back in the car. The snowfall had grown more intense and the road was a pale, curtained obscurity. "I assume you know how to do that?"

"He's in Missouri, according to his letter."

The letter Ethan had collected from his mailbox as they fled the farmhouse. "Did he have anything else useful to say?"

"You can read what he wrote when we find a place to stop."

"All that stuff the sim said. What do you think? You believe any of it?"

Ethan shrugged. "Some of it might have been true. Some of it sounded plausible, at least."

There was a quotation Nerissa recalled, something from a Greek philosopher named Xenophanes. Ethan used to admire the way she could dredge up fragments of poetry and prose from her catch-all memory. But it wasn't a talent, it was a freak of nature. Her own tawdry little magic trick. "*And even if by chance he were to utter the perfect truth, he would himself not know it, for all is but a woven web of guesses.*"

"Yeah," Ethan said, "that sounds about right."

13

Cassie wasn't surprised by how easily Leo managed to steal a car. Boosting cars was a skill he had learned from his friends back in Buffalo—not his Society friends but the east side musicians and petty criminals he hung out with on weekends. The company he kept was one of the reasons Cassie had never taken him seriously, and why Beth's fascination with him had seemed so shallow. But now that Cassie was a criminal herself, she appreciated the skills Leo had learned.

Armistice Day had brought a lot of cars into Jordan Landing from neighboring farms and rural routes, which presented a wealth of opportunities. Leo waited until after midnight, then selected a late-model white Ford Equipoise, an economy vehicle common in these parts, parked in the lot of a motel a half mile north on the main strip. The owner of the car was probably asleep and likely wouldn't report the theft until morning, which would give them a decent head start. He broke off the car's radio antenna and used it to jimmy open the driver's-side door. Firing up the ignition was a more serious obstacle, but there was a tool kit in the glove compartment—tire-pressure gauge, needle-nose pliers, a screwdriver with inter-changeable bits—and with these Leo somehow con-trived to start the engine. Thankfully, none of this attracted any attention. God bless the peaceful little towns of this peaceful land, Cassie thought, and God bless their honest and trusting inhabitants.

By dawn they were a couple of hundred miles west and within an hour's drive of their destination. They were headed for an auto-repair shop called Dowd's, on a flat strip of Kansas highway between Salina and Great Bend.

Dowd's AUTOMOBILE SERVICE AND PARTS, the sign said.

It wasn't much of a sign: a slab of whitewashed plywood on which the letters had been stenciled with orange paint. It had been tacked to what looked like a converted barn, the only visible structure from ho-rizon to horizon where Federal Turnpike 156 crossed the exit for a town called Galatea. The unpaved yard where they parked was littered with rusted engine parts and the shell of what Leo said was a 1972 Pack-ard, and the only thing moving was a set of cut-tin wind chimes hanging from a bracket screwed to the building's aluminum siding.

At the sound of Leo's horn a man emerged from

the darkness behind the corrugated-steel door of the garage, wiping his hands on a blackened rag and blinking at the morning sun. The man was tall, skinny except for the slight paunch under his coveralls, and somewhere in the neighborhood of thirty years old. His moustache and the sweep of brown hair dangling over his collar made him look like he'd stepped out of a Civil War daguerreotype.

Cassie climbed out of the car, Thomas beside her. She desperately needed to pee, though she dreaded to imagine what might pass for a restroom in this establishment.

The man came to a stop a few cautious feet from the car. "What can I do for you folks?"

Leo said, "Are you Eugene Dowd?"

The man stopped wiping his hands and tucked the rag into the hip pocket of his coveralls. "I guess I am. Who might you be?"

"My name's Leo Beck. I think you know my father."

Dowd remained expressionless. The wind gusted, and Cassie heard the clatter of the wind chimes—like music that forgot how to be music—and the creaking of the Packard's loose hood. Finally Dowd said, "Is this your car?"

"Not exactly."

"Uh-huh. I was afraid of that. I dislike having a stolen vehicle on my property. Bring it inside where it won't be so damn obvious. Can you prove you're who you say you are?"

"I think so."

"Well, we'll talk about that. All you lot get inside too."

"Is there a bathroom?" Cassie felt compelled to ask.

Eugene Dowd gazed at her. "Toilet around the back. It's nothing fancy."

No doubt, Cassie thought.

Leo had first mentioned Eugene Dowd during the night's drive. Cassie had asked whether he had learned the name from the papers stashed under the floor of his father's house.

Leo had nodded. "The name, not much else. His instructions were to take the key to Eugene Dowd, at a certain location in Kansas."

Typical Correspondence Society subterfuge. Aunt Ris had once described this kind of reasoning as "paranoia—*necessary* paranoia, maybe, but still, a kind of mental illness." And Leo's father, Werner Beck, was even more systematically paranoid than most Society members.

"So what else is in those papers?"

"A lot of it is statistics he compiled, plus photocopies of newspaper and journal articles . . ."

"Like what?"

"All kinds of things. Statistics on mining in China, shipping in the Pacific. Imports and exports of minerals and rare earths. Newspaper clippings from the last twenty years, some of them about unexplained deaths. Technical articles. Notes from his studies of simulacrum biology. Maps."

"Maps of what?"

"Argentina, Chile, Bolivia, Peru."

"Why, what's there?"

Leo shrugged. "I think it's in case something happened to him, maybe somebody else in the Society could make sense of it."

Beth had somehow found the courage or the insensitivity to ask, "Do you think your father's dead?"

Leo kept his eyes on the road. Night on the turnpike, empty prairie, nothing to see but the periodic glare of passing headlights. "There's obviously some reason he left the house in a hurry. As for whether he's still alive, I don't know. There's no way to know."

"So maybe Eugene Dowd can tell us," Beth said.

"The first thing I got to do," Dowd said to Leo, "is make sure you're the real deal. I will admit, you kind of resemble your old man. But that's not proof one way or another. You might not even be a human being."

The interior of the garage consisted of a complexly stained concrete floor under a cavernous arched roof. A sort of second-story balcony running along one wall had been partitioned into crude rooms—maybe Dowd lived up there, though Cassie found the thought depressing. The workspace was equipped with hand tools and power tools, large and small, none of which she could identify, and a trestle table of rough-cut two-by-fours on which a partially disassembled automobile engine sat. Chains and pulleys dangled from overhead beams. The air smelled of gasoline and of the chemical toilet out back, which she and Beth had hurriedly used.

She sat next to Leo on a torn leather sofa apparently rescued from a trash yard. Beth and Thomas squeezed in beside them. Eugene Dowd pulled up a wooden chair and straddled it.

Dowd was no Society member, Cassie thought, or at least he was unlike any Society member she had ever met. Obviously, he wasn't a scholar or a scientist. He sounded exactly like what he appeared to be: a rural-route auto mechanic with a chip on his shoulder, unimpressed by the four city-bred young people who had arrived uninvited on his doorstep.

"How am I supposed to prove I'm human?"

"Well, we could stick a knife in you and see what color it comes out. That generally works."

"Very funny."

"Or you could show me a certain key."

Leo stood up, fumbled in his pocket—*What if he lost it?* Cassie wondered for one terrifying moment— then produced the key from his father's safe.

"Okay, let me see," Dowd said.

With obvious reluctance Leo put the key in Dowd's open hand. The lines in Dowd's palm were etched with motor oil. His thumb was callused, his nails cut clinically short.

"Good enough?" Leo asked.

"Not yet it isn't. We'll see if it opens what it's supposed to open. Come on."

Dowd led them to the rear of the garage. He pulled away a tarp that covered a white unmarked delivery van, some years old. The dust released by this gesture hung in the air and tickled Cassie's throat.

Dowd applied the key to the driver's-side door of the van. It slid into the lock and turned. He pulled the door open.

"Well, then," he said. "Well, then."

The van hadn't been open in quite a while. Stale air with the tang of vinyl upholstery gusted out. "It looks like any old van," Cassie said.

"It's what's in back that matters."

"So what's in back?"

Eugene Dowd pocketed the key. "We'll talk about that later."

Dowd escorted them up a flight of stairs to the loft he used as an office and bedroom—a few chairs, a table, an ancient refrigerator, sink and hot plate, a mattress on the floor—and asked if they wanted lunch. Cassie looked at the unwashed plates stacked on a sideboard. "Don't worry, girl," Dowd said. "All's I got to offer you is canned chili and some wrapped sandwiches from the 7-Eleven in Galatea. Fresh enough you won't poison yourself, if that's what's worrying you."

Thomas said he was hungry, and Cassie had to admit that she was, too: hungry enough to accept a chicken salad sandwich, as cold as Dowd's wheezing refrigerator could make it. Thomas took the same, as did Leo and Beth. Dowd offered them Cokes and took a bottle of beer for himself.

He levered the cap from the bottle. "So, Leo—I bet you could have opened the door of that van even *without* a key, isn't that right?"

"I don't know. What do you mean?"

"Don't be bashful. Your daddy told me you got hauled into juvie court one time for vehicle theft, attempted."

"It was stupid. I was showing off."

"That's why they let you go with a fine and a lecture?"

"I guess my father told you that, too. Is he here?"

"Your old man? No."

"Then where is he?"

"Werner Beck doesn't post his whereabouts with me, at least not on a regular basis. But since you showed up without him, I doubt the news is good. I was told you wouldn't come here without him unless something unexpected happened."

"So how do you know my father? And what's so special about that van?"

"Well, Leo, it's a kind of a long story. Which I expect you need to hear. It was your father who come to me, by the way, not the other way around. I was living in Amarillo, this was most of ten years ago.

Had a little one-room apartment, making ends meet with federal Work and Welfare checks. Your old man just knocked at the door one day and introduced himself. He said he'd seen a story about me in a local paper and he wanted to know if it was true."

"If *what* was true?"

Dowd ran his thumb along the label of the beer bottle and looked off into the dim cavern of the garage. "I need to start at the beginning. But I guess you got time. We'll talk a little. Then we'll do some work on that car you stole, so it won't be so easy to identify. Because pretty soon we need to leave here, and we won't all fit in the van."

"Leave and go where?"

"A place I dearly hoped I'd never see again. But life shits on hope." He took a long drink. "Isn't that the truth?"

14

Interstate 80 passed through the college town of Montmorency, Pennsylvania. The Federal College at Montmorency—one of the colleges established by the Wallace administration in the 1930s—was the town's biggest business, apart from a couple of manufacturing plants and a limestone quarry. The town was peaceful in the long light of an end-of-November afternoon, many of its neat wood-frame houses flying American flags from front-porch stanchions. It looked like a nice place to live.

But the town had another distinguishing feature: Montmorency had been the home of the late Winston Bayliss, according to the ID Ethan had collected from the dead sim's wallet.

He had been surprised when Nerissa suggested they drive by the address listed on Bayliss's driver's license. "It'll take us out of our way."

"Only a little."

"I thought you wanted to get to Werner Beck as soon as possible."

"I do. But this might be important."

"Why? What's the point?"

She shrugged and looked away.

"It might also be dangerous," he added.

"Everything we're doing," she said, "is *dangerous*."

Last night he had talked to Nerissa—more or less for the first time—about their plans.

She had left Buffalo in a furious but unfocused state of mind, determined to enlist Ethan in the hunt for Cassie and Thomas. He understood that. And he understood the guilt she must be feeling. The careful precautions she had put in place after the murders of 2007 had backfired, badly. Cassie and Thomas had left home under the impression that a full-scale second-wave attack was underway. Following protocols, they had gone to the nearest Society member, who happened to be Leo Beck. Leo (and Leo's girlfriend, a young woman named Beth Vance) had left town, most likely to find Leo's father. Nerissa was tormented by the idea that Cassie and Thomas might believe she was dead, and she was reasonably afraid that connecting with Werner Beck might put them in even greater danger.

Ethan also knew she had never cared for Werner Beck. She had met him at a couple of Society gatherings. "Even in a community of paranoids," she said at one of those meet-ups, "this guy is scary-paranoid."

"He's right about a lot of things," Ethan had said.

"He's produced more valuable research than any-body else."

"He thinks the Society is the vanguard of some kind of human insurgency. We'll be lucky if he doesn't get us all arrested."

"Maybe he is a little crazy. But he's smart, and he has deep pockets."

"And you think that's a *good* combination?"

So Nerissa was worried about Cassie and Thomas coming under the influence of Werner Beck, more so since the sim's baleful confession. And Ethan more or less agreed with her. Find Cassie and Thomas, let Nerissa protect them, leave Beck to fight his own wars—fine. Ethan was on board with that. But after-ward?

Everything had changed. The dead sim was hardly a reliable source of information, but the attack at the farmhouse suggested that at least some part of what it had said was true: there was internal conflict in the hypercolony. And although the Society survivors had tried to remain hidden, they had self-evidently failed: the simulacra had obviously known exactly where to find them. So going back into hiding wasn't an op-tion. They had never really *been* in hiding.

So, even assuming he and Nerissa successfully reconnected with Cassie and Thomas, what then? Nerissa had been living on the inheritance she had received after the death of her parents in 1998. Ethan had cashed out all his investments in 2007 and had been spending frugally (apart from a few high-dollar weapons and security purchases) ever since. Between the two of them, their resources amounted to very little. Both of them would have to find new ways of making a living and of defending themselves (and Cassie, and Thomas) from future attacks.

Should there be any such attacks. If the sim was to be believed (which of course it was not), the hypercolony was dying. If the hypercolony's death resulted in a global communications collapse, the consequences would be catastrophic, at least in the short run. And while such a disaster could be overcome, there remained the question of how the world would fare without the hypercolony's subtle suppression of human bellicosity.

Ethan and Nerissa were facing the same problems, and it seemed to Ethan that they could help each other out, but that was hardly a plan—it was barely more than a wistful thought. He had been married to this woman for ten years and physically separated from her for seven. And although in many ways she was still the woman he had loved and married, in other and significant ways she had changed. He no longer knew what to expect from her. Their old, easy intimacy had evaporated. She was nine-tenths a stranger to him.

Winston Bayliss's house—that is, the house at the address on the simulacrum's license—was a small home on a street of similar homes. Like many of these houses it featured a wooden front porch in modest disrepair. The lawn had turned patchy and yellow with autumn. A faux-rustic peach basket, planted with geraniums that had died in the last frost, substituted for a garden.

Nerissa had opened the car door before Ethan could say, "Whoa—where are you going?"

"It looks like somebody's still living here. Maybe it's the *real* Winston Bayliss. I want to knock on the door and see who answers."

"Why?"

But she didn't answer, and he had no choice but to hurry after her as she strode determinedly up the driveway and onto the porch. She rang the doorbell, then pulled back the screen door and knocked.

Should have brought the pistol, Ethan thought—what if there was another sim inside, what if the house was some kind of sim factory?—but the door creaked open to reveal a stoop-shouldered elderly woman leaning on a walker. She peered at them through bottle-glass lenses and said, "I thought you might be Outpatient Therapy. But you're *not* Outpatient Therapy, are you?"

"No, ma'am," Nerissa said, apparently unfazed.

"No, of course you're not. Therapy comes on Wednesdays. I'm sorry. So what can I do for you folks?"

"Maybe this is the wrong address. We're looking for Winston Bayliss?"

"Oh! Well, not the wrong *address*, but the wrong

door. Winston has a separate door around the side. He lives in the basement. He has his own apartment down there. He did the renovation himself."

"Ah . . . is he home today?"

"Afraid not. He's at a conference in Boca Raton and he won't be back until next week. Something to do with his work. He explained it, but I don't really understand."

"You're Mr. Bayliss's landlady?"

She grinned. "I'm sorry, but that makes me laugh. No! I mean *yes,* Winston gives me a monthly allowance for the use of the basement. But I'm not his landlady, I'm his mother. Amanda Bayliss. Mrs. Carl Bayliss, though Carl's been gone five years now. What did you want to see Winston about?"

"We're from the Blue Horizon Insurance Agency. Mr. Bayliss contacted us a while back about the possibility of taking out a policy. We were hoping to follow up on that."

"Well, that can't be true," Mrs. Bayliss said.

To her credit, Ethan thought, Nerissa didn't miss a beat. "Really? Why not?"

"I apologize, but it makes me tired to stand . . . will you come in for a moment? Though I don't believe I'll be buying any insurance from you."

"Of course," Nerissa said.

"I would offer you coffee, but I don't drink it anymore. My doctor recommends I don't." Mrs. Bayliss frowned. "There might be some instant up in the cupboard. I could boil water, if you like."

"No, ma'am," Nerissa said. "Thank you all the same."

Mrs. Bayliss's front room was a time capsule in which no item of furniture appeared to be less than thirty years old. The pictures on the end tables bracketing the sofa featured a man who might have been the late Carl and a child who might have been Winston (if Winston Bayliss had ever really been a child). The room's double-paned windows had been shut and the curtains drawn, enclosing a silence in which the ticking of a mantel clock seemed absurdly loud.

There was nothing to suggest that the house was anything more than the longtime residence of an elderly woman who had been widowed some years before. But that didn't mean Mrs. Bayliss was necessarily any more human than the creature she claimed as her son.

"You said you doubted Winston would consider a policy with us," Nerissa said. "May I ask why?"

Mrs. Bayliss looked at Ethan. "Do you talk at all, mister, or are you just for decoration?"

"I'm, ah, in training," Ethan managed. "I'll chime in if I'm needed."

"Just wondered. Anyway, no. No, I can't see Winston wanting to take out insurance. I assume it's *life* insurance you're selling? But that generally calls for a physical, and Winston won't see a doctor for love or money. Thankfully, he's healthy as a horse."

"Well, that's good," Nerissa said. "I hope you're the same, Mrs. Bayliss, although I see . . ."

"The brace I'm wearing on my leg? That's why Outpatient Therapy comes by every week. I had a knee replaced in September. Arthritis. I think it's wonderful what they can do nowadays. Not that it was such a breeze, the surgery I mean. The physiotherapy's no fun, either. Though I do like the State nurse who helps me with it. She tries to sound tough, but she's a sweetie."

"Winston didn't get his fear of doctors from you, then."

"Nor from his father. But he's had it all his life. That's why I can't picture him volunteering for a physical. Even when he was younger, back when he was in school . . . but I don't imagine you want to hear these stories."

"I don't mind," Nerissa said. "Frankly, it's nice to get out of the cold and chat a little. Just don't tell my supervisor." She chuckled, and Mrs. Bayliss laughed agreeably. "Every once in a while we pull a name from the wrong list and end up calling on someone who's already declined our offer. Probably Winston is one of those. I'll have a word with my boss about it. It doesn't do us any good to bother people who aren't interested in what we have to sell. Though I have to say, it's an attractive policy package at the price."

"I'm sure it is."

The ease with which Nerissa told these lies surprised Ethan. He guessed it was a skill she had taught herself since 2007, the way he had taught himself marksmanship.

"Fear of doctors," she said, "is more common than you might think."

"Winston must have been born with it. Fortunately he was a healthy child. Maybe a little too cautious. He always disliked sports, or anything rough-and-tumble. But he seldom caught cold and never came down with anything more serious, even though he wouldn't submit to vaccinations. The one time he *did* hurt himself—well, that was probably harder on me and Carl than it was on him."

"How so?"

"He was walking home from school one day when a car clipped him. Winston was ten years old, and the car driver—we never did find out who it was, but I suspect it was one of those high-school boys—Adlai Stevenson High is just four streets away and I've seen how they drive, boys with their first license in their pocket—anyhow, Winston wasn't badly hurt, but he was skinned up pretty good and he broke a bone in his arm."

"So he must have seen a doctor."

"Well, no—not that we didn't try to take him! I can't even say for sure the bone was broken—I'm no expert—but he couldn't use the arm right and there was a lump up above the elbow and real serious bruising, his whole arm was practically green with it. So I called the doctor and he said to bring Winston in, but while Carl was warming up the car—and this was in the dead of winter—Winston tore out the back door and ran off."

"Ran off?"

"Disappeared for, believe it or not, *five days*. We had the whole town looking for him. It made the news. Lost boy, probably injured, out in the cold. Honestly, Carl and I were prepared for the worst."

"But they found him?"

"In fact they didn't. Winston came home all by himself. Walked in the door five days later as if nothing had happened. Of course, all hell broke loose. He said he'd been hiding in an old barn on one of the rural routes and that he kept warm by building a fire at night. And when we asked him why he'd done all this—and believe me, we asked him that question more often than he cared to hear it—he said it was because he didn't want to go to the doctor."

"Even with a broken arm!"

"Well . . . we sure *thought* it had been broken. But it was healed by the time he got back. So he must have just sprained it. And although it probably would have been wise to get him checked out anyhow, we didn't insist. Does that sound foolish?" She shook her head. "Carl and I only had the one child and we probably indulged him more than we should have. Some days I think that's why Winston never married. We coddled him into a lonely bachelorhood. But as my husband used to say, all you can do is the best you can do. There are no guarantees in this life. Not even"—Mrs. Bayliss smiled at her joke—"if you take out insurance."

The conversation drifted from Mrs. Bayliss's son Winston to the weather lately, and Nerissa checked her watch and said they had another appointment to keep. Mrs. Bayliss saw them to the door (a little abashed, Ethan guessed, at how garrulous she had been) and wished them well. "I'll let Winston know you stopped by."

"Thank you."

"You want to leave a card or anything?"

"It doesn't sound like your son is a likely prospect for us. When do you expect him back?"

"He said he'd let me know. He hasn't phoned in a few days. That's not like him. But he's probably just having a good time down there in Florida. Last time I saw him he was cheerful as a chipmunk."

And the last time I saw him, Ethan couldn't help thinking, he was lying in a bed of fallen leaves, eyeless, dying.

Nerissa was somber in the car, and Ethan respected her silence as he drove back onto the turnpike. The sun beat through the windshield with a clarifying light.

Eventually she said, "So Mrs. Bayliss isn't a sim."

"Her knee, you mean."

"Surgery or even an X-ray would have exposed her. And she wasn't faking it. You saw the scar?"

He hadn't, but Nerissa said she caught a glimpse when Mrs. Bayliss first sat down, the cotton skirt briefly rucking up to expose a line of suture marks stark as railroad tracks. "Obviously *she's* not afraid of doctors."

"But Winston was."

The nature and origin of the simulacra had been debated by the survivors since 2007. Most assumed the sims were manufactured in their final adult form. But that had never been more than an assumption. Apparently a baseless one. "So what he told us was true," Ethan said. "He was born to a human mother."

"I guess so. But it's a horrifying idea. That she actually gave birth to this thing, nurtured it, dressed it, sent it to school, and never noticed anything unusual beyond its reluctance to visit a doctor. . . ." Nerissa shuddered. "That's incredibly fucking creepy."

"But it's possible," Ethan said. "The sims aren't just approximate copies of human beings. In every detail except their internal structure, they're *perfect* copies. It's tempting to think that if you knew a sim intimately enough something would give it away, some subtlety it hadn't quite mastered. But that's wrong. Even Mrs. Bayliss couldn't guess."

"I suppose I thought the sims were made for a purpose—to be assassins—and after they did their jobs maybe they just, I don't know, dried up and blew away in the wind. But if what she said is true, it means they can pass for years without being noticed. *Anyone* could be one."

"Not you."

She gave him a sharp look. "What do you mean?"

"It's been a while," Ethan said. "But the appendectomy scar."

She surprised him by blushing. "Yes, okay. True. And you had chest X-rays the winter you came down with pneumonia. So we can trust each other."

"It's the rest of the world we can't be sure about."

"Also, if Mrs. Bayliss is human and gave birth to a sim—how's that work? Was her husband a sim, too? But that only pushes the question back a generation."

"It's not uncommon for one species to exploit the nurturing functioning of another species. It's called brood parasitism." In fact it was the same kind of parasitism Bayliss had claimed was happening within the hypercolony itself.

"But what's the *mechanism* exactly? How does a perfectly ordinary woman in a perfectly ordinary town give birth to a non-human child?"

Ethan had no answer.

"And if they're so perfectly human, we can't even be sure about the Correspondence Society. You guys were always careful about using the U.S. Mail so the hypercolony couldn't listen in, but what if you had a ringer among you? What if a sim was reading your monographs all along?"

He had thought about this. "There's no way to rule out the possibility. It might be true. Even though we were in hiding, the sims had no trouble finding Cassie and Thomas. Or me. And Bayliss seemed to know exactly how much *we* knew about the hypercolony. So it would probably be smart to assume that the Society has been infiltrated."

"So who can we trust? You, me—"

"That's two. And probably Werner Beck."

"Beck!" Nerissa said scornfully. "I never did trust Beck."

15

DOWD'S GARAGE

One part of Eugene Dowd's converted barn had been set aside for paintwork, and Cassie watched with fascination as he worked on the stolen car. Even more fascinating—in a much scarier way—was Dowd's running monologue.

First he unbolted the car's license plates and set them aside on his workbench. The plates were evidence, he said, and he would cut them apart with tin snips and bury the pieces in the yard before they left. Then he snapped off the Ford's removable trim and moldings and used a power sander to rough up the paint. "Ordinarily," he said, "I'd sand down to metal, but we're in a little bit of a hurry here." Cassie guessed this wasn't the first vehicle he'd repainted, probably not the first *stolen* vehicle he'd repainted.

When Dowd bent to sand the side panels she could see the blades of his hips working under the denim sprawl of his jeans. Paint dust roiled up around him, but he wasn't wearing a mask and didn't appear to care. When he spoke (between bouts with the noisy sander) he kept his eyes on the Ford, as if Cassie and Thomas and Leo and Beth weren't fully present, as if his words were addressed not to them but to something invisible that lived in the motor of the car.

I was in a little town outside of Amarillo, name of it doesn't matter, when Werner Beck found me. This was, let's see, five going on six years ago now.

The town was where I grew up but I'd been gone a long time and I came back because I didn't know where else to go. I'd been doing odd jobs, carpentry and electrical work mostly, out of the country, but I was done with that, for reasons I'll get to shortly.

So there I was, back in town and out of work. Since I left both my parents had died, but I didn't know that till I got back. I wasn't real good about keeping in touch. So the news was kind of a shock. Not that they were much of a family. My daddy drank when he wasn't digging foundations and my mom worked as a beautician all her adult life. Cancer took her, and sometime later my daddy shot himself. Their house was sold off for back taxes. I came home to nothing, in other words. All I wanted was to curl up in a safe place and forget what I'd seen down in the Atacama, and all I got was more fuckin' grief.

I rented me a little place at the edge of town and I guess I meant to sit there smoking weed and watching shit on TV until my savings ran out, but one day Werner Beck knocked on the door. At the time, I didn't know who the fuck he was. I figured he wanted to collect a debt or sell me a Bible. But what he said was, Are you the Eugene Dowd who saw some unusual things in Chile last year? Which made we want to reach for a gun, except I didn't have one. Relax, he tells me, I'm red-blooded all the way through. And I knew what that meant. So I told him to come in.

Naturally I wanted to know how he'd found me. He said he'd seen a piece in the local paper. He subscribed to what he called a clipping service. Clipping service sends him pieces from newspapers all over the country, big and little newspapers, if the article mentions certain words or phrases.

He didn't say what those words or phrases were. But I knew the piece he was talking about. A column in the local rag, which is barely a real newspaper, mostly grocery coupons and classified ads. Well, some bored fucker wrote a column about what he called "colorful characters," and I'd had the misfortune to run into this guy at a bar when I was too pissed for my own good—I told him a few things about the Atacama and he wrote it up like it was some big fucking joke. Local loser sees green men, that kind of shit.

Yeah, I told Beck, that's my story, or part of it, but the paper didn't use my name, so again, how'd you find me? I asked around, Beck says. Lot of trouble to go to, I say. Yeah, he says, but the thing is, Mr. Dowd, I believe you.

Well, there really wasn't much in that newspaper column to believe, it seemed to me. The column told how I'd said there were Martians living in South America, which I didn't. It even had a punch line. Like this: "I asked my newfound acquaintance whether his Martians were green, as in the comic books. 'Yes,' he confided, 'green as grass—but only on the inside!'"

Fucking humiliating.

Beck saw the expression on my face and said, Look, Mr. Dowd, I'm serious about this. I know all about people who are green on the inside. And one thing I know is, they don't think twice about committing murder. They killed a bunch of my friends. They tried to kill me.

Which made me realize he was serious. I said, How do I know you're not one of them?

He told me that was a smart question and he loosened his belt and lifted up his shirt and showed me a scar where he had his appendix out. I asked him what that was supposed to prove. He said the hospital where he was treated would've noticed if he'd been bleeding green. Then he says, How about you?

I didn't feel like showing him any scars, but he said that was okay, he'd take me at my word. At least for now. The word he used was "provisionally."

Then we got down to business. Given what he'd already said, I asked him what he wanted. I want to hear your story, he says. And then I'll tell you mine.

* * *

Once he had sanded the original paint Dowd washed the car with soapy water, dried it, and rinsed it again with a solution of mineral spirits. Then he taped off the parts he wanted to protect—windows, bumpers, trim. In the occasional silences, when Dowd wasn't talking or operating power tools, Cassie heard wind rattling the corners and hollows of Dowd's garage. Winter coming. She wasn't sure what winter meant in this part of the country—probably not what it meant in Buffalo, where snow sometimes shut down the city for days.

Dowd broke for lunch as soon as the car was prepped for spraying. Lunch today was a rerun of lunch yesterday: convenience-store sandwiches. Cassie watched Dowd as he crammed a ham sandwich into his mouth, crumbs collecting in his moustache. He caught her looking and gave her a grin that wasn't entirely friendly. *Werner Beck trusts this man,* Cassie reminded herself. But how much did she really know about Leo's father?

"Had enough to eat?" Dowd asked, still gazing at Cassie.

She nodded.

Leo said, "You were going to tell us what you told my father."

"Yeah." Dowd wiped his mouth on the sleeve of his shirt. "I guess I was."

* * *

I was sick of Texas and I wanted to travel, which is how I ended up on the Trans-American Highway—parts of it brand new in those days, all those tunnels and bridges through the Darien Gap—working my way south from the Canal Zone picking up odd jobs. Mostly construction and electrical, like I said. Or whatever came to hand. I slept rough from time to time but I was young and that was all right with me as long as I could move on when I felt like it. Just heading south, like some kind of migrating bird.

I was in Antofagasta, that's in Chile, when I hooked up with a Dutch company that was doing some work out in the Atacama Desert. Building and running a supply depot for a copper mine, supposedly. Crew was mostly local but the company had an arrangement with the unions that let them hire a few foreigners, a handful of Ecuadorian and Colombian guest workers and one American, me—the crew boss liked that I had a U.S. electrician's certificate, which is pretty much the gold standard. So they bused us over the Coast Range and up the Atacama Road, then along one of those old roads that used to service nitrate mines, to a flat place where a little spur of the Ferrocarril ran out—the real high desert, dry as glass and air so thin you could practically see the stars by daylight.

In a couple of months we had four air-conditioned buildings up and running. More like warehouses than anything else. And it was all kind of a mystery. There was no copper mine in sight, far as I could see. The Dutch crew boss spoke Spanish and a little German but he liked to practice his English on me in the off-hours, so I asked him about that one time. Get a little Jenever into him and he was pretty friendly. But he didn't have much to say. He'd been told the site was a depot to store supplies on their way from the railhead or the road to the mine—the mine itself being a ways east. And no, he said, you couldn't see the mine from here, but some nights you could see a light, like a spotlight or what do you call it, one of those lights they shine at movie theaters, know what I'm talking about? A shaft of light going up into the desert air. What kind of mine has a light like that? I asked him. But he didn't know. It wasn't his business to know.

We, I mean the work crew, slept in temporary shelters, plywood bunkhouses with canvas roofs and the wind for ventilation. Some nights when I couldn't sleep I went out to look for that light the crew boss talked about. I saw it once, a shaft of light coming up from the horizon, almost too faint to see. Straight-up vertical. It lasted about three minutes. Not real impressive, but it had no business being there.

Anyway, I stayed on after the construction was finished. The Dutch company'd been contracted to operate the depot once they'd built it, and they needed hands for cartage and security. And I didn't have anything better to do and actually, strange as it sounds, I *kind of liked it out there in the high desert. At least at first. It felt like time went slower there. Cities sort of rush you along, if you know what I mean. Whereas in the desert an hour goes by and nothing happens but maybe the wind blows a few grains of sand across the* salares. *The salt basins.*

I made friends with a guy named Bastián. Bastián was a forklift driver from the south of the country, spoke English, claimed to have a grandmother who spoke Quechua, which meant fuck-all to me. Skinny little guy but strong for his size. Dark-haired. He had a sense of humor, which I appreciated. When I told him about the light on the horizon he grinned and said, Shit, Eugene, that's the alicanto.

We were off behind the depot buildings in the shade, sharing a smoke where the crew boss wouldn't see us. I said, Well, what's an alicanto?

It's a bird, he says. It's got metal wings and it lives in caves and eats gold and silver. Its wings light up at night, all different colors.

Bullshit, I say.

Yeah, obviously, Bastián says. Or no, not bullshit exactly but a myth. A legend. The alicanto's good luck for miners. Follow it to find silver or gold. But if it sees you, it leads you nowhere. It lets you die in the desert.

I'm no miner, I tell him. And I don't believe in any fucking alicanto.

Fair enough, he says. I don't believe in your light.

So I told him, next time I saw it I'd wake him up and show him.

But we got pretty busy about then. There were big shipments coming through. How it worked was, goods were trucked in from the railhead. Some of it was food but most of it was hardware. Electronics: integrated circuits, transformers, microwave generators. And some large-scale stuff. Machines for working metal. Aluminum parts. Tubes and piping. Crates listed on the manifest as powdered silicon carbide. Pressurized hydrogen. Mirrors, huge ones. Graphite. I mean, what the fuck? I'm no expert, but why does a copper mine need mirrors and graphite?

And it was a strange arrangement all around. These shipments were delivered from the Ferrocarril and the crates would sit in our storehouse for a couple of days, then a fleet of trucks would come down the road from the east and we'd load 'em up. It made no sense. Why not just deliver it all straight to the mine? Also, the guys who drove those trucks—copper miners, supposedly—never talked to us. They'd nod if you said hello, but they were all about their manifests. They didn't socialize. They never even stepped out back of the shed for a smoke—none of them smoked. Guys in white shirts and jeans, neat and clean as fucking Mormons. Eyes on the clipboard at all times.

What I figured out was that we were there to sanitize their operation. You know what I mean? So nobody from outside ever got to see the mine. Whatever they did there was always out of sight, over the horizon. We were as close as anybody was allowed to get—and all we *ever saw were these guys in their unmarked trucks.*

Which made me curious.

Bastián, not so much. It was just a job to him, he didn't give a fuck how the mine worked. Not until one night, one of those nights without a breeze of any kind, I woke up, it might have been three or four in the morning, I couldn't sleep, so I stepped out of the bunkhouse to get some air, cold as it gets at night even in summer in the Atacama, and the light was shining again, like a candle on the horizon. So I went and woke up Bastián. There, I told him. See? There's your goddamn alicanto.

I don't know what that is, Bastián says, serious for once. Maybe some kind of smelter they're running. But he knew better than that.

I could tell he was curious. We talked it over now and then for a couple of weeks. But it was busy times. Lots of supplies going into the mine. And something else strange: nothing ever came back the other way. No copper, no ore, nothing raw and nothing refined. One time I asked one of those white-shirt truck drivers how that worked. Did they dig a dry hole or what? And he looked at me like I was something that crawled into his boot during the night. No, he says, we're still getting it up and running. Meanwhile staring at my name where it was stitched on my shirt. Making notes.

The next day the shift boss took me aside and gave me a lecture about minding my own business, do my work and let the truckers do theirs, etcetera. And if I wanted to keep my job I should shut my mouth and get on with it. Which didn't really bother me because I'd got to the point where I'd saved enough of my salary to move on. And it looked like there'd be no hard feelings if I did.

Which might have been the end of the story if Bastián hadn't spent one of those Chilean holidays, I forget which one, Feast of the Virgin, Feast of Peter and Paul, Feast of Whatever, in Antofagasta with his buddies from the port where he used to work. He came back with a couple of bottles of Pisco. No drinking allowed in the camp but he bribed a guard. So he and I sat up one Friday night and shared a bottle, out behind the warehouses where there was nobody to see us. Getting steadily drunker and complaining about the job. When up comes that light again, brighter this time. Like a wire strung between the desert and the stars. And somehow we get the stupid idea of taking one of the Toyotas in the motor pool and driving east, at least a little ways, just to see if we can see what's going on.

You know what they say about curiosity, right? Killed the fucking cat.

Eugene Dowd interrupted his monologue to attend to the actual painting of the car, and the noise of the compressor and the stink of the paint drove Cassie outside. Thomas was fascinated by Dowd's work on the car, and Cassie agreed to let him watch as long as he stayed behind the glass door of the upstairs office—a ventilator built into the wall of the garage sucked most of the urethane mist out of the building, but Cassie didn't want him breathing even a little of it. Beth volunteered to stay with Thomas where she, too, could watch Dowd. She had been watching Dowd all day, Cassie had noticed, and Dowd had returned every one of her frequent glances, with interest.

Outside, the sky was cloudless and the air was tolerably warm for December. Cassie walked past Dowd's noisy wind chimes, around a corner of the garage to a patch of packed brown earth, sheltered from the wind, where a pair of ancient lawn chairs had been set up. She was surprised to find Leo in one of them, reading.

Reading a book. Reading the book her uncle had written, *The Fisherman and the Spider*. She gaped at the tattered yellow jacket. "That's *mine*, Leo—where'd you get that?"

He looked up, startled. "Hey, Cassie."

"The book," she said grimly.

"Oh. Sorry. Yeah, it's yours. I grabbed it from the hotel room in Jordan Landing."

Cassie had thought the book was lost. She didn't know whether to be grateful to Leo for saving it or angry that he hadn't bothered to give it back.

He added, a little sheepishly, "I didn't think you'd mind . . ."

She sat down in the brittle webbing of the second chair. She imagined herself falling through, getting her behind stuck in the aluminum struts. That would be graceful. "No. I mean, I guess it's okay. But I do want it back. You're actually reading it?"

He raised an eyebrow. "Yeah, this is me, actually reading it. That surprises you?"

"I don't know. I just never pictured you . . ."

"Reading books?"

Frankly no, though she was less surprised now than she once would have been. His finger marked his place in *The Fisherman and the Spider,* about halfway through. She said, "Well, what do you think of it?"

"It's your uncle's book, right?"

"Right."

"About insects."

"He studied them."

"But really about the hypercolony."

She was pleased that he understood this. "In a way, yeah."

He turned his head up toward the sky. "I was thinking about the way they talked about it in school. The great discovery. Marconi bouncing signals from Newfoundland to France. The *radio-propagative layer.*"

Cassie nodded.

"But it's alive. And that's what your uncle's book is about, at least between the lines. The hypercolony as a kind of insect hive."

It was an idea Cassie had struggled with for a long time. She could grasp that the hypercolony was a diffuse cloud of tiny cells surrounding the Earth, each cell functioning like a neuron in a kind of brain. A huge, peculiar brain, surrounding the Earth. Okay, she got that. And it intercepted human radio signals, analyzed them, subtly altered them, and bounced them back in ways people found useful.

All that was basic Society stuff. And since the hypercolony was a sort of brain, she accepted that it might be intelligent. It *had* to be intelligent, to do what it did. Some early Society theorists had even tried to make contact with it: they had broadcast signals on dormant frequencies, sending out simple mathematical formulas or even questions in basic English, hoping for a response. But no response had ever come.

It was the Society's mathematicians and cyberneticists and in no small part her uncle who had come up with an explanation: the hypercolony functioned without conscious volition of any kind. The hypercolony didn't know anything about itself or its environment, any more than a carrot understands the concept of organic farming or the color orange. It just lived and grew, mindlessly exploiting the resources available to it: vacuum, rock, sunlight, other living things. Its powers were in some respects almost godlike, but it was an insect god—mindless and potentially deadly. Her uncle had known that, and though he couldn't mention the hypercolony by name in his published book, Leo was right: it was there between the lines, on every page.

He gave her a brooding look. "You'd think it would be hard to hate something you can't see or touch. But it's not. I *do* hate the fucking thing. I hate it as much as my father does. He used to say, given that we know what we know, the only honorable thing to do is declare war."

"In a way, isn't that what we've done?"

"More than *in a way*. The man I shot . . . he was a casualty of war. Along with everybody who died in '07 and everybody who died last month."

Of course Leo was still dwelling on the man he'd shot. So was Cassie. She thought the act was forgivable even if their defense would never stand up in a court of law. She accepted her share of responsibility, and she knew that in Leo's place she might have behaved the same way. But the memory was still too awful to contemplate. The blood, the furtive way they had tried to dispose of the body. And in the end, even if they shared responsibility, it was Leo who had pulled the trigger.

He looked at the book in his hand, then offered it to Cassie. She shook her head. "Finish reading it if you want."

"You ever meet your uncle?"

"A few times. Before '07. But I don't remember much about him. Uncle Ethan and Aunt Ris visited sometimes, back when I lived with my parents. He was just a quiet guy who smiled a lot and didn't say much." And since Leo had raised the subject, Cassie allowed herself to broach a delicate subject: "My uncle was pretty close to your father. According to Aunt Ris, Werner Beck was pretty much the head of the whole Correspondence Society."

"I bet she said more than that."

"Well—"

"It's okay, Cassie. I know my father has enemies."

"I'm not sure *enemy* is the word. She said he was brilliant." Which was true, though her other words had included *arrogant* and *narcissistic*.

"He's not shy about telling people things they need to hear, whether they want to hear them or not."

"He wrote to you, right?"

"Once a month. Long letters. He called it my real education."

"How come you didn't live with him?"

"After '07, he figured I wouldn't be safe anywhere near him. He sent me to live with a cousin of his in Cincinnati. A married couple, no kids, they didn't know anything about the Society. He paid them pretty generously to look after me. They put me up in a spare room and enrolled me in school. Decent people, but they didn't really want me there . . . and it wasn't where I wanted to be. So as soon as I was legal I bought a bus ticket to Buffalo and got a job washing dishes. I knew there were survivors there who could help me out. My father told me about your aunt and the people she was connected with, how to get in touch with them. He didn't really approve, but I think he understood."

"But we weren't what you hoped we'd be?"

"Well. You know what my father used to say about the Society? He said it was a social club when it should have been an army."

Possibly true. "That changed in '07," Cassie said.

"No, not for the better. The murders were obviously meant to drive the Society into hiding, and that's what happened. We cringed like dogs. Quoting my father. Which is what I found in Buffalo, a bunch of whipped dogs . . ." He gave Cassie a look that seemed both sheepish and defiant. "Anyway, that's how it seemed. Don't do anything rash. Whisper. Mourn, but don't get angry."

"Some of us did get angry, Leo. Even if it didn't show. Some of us were angry all along."

"Yeah, I suppose so." He shifted his legs, making the ancient lawn chair creak. The only other sound was the wind furiously tangling the wind chimes. "Anyway, what could I say? My father survived '07. I wasn't an orphan. I could hardly complain to someone like—"

"Like me?"

"Someone who'd seen what you'd seen."

Well, yes, Cassie thought. She had caught one indelible glimpse of her parents' slack and bloodied bodies before Aunt Ris covered her eyes and pulled her away. You can't unsee something like that. But what did that buy you? Only bad dreams and guilt. A clinging sadness she could never quite escape.

But anger, too. *We never lacked for anger.* "Well," she said, "we're in the same boat now."

"Orphans?" Leo asked sharply. "Is that what you mean?"

"No. I mean—"

"I don't know for sure he's dead. But whether he is or whether he isn't, he wouldn't have sent me here unless he wanted me to finish his work."

"You really think Eugene Dowd can help us do that?"

"Dowd seems to think we're here to help *him*. But my father trusted him."

"To do what?"

"I guess we'll find out," Leo said, "when he finishes his story."

16

ON THE ROAD

Somewhere on the turnpike west of Columbus, Ohio, the events of the last few days settled on Nerissa like an unbearable weight. Suddenly breathless, she asked Ethan to pull over. She was out of the car before he finished braking, falling to her knees next to a weed-clogged drainage ditch. A barrel hoop had tightened around her chest. Her head felt heavy. The sun was viciously bright, the noise of passing trucks cruelly loud. She put her hands into the yellow grass, leaned forward and vomited up the remains of this morning's breakfast.

When the spasm passed she shut her eyes and took small sips of the chilly December air. The darkness that formed behind her eyelids was cavernous and oddly comforting. She didn't move until she felt the pressure of Ethan's hand on her shoulder.

"Ris? Are you all right?"

Obviously not. But in the sense he meant . . . well, she was recovering. "Help me up, please, Ethan."

She leaned into him until her dizziness passed.

Back to the car, then, where she rinsed her mouth with bottled water, spitting it onto the verge.

Funny how this feeling had snuck up on her. It wasn't the memory of the sim's awful death that had triggered it. It wasn't even the horrific inference she had drawn from her meeting with Mrs. Bayliss, the idea that a human womb could be shanghaied by an alien organism. What had sent her reeling out of the car was simply the thought of her niece and nephew, of Cassie and Thomas, friendless and vulnerable and believing she was dead.

Not that it was exactly a *new* thought, but she had kept it at a safe distance in the frenzied activity of the past few days. But time, or the drowsy, sun-warmed comfort of the moving car, had lowered her guard.

She allowed herself another sip of water as Ethan steered back into traffic. A pair of eighteen-wheel trucks barreled past, lords of the turnpike on this chilly weekday afternoon. She found herself thinking of the custody hearings back in '07, held in the aftermath of the massacre. A panel of Family Health and Social Welfare workers had reviewed Nerissa's suitability as a caregiver for her orphaned niece and nephew. Nerissa had testified to her willingness to make a new home for them, had promised they would receive any counseling or therapy they might need. And those vows had been authentic; she had made them without reservation, though she was less than certain of what FHSW called her "parenting potential." In the end, the tribunal had expressed more confidence in her ability to raise two kids than she actually felt.

She had always admired her sister's devotion to her children, even occasionally envied it; but children had never been on Nerissa's agenda, except in a vague maybe-someday sense. Her career and her troubles with Ethan had rendered the question moot. Then, suddenly, she found herself responsible for two traumatized children. She had taken a leave of absence from the University after the murders and she knew that going back would make her a sitting target, should the killers return. A new city, responsibility for Cassie and Thomas, the unfathomable threat hanging over them all, not to mention her own burden of traumatic memories . . . some nights she had come awake in the sweaty certainty that she couldn't handle *any* of it: the kids would despise her; she would be reduced to poverty; they would all be butchered in their sleep.

But it hadn't happened that way. The kids had slowly adapted. For months Cassie had covered her ears at the slightest mention of her parents; she had been clingy, reluctant even to walk to school by herself. Slowly, however, her confidence had crept back. And so, in equal measure, had Nerissa's. It was as if they had learned a silent magic: how to draw strength from each other in a way that left each of them stronger. Thomas, though he was younger than Cassie, had recovered even more quickly. There were difficult

moments, of course, sudden and unprovoked out-
bursts of tears or anger, demands to be taken back to
his *real* home, his *real* mother ... but Thomas had
been willing to accept Cassie's consoling hugs and,
later, Nerissa's. She remembered the first time he had
come crying into her arms. The surprising warmth
and weight of him, the damp patch his tears left on
her shoulder.

Protecting them had become the central business
of her life. It was what was left, after so much else
had been taken from her. And it was a job for which
she possessed, to her surprise, a certain aptitude.

But ultimately she had failed at it. She had been
away from home the night the sims came back. And
for purely selfish reasons. An evening at the theater
with John Vance—Beth's father, who was one of the
Society's singletons, widowed in '07. They had seen a
Performing Arts Center production of *Twelfth Night*.
Then drinks at John's place. And then to bed, in the
secure knowledge that Cassie could look after Thomas,
that it was good for Cassie to feel in charge once in a
while, to take on some of the responsibility she was
beginning to assume as an adult ... and other self-
serving rationalizations.

You let your vigilance lapse, Nerissa thought. She
had felt safe enough to let a little buried resentment
leak out—resentment of a duty she had never wanted
but couldn't refuse; resentment that she had been
relegated to a supporting role in the lives of these
children rather than a starring role in her own. She

had chosen to slake her loneliness in the company of a man for whom she felt nothing more than a passing affection. And as a result Cassie and Thomas were gone. Not dead *(please God, not dead)*, but out there somewhere in the company of Werner Beck's cocksure son and John Vance's sullen daughter— bound, in all likelihood, for one of Werner Beck's safe houses. Assuming Beck himself hadn't been killed. The sims had been more selective this time around, but surely Beck was one of their primary targets. Because Beck, as Ethan had always insisted, was the heart of the Society. Its mainspring, its motivating force. Its most dedicated and most dangerous member.

The turnpike ribboned through Ohio into Indiana. By dusk the sky had grown clear, the air colder. Outside Indianapolis they passed a local radio station, its broadcast antenna aimed like a steel flower at the meridian, whispering to the radiosphere, which would whisper its message back to the neighboring counties and suburbs . . . to the entire world, given a powerful-enough signal.

Ethan tuned in the station in time for a newscast. The world was facing a nervous and unusual Christmas. In northern Africa, General Othmani's forces had encircled and destroyed a brigade of League of Nations peacekeepers. In Europe, a conference on the Balkan crisis had adjourned without reaching an accord. And the Russian Commonwealth and the Pan-Asian Alliance were butting heads over an oil port on the Sea of Okhostsk, with reports of an exchange of artillery fire.

None of these small crises was unusual in itself, but the combination seemed ominous. "Sometimes I wonder if it's starting to unravel," Ethan said. "The peace they gave us."

"Imposed on us. And I'm not sure we should call it peace."

Pax formicae, she thought. The peace of the anthill.

"If any of what Bayliss said is true—if the hypercolony is infected and at war with itself—that would obviously affect the way it manages the world."

"Or else it'll all be resolved by New Year's." Nerissa shrugged. "No way of knowing."

Then the state and local news. The Indiana legislature had passed a budget extension. The Farm Alliance was threatening to boycott the Midwest Corn Exchange unless prices stabilized. State Police were participating in the search for four young persons sought in a murder-assault case. The weather would be clear and seasonally cool for the next few days.

"If we drive through the night," Ethan said, switching off the radio, "I think we can make Werner's place by morning."

She had met Werner Beck for the first time at a Correspondence Society gathering in Boston before the massacres of '07. Brief as it was, the meeting had soured her on the Society and helped derail her relationship with Ethan.

The Correspondence Society, true to its paranoid principles, was really two organizations. The majority of its members were academics or scientists who used the mailing list to share unpopular or even whimsical ideas related to their research. For those people it was little more than an academic equivalent of the Masons or the Shriners: a notionally secret social club, useful as a way of networking with other professionals. They weren't required to take seriously the idea of the radiosphere as a living entity.

Those who *did* take the idea seriously were more likely to be members of the Society's inner circle, numbering no more than five hundred individuals in universities and research facilities throughout the world. Invariably, their work had confronted them with evidence they could neither safely publish nor honestly ignore. Ethan, for example. Ethan had been one of those outer-circle Society academics until his work with Antarctic ice cores. He had shared some of his results with Werner Beck, who had pushed him into conducting isolations of the chondritic dust he discovered in his samples. It was Werner Beck who had recruited him into the inner circle.

The inner circle didn't hold conferences in the conventional sense, but every few years there was an informal gathering somewhere in the world. That year, Beck had booked rooms in a motel in Framingham outside of Boston. It wasn't necessary to rent function rooms—the Society attendees amounted to seven men and one woman (four from the U.S., one from Denmark, two from China and one from France); the entire gathering would fit comfortably in a single hotel room. Each delegate was scheduled to present a paper deemed too sensitive for the larger Society mailing list. Ethan would be reporting on his work with the ice cores; Beck, on the cultures he had succeeded in growing from Ethan's extractions.

Ethan had introduced her to Beck in the motel's coffee shop. She had expected someone slightly larger than life. And maybe he was, but only in the metaphorical sense: Beck was no taller than Nerissa herself, and she topped out at five and a half feet. His hair was dark and thinning. He wore a beard: a uniform quarter-inch of facial hair so carefully manicured that it had a topiary quality. He dressed casually, in spotless jeans and a white shirt open at the neck, and in contrast to most of the attendees he looked as if he'd spent some time at the gym—broad shoulders, thick upper arms.

His eyes were his most striking feature. There was nothing nervous or tentative about them. He looked at her steadily and with a bluntness that began to make her uncomfortable. Then he smiled. "You must be Mrs. Iverson."

Ethan, typically, had forgotten to introduce her. "Nerissa," she said. "Hi."

"Werner Beck." He shook her hand briskly and

briefly, then turned to Ethan. "Last time we met you were single. You've done all right for yourself."

"Thank you," Ethan said—a smidgen too obsequiously, Nerissa thought.

"It's unusual to bring a spouse to one of these events."

"We're both on a sort of sabbatical. Well, a vacation. After this weekend we're headed to Hawaii. Two weeks at Turtle Bay."

"Sounds nice. Anyway, welcome, Ethan. We have a lot to talk about. Mrs. Iverson, I hope you don't feel left out. But Boston's a big city. I'm sure you can keep yourself busy."

It was a dismissal, and not a particularly gracious one. Nerissa fought the urge to say something condescending in return. She had hoped Ethan might stick up for her, but all he offered was a nervous laugh. "Ris knows the city pretty well—she's lived here most of her life."

"I'm sure. Anyway, we have our first gathering this afternoon at one. It's Wickramasinghe's session—he'll be talking about organic inclusions in meteorite fragments. A great lead-up to *your* work." Beck's eyes flicked back to Nerissa. "Nice meeting you, Mrs. Iverson, and I hope to see you again soon."

"Well?" Ethan asked, after Beck had left the table.

She shrugged. "He's well-groomed."

"That's your impression of him? Well-groomed?"

"A little oily." *Since you ask.*

"He's just trying to make a good impression."

"On the unexpected spousal baggage?"

"That's not fair."

Perhaps not. The Society, Ethan had told her, didn't have a strict policy on how much information members could share with their families. But it was understood that talking too freely could endanger one's career—that was why the Society had come to exist in the first place. And much of what the Society's inner circle had learned would have sounded bizarre or even irrational to an outsider. Nerissa understood that she would have to tread carefully here, perhaps especially around a key player like Werner Beck.

But she resented being treated as an interloper. Or worse, a potential spy. As if she *cared* what these people discussed at their meetings. As if their ideas would ever be more to her than an unsettling and highly speculative hypothesis.

"Anyhow," Ethan said, "it's his ideas that count. And he's a solid researcher. Since his wife died a few years ago, his work is all he has. And he can afford to devote himself to it."

"He's a widower?"

"Raising a son by himself."

She allowed Ethan to change the subject. They talked about their plans for Oahu. Nerissa imagined a room with bamboo furniture, a breeze, the distant sound of the sea. And herself on a shaded veranda with a drink (something with gin and an umbrella in it) to extinguish any lingering thoughts about the forces that influenced human events.

On Saturday she wandered through the secondhand bookshops in Old Boston. Nerissa found bookstores soothing, especially antiquarian bookstores—the smell of old ink, the muted acoustics. She wanted something smart but not too challenging, and she eventually settled on a tattered second printing of Raymond Chandler's *The Little Sister*. Back at the motel she staked out a table by the window of the bar and began to read. She had not reached the end of the first chapter when she became aware of a looming shadow. A woman of, she guessed, forty-something, carrying a drink and blinking from behind an impressively dense pair of eyeglasses. "You're Ethan's wife, right?"

Nerissa nodded cautiously.

"I thought so. I saw you with Ethan and Beck the other day." Her voice was small (*birdlike,* Nerissa thought) and she spoke with a French accent. "I'm Amélie. Amélie Fournier. I'm one of the—well, you know. I'm with the Society. Do you mind if I sit with you? Or if you'd rather be alone—"

"No, please sit. I'm Nerissa."

Amélie lowered herself into a chair. "Thank you. I'm playing hooky from the meeting. Is that the right expression? Playing hooky? I find I can endure only so much of staring into the abyss."

"The abyss?"

"I mean the deep of the sky. And what lives there."

Amélie wrinkled her face, an expression not quite approximating a smile. "Of course, I don't know how much Ethan has discussed with you . . ."

"My husband and I don't keep secrets."

"Really? That would be unusual. But of course I shouldn't be talking about these things at all. Mr. Beck would be upset with me. But I discover I don't really care. I'm tired of Mr. Beck. I prefer the company of the unenthusiastic. By which I mean someone who is not so highly partisan. Mr. Beck considers himself a warrior. In his eyes we are all unsatisfactory soldiers. Some of us are reluctant to be soldiers at all, much to his disgust. I'm sorry, would you rather talk about something else? I can be a bore when I drink. People tell me so."

"Not at all. It's refreshing to get another point of view."

"As opposed to your husband's?"

"My husband's opinion of Mr. Beck is somewhat higher than yours."

"Yes, I am in a minority. I admit it. I think there are truths Mr. Beck is unfortunately ignoring."

"Such as?"

Amélie hesitated. She ran a hand through her hair, which was cut in a style Nerissa hadn't seen before, like sleek dark wings. "Each of us at this meeting represents a certain discipline. Mine is astronomy. I am an astronomer. Have you ever looked through a telescope, Nerissa?"

"Once or twice."

"Optical telescopes are old-fashioned. Nowadays we look at the sky at invisible wavelengths. Or with photographic plates. The naked eye is an unreliable observer. But I was raised by a man whose hobby was astronomy. We lived in Normandy, in the west of the country. My father owned a large property there. Farmland. Far from the cities. The sky was dark at night. The stars were a constant presence. I became fascinated with the stars, as was my father. He used to say that there was something noble about the act of looking through a telescope. Human beings are small animals on an insignificant planet, but when we look at the sky—when we understand that the stars are distant suns—we begin to encompass an entire universe.

"As a child I was enthralled. Of course, I thought about the possibility of other worlds circling those distant suns. Inhabited worlds, perhaps. Planets perhaps with civilizations like our own, but more primitive or more advanced. Childish fantasies, but even a scientist may entertain such ideas.

"As an adult I discovered that a career in modern astronomy was more prosaic than I expected. My post-graduate project was a study of the propagative layer, the radiosphere, using high-frequency interferometry. My work met with resistance. It was hard to get cooperation or research time on the larger dish antennae. The details don't matter— a tenured colleague from another university became aware of my work and introduced me to the

Correspondence Society." Amélie smiled ruefully. "Much was explained."

"You believed what they told you? About the radiosphere being alive?"

"They offered me the evidence and allowed me to draw my own conclusion. Don't you believe it?"

"I'm not a scientist. I guess you could say Ethan convinced me. His *conviction* convinced me."

"Life," Amélie said, "not of this world, and almost near enough to touch. At first it was only a surmise, but the evidence is now conclusive. Thanks in part to the work of your husband. The small seeds embedded in ancient ice cores. Think of that, a sort of gentle snow of alien life, very diffuse, sifting down from the sky, accumulating over centuries. And not dead, but still in some sense living. We are enclosed in an *organism*, which facilitates our communication and moves us, as a species, in a certain direction."

Herds us, Ethan had once said, *the way certain ants herd aphids.*

"It's a marvelous, a terrifying, an utterly unpalatable truth." Amélie waved a hand at the sky—well, the ceiling—and came within an inch of knocking her drink to the floor. "For some years now we have consoled ourselves with the idea that the relationship between ourselves and this entity is *symbiotic*. Do you know that word? Mutually beneficial. It preserves and enhances the peace of the world, and in return . . . ah, what it takes in return is a matter of some debate. But Mr. Beck is more pessimistic. He suspects the relationship is purely parasitical. What the hypercolony wants, it will eventually take. Its intervention in our affairs is entirely selfish. If it wants us to be unwarlike, it's so we won't develop the weapons we might use to defend ourselves."

"You think that's true?"

"I don't know. The evidence is controversial. But consider the implication, if what Mr. Beck believes *is* true. There is a form of life that is distributed throughout galactic space, and it depends for its survival on the exploitation of civilizations like our own. What does that mean?"

"I suppose . . . well, that civilizations like ours must be relatively common."

"Yes, perhaps. At least common enough to have played a role in the evolution of this entity. This *parasitical* entity. This *successful* parasitical entity. The parasite is here, all around us—" Amélie leaned close enough that Nerissa could smell the alcohol on her breath. "But *where are its previous victims*? Where are these other civilizations like our own? Why haven't they warned us against it? Why aren't they here to help us?"

"I don't know. Maybe it isn't practical, or maybe they don't care . . ."

"Or maybe the predator, having devoured its victim, leaves only a corpse behind."

The bar was aggressively air-conditioned. Nerissa shivered.

Amélie nodded. "You understand, I think. And

this is what has destroyed the pleasure I once took in looking through the telescope. All those wonderful possibilities. But now when I see the stars I think, death. Killing. Nature, red in the tooth . . ."

"Red," Nerissa corrected her, "in tooth and claw." Amélie was quoting Tennyson, whether she knew it or not. A passage about "man," that Victorian abstraction, *Who trusted God was love indeed / And love Creation's final law— / Tho' Nature, red in tooth and claw / With ravine, shriek'd against his creed* . . .

"'In tooth and claw.' Exactly."

"And you blame Beck for changing the way you look at the sky?"

"Blame Beck? No, not for *that*." Amélie smiled bitterly. "No. I blame Mr. Beck for propositioning me very crudely when we were alone in his room, and then belittling my work because I refused his advances. But that's the kind of man he is." She stood up suddenly, her chair teetering behind her. "I think Mr. Beck is as deluded as the rest of us. He simply cherishes a more militant delusion. Watch out for your husband, Nerissa. I mean to say, be careful of him. Protect him. Because he seems terribly impressed with Mr. Beck's ideas. And I think Mr. Beck's ideas are frankly dangerous."

Nerissa saw Werner Beck once more that weekend, at a group dinner at the end of the conference. All technical discussion was banned for the duration of the meal. It was meant to be a social evening, though Nerissa was the only woman at the table: Amélie Fournier had booked an early flight to Louis Blériot Airport in Paris.

Conversation was shallow and often awkward. Maybe it hadn't been a good idea to ban discussion of the single subject these people had in common. What was left? Books, films, politics, trivia. Nerissa said little and allowed her attention to drift, but she was impressed by Beck's obvious domination of the event. The Correspondence Society was supposedly nonhierarchical and Beck held no official position, but it was Beck who called for menus, Beck who refereed minor disagreements, Beck who had organized the dinner in the first place.

And it was Beck who declared it over as soon as the dessert dishes had been cleared away. He held his hand out to Nerissa as she left with Ethan. "Pleasure meeting you, Mrs. Iverson." His handshake was firm and his smile radiated a perfect confidence. She managed a smile in return, perhaps not very persuasively.

Later, in their room, she told Ethan what Amélie had said about Beck.

Ethan frowned. "It must be some kind of misunderstanding."

"Amélie seemed clear on what happened."

"Her work on microwave echoing was pretty thin gruel. Beck was a little dismissive of it in discussion, but I don't think he said anything unfair. It was Beck who delivered the bombshell at this conference. He managed to detect signaling mechanisms in chon-dritic cells in culture."

"And that's important?"

"Like pulling down a piece of the sky and putting it under a microscope. If we understand how these cells communicate, it should be possible to monitor that communication or even interfere with it. I mean, if we choose to."

"And the fact that he propositioned her?"

"Well, did he? He may have said something cal-lous, which she amplified out of, you know, profes-sional jealousy—"

"So she was lying?"

"Come on, Ris! Not necessarily lying, but . . ." He shrugged impatiently. "And no real harm was done. I don't know why we're even discussing this. She produced some trivial work, it got the attention it deserved, and she resented it. Maybe Beck didn't conduct himself like a perfect gentleman, but even if that's the case, does it really matter?"

At least take it into consideration, Nerissa thought. Don't dismiss it out of loyalty to Beck. Don't make excuses for him just because his research is impres-sive. But she didn't say any of those things, only frowned and turned away.

The disagreement cast a shadow over their vaca-tion. Oahu was predictably beautiful. They hiked Mokuleia, they sunned for blissful hours on the white sand of the hotel's beach. But Nerissa had seen a side of Ethan (and of the Correspondence Society) she didn't like and couldn't altogether dismiss. And although the stars over the North Shore were lovely, she was haunted by what Amélie had said. *Nature, red in tooth and claw / With ravine, shriek'd against his creed* ... And against Amélie herself, apparently. Amélie had been one of the first to die in the murders of 2007.

"Ris, wake up."

For a moment she thought she was back in Hawaii. But no. She had slept in the car. She blinked her eyes against a gray dawn, hardly tropical. When she sat up, every joint in her body voiced a separate complaint.

Ethan had parked in front of a bungalow on some dusty street near a railroad crossing. She began to ask where they were, then realized she didn't have to. This was one of Werner Beck's many so-called safe houses, the address of which he had given Ethan in the letter that had arrived the day they left the farmhouse. *Evidence of heightened radiosphere activity,* Beck had written, *take all precautions, you can reach me at this address.*

And the man just now stepping out the door and down the porch steps was Werner Beck himself. He hadn't changed much in the years since Nerissa had last seen him. His posture remained militarily erect, though his hair and beard were grayer. He wore loose khakis and an untucked red flannel shirt. And he was cradling a shotgun, though he offered a tight smile when Ethan rolled down the window.

Please let them be here, Nerissa thought. *Please let them be inside the house, Cassie and Thomas, and Beck's son, Leo. Let them be watching from a window. Let them come running out when they see me.* She opened the car door. She stood up. Ethan did the same.

"You'd better get inside," Werner said.

And from the house there was nothing. Only a pale light, an empty porch, a motionless door, the vacant silence.

17

DOWD'S GARAGE

Eugene Dowd's spray paint had turned the car Leo had stolen from white to metallic blue. With its windows and trim still masked it looked almost fake to Cassie's eyes, a trompe l'oeil automobile, a magic trick at the point of unveiling. Dowd said he would give it a buff and a clear coat in the morning—there wasn't time for anything better, and the only purpose of all this work was to make sure the car no longer fit its original description. A hasty coat of paint and new plates was the best he could do. Then they would have to get on the road.

Of course Cassie wanted him to finish his story about Chile, about the desert called the Atacama and the strange lights he had seen there. But Dowd wasn't in the mood. Tomorrow, he said. He talked better when he had something to do with his hands. In the meantime he meant to drive his truck into Salina to pick up supplies, and did anybody want to come with him?

Beth volunteered at once. Dowd nodded and escorted her out of the garage.

Cassie, Leo and Thomas adjourned to Dowd's office upstairs, where the grimy window was orange with the glow of the sunset. They were too hungry to wait for Dowd and Beth to get back, so they assembled dinner out of the leftovers in Dowd's refrigerator. Leo switched on Dowd's little transistor radio and let it play for a while—mostly Christmas music, since that was the next big holiday on the calendar. The tinkling bells and choral arrangements were cheerful for a time, but after dark the music began to seem as sad and distant as a signal from a ship at sea. Cassie wondered whether she would ever celebrate Christmas again. Aunt Ris had not been particularly religious, but every December she dragged a dwarfish pine tree up the stairs to the apartment and installed it in a tin basin over a white sheet, where its fallen needles would collect in prickly drifts. Cassie supposed the apartment was empty now—past-due notices in the overflowing mailbox, food rotting in the refrigerator, dust sifting out of the still air.

Leo switched off the radio. Thomas sat glumly at the window. "Wish I had something to read," he said.

Cassie agreed. Even a magazine would have been better than nothing, but a search of Dowd's premises had proved fruitlesss. "All we have," she said, "is one of Uncle Ethan's books, and Leo's got dibs on that."

"I could read it out loud," he said.

Cassie had to stifle a laugh when she realized he

was serious. It seemed comical to her, the idea of chain-smoking Leo Beck reading to them from a work of popular science. But it was a nice thought. (And, come to that, when was the last time she'd seen him smoking a cigarette? He must have finished his last pack, and he hadn't asked Beth to pick up more.)

Thomas seemed intrigued. "Really?"

"Yeah," Leo said. "Sure." He flashed Thomas a smile, then opened the book to its first chapter. "*Consider a fisherman—let's say, a young man who owns his own boat and weaves his own nets. . . .*"

In Leo's sonorous and surprisingly confident voice it sounded more like a story than an essay. Cassie watched Leo's face as he read, the attention he paid to the text, the way he glanced up from the page to make eye contact with Thomas, who leaned forward with obvious interest. It was a charitable act, she thought. A nice thing to do. Apparently, somewhere inside Leo Beck was a man Cassie might be able to respect.

Dowd and Beth returned after midnight, both of them a little drunk. Dowd left a box of canned goods by the door and brought a few perishables up to the refrigerator in his office. "Supplies for the trip," he said, and stalked out again before Cassie could ask the obvious question: *What trip? Where are we going?*

Leo and Thomas and Cassie had already unrolled

their sleeping bags on the floor of the office. "You're closest to the switch," Leo said. "Will you turn out the light?"

"Okay, but what if Beth comes in later?"

"She can find her way around."

From downstairs, the sound of hectic laughter.

A few miles down that road—and it wasn't much of a road, just gravel and dirt blown over with sand—me and Bastián realized we were doing something stupid.

Morning had dawned cold, with a few flakes of snow drifting from a thickly overcast sky. The air in the garage smelled of urethane and stale beer and motor oil. Dowd had stripped the car of its masking and now he had it up on a lift, inspecting the tires and undercarriage in case it became necessary to drive through bad weather. On their way to where, exactly, Dowd still hadn't said.

Stupid because we didn't know what we were getting into, and stupid because we'd almost for sure be fired. But it didn't matter. It was one of those situations where you just say fuck it. Fuck the job, fuck management. The pay was decent but living in a bunkhouse in the middle of the world's driest desert, staring at the salares and the cordillera all day, makes you a certain kind of crazy. I don't know about Bastián, but I was ready to go back where people actually lived. See something vertical for a change. Talk to a woman who wasn't an overseer or a forklift driver.

So we drove on even after the Pisco ran out. Bastián started talking about copper mining. He said he had a cousin who had worked at Chuquicamata and Escondida. Whatever these people were doing out here, he said, they weren't mining copper. To mine copper you need water, but there was no river or aquifer. Big tanks of water had come through our compound, but not enough for serious ore extraction. And if they were doing heap-leaching there would have been bulk shipments of sulfuric acid and chemicals like that. Hell, we should have seen the tailing dams by now. Or at least smelled them. Because we were getting close.

What we did see was all kinds of garbage on the side of the road. That's the thing about the desert, nothing rots or gets overgrown or sinks into the earth. You throw something away, it just sits there. We drove past these little piles of fractured aluminum tubing and cut metal and broken machine parts and colored glass and cracked ceramic insulators and shit like that. It was past midnight, there was a half-moon in the sky and all kinds of stars, so it looked pretty strange, sort of Martian, if you know what I mean—these trash piles with rebar and steel girders sticking out. Six feet high, some of them, then ten feet high, until we were driving down an alley made of trash, and Bastián slowed up and started to look *worried. Eugene, he says, this is not a normal operation. No shit, I said.*

I don't want to be seen here, he says. Whatever these people are doing, they don't want company. Well, I say, and it was probably the Pisco talking, I came out here to see and I mean to see.

Okay, but on foot, Bastián says. Toyota makes too much noise.

Okay. So we get out and climb up an embankment that's mostly industrial refuse. Slipping on sheet plastic and grabbing rebar like it was tree branches, all in all probably making more noise than we would have if we just kept driving. But it turns out Bastián picked a good place to stop, because from the top of that ridge we could see the whole installation.

If you want to call it that. The compound. Whatever. That's no mine, Bastián says. Yeah, I said, that's pretty fuckin' obvious.

It was a patch of desert the size of a small town, with this trash heap around it like the side of a bowl. Most of the buildings in it were long sheds, tin roofs, plywood or cinderblock walls, no marks on them. In the middle there was a tower, not very tall and kind of squat, holding up what looked like a ten or twelve big mirrors arranged like the petals of a flower. You could tell they were mirrors because they reflected the lights from the buildings and also the stars overhead. Real industrial-looking. Around it there was a bunch of pumps and pressure tanks full of god-knows-what and fat electrical cables, all told taking

*up about as much space as a regulation football field.
That was where the light came from, the light we
saw all the way back at the depot where we worked.*

"How do you know that's where it came from?"
Thomas suddenly asked. Dowd gave him a shut-the-
fuck-up look and paused. Cassie put a protective arm
around her little brother.

*We knew because it came on while we were watch-
ing. Nearly blew us back down the trash heap. I
mean it wasn't loud or anything, there wasn't any
noise at all except what might have been a compressor buried somewhere underground. But bright, oh,
Jesus! Maybe thirty seconds before I could see anything but the glare. Bastián put his head down, but I
couldn't help sneaking looks. The beam of light went
straight up, and it didn't spread out like a spotlight,
it was straight as a pencil all the way up to where it
disappeared. The air started to smell electric, like hot
metal and burning insulation.*

*Bastián said in a sick little voice he wanted to get
back in the Toyota and go home. And I thought that
was a good idea. Because with all that light we were
pretty conspicuous, and worse . . . I could see things
moving. Moving toward us. Look, I said.*

*People down there, he says. Anyway we guessed
they were people. Between the glare and the shadows it was hard to tell. The way they moved, they
might have been animals. Big ones. So. Come on, he
says, let's get the fuck out of here. So we scramble
down the dark side of the trash heap, half-blind,*

tripping over shit. I cut myself on a piece of sheet metal and didn't even feel it till later. Still got the scar—see?

Dowd lifted his T-shirt to expose his torso. The scar ran at right angles to the staves of his ribs, a pale irregular line.

Then Bastián says stop, I hear something. So we stand still. The wind had come up, so I could hear scraps of roofing paper and torn plastic rattling in the trash pile, plus industrial sounds from the compound, that compressor or whatever it was beating like a drum, and over that—this is what Bastián was talking about—a kind of scrabbling sound, like a dog might make digging through garbage. Getting louder. Bastián looks up at the ridgeline of the trash heap and kind of gasps, and I look where he's looking, and there's this, uh, thing up there—

"What do you mean?" Leo asked. "What kind of thing?"

Dowd gazed abstractedly at a torque wrench he had picked up.

Well, that's a good question. I don't know what else to call it. It was something about halfway between an ape, a spider, and a Swiss army knife.

Thomas emitted a bark of laughter, more nerves than anything else. Dowd ignored him.

Moved like a spider or a crab. Had about that many legs. But it bent up at the middle, I mean it had a kind of a waist, and arms above that, but not hands—more like tools, blades and pincers and shit like that. And it had a head, which was the only human thing about it. Not a human head exactly. But eyes, a mouth.

So it comes down the side of that trash pile, headed straight for Bastián. Bastián starts looking around for something he can use to defend himself. Grabs a piece of rebar that's sticking up but it's buried too deep, he's like desperately tugging on this iron rod, doesn't take his hand off it until the thing is on top of him. Then he tries to back up but he's on a slope and he can't move fast enough and the thing just— well, it basically took him apart. Three quick moves. Snip snip snip. Three pieces of Bastián rolled past me, leaving blood trails.

Then it came for me, but I'd had a little more time get ready. Or else I just got lucky—the Lucite rod I grabbed out of the trash had about the weight and heft of a baseball bat. The thing had long arms and those fingers, or blades, or claws, were fast as lightning, I got a couple more scars I could show you but I'd have to drop my pants—anyway I managed to bring that rod down on the thing's head, maybe not hard enough to kill it, I don't know, but maybe I did, it dropped like all its strings had been cut and I proceeded to move the fuck elsewhere.

Got to the Toyota. Did a crazed U-turn and as soon as I'm pointed the right direction I see a half-dozen more of those things in the mirror, gaining on me. Stepped on the gas so hard I nearly ran the fucking vehicle off the fucking road. Kicked up a big cloud of dust and sand, which in the glare of that light was like a smokescreen.

The next thing I see is in front of me, and this time at least it's a human being, a guy in jeans and a white shirt standing in the middle of the road trying to flag me down. Which was almost reassuring, except the guy has a pistol in a holster and he's starting to reach for it. I mean, to me he looked like a mall cop. But what am I gonna do, pull over? So I stand on the gas pedal.

The guy looked weirdly calm, and I could see him real clear in that freaky light, trying to level his pistol before the Toyota hit him. Like it was a race between the pistol and the Toyota. The Toyota won. I hit him full-on.

Which pretty near killed me. Any of you ever been in a car when it runs into a large animal, maybe a deer? No air bags on that vehicle. No seat belts. If my legs hadn't caught on the steering wheel my head would have gone through the windshield. As it was I took a nasty crack on the dashboard. Lost control. The vehicle went up on two wheels, almost turned over. It was halfway up the embankment before I got control of it again. Big dent in the front end and the engine making a sound like a circular saw with a bent blade.

But the mall guard was dead. I knew that because he was all over the fucking windshield. He pretty much exploded on contact. Green shit everywhere. I mean I had to turn on the wipers just so I could see.

*Clots of red and yellow, yeah, like blood and I guess
body fat, but mostly green—I guess you know what
I'm talking about.*

"He was a simulacrum," Thomas piped up, need-
lessly.

*Yeah, a sim. But obviously I didn't know that then.
It was just more weirdness. I was being chased by
spiders with blades for hands, Bastián was dead, the
mall guard was made of snot, and all I wanted was
to be anywhere else in the world but this fucking
desert. Kept my foot on the gas even when smoke
started coming out from under the hood. Long as
the wheels turned. One eye on the mirror at all times.*

*Pretty soon they switched off that tall beam of
light. And I killed the Toyota's lights and drove by
the moon, just to be less conspicuous. I expected to
be chased, but that didn't happen. At least not right
away. And then I thought, well, where do I go? Back
to the depot? Tell an overseer I totaled a company
vehicle and by the way Bastián was cut in three
pieces by a giant crab?*

*Since there was nobody on the road back of me far
as I could see—and in the Atacama that's a long way,
even at night—I stopped the vehicle and tried to take
inventory and come up with some kind of plan. Took
off my shirt and tied it around my ribs to stop the
bleeding. Obviously the Toyota wasn't going to make
it much farther. Smoke kept coming even when I
turned the engine off. I got out and opened the trunk.
Found a spare tire—useless—a tire iron, the four-way*

kind—also pretty useless—and a jack. The jack had a detachable steel handle, which was better than nothing, so I took that. A knife would have been better. Even a box cutter. Anything. But the jack handle was the best I could do.

Then I rolled the Toyota off the road and pointed it across the salt flats, got the engine running— barely—put the transmission in neutral, braced the tire iron against the gas pedal, put it in first gear and jumped the fuck out. The vehicle rolled out into desert on a slow curve, probably would have come right back to me except the engine died when it was a couple of hundred yards off in the flats. Engine caught fire. Pretty soon it looked like a bonfire, burning out there. I hoped it looked like I'd driven off-road and maybe died in the fire. Or at least that somebody might think that from a distance. Then I hunkered down behind the little dirt-and-pebble embankment at the side of the road, which was the only thing to hide behind, which wasn't much.

Still trying to make a plan. The moon was close to setting and dawn was about an hour away. If more mall guards showed up I thought I might have a chance, but if a posse of those spidery things came down the road I figured I'd be better off slitting my own throat before they did me the favor . . . But then I saw headlights in the distance.

It was just one truck. A four-wheel-drive Ford with roll bars and a pickup bed. It slowed down, probably because the driver saw the Toyota burning

like a motherfucker out there on the salt flats.
Stopped a few yards away from where I was hiding.
Looked like there was two guys inside. One of 'em
gets out. He's a mall guard—same clothes, same pistol on his hip. Flashlight in his right hand. He's looking down at the road, shining that light on the gravel,
checking out the tire tracks where the Toyota veered
into the *salar*. And every step brings him a little closer
to me.

So while he's staring at the ground I get up and
run at him. All I have on my side is surprise. He sees
me coming, of course. He drops the flashlight. Reaches
for his pistol. But I swing the jack handle before he
even touches the weapon. He dodges real quick, but
I manage to stun him. So I hit him again, a home-run
swing to the side of his head, which drops him like
a bag of sand. I go down on my knees and take the
pistol out of his holster.

In those days I didn't know a lot about firearms,
but I'd handled my daddy's old .45 a few times. So I
switch off the safety and pray the fucking thing's
loaded, because the second guy is getting out of the
Ford in a hurry, and he's definitely armed and dangerous. I get off one shot, which goes through the Ford's
windshield. Useless. Second shot clips the guy's shoulder, which turns him around. I'm up and running, he's
still trying to bring his weapon up though his arm
don't work right, third shot is to the head and boom,
he's down.

Another head shot for each mall guard, just to

*make sure. Which causes blood and green goo to
leak all over my shoes.*

*Then I get in their truck and drive. Full tank, reli-
able vehicle, and by this time I'm so high on adrena-
line I start to feel pretty good about myself, all things
considered. Back of me I can see more headlights,
but I'm way ahead of 'em. I blow past the depot
where Bastián and I worked, and by the time the sky
gets light I'm halfway to San Pedro de Atacama and
if anybody's following they're well out of sight.*

*In San Pedro I traded the Ford to a guy no-
questions-asked for his little piece-of-shit ten-year-
old Hudson, which for some reason there are a lot of
in the Atacama, somebody must've opened a dealer-
ship once . . . a plain dumb car, which I managed to
drive all the way to Antofagasta before its tranny
seized up. Laid low for a while, did day labor at the
puerto until I could afford a plane ride back to the
USA. Back home I spent a year or so trying to chase all
this shit out of my head with Jack and Coke, hold the
Coke, until I shot off my drunken mouth to that
writer. After which Werner Beck showed up and
more or less explained things to me.*

And that's my story.

"But that doesn't explain anything," Leo protested.

"What do you need explained?"

"The light in the desert? The spider things?"

"You should ask your daddy about all that, Leo. Assuming you ever see him again."

"Also, what's in the back of your van that's so important?"

"Your daddy should've mentioned that, too." Dowd grinned, displaying a row of crooked teeth. "You could call it a secret weapon. Or *part* of one."

"And you keep talking about getting on the road. Road to where?"

"Do you really have to ask?"

Leo shook his head. "This is crazy."

Dowd's grin expanded. "Amen, brother," he said. "No argument from me."

18

Ethan's first concern was for Nerissa, who was hugely disappointed to discover that Cassie and Thomas and Leo hadn't shown up at Werner Beck's safe house.

Ethan was disappointed too, of course. But Ris seemed to lose all the fierce energy she had been drawing on for days. She looked suddenly years older, and the tone she took with Beck was querulous and irritable. "So where *are* they—do you have any *idea* where they are?"

Beck escorted them to a plain pine table in the kitchen of this small, plain house. "Sit down," he said.

"And Leo! He's your *son*, for Christ's sake! Are you telling me you can't find him?"

"We made plans for this contingency."

"What plans? What do you mean?"

"If Leo's doing what I told him to do, we should be able to catch up with him. And if Cassie and— what's the boy's name?"

Nerissa shot him a poisonous look. *"Thomas."*

"If Cassie and Thomas are with him, that will be your opportunity to take them out of harm's way. But obviously, Mrs. Iverson, I don't know with any certainty where any of them are right now. I can't snap my fingers and make them appear in front of you. You need to exercise some patience."

"Do you care to explain any of that?"

"I'm as concerned about Leo as you are about your niece and nephew, and I'll do everything I can to guarantee their safety. The situation is complex, and I'd be happy to talk about it, but in the meantime maybe you'd like to have a shower and a change of clothes? No offense, but you look like you could use it. I'll put together a hot meal for all of us as soon as you're refreshed. How about that?"

It was testimony to her fatigue that she sighed and nodded. Beck told her how to find the bathroom.

"I understand why you brought her here," he said when she left the room. "But it's frankly a little awkward."

Ethan didn't want to get into that discussion, at least not yet. "How many houses do you own, Werner?"

"Enough. They're only tools. You could say, weapons of war."

"The sims came for you, didn't they?"

"I got out of my place in Illinois minutes ahead of them. I'd been there too long in any case—I knew it was probably compromised. I was packed and ready to go when they came to the door. They didn't see me leave."

Ethan had heard speculation about Beck and his money—especially his money—for years before Beck confided in him. It was rumored that Beck had patented some useful invention. Or that he had inherited a fortune back in the 1990s. Or that he had criminal connections. Or all three.

That he possessed both deep pockets and useful connections was undeniable. It was Beck who had organized and paid for the annual gatherings of Society members; it was Beck who had funded key research projects when educational institutions backed out; and after the murders of 2007 it had been Beck who helped out the survivors and their families, with cash and when necessary with goods otherwise unobtainable: new names, social security numbers, passports.

Not to mention his apparently inexhaustible supply of safe houses, properties he owned but kept unoccupied so that he could relocate himself or others on a moment's notice. More than one Society member had called Beck paranoid, and maybe they were right. But it was, Ethan thought, at least a *well-funded* paranoia.

"The thing is," Beck said, "you more or less walked into a war zone."

"The war came to us. And you supplied the address, Werner."

"Because we need to stay in touch. But I didn't expect you to turn up on the doorstep."

"It seemed like the logical thing to do, given that Cassie and Thomas are traveling with Leo."

"I understand. But the situation is more complicated than you realize. I've been working with people who aren't part of the Society. The Society was never more than one aspect of this war, Ethan. You can think of the Society as a kind of intelligence service, gathering information about the enemy. That's good and useful work. But wars have to be fought. And they have to be fought by soldiers, not scholars."

Ethan sat back in his chair as Beck got up to make coffee. The coffee machine on the faux-marble counter looked as if Beck had bought it yesterday. And maybe he had. The house itself still smelled untenanted, redolent of stale air and the chemical exhalations of undisturbed carpets and furniture. Ethan had a momentary vision of Beck as the kind of furtive animal that nests in abandoned buildings. But he looked martially efficient as he filled the machine's reservoir and dropped a filter into its basket. He was fifty years old, Ethan guessed, maybe older, but he could have been a weatherworn drill sergeant, still able to hike as far as any recruit and count off twice as many push-ups. "You always were unhappy with the Society,"

Ethan said. In fact Beck's private letters had so often dripped with contempt for his colleagues that Ethan occasionally wondered why Beck bothered with them at all.

"Well, I don't really blame the Society. So much of what we believed was essentially speculative. Before you turned up those ice-core inclusions all we really had was some anomalous data, a history of academic persecution, and a mother lode of surmise. The Society connected the dots, and what emerged was this frankly *ludicrous* idea, that the radio-propagative layer was also an organism. From elsewhere. From outer space. Even before '07, nobody wanted to say that out loud. A few of the old lions took it seriously—Fermi, Dyson, Hoyle—but even those guys never contemplated doing anything about it."

"What *could* they do?"

"As I said, I don't blame them. You learn to fly under the radar. Fine. But there's something to be said for facing facts. And since 2007 we've been forced to face a few." Coffee began to seep through the filter and drip into the pot, a metronomic sound. "Or anyway, I have. You want anything harder than cream in your coffee? You look like you could use it."

"No. Thank you." Ethan cleared his throat. "I was seven years in Vermont, living in a cabin in the woods. Does that count as facing facts?"

"You killed some sims, you said?"

He had already given Beck a partial account of events at the farmhouse. "Four altogether."

"Well, good. You did what you had to. But that's self-defense. You were planning for the next attack, but not beyond it."

"I managed to survive."

"Right, but what now? What next? Find a new place to hide? Somewhere even deeper in the woods?"

Ethan shrugged.

"I wasn't willing to settle for that," Beck said. "What I've done these past seven years is make contact with people outside the Society, people who've had direct experience of the hypercolony or the sims."

"I wasn't aware such people existed."

"You think it's only scientists and scholars who can draw an inference or trip over a dangerous piece of knowledge? Think about it. I have reason to believe the sims constitute a tiny fraction of the human population, far less than one in a million. But there are at least a few doctors and coroners who've examined unusual bodies. Police officers who've witnessed perplexing deaths. And plenty of people who asked awkward questions and received unsatisfying or threatening answers. I made it my business to find those people."

"How?"

"All sorts of ways. Small-town and local newspapers are a good resource. Local stories usually make it to print before they can be filtered through the radiosphere—the copy goes straight to the composing desk. The press services would never pick up an item about a traffic accident that left green matter all over the road, or, if they did, the story would get lost in transmission—but local papers often publish it."

"So you run down believe-it-or-not stories in rural newspapers?"

"Much more than that. I have contacts on three continents. I've been able to put together a network of people who understand what we're dealing with—understand it viscerally, not just theoretically—and who are motivated to take action."

"What kind of action?"

"Every living thing is vulnerable, Ethan. Even the hypercolony."

"You honestly think you've discovered a way to hurt it?"

"If it couldn't be hurt it would never have expended so much effort attempting to hurt *us*."

"Do you realize what you're admitting?"

Ethan looked up, startled: Nerissa stood in the kitchen doorway, wearing fresh clothes and carrying a towel. Beck displayed a thin-lipped flush of irritation, quickly suppressed. "I hope you're feeling better, Mrs. Iverson. What is it you think I'm admitting?"

"That you provoked it—the hypercolony. It isn't just afraid of what we might know, it's afraid of what you might do with that knowledge."

"If that's true, I hope its fears are fully justified."

"And the people who died?"

"I didn't kill them."

"You've involved your own son in this."

"I could hardly exempt him."

"And Thomas and Cassie?"

"Please don't misunderstand. I want them out of harm's way as much as you do. Your niece and nephew are of no use to me."

Ethan let Nerissa tell the story of the sim Winston Bayliss: what he had said, how he had died, and especially what they had discovered when they visited his home in Montmorency. "Mrs. Bayliss had had recent surgery, so she must have been human. But her son was a sim. How is that possible? Do you know anything about that?"

Beck was silent for so long a time that Ethan wondered whether he might refuse to answer. Then he said, "I can show you some recent research. You too, Ethan. This is work you haven't seen. Come with me."

They followed Beck to the small living room of this small house and waited as he sorted through the contents of a cardboard filing box stashed behind the sofa. He extracted a manila folder and put it on the low coffee table. Ethan and Nerissa sat down while Beck pulled up a chair. "I should warn you. Some of the photographs are graphic."

The folder contained records of the work of an English veterinarian named Wyndham. According to

Beck, Wyndham had been culturing pseudochondritic cells to explore their interaction with living tissue. For that purpose he had equipped a laboratory with cages of white mice and a few larger animals.

He had begun by introducing the foreign cells to cultivars of yeasts, fungi and bacteria, without any useful result. Tissue samples from metazoans were slightly more responsive, but the cultures quickly became necrotic.

When Wyndham injected the pseudochondritic cells directly into living mice, the effect was quickly lethal—a simultaneous eruption of multiple aggressive tumors. (The file contained a photograph of a euthanized mouse on a dissection board: the tumors with which its body was riddled looked to Ethan like bloody raspberries.) But when Wyndham dosed the creatures with the same cells in an aerosol preparation—when he put the mice in a sealed chamber and allowed them to inhale dry, extracted spores—they showed no obvious ill effects over weeks and even months.

Not that they were unaffected. Wyndham's dissections revealed that the foreign cells had migrated to the reproductive system of the mice. Gametes of both sexes were significantly altered. Under the microscope (and here was another, thankfully less visceral photo), haploid cells appeared fatter and included new and unusual organelles. "But the truly significant effect," Beck said, "was on the next generation."

Another photo of a dissection—a messy one. Nerissa made a disgusted sound and recoiled. Ethan was queasily reminded of what he had seen after the raid on his farmhouse.

Once again the dead mouse had been splayed on a dissection board. It possessed what appeared to be a complete set of internal organs, reduced in size and displaced to the borders of the abdomen. The bulk of the body cavity was occupied by a gelatinous green mass, some of which had already liquefied and begun to drain away as the photograph was taken. Tendril of this mass passed into and among the otherwise normal organs. A partial dissection of the skull revealed a hollow sphere of neural matter surrounding the same gelatinous green core.

"God, enough!" Nerissa said, grimacing.

Beck gathered up the photographs. "This would appear to be how sims are created. Pseudochondritic cells are shed by the orbital mass of the hypercolony. Some fraction of them survive entry into the Earth's atmosphere. Counting the enclosures in the ice cores lets us estimate the number of spores reaching the Earth's surface in an average year. Inevitably, some small fraction of those spores will be inhaled by animals or human beings. Assuming even a single aspirated cell is able to alter all the gametes in a given individual, and given the density and distribution of fertile adult humans across the globe, there can't be more than two or three hundred sims in all of North

America—maybe four thousand altogether on the planet. Plus a population of altered animals, probably irrelevant but worth taking into consideration."

Ethan said, "And the sims . . . are they fertile?"

"Do they breed more sims? No. Wyndham's mice were sexually functional but genetically sterile. So were his dogs and other higher mammals. There are more photos—"

"*No,*" Nerissa said.

"Wyndham refused to work with primates, but we have every reason to believe the results would have been the same."

"And these animals were otherwise normal?"

"Functionally and behaviorally. There was no way to tell a normal mouse from a sim, except with a scalpel."

"Then Mrs. Bayliss wasn't lying," Nerissa said. "She really did give birth to that *thing.*"

Beck took two more photographs from his files. Ethan was relieved to see that they were micrographs, not images from a dissection table. "We've learned more about how the spores operate on the cellular level—this should interest you, Ethan."

Whoever had produced these images must have had access to some very sophisticated equipment, maybe one of the new scanning electron microscopes, a technology that had only just become available when Ethan began to isolate ice-core specimens. "It's a busy little factory," Beck said. "But it would have to be, wouldn't it, when you consider what these things are capable of. Some of its chemical constituents are familiar enough. The so-called genetic molecules: nitrogen, carbon, phosphorous. Purines, pyrimidines. Plus arsenic, some trace metals. But what stands out is the level of *organization* in the cell. These unfamiliar filamentous structures, you see them? Fractally folded threads of conductive carbon embedded in a sub-membrane, with dendritic extensions that seem to affect every part of the cell in some fashion—"

"Some of us aren't biologists," Nerissa said. "If you want me to understand this, you'll have to dumb it down a little."

"The details don't matter as much as the function. Think about what these cells do. They travel immense distances through the vacuum of space. They duplicate themselves—at least so we surmise—by absorbing minerals and trace elements from the rocky or icy surface of asteroids, comets, planetesimals. They do this at temperatures far below the freezing point of water and with no driving force apart from faint sunlight and slow catalytic chemistry. They communicate with one another over enormous distances by generating microbursts of narrow-band radio-frequency energy. Which would be remarkable enough. But they do something that's even more impressive. In our case, they tacked inward toward the sun and occupied a stable orbit around the Earth. Ethan's research suggests they were present as much as forty thousand years ago, possibly longer. And once their numbers reached some critical threshold, they began to function as a coherent network. Do you understand what that means, Mrs. Iverson?"

"Only vaguely."

"Their intercommunication became complex. The pseudochondritic cells interact with each other much the way brain cells do. And as soon as our species began to generate radio signals of its own, the so-called radiosphere started to function as a vast distributed transceiver, relaying radio waves around the globe but also *analyzing* those signals, making of itself an analytical computer more sophisticated than any such device we've ever dreamed of building."

"So are they some form of life, or are they machines?"

"At the chemical level all living things can be construed as machines. We have no evidence that anyone *designed* these objects, though it's possible. The likeliest scenario is that they evolved over an immense span of time and gradually acquired the characteristics they now possess. On the cellular level they're immensely sophisticated; more importantly, the network they form is itself a unitary entity. The hypercolony. The hive, to borrow Ethan's description. It's the hypercolony that has learned to comprehend and manipulate human society, and it's the hypercolony we have to destroy."

If that was even remotely possible. Ethan inspected the micrographs. Cyberneticists had estimated that just one of these tiny cells was capable of faster and

subtler calculations than even the massive transistor-
ized computers operated by insurance companies or
the Internal Revenue Service. The Society's physicists thought the processing must operate at a deep,
fundamental level of reality—the "quantum" level, a
term Ethan didn't entirely understand. But a more
immediate question was vexing him. "Why haven't
I seen these micrographs before?"

"Why should you have?"

"Well, the Society—"

"Ethan, *this isn't the work of the Society*. Wyndham is an independent researcher. I underwrote his
work myself."

"Nevertheless, I would have liked to have seen
them."

"I chose to limit the exposure of this information."

"Why?"

"In order to protect it. Isn't that obvious? For
years we assumed the precautions the Society took
were good enough to hide our work from the hypercolony. But the events of 2007 proved that theory
disastrously wrong. We have no secrets and probably
never did. The only conclusion I can draw is that the
Society itself has been corrupted and infiltrated."

"So you set up another circle of researchers."

"More than one, and I've put up firewalls between
them. If one circle is compromised, the others remain
secure. And where the Correspondence Society was
basically a club for frustrated scholars, my people
are better motivated."

"Why, what motivates them?"

"Anger," Beck said. "Fear."

Beck repeated his promise that he would take Ethan and Nerissa to rendezvous with Leo (and presumably with Cassie and Thomas). But he refused to say anything more specific, except that it would be "a long trip." Nerissa continued to press, which made for a sullen evening meal, after which she and Ethan retired to the upstairs bedroom.

The room was as spare as every other room in this barely-inhabited house. A single bed, muslin curtains over the window, a layer of undisturbed dust on the uncarpeted parquet floor. "He's insane," Nerissa said.

"He's been right in the past."

"I notice that's not a denial."

"If he's paranoid, is that so hard to understand? Given the life he's led?"

"A ridiculously privileged life. Heir to millions."

True, but the whole story, at least as Ethan understood it, was more complex. Yes, Beck's parents had been wealthy. Beck's father had immigrated from Poland in the 1960s with a degree in engineering, some experience at the Nagórski plant in Starachowice, and an ambition to work with aircraft. Within a few years he had generated three modestly profitable patents and owned a small manufacturing facility in Portland that supplied parts to Boeing. He

had married an American woman who died of pancreatic cancer after giving birth to their only child,
Werner, and he had never remarried.

Beck's father had been frugal by nature and had
raised his son that way. When he died at the age of
fifty-seven, he left Werner Beck a staggeringly diverse
portfolio of investments, sole ownership of a successful company that was about to go public, and a
work ethic only slightly less demanding than the dis-
ciplines practiced by Tibetan monks.

The fortune hadn't diverted Beck from his academic career, which he had conducted with the same
Spartan intensity. When Beck discovered the Correspondence Society he had immediately diverted some
of his wealth to the support of clandestine research.
And if Beck felt his generosity entitled him to a certain amount of deference, a little centrality in an otherwise decentralized organization, who could say he
was wrong?

In 1990 Beck had married a former student who
gave birth to one child, Leo, and who had little to do
with the Society. She died in a car accident when Leo
was very young. Her death must have been traumatic
for Werner, but that was pure surmise on Ethan's
part: Beck had never spoken about his feelings and
had seemed reluctant even to mention the loss. But it
was after the death of his wife that Beck severed all
contact with conventional academia and began to
devote himself exclusively to the Society's business.

"And the only reason you know any of this,"

Nerissa said, "is that Beck told you. He could have been lying."

"Why would he lie?" The money was real, Ethan thought. The work was real.

"He may not be clinically paranoid, but he's almost certainly narcissistic. He needs to feel special, like he's fulfilling some grandiose destiny. On bad days, he probably suspects his own inadequacy."

"And you're making that diagnosis based on what exactly?"

"Jesus, Ethan, think about it! He wants us to think he's fighting a clandestine war, that he has a cadre of secret soldiers, that he's figured out the hypercolony's weaknesses . . ."

"Maybe it's true."

"It doesn't *feel* true. It doesn't even feel *likely*. What are you saying, you think he's completely sane?"

"No. But I'm not sure any of us rises to that standard."

There was nothing left to do but sleep. Ethan turned down the bed, stripped to his underwear and lay down. Nerissa curled up beside him and adjusted the blankets. Within minutes her breathing steadied into a gentle burr.

They had grown accustomed to sharing a bed during the drive to Joplin. Given the circumstances, that hardly represented an erotic opportunity. It was, however, a small reminder that they had never been officially divorced. Separated and *effectively* divorced, divorced in all but name; nevertheless, he was lying here next to his legally-ordained wife, feeling a different uneasiness than he would have felt with a stranger. He couldn't suppress all the memories she provoked. She had changed in seven years. But she smelled the same, and he found himself imagining she tasted the same—her mouth, her skin . . . not a wise thought.

He rolled away from her, toward the window. Nerissa had opened the curtains before she turned in, a habit of hers. She used to say that a view of the sky made her feel less confined. Apparently that was still true. But all Ethan could see was blackness and a few pale stars. Of course his old enemy was up there, too, ethereal and tirelessly observant, as enigmatic and as perversely fascinating as ever. Did he hate the hypercolony the way Beck claimed to? Of course he did. It had taken away everything that mattered to him. It was relentlessly, tirelessly lethal.

The difference was that he knew it didn't hate him in return. He didn't believe the hypercolony was capable of that or any other emotion. It had the magnificently indifferent lethality of a poisonous mushroom or a venomous insect.

He hated it, but he respected it. Maybe even admired it.

Would he help Beck exterminate it, if that was possible? Yes. And in the unlikely event they succeeded, he would rejoice. But unlike Beck, unlike Nerissa, he would also grieve for the passing of an extraordinary living thing.

And maybe that made him an unlikely soldier. And maybe Beck had known that about him all along.

19

ON THE ROAD

They set out in a two-vehicle convoy, Eugene Dowd driving the white van and Leo at the wheel of the repainted Ford. Cassie and Thomas chose to ride with Leo, while Beth, to no one's surprise, elected to ride in the van with Dowd.

Cassie watched the way Leo drove. He was careful to keep the van in sight as they followed the long road from Salina through Great Bend and Dodge City and across the northwestern tip of Texas, out into the dry lands under a flat December sky. If Dowd stopped for gasoline or a bathroom break, Leo would pull in behind him. If Dowd crept too far ahead, Leo would accelerate until the van was back within a comfortable distance. He was as grimly vigilant as a hunting animal.

At first Cassie wondered whether this was because of Beth—because Leo was jealous, in other words. Their relationship had cooled since they left Buffalo, but Leo might still resent Dowd for moving in on his girlfriend. Which Dowd had done as quickly and gleefully as if she had been gift-wrapped and delivered by a generous providence.

But it was more likely the gear in the back of the van Leo was concerned about. Maybe because it had seemed so fragile and incomplete, considered as a weapon. Maybe because it was the only meaningful weapon they possessed.

The highway was one of the flagship federal turnpikes constructed under the Voorhis administration more than fifty years ago, wide and well-maintained. It crossed the desert like a dark ribbon, making silvered oases where hot air mirrored the sky.

After sunset they stopped at a public campground in Arizona. The December evening was cool—cold, now that the stars were out—but they built a fire in a stone-lined pit and roasted hot dogs they had bought at a convenience store outside Tucumcari. Dowd had supplied himself with a six-pack of beer, which he shared with Beth. He talked incessantly, but not about anything serious, and after a few beers he sang a couple of country-and-western songs and encouraged Beth to come in on the choruses. Then he put his arm over Beth's shoulder and led her toward the canvas tent he had pitched. Beth spared one gloating look for Leo, who refused to meet her eyes.

Cassie made a bed for Thomas in the car: a sleeping bag on the backseat, windows open a crack to let in some air. Then she went to sit beside Leo, who stirred the embers of the dying fire. "Dowd's an ass-hole," she said.

Leo shrugged. "I guess he serves a purpose. My father trusted him. Up to a point, anyway."

Dowd had expressed his belief that Leo's father was still alive and that they would meet him some-where in Mexico or farther south. That was the plan, anyway. The plan had been in place for a couple of years, a private arrangement between Dowd and Werner Beck, and Leo's arrival had set it in motion.

Cassie tried to ignore the faint but unmistakable sounds of Dowd and Beth making love in Dowd's tent. She hoped Leo couldn't see her blushing. To make conversation, or at least a diverting noise, Cassie talked about her family—her original family, back before '07, and the house they had lived in, what little she could remember of that ancient, fragile world. Leo seemed willing to listen. He even seemed inter-ested. And when Cassie fell silent he stirred the ashes of the fire and said, "I lost my mom when I was five years old. A car accident. I survived, she didn't. The thing is, I can't even remember what she looked like. I mean, I've seen pictures. I remember the pictures. But her face, looking at me, those kind of memories? Not even in dreams."

Cassie nodded and moved closer to him.

She shared Leo's tent that night—chastely, but she was conscious of his long body beside her as he turned in his sleeping bag, the warmth and scent of him hovering under the canvas.

She thought about Beth's defection to Dowd. It wasn't really so surprising. Beth was a Society kid, and one thing that marked Society kids was a heightened sense of personal vulnerability. Maybe for that reason, Beth had always been drawn to guys who seemed powerful or protective. Which was how Leo must have seemed to her, back when he was boosting cars and hanging around with petty criminals. But Dowd was older, had traveled farther, was more persuasively dangerous.

Sometime after midnight Cassie snuck out to pee, squatting over the sand behind a mile marker. The highway was empty, the desert a vast silence. A quarter moon leaned into the shoulder of the western mountains. Mexico, she thought. Or somewhere farther south. A rendezvous with Leo's father. And what then?

In the morning they crossed the Colorado River at Topock and pushed west, heading for what Dowd called a "mail drop" somewhere in Los Angeles. Strange how peaceful the desert seemed, Cassie thought. Something about the sunlight, the solemn authority of it. Then through Barstow, where they stopped at a roadside store and Thomas gawked at a terrarium populated by pea-green lizards, and across the San Gabriels into the Los Angeles basin, the distant city white with gneiss and marble. "Where they make movies," Thomas said, and yes, Cassie said, Hollywood wasn't far away, nor were the vast industrial plants that manufactured commercial aircraft, including the planes her little brother excitedly pointed out in the cloudless sky: six-prop passenger aircraft arriving or departing from Los Angeles International Airport, even a few of the new jetliners. The mail drop turned out to be a box-rental place in Vernon, and there was nothing to pick up but a set of export permits and cartage documents that covered the contents of the van—but that was okay, Dowd said; there would be other mail drops along the way, maybe with news from Leo's father. From there they drove south past thriving farms and olive orchards, road signs not just in English but in Spanish and Japanese, enormous federal aqueducts that soared above the road, seasonal-workers' housing complexes with stucco facades in rainbow colors. How much of this would survive, she wondered, if the machine in the back of Dowd's van did what Dowd believed it would do? Because, like any other good and necessary act, destroying the hypercolony might have unintended consequences.

But she thought of her parents as she had last seen them. Murdered, though they were guilty of no crime but the possession of unauthorized knowledge. Her own life distorted, Thomas's future in doubt . . . It wasn't revenge she wanted (though she wanted that too: yes), it was justice. But justice would come at a price. Inevitably. And persons other than herself might be forced to pay it.

On the radio the local stations were playing *villancicos*: Christmas carols. *Los peces en el río. Hoy en la tierra.* Ahead, as the afternoon shadows lengthened, Dowd's van began to slow. They were close to the border now, and they needed a place to stay for the night.

Back in his Kansas garage, Dowd had thrown open the rear doors of the dusty white van and smiled like an impresario. Cassie, peering into that windowless metallic enclosure, had seen what looked like a piece of hand-wired radio gear about the size of a shipping trunk. Leo said, "That's it?"

"You don't know what you're looking at," Dowd said. "I don't understand it myself. But it was your daddy who delivered it to me. Your daddy did a lot for me. Bought this garage for me to work and live in. No charge, as long as I was willing to be a soldier when the time came. He delivered this piece of equipment just last summer. *Keep it here,* he says, *and when you get the cue, take it and yourself down to Antofagasta for a meet-up.* You showing up, that was the cue. Time to go."

"All right," Leo said dubiously. "What's it do?"

"By itself it doesn't do anything. It's part of something bigger. You're not the only soldier in the army, your daddy told me. Other folks'll be coming with other kinds of gear. Pieces of a puzzle. Best if you don't know anything about that. What you don't know, you can't tell. But it's a weapon—part of a weapon. He was pretty clear about that."

"Doesn't look like a weapon."

"I trust your daddy's judgment," Dowd said, smirking. "Don't you?"

They rented two rooms in a Chula Vista motel where fan palms stood like liveried doormen between the swimming pool and the highway. Dowd and Beth took one room, Cassie and Leo and Thomas the other.

Thomas slept on a roll-out by the door. Cassie and Leo shared the double bed. Thomas was a heavy sleeper, fortunately, and Leo turned on the room's radio at low volume to disguise any other sounds. *Noche de paz,* some choir whispered. *Todo duerme en derredor.*

It was the first time they kissed. It was the first time Cassie touched Leo, the first time she allowed herself to be touched. An exploration, she thought. The exploration of Leo. His mouth tasted of cinnamon and smoke. His hands, she discovered, were generous and wise.

In the morning they gathered in Dowd's room for a planning session.

"I've got ID for myself and a commercial permit for transporting radio gear," Dowd said, "so I'm good for the border. You all have identification you haven't used yet, so use it today. Beth can ride with me. But it's too dangerous to cross in a stolen vehicle, even with new plates and a paint job. So we ditch the car and you guys buy yourselves bus tickets, San Diego to Tijuana. We'll meet up at the depot on Avenida Revolución. Leo, you still have that pistol you shot a guy with?"

Leo gave Eugene Dowd a cold stare. Beth must have told him the story. "Yes."

"Give it to me."

Leo didn't move, though his eyes darted to the green duffel bag he had carried all the way from Buffalo.

"Come on," Dowd said. "What are you gonna do, cross the border with a gun in your luggage? That's just stupid. Give me the pistol and we'll ditch it along with the car."

"What if I need to protect myself?"

Beth, standing next to Dowd with a proprietary hand on his arm, said, "You should listen to Eugene. He knows about these things."

Leo scowled but retrieved the gun from his bag and handed it to Dowd, who checked the safety before tucking it into the waistband of his jeans.

"One other thing," Dowd said. "I know your daddy gave you my Kansas address, and he told me I should watch out for you if you showed up. That's fine. That's part of the deal. But he didn't say anything about *her*," Cassie, "or *him*," Thomas. "And I'm not real happy about looking after children on this junket, especially when we have a few thousand miles of the Trans-American Highway ahead of us."

"They don't need you to look after them," Leo said. "They're with me."

"Well," Dowd said, "leaving them behind isn't safe either, considering they're wanted criminals. I suppose we could shoot them." He smiled to show this was meant as a joke. "But once we're in Mexico you might fix them up with a little hacienda and a cash stake for the duration. Safer for all of us."

"No!" Thomas said before Leo could answer.

"Didn't ask your opinion," Dowd said.

"They're with me," Leo repeated, "at least until I can talk to my father."

"Yeah, well . . ." Dowd shrugged. "The next mail drop's in Mazatlán. I guess they can tag along that far. But then this business gets serious. Everyone clear on that?"

They were all clear.

At the San Ysidro crossing a bored customs agent strolled down the aisle of the Greyhound bus asking desultory questions and examining papers. Cassie sat with Thomas, and for the purpose of the crossing they were brother and sister en route to visit their uncle in Rosarito Beach. The guard gave their documents a cursory look—the Common Passport Accord had made this a formality—and moved on. Neither Cassie and Thomas nor Leo a few rows back appeared to arouse his suspicion.

The bus idled a little longer in a cloud of diesel fumes, then grunted into motion. Cassie listened to nearby passengers chatting in Spanish as they passed under the Port of Entry gates and crossed the brown Tijuana River. "You going to Rosarito?" a woman asked her as the bus pulled into the station on Avenida Revolución. "I heard you say."

Cassie stood to shuffle out, taking Thomas by the hand. "Rosarito, yes."

"Very nice! ¡Feliz navidad!"

Rosarito, no, she thought. No, we're not bound for Rosarito Beach. We're bound for Antofagasta, Chile. We're bound for the Atacama Desert. We're bound for the end of the world.

20

"We might be able to intercept them in Sinaloa," Werner Beck said. "Failing that, we'll meet them in Antofagasta."

He had explained about Chile, about the facility the hypercolony had supposedly constructed in the Atacama Desert, the beams of high-intensity light. He hadn't seen it himself, but he had talked to an eyewitness, and there was plenty of corroborating evidence: from shipping manifests, from suppliers of industrial parts and rare earths, from inexplicable lacunae in the routes by which commercial aircraft passed from Chile to Bolivia and Brazil. Beck had made a study of it.

The facility in the desert, he insisted, was the hypercolony's reproductive mechanism. Strike there and you strike at the heart of the beast. *Or at least,* Nerissa thought, *its balls.*

Ethan seemed convinced. Nerissa wasn't, but that didn't matter. What was important was that she might at last be able to put her arms around Thomas and Cassie and shelter them from Beck's militant fantasies.

While Ethan was showering she sat in the kitchen with Beck and raised a question that had been troubling her. It was about what the sim Winston Bayliss had said, that there was a parasite at work in the hypercolony, that the hypercolony was divided against itself. Could that be true? If not, why had Bayliss been attacked in Ethan's farmhouse by a different party of sims?

"It's possible," Beck said. "There are certain signs."

"Such as?"

"All the cultures from Ethan's ice cores are identical and compatible. But we've cultured fresher strains, and the two samples sometimes compete for resources in vitro until one is eliminated. But I'd hesitate to draw any conclusions from that."

"Still, what Bayliss said—"

"Nothing a sim says is trustworthy, Mrs. Iverson. And all warfare is based on deception."

"You're quoting Sun Tzu."

"I suppose I am. Of course, what emanates from the hypercolony isn't even a *conscious* lie."

Nerissa's busy mind turned up a different quote, from Boswell's *Life of Samuel Johnson: But if he does really think that there is no distinction between virtue and vice, why, Sir, when he leaves our houses let us count our spoons.* "So it is possible there could be some kind of internal conflict going on."

"Sure, but it's impossible to know."

Ethan came into the room fully dressed and with his suitcase in hand. "Packed and ready."

They waited while Beck built a fire in the living-room fireplace and systematically burned the contents of his files, including Dr. Wyndham's ghastly photographs. Nothing must be left behind to fall into the hands of the enemy.

Beck drove one hundred and fifty miles to the international airport in Kansas City, where he paid for long-term parking in a lot where the car wouldn't be disturbed for at least three weeks. At the terminal he booked seats on the next available flight to Mazatlán.

Not long after dark, a gleaming six-prop aircraft lofted them into the night sky. Nerissa, sleepless in a window seat, watched prairie towns pass beneath the plane like luminous maps of a world she could no longer inhabit and which her traveling companions had sworn to dismantle. Several times she caught Beck looking at her with an expression she couldn't quite read—suspicion? Curiosity? As if he wondered what secret motive she might be concealing.

But her motives weren't secret, not secret at all. Let Beck conduct his war against a hostile abstraction; let Ethan join him, if that was what Ethan wanted to do. She would follow a certain distance down that road. But she was fighting a different war, for a different cause. And maybe Beck understood that truth about her. And maybe that was why she was so frightened of him.

21

MAZATLÁN

The Mexican holidays had prevented Eugene Dowd from checking the prearranged mail drop for three days now, and he resented it.

Mazatlán was a pretty town, but the concept of "silent night" was lost on the locals. The Christmas Eve street party had nearly deafened him. Live bands, fireworks, noisy crowds in the Mercado, after which everything shut up tight for Christmas Day. The mail drop was just an ordinary storefront mailbox service on a side street near the Centro Histórico, where Eugene was supposed to check a certain box number before proceeding to Antofagasta. But the business had been consistently closed, nothing to see but a locked door and a cardboard sign on which the words CERRADO POR NAVIDAD were printed in green crayon.

So he had been closeted in a three-story tourist hotel with Beth, Leo Beck, and what he continued to think of as the two kids, Cassie and Thomas. (Cassie wasn't much younger than Beth, but her flat face and unimpressive figure made her look like a child to Eugene.) He shared his room with Beth, which helped pass the empty hours, but Beth's charms had already begun to wear thin: she was clingy, easily frightened, and not half as smart as she liked to pretend.

Today Mazatlán was finally open for business. Eugene left the hotel at ten in the morning and began walking toward the historical part of town, Leo Beck tagging along behind him. Eugene would have preferred to do this alone, but Leo, whose poorly-concealed hostility toward Eugene probably reflected the haste with which he had been dumped by Beth, had insisted on coming with him. And since Leo was Werner Beck's son—it would be a mistake to forget that—Eugene had grudgingly agreed.

The street was crowded with the local golf-cart taxis called *pulmonias,* most of them ferrying tourists to and from the Zona Dorada. The sky was faultlessly blue above the brick-and-stucco storefronts, the temperature 70 degrees Fahrenheit and gliding steadily higher. The sheer pleasantness of the day was an invitation to relax, which Eugene was careful to decline. Everything he had seen and done in the Atacama, plus Werner Beck's lectures on the nature of what he called the hypercolony, had been Eugene's education in the operating principles of the world. All the pious high-school bullshit about the Century of Peace had been revealed for what it was: as artificial as a plastic nativity scene and as hollow as a split piñata. The world was peaceful the way a drunken coed passed out at a frat party was peaceful: it was the peace that facilitated the fucking. These kids he was traveling with, they claimed to know that; but did they? No. Not the way *he* knew it.

They were within a block of the mail drop when Leo grabbed Eugene's arm and said, "Wait, hold on. . . ."

"What is it?"

Leo had come to a full stop and was squinting back down the avenue at the traffic of tourists and locals. Eugene hated being made conspicuous, especially in a strange place when he was in a state of high vigilance, and passing pedestrians were already craning their necks in an instinctive effort to see whatever this excitable *turista* was gawking at. He wished Leo had inherited even a fraction of his father's sensible caution.

"Thought I saw someone," Leo said, sounding a little sheepish now.

"Yeah? Who?"

"I don't know. A face. A *familiar* face."

"Familiar how? Someone you recognize?"

"No. I guess not." Leo shrugged with obvious embarrassment. "Nobody I could name. Just a feeling, like, you know, I've seen that guy somewhere before. . . ."

"A guy?"

"If I had to guess, I'd say an American. Not much of a tan. Forty or fifty years old."

"Okay," Eugene said. "I'll take that under advisement." Probably it meant nothing. Probably Leo was just nervous. But Eugene was carrying a pistol—the same pistol he had taken from Leo before they crossed the border, and which Eugene had brought into Mexico in a concealed compartment built into the dash of the van. It was tucked into a sling he had made from torn pieces of an old shirt attached to his belt, hidden under the XL tee he had worn to obscure its presence, and he was conscious of its weight.

Eugene's father had taught him to shoot. The Dowds were farmers from way back, well-acquainted with long guns, but Eugene's father had also been fascinated by pistols and he'd been an experienced target-shooter. He had owned a fully-registered antique Colt revolver, which he had treasured and which he had eventually used to take his own life after Eugene's mother lost her fight with pancreatic cancer. Eugene blamed his father's grief for the suicide, not the weapon. Eugene felt a sentimental attachment to the gun and wished he had inherited it; but he had been in Chile when his father used it to blow a half-dollar-sized hole in his left temple, and the Colt had been handed over to the police for lawful disposal. At the moment Eugene didn't even have a license to carry. He had applied back in Amarillo, but by that time there were too many DUIs on his record. The laws around gun possession were annoyingly strict even in Texas.

The fact was, Eugene had come back from the Atacama kind of fucked up. How do you process an experience like the one he'd had in the Chilean desert? Finding both his parents dead, his mother of cancer and his father of .45-caliber self-administered euthanasia, had only compounded the problem. For a while it had seemed to Eugene that he was fated to end up a chronic drunk, pissing away his dole money in a secondhand Fleetwood trailer home, and that had been unsettlingly *okay with him*. The unexpected advent of Werner Beck was what changed everything. Or, no, not Beck himself, though Beck's can-do attitude was bracing—it was the prospect of *taking action,* of recalibrating the mysteries of the Atacama as a personal attack and bending himself in the direction of revenge. Of going back to Chile, not as a victim but as a soldier. With other soldiers beside him and a suitable weapon in his hand. That was another promise Beck had made: there would be a weapon, one to which the green-on-the-inside men and the spiders-with-faces were uniquely vulnerable.

He turned the corner from the *avenida* into the narrower *calle* where the mail drop was located. The stores here were doing brisk business, clothes racks and laden tables crowding the sidewalk, catering to tourists who had missed the dense knot of such establishments in the Zona Dorada. Eugene was still rattled by what Leo had said about a familiar face, and he moved cautiously, peering into shop windows as if he were debating the purchase of a seashell necklace or a picture postcard. Windows were useful because their reflections let him scan the passing crowd without being noticed. Leo shifted impatiently from foot to foot as Eugene conducted this methodical surveillance, but that was okay, it was plausible behavior for a young guy who had been, say, dragooned into a shopping expedition when he'd rather be down at the beach. Across the street and half a block away, the CERRADO sign had vanished from the door of the mail drop.

Eugene was about to turn away from the shop-window reflection when he caught sight of someone moving through the throng of tourists with suspicious directness and determination.

The man wore jeans, a denim shirt with the sleeves turned up, a sweat-stained *DIABLOS ROJOS* baseball cap, and a pair of black-rimmed glasses. None of that distinguished him in any meaningful way from the other locals Eugene had seen. It was his trajectory—a straight line aimed at Leo Beck—and his body language that set off Eugene's alarms. Not least, the way the man held his right arm stiff at his side. "Leo," Eugene said.

"What?"

"Leo, you might want to—oh, *shit!*"

The object the man had been concealing under his right arm was a long-bladed knife. He brought it out and broke into a sprint, closing the distance between them with alarming speed. Eugene whirled, fumbling under his shirt for his pistol.

Meanwhile Leo was still staring at him. Eugene used his free hand to give the kid a shove. Leo stumbled to the left, which was good, because the assailant was within cutting range now and had started a slashing movement that would otherwise have opened Leo's belly. Eugene managed to haul the handgun out of his trousers and disable the safety just as the man in the baseball cap turned toward him. The tip of the knife found him, a glancing slash that rebounded from his hip bone and felt like the touch of a frigid finger. Eugene leveled the pistol and pulled the trigger.

Eugene had never shot a man, given that the creatures in the Atacama weren't actually human beings. He looked at the pistol as if it had appeared from some distant dimension. He felt the recoil burning in his wrist. He became aware of the panic that began to spread through the crowd, gasps and shouts, people starting to careen into one another like wobbly bowling pins.

Then he looked at the man he had shot, who had fallen to the sidewalk and was leaking, in addition to blood, a green fluid that smelled like garden fertilizer.

Eugene *still* hadn't killed a human being.

"Run," he told Leo.

Blending into the panicked crowd was relatively easy. Eugene stuffed the pistol under his waistband and pushed through a ring of horrified gawkers, made sure Leo was behind him, then broke into a sprint.

Once they were under speed they were indistinguishable from a dozen other tourists whose reaction to the shooting and the sim's red-green bleed-out had been to dash for safety. After a few uncalculated and therefore usefully random changes of direction, Eugene slowed to a walk and waited for his breathing to return to normal. The injury he had sustained from the sim's knife was messy and increasingly painful, but so far his jeans were staunching the wound and soaking up the evidence. A cautious reconnaissance revealed no pursuing *policías*, though he could hear multiple sirens in the distance.

At the hotel, fortunately, Beth and the two kids were killing time in the lobby restaurant; he didn't have to hunt them down, only herd them back to their room and order them to pack up their gear. Time had become centrally important. The mail drop, no matter what instructions Werner Beck might have left there, had been compromised and was therefore unapproachable. In which case the agreed-upon protocol was to proceed to Antofagasta for the meet-up. Maybe there had been some revision to that plan, and maybe Beck had used the mail drop to communicate some such change, but as Eugene's mother used to say, *might and maybe don't put money in the bank*.

Eugene stripped to his shorts. The sim's knife had pricked him neatly but not deeply, and he allowed Cassie to tape gauze over the wound. She bent to the work with the eyes of a forest animal blinking into the headlights of an oncoming car, but her hands were steady and she didn't flinch at the blood. He had begun to understand that she was maybe more reliable than Beth and that Cassie's slightly froglike exterior concealed a capable human being. Not so surprising, then, that Leo had begun poking her on the rebound.

A couple of stitches, even amateur stitches with a sterilized needle and thread from a sewing kit, would probably have been wise. But there wasn't time for that. Better by far just to get on the road. After Cassie finished taping the bandage she started to pack, hesitating over the contents of her duffel bag as if it mattered whether her underwear was folded. "Just pack the fucking thing!" Eugene snapped. Did she not understand the significance of what had just happened? The dead sim had known Eugene and company were in town and had known where to ambush them. Sims were few and far between, Beck had once told him, but they were clever and they operated strategically, so there might be more than one of them in Mazatlán—they could be closing in on the hotel at this very moment, an army of them, for all Eugene knew.

"No, stop," Leo said, which only piqued Eugene's simmering annoyance.

Leo was staring into Cassie's bag. He reached past her and pulled out something she had just dropped there: a book.

"Back in the street," Leo said, "when I thought I recognized someone?"

"Yeah? So? What about it?"

Leo held up the book. It was called *The Fisherman and the Spider*. There was no fisherman on the creased and soiled cover, but there was a spider—an impressionistic rendering of what Eugene guessed was supposed to be a black widow, judging by the red hourglass on its abdomen. Leo turned the book over and held it close enough for Eugene to see the back. In the lower left-hand corner there was a black-and-white photo of the author, Ethan Iverson, some relation of Cassie's: a lean-looking guy with a crown of dense gray hair.

"That's where I saw him before," Leo explained. "That's the man I saw before we were attacked."

Cassie gasped. "He's here? Uncle Ethan is *here*?"

"Just fucking *pack your bag*," Eugene said. "If he was here, he's probably on his way to Antofagasta by now. Just like us."

"But we should try to find him—!"

"We should stick to the fucking plan is what we should do."

Cassie gave him an angry glare before she relented and went back to filling her duffel with wadded clothes.

Steely little bitch, Eugene thought. More sure of herself than she liked to let on. He would have to keep an eye on her.

22

"Were they there?" Nerissa demanded.

Cassie and Thomas, she meant. Ethan had just come back from the street near the mail drop. He said he had been loitering there, watching traffic in the *calle* before making an approach, when he heard a pistol shot. He had fought his way through the crowd to the place where a wounded sim was dying, oozing fluids onto the sidewalk in front of a tourist shop. But he hadn't been able to see the attack as it happened. "I don't know who was involved," he said.

Could Cassie have been there? Nerissa couldn't picture her niece with a handgun, but the boy with whom she had left Buffalo, Leo Beck, was probably reckless enough to carry one. "So what do we do?"

"We go on," Werner Beck said flatly, before Ethan could answer.

So they went on. Because Beck said so. Even though, in Nerissa's opinion, Werner Beck was subtly mad.

She had been exercising a grim patience, cooperating with Beck because Beck had money for travel and a plan that might reunite her with Cassie and Thomas. Or at least with Beck's son, Leo. It was possible that every step she took was carrying her farther from her niece and nephew, but it was equally possible (she hoped *likely*) that she had begun to close in on them—thus her patience.

But Ethan's news about the killing of a sim unhinged all that studied calm. She wanted to run into the street and look for Cassie and Thomas, wanted to call out their names. She restrained herself from making that or some other stupid and impulsive gesture. Because, at least in this, Beck was probably right. The best they could do was to go to Antofagasta and make the connection there. Because that was where Leo was headed. Assuming no sims interfered. Assuming Cassie and Thomas survived the journey.

And then what? A chilling thought occurred to her: What if Cassie had acquired through Leo a dose of Werner Beck's madness?

Because it *was* madness—she was increasingly sure of that.

Beck bought seats on a commercial flight to Santiago with a connection to Antofagasta. Their documents were cursorily examined as they moved through the airport, and the aircraft they eventually boarded was a sleek Fanaero United four-prop liner that stood into the cloudless sky and made a banking turn to the south.

Nerissa longed to discuss her fears with Ethan, but they had enjoyed very little privacy since they had arrived on Werner Beck's doorstep. She could tell Ethan's faith in Beck had been shaken by prolonged exposure at close quarters. "He's not the man I knew ten years ago," Ethan had admitted when they had a rare moment alone. "But no one else knows what he knows or has his kind of leverage."

Maybe so, but what had Beck really accomplished? He talked about a worldwide network of researchers and proto-soldiers, all primed to confront the hypercolony and to destroy its facility in the Atacama Desert, which was wonderful, and maybe, at a stretch, even *plausible,* but the details were suspiciously sparse. Beck had offered Wyndham in England as a typical researcher, and he had cited Eugene Dowd, the man Cassie and Leo and Thomas were supposedly traveling with, as a typical soldier. But that hardly constituted an army. And it was little more than speculation on Beck's part that an attack on the Atacama site, even if it succeeded, would materially damage the hypercolony. There could be other such facilities elsewhere in the world. Beck said not—but pressed to explain his reasoning, he became evasive.

He had been generous with his money over the years, but according to Ethan it was money he had more or less inherited; all Beck himself had done was to create a network of front companies and dummy accounts that allowed him to administer his own income without leaving an obvious electronic trail. And she wondered how secure that income stream really was. Beck's safe house had been a little shabby, and so was his customary wardrobe of tweed jacket and denim trousers.

None of this amounted to *madness*, but how should she parse his style of conversation (mannered and condescending), his monomania, his obsessive attention to the minutiae of privacy and security? All the surviving families of the victims of '07 shared these traits, to one degree or another, but at least they had tried to build lives outside the boundaries of their necessary paranoia. Beck was entirely enclosed by it. Even Ethan, whose isolation in his Vermont farmhouse had been nearly as complete as Beck's, had managed to retain his sanity—maybe because he was objective enough to question it. Beck allowed himself no such unmanly doubts.

And that was the crux of the matter. Beck was impervious to doubt. He believed in his army of followers, his implacable enemy, and his invincible strategy; and to question any of that was not only stupid but, in Beck's eyes, a betrayal so heinous as to be unforgiveable.

Ethan, dozing next to the window, had left Nerissa with instructions not to wake him. The flight attendant served lunch as the plane curved over the Pacific west of Panama, but it was typical airline fare; he wasn't missing anything. She found her attention drawn to Beck's tray as he ate—the way he tugged the foil cover from the tray and folded it in thirds, likewise the wrapper from which he had extracted the cutlery. He took a sip from his thimble-sized cup of black coffee after every four bites. She counted. Four bites. *Sip*. Four bites. *Sip*. It was metronomic.

"What are you looking at, Mrs. Iverson?"

She jerked upright like a guilty schoolgirl. "Nothing . . . sorry."

Beck glanced at Nerissa's tray, now a clutter of torn packaging and half-eaten food. "The attendant should be around shortly to pick that up."

She forced a smile and hoped it would end the conversation. Beck shifted his gaze to her face, but his expression of disgust hardly changed. "Since we have a moment, can I say something?"

"Of course."

"I want to put this to you directly. Bluntly. Because it's obvious you're skeptical about what I mean to do in Chile."

"I wouldn't say—"

"All *you* want to do is reclaim your niece and nephew. And I have no problem with that. You're not a soldier, and neither is Cassie or Thomas. If they're in the company of Leo, they're only an impediment to his work. Taking them back to the States is probably the most useful service you could perform."

Wake up, Ethan! Nerissa thought. But Ethan didn't stir. The plane lurched through a patch of turbulent air and she reached out to steady her coffee cup.

"But you're wrong about what we're doing in the Atacama. Others have expressed similar reservations. I've heard the argument for accommodation more often than I care to remember, though less often since 2007—the idea that the hypercolony has given us something valuable in exchange for a trivial diversion of resources. The idea that interfering with that puts both parties at risk and even constitutes a threat to world peace. I have to say, it's a contemptible attitude."

"I saw my sister and her husband murdered. I'm not inclined to forgive that." Where was the flight attendant? The entire plane seemed to have been enveloped in a kind of sunny afternoon coma.

"I know. But you've wondered, haven't you, what we stand to lose if I'm successful?"

Sure she had wondered. If it was true that the hypercolony had molded the world the way a potter works wet clay on a wheel—if it had actually coaxed prosperity out of poverty and made a tractable chorus of the world's discordant human voices—then yes: "Of course I wonder about the consequences."

"As I see it, humanity will be forced to take responsibility for its own future."

"For better or worse."

"All of us who survived 2007 bear a heavy burden.

People around us are allowed to go about their lives, while we carry this unspeakable knowledge. So we try to cope. We do what we have to do. You've elected to stand back and look after the children while others fight. That's your choice, and it's a good and useful one. But as a civilian, the *consequences* of what we do are not your concern. You need to let the soldiers fight the war."

Between planes at Pudahuel Airport they sat in a lounge nursing drinks—mineral water for Beck, beer for Ethan, rum and Coke for Nerissa. She passed the hour between flights listening to an English-language news broadcast on a TV set behind the bar.

Was the control of the hypercolony already faltering, as Winston Bayliss had suggested? More Russian and Japanese troops and gunships had been dispatched to Magadan on the Sea of Okhotsk. There was footage of brick buildings collapsing under mortar fire. Such outbreaks were not altogether unknown and were usually tamped down as soon as they started, but this one might be different. The diplomatic saber-rattling continued to intensify and the League of Nations seemed helpless to intervene. Shattered walls, broken bodies: was that what the world would look like in five or ten or fifty years?

She stole another glance at Beck. Give him his props, Nerissa thought. He was a clever and persuasive salesman. As toxic and as fraudulent as his worldview might be, he had successfully peddled it to a number of intelligent people, apparently including Ethan.

In other words, he was a natural leader. But maybe that was what had made the last century so peaceful: an enforced vacation from natural leaders. And if the hypercolony were destroyed they would come storming back—our Napoleons, she thought. Our Caesars. Our terrible and rightful rulers.

A smaller single-prop plane carried them from Santiago to Antofagasta, and as it bent down to the Cerro Moreno runway strip she caught her first glimpse of the coastal mountains that bordered the high salt desert of the Atacama.

The driest place on Earth. More than forty thousand square miles of sand, salt and ancient pyroclastic debris. A great place to put an observatory, if anyone had been funding observatories, because the skies were so consistently clear.

It was the place (if Beck was to be believed) in which the hypercolony had built its breeding ground. She tried to imagine that entity, to think about it without hatred or fear. Perhaps the way Ethan thought of it, as an organism of great age and complexity. It was intelligent, Ethan and Beck believed, but not self-aware. It didn't think, in human terms, but it *calculated*. It was like the computers the utility companies used, but infinitely more subtle, programmed by its own unfathomably long evolutionary history.

And out there in the Atacama it had assembled

some means to deliver itself to new, distant worlds. Using rockets, maybe, like the ones in the paperback science-fiction novels Cassie used to jam into her schoolbag, or something better than rockets. Something to do with beams of light. Something that could be constructed only with the resources of a technologically adept culture.

If you looked at it that way the hypercolony wasn't really an enemy, at least in the sense of a malevolent, conscious opponent. And maybe that was what Beck had failed to understand. There was no more malice in the hypercolony than there was in a natural disaster . . . and it wasn't even necessarily a disaster, Nerissa thought, except for those of us who, like willful children, poked our fingers into the lethal business of the hornet's nest.

Antofagasta was a busy industrial city. Copper refineries and cement factories etched parallel lines of smoke on the northern sky; a huge port dominated the harbor. Nerissa, Ethan and Beck took a taxi from the airport to a three-bedroom row house on the fringe of the hotel district.

Night had fallen by the time they finished unpacking. Ethan turned on the TV, and a *Televisión Nacional* newscast began to repeat what Nerissa already knew about the fighting in Magadan. She crossed the street to a tiny *Líder* store and exchanged some of the pesos they had bought at the airport for basic groceries. Back in the kitchen she fried fish and vegetables for three but ended up eating very little of it herself. Her appetite had been fragile since she left Buffalo and she had lost a few pounds already.

There was no evidence of the army Beck had said would be waiting for him. No cryptic messages, no hooded partisans knocking at the door. When she asked him about that, Beck said he'd contact "some people" tomorrow. And Nerissa carefully refrained from rolling her eyes.

She and Ethan shared a bedroom. What made this especially unsettling was that tonight might be one of their last nights together. Sooner or later Ethan would be off to the interior of the Atacama, Sancho Panza to Beck's Quixote, and with any luck she'd be back in the States with her niece and nephew. She might not see Ethan again even if he survived. She wanted him to survive, of course, but did she want something more than that? How much of their shipwrecked marriage might it be possible to salvage? If they were together under less dire circumstances, if they were granted time enough to discover what they had become after seven years of separation . . . what might be possible?

He opened the curtains and turned down the bed. Nerissa repeated some of what Beck had said on the airplane and asked Ethan bluntly whether he still believed in Beck's plan.

Ethan frowned. Even that small gesture was hauntingly familiar. The creases at the corners of his eyes. The buckled *V* between his brows. "I think it has a chance."

"So you buy all that stuff about radio waves?" Nerissa understood the concept only vaguely, but Beck claimed to have isolated key frequencies at which the orbital cloud of the hypercolony communicated with itself. He believed he could disrupt those signals—not globally, but locally, at the Atacama site. Which would have the effect of isolating the Atacama facility from the orbital hypercolony. Which would render the resident simulacra inert, perhaps even kill them. Supposedly.

"It wasn't just Beck who did the research. If he can suppress activity at the site long enough, then yeah, we can get inside and damage it. Whether that will have any lasting effect is hard to say. It depends on which theory of the hypercolony's life cycle you accept."

"So even if it works, nothing might happen."

"I'm pretty sure *something* will happen."

"But the hypercolony might have a way of defending itself."

"Also possible."

"But you think it's worth doing?"

He shrugged.

Lying in bed, exhausted but sleepless, she found herself recalling a film Ethan had shown her years ago. A home movie, basically, made by one of his undergraduate students during a research trip to Japan. Ethan had been working with a nest of Asian giant hornets, insects that were also called "yak-killers"—the species was responsible for an average of forty human deaths every year. This particular nest was in a forest close to a settled community in Kanagawa Prefecture, and it would have to be destroyed once Ethan had secured specimens. Ethan approached the nest in protective clothing as carefully sealed as a diving suit. His face through the plastic visor looked tense but not frightened, and his movements were calculated, deliberative. *Respectful* was the word that came to mind.

As he approached the nest it detected his presence and reacted to it. Dozens of wasps swarmed out and darted directly at him. The camera wavered but the cameraman stood his ground; two of Ethan's other students panicked and ran. Ethan did not. Even as the fist-sized hornets clustered on his visor, struggling with the selfless lethality of a suicide bomber to reach his face, he went about his work. And when he was done taking samples, he poisoned the nest with the same impersonal efficiency.

She woke an hour before dawn from a terrible dream. In the dream Ethan had been back in Japan, but the hornets were as big as people and they had faces like the face of Winston Bayliss. She came to herself *(I came to myself in a dark wood where the straight way was lost)* convinced she had heard some ominous noise, but when she went to the window there was no one in the alley behind the house, only a cat digging through a drift of refuse. "Don't go," she said.

She wasn't sure whether she meant to wake him. She heard him turn over in the bed.

"Don't go. The only reason you can't see how crazy this is is that we've been neck-deep in crazy for years. Beck is delusional. There is no army. He doesn't know what's out there in the desert or where it came from or what it wants or how it can hurt you. Don't go."

Enough of the ambient light of Antofogasta seeped through the window that she could see his head against the pillow, eyes closed. She assumed he was asleep, but he startled her by saying, "Come back to bed."

"Ethan?"

He didn't move. Maybe he still wasn't altogether awake. "I don't have a choice, Ris." His voice thick, words like an extended sigh. "This is what I have to do. There's nothing else. Come back to bed."

The cat pricked its ears and chased something invisible down the alley and out of sight. Nothing else moved. The air itself seemed sterile and empty. *Then I'll find my own way home,* she thought.

23

They followed the highway in two vehicles: Eugene Dowd's white van, with Dowd and Beth in it, and a sky-blue Ford Concourse Dowd had rented with the promise that he would return it to the rental agency's Valparaiso branch. Cassie took turns at the wheel with Leo, occasionally checking the mirror to see if they were being followed.

The Trans-American Highway was an advertisement for the success of the Pan-American Common Market. It passed through some of the hemisphere's most rugged and beautiful terrain, and it was a feat of large-scale multinational engineering to rival the Channel Tunnel, the Danyang–Kunshan Bridge, or the Jordanian desalinization towers. Under other circumstances Cassie might have relished the trip. As it was, her connection with Leo Beck made it at least bearable.

Had she adapted to Leo, or was it the other way around? But it seemed to Cassie that there was no compromise in their unfolding relationship, only a series of surprising discoveries. Cassie had been with boys before, on what she preferred to think of as an experimental basis. Well, two boys. There had been Rudy Sawicki from high school, a math prodigy with bad skin who was nevertheless sweet and gently lascivious when they were alone together. But he wasn't Society, and their relationship had collapsed under the weight of unspeakable truths. And there had been Emmanuel Fisher, whom everyone called Manny: he *was* Society, and for a year they had seen each other every weekend. But the closer she got to Manny, the more he felt entitled to make decisions on her behalf or to overrule decisions she had made. Eventually, after a trivial argument about homework, he had called her a bitch and thrown her copy of *Wuthering Heights* against the wall so ferociously that the school librarian complained about the broken spine. By mutual consent, they hadn't dated after that.

From a distance Leo Beck had seemed like just another nervy, chain-smoking Society boy. Undoubtedly that was what Beth had imagined him to be. (Cassie was tempted to wonder what *Leo* had seen in *Beth*, but that was a mean thought.) So it had surprised her to learn that Leo was a habitual reader; it had surprised her to see how easily he related to Thomas. In bed, during the few but precious opportunities they shared during the drive south, Leo was gentle when she wanted him to be and fiercely eager at exactly the right moment—and he was good company afterward. With Leo beside her she could sleep soundly, even in a dark room in a strange country. As her eyes closed he kissed her ear or her forehead and whispered, "Sleep well." Simple, comforting words. She cherished them. *You too,* she thought. *Sleep well, Leo.*

The Trans-American Highway crossed the Darien Peninsula on the Pacific side of the peninsula's mountainous spine. Often she could see the highway winding ahead of them, a high steel ribbon where it spanned marshes and gorges or hugged rocky scarps, though as acts of engineering the tunnels were even more impressive, cutting through massive rock-faces as cleanly as a bullet. As the day approached noon Dowd signaled his intention to pull over at the next rest stop, which turned out to be a wide space at the side of the road featuring a cafeteria, four pumps marked GASOLINA SIN PLOMO, a gift shop, and a view that rivaled anything Cassie had ever seen in Aunt Ris's back issues of *National Geographic.*

For most of the morning she and Leo had talked about her uncle Ethan's book, *The Fisherman and the Spider.* Leo was convinced the familiar face he had seen in Mazatlán was Ethan Iverson, and Cassie was eager to believe him. If Uncle Ethan had been in Mazatlán—if he had been haunting the same mail drop where Eugene Dowd was supposed to look for instructions or updates—that meant he had survived the latest attack on the Society and was maybe even trying to connect with Cassie and Thomas. Which meant there might be *other* survivors, maybe even including Aunt Ris. It meant she and Thomas were doing the right thing by traveling with Dowd to Antofagasta: Leo's father really would be there, or if not him then someone from the Society, possibly her uncle.

Leo wanted to know more about Uncle Ethan, but Cassie couldn't tell him much. She knew him best through his books. Leo had liked *The Fisherman and the Spider*: it was pretty interesting, he said. He had given much thought to the questions the book had raised. "I studied the technical stuff pretty closely," Leo said, "because my father sent me all those monographs. I mean, I always knew the hypercolony was a living thing. But before I read your uncle's book I never wondered what it was like to *be* the hypercolony."

"I'm pretty sure it's like nothing at all," Cassie said. "That's like asking what it feels like to be a light switch. Or whether a virus is happy when it invades a cell."

"Evolution writing on an empty page. So your uncle says. You think he's right about that?"

She was no scientist, but had gleaned a few things from the monographs in Aunt Ris's closet. "The signals the cells of the hypercolony generate are apparently pretty basic."

"You could say that about a brain cell, too. But if

you hook enough of them together you get a think-ing, feeling human being."

"Yeah, but it's a different kind of what they call *connectivity*. The mathematicians think my uncle's right, that the hypercolony functions in what they call a hive mode."

"But they could be wrong."

Nothing in science was more than provisionally true and all theories were subject to revision, so sure, they *could* be wrong. But Cassie hadn't seen any convincing evidence of that.

"An organism like the hypercolony," Leo said, "when you think about how it supposedly spreads across space, how it manipulates civilizations, how incredibly fucking *old* it must be . . . don't you some-times wish you could talk to it? Ask it a question?"

"That's impossible. Even if you *could* talk to it, you wouldn't learn anything. All it would tell you is what it wanted you to hear. Or no, not even what it *wants* you to hear; it would generate words that in some kind of model of possible outcomes produce a result that enhances the likelihood of its reproduc-tive success."

"I do that too," Leo said. "From time to time." Smiling.

"Smartass," Cassie said. "Anyway, we're not going to talk to it, we're going to kill it."

"I know. It's not like I feel sympathy for the fuck-ing thing. I know how many people it murdered." He gave her a quick look. "And another thing. We don't just need to kill it, we need to know how to kill anything *like* it. Because the sky's a kind of forest, and whoever heard of a forest with just one tree? Or just one anthill? Or just one wolf?"

Eugene Dowd opened the hood of the parked van, poked the gauge rod into the oil tank and scrutinized the results. He wiped his hands on a soiled rag and went to buy a can of oil from the gas-station attendant. Cassie followed Beth into the gift shop that adjoined the restaurant.

Beth poked through a stack of souvenir hats, mostly baseball caps with TAPÓN DEL DARIÉN or I DROVE THE DARIEN GAP printed on them. Cassie realized why Beth was interested when she saw her trying one on: it hid a bruise on her forehead just under the hairline.

"Did Eugene do that to you?"

It was no secret that Dowd's behavior toward her had grown increasingly sullen and dismissive. Cassie was pretty sure the question would prompt a hasty denial, followed by a heartfelt invitation to fuck off. Beth frowned sourly, and Cassie braced herself. But the frown wilted into a sigh. "Might as well admit it. Yeah, that was Eugene."

"What happened?"

"I don't know. I started my period. I guess he finds that inconvenient." Beth put down the cap. "You want to go outside a minute? While he tinkers with the engine?"

They walked to the stone wall meant to keep tourists from tumbling down a vertical precipice into the Pacific. Below, in a mist of breaking waves, gulls prospected salt-rimed boulders for shellfish.

Beth leaned against the wall. "People say I like the angry ones. When it comes to guys, I mean. And I was never sure how to take that. It sounds, I don't know, slutty or stupid. But it's not the angry ones I like, it's guys who know who they are and what they mean to do. Who believe what they believe, full stop. Because it's reassuring. Because if you stand back and squint, all this Society stuff looks pretty crazy. Not to mention scary as hell. And driving into the desert with some radio gear to kill the thing? *Batshit* crazy. You know what I mean?"

"I guess so."

"See, you're different. You're on the outside looking in, and that's okay with you. . . ."

"Maybe not completely okay."

"Leo had the balls to go down to the South Side with his friends and boost cars. Full of his daddy's ideas about the hypercolony and how to kill it. I wanted to take a fucking *bath* in all that courage. But apparently he finds you more interesting than me. Little old raccoon Cassie Iverson. Because you have your own kind of courage, don't you? Under that dweeby exterior. *Like calls to like,* my mother used to say."

"Did Eugene call out to you?"

"The mother lode of dopey self-confidence! Killed a bunch of sims and wants to kill more. But what I learned lately about all these brave boys and men? They're not as sure of themselves as they want you to think."

Cassie nodded. "Well, in a way you're right—all this Society stuff *is* crazy. It just happens to be true."

"'Martians,' my father called them. He thought 'simulacra' sounded pretentious. Obviously, he knew they weren't from Mars. Or I guess he knew. I don't think he gave a shit, really. It was my mom who was Society—my dad was just the guy she married. She never told him much about it, and he didn't take any of it seriously until the day she was killed. After that, as much as he hated the Society, he needed the financial help. Before 2007 he made a little money as an independent real-estate agent, but it was my mom who paid the bills. She was a research chemist."

Alice Vance. Aunt Ris had talked about her. Worked for a pharmaceutical firm before '07, but she'd done Society work on the side.

"Fucking sims. I used to wish—" Beth raised her hand to the bruise on her head, brushing it with her fingers. "It sounds awful, but I used to wish the sims had taken him instead of her. My father I mean. But *instead*, right? Not *also*—I never wished for *that*."

"We've all wished for some pretty awful things now and then."

"Don't try to comfort me, Cassie. I don't think I could take it."

"You don't have to ride with Eugene today. I can convince Leo to trade places."

"It's okay. Thanks, but I know the score. I won't provoke him. Anyway, please don't mention any of this to Leo. Should never have opened my big fucking mouth. Right?"

"Right."

"We ought to break this up."

Cassie looked over her shoulder. Eugene was wheeling his arm in an impatient get-on-back-here gesture. Beth surprised Cassie yet again by taking her hand and squeezing it. "I think Leo's the real soldier here."

"Maybe."

"Funny how you can want a person so bad you end up pushing him away. People are pretty screwed up. You think the hypercolony knows that about us?"

Cassie shrugged.

Beth kicked a pebble toward the parking lot. "Stupid question. Of course it does."

In Ecuador, near Quito, a stone column at the side of the highway marked the approximate position of the equator. Dowd didn't stop and Cassie didn't blame him: it was only an imaginary line. But it was a crossing nevertheless: a reminder of how far she had come from everything familiar and predictable. That night, in one more motel room (not quite an "anonymous" room, because each room seemed to her distinctive in some memorable way: this one featured a framed antique map of Pichincha Province and muslin curtains dyed a vibrant shade of green), Leo asleep beside her, she wondered whether a different but more important imaginary line had been crossed.

Dowd had insisted on a room to himself. Beth had generously and surprisingly offered to share her room with Thomas, which meant Cassie and Leo's lovemaking was fierce and for the first time truly uninhibited—yet still sweet for all that. Like opening a door into a forest, rich with rain and green things growing. And the question she found herself asking now that Leo was asleep beside her was: had she fallen in love?

Because that was how it felt. But only a few minutes ago her body had exploded into an orgasm so intense that it probably registered on the Richter scale, so maybe her judgment wasn't entirely unbiased. Could she conceivably share more than a terrifying car trip and some terrible memories with the man who was breathing gently by her side— moonlight glinting where a drop of sweat, his or hers, had lodged in a down of fine white hair on his chest?

Well, maybe.

Assuming Leo felt the same way.

Assuming he wasn't killed in whatever battle Werner Beck contrived to wage against the hypercolony in the Atacama Desert.

She turned her pillow cool-side-up and nestled her head against it. Leo stirred long enough to drape an arm across her waist. "Sleep well."

You too, Cassie thought.

Down into the dry country, then, where the highway hugged the coast for more than two thousand miles. They spent more nights in motels or cramped *albergues*, more days of monotonous driving as they neared the border between Peru and Chile.

The morning of their last day's drive—they were already approaching the northern fringe of the vast Atacama Desert—Eugene Dowd spread a gas-station map of the city of Antofagasta on the restaurant table from which a sleepy *camarera* had just cleared breakfast dishes and empty cups. He circled three intersections clustered in the center of the city. Then he wrote three addresses on a napkin and passed it to Leo. "First address is where we meet your father. The next two are fallbacks, in case the first site is compromised or if nobody's home. Keep this in case anything happens to me. And some ground rules. We don't just park and wave hello. We do a drive-past to scout the location, and if it seems safe we leave the vehicles and one of us approaches the building alone. You all understand that?"

Thomas surprised Cassie by speaking up: "What if we go to all these places and there's nobody home *anywhere*?"

Dowd gave him a nasty smile. "Well, then, I guess we're fucked for good and all."

They came into the city from the north, where refineries processed ore delivered by rail from the Atacama and where chimneys as tall as skyscrapers emitted chemical gasses that seeped into the car and made Cassie's eyes water. She guessed these factories were what her high-school civics teacher had once called the mills of South Buffalo and Lackawanna: "engines of prosperity." Ugly, smelly engines. She wondered whether all of Antofagasta would be like this.

But no. The road carried them through a brightly-painted borderland of workers' housing to a city of broad avenues and glass-walled business towers, down narrower residential streets where water had been lavished on small lawns and riotously colorful gardens. To the west she could see harbor cranes turning in tandem, a ballet performed by stiff-limbed giants.

Conversation with Leo and Thomas had been sporadic all morning, and they fell silent as they approached the first meeting point. Leo was still shadowing Eugene Dowd's white van, and Cassie restrained herself from pushing her nose against the glass of the passenger-side window as the car cruised by the designated address. There was nothing unusual to see—and that was a good thing, right?—only an old stucco-walled building with ornate iron balcony railings adjacent to a concrete parking garage. Still, she felt her heart beat harder as the car slid past.

Leo followed Dowd's van into a commercial lot in the shopping district some three blocks from the apartment and parked there. They walked back by the same route, until Dowd called a halt and said, "I'll knock. You watch." His voice sounded as if someone had driven a nail into his throat.

She waited with Beth and Leo and Thomas at the mouth of an alley next to a grocery store on the opposite sidewalk. Dowd had told them to "act natural and don't attract attention," but Cassie couldn't help staring at the door as Dowd approached it. A quick knock. Dowd waited for a response, his right hand at his side in case he needed to reach for his pistol.

Then the door opened and Cassie saw a face loom out of the shadow—an older man, no one she knew, though it could only have been Werner Beck, because Dowd squared his shoulders and actually *saluted*.

"My father," Leo whispered.

A second figure emerged behind him, and this time it was Cassie who couldn't catch her breath. Aunt Ris!

Without thinking she dashed across the street. It wasn't a busy street but she nearly stepped in front of a car that swerved, horn screeching, to avoid her. Cassie, still barreling toward the door, couldn't help remembering what she had seen from her bedroom window in Buffalo that night in November, the night the sim had been splashed across Liberty Street: how grimly strange if she were to be killed in the same fashion . . . but that unpleasant thought went out of her head as she ran and now *leapt* into the arms of her aunt.

She was only dimly aware of the others following behind her, of Thomas as he joined the embrace, of her own involuntary sobs. Minutes passed before she could step back and swipe her sleeve across her eyes.

She found Werner Beck giving her a hard look. "Not very smart, running across the street like that."

Cassie ignored him and asked her aunt, "Is Uncle Ethan here?"

"He was," she said. "But he had to leave."

PART THREE

BURNING PARADISE

What is intelligence, exactly? Maybe that sounds like a simple question. We know—or think we know—what our own kind of intelligence is like. After all, we experience it on a daily basis.

But there are other kinds of intelligence. There is the intelligence of the hive—the complex behavior that arises from individually unintelligent organisms following a few simple behavioral rules in response to cues from the environment. And there is a kind of intelligence that inheres in the ecosystem as a whole. Evolution, over time, has created entities as diverse as crinoids and mushrooms and harbor seals and howler monkeys, all without a predetermined goal and without devoting even a moment of thought to the subject. You might even conclude that this kind of thoughtless intelligence is more powerful and patient than our own.

What are the limits to mindless intelligence? Or, and here's an even more striking question, could mindless intelligence successfully mimic mindful intelligence? Could an entity (an organism, hive, ecosystem) learn to speak a human language, perhaps even deceive us into accepting it as one of our own and allowing it to exploit us for its own purposes?

Such an entity would lack real self-awareness. It would never experience the inner life we discussed in a previous chapter. But given an adequately broad sample of human behavior to mimic, it could almost certainly conceal those deficits from us.

Why would such an entity want to fool us? Perhaps it wouldn't. But mimicry is one of the common strategies by which a species gains an advantage over its competitors. We may hope the question remains forever hypothetical. But the possibility is real.

—Ethan Iverson,
The Fisherman and the Spider

24

Later—after stories had been told on both sides, mistaken assumptions corrected, difficult truths shared—Nerissa asked Cassie to help her put Thomas to bed.

"I can go to bed by myself," Thomas said, but it was a token protest, and he seemed secretly relieved when Nerissa led him upstairs. She took him to the room she had shared with Ethan until he left, where she separated the single beds, one for Thomas, one for Cassie. Nerissa planned to spread a blanket on the carpet and sleep by the door, guard-dog style.

Cassie made no objection, though she seemed slightly miffed at the idea of being relegated to a room with her little brother. Nerissa had seen the looks that passed between her niece and Beck's son Leo, and she could guess what might have happened during the journey from Buffalo to Antofagasta. That was dismaying but not surprising, and Nerissa withheld judgment. But it was hardly practical to allow Cassie and Leo to share a room . . . and Werner Beck would have vetoed the idea.

Nerissa remembered Leo as a truculent adolescent with an unfortunate penchant for petty crime, but maybe he'd changed. Or maybe his truculence had been an understandable reaction to his status as his father's son. The awkwardness between Beck and Leo suggested the latter. Still, she would have thought Beth Vance was more Leo's type. But Beth had apparently been more attracted to Eugene Dowd, the semi-literate garage mechanic Beck had shanghaied as one of his "warriors."

At least Dowd—unlike the rest of Beck's supposed army—had actually shown up for the battle.

Thomas's eyes closed and his breathing steadied almost as soon as his head hit the pillow. Nerissa tucked the blankets around him while Cassie stood at the window, looking past the wrought-iron balcony railing to the dusty back alley where a garbage truck groaned through the heat. "The next thing we need to do is get you and Thomas back to the States."

Cassie closed the curtains. "Really? Is that even safe? After what happened with the man we killed—"

"The man *Leo* killed." Nerissa had cringed when she heard this part of their story, but she hadn't shied away from dealing with it. "There won't be any legal problems. If it happened the way you said it did, there's no substantial evidence to connect you or Thomas to the crime."

"Except for the man who saw us . . . the man Beth hurt."

"At best, the police might have a vague description. And even if, somehow, they *did* come after you, it wouldn't be hard to put together an alibi. But you won't need one."

"If the sims find us it hardly matters about the police."

That was unfortunately true. "But it's not you they're after. You're in far more danger here than you would be back in Buffalo."

"No." Cassie shook her head. "You're wrong. It was me they came for. The sim that got run over on Liberty Street was looking for me."

"You don't know that. It might have been coming for me, or it could have been a ruse, or a feint, or even a way of getting at Beck through you and Leo."

"I saw it looking at me from the street. It knew I was there."

She seemed unwilling to admit any other possibility, and the discussion was making her agitated. "Okay, Cassie, but even so, all we can do is take care of each other the best we know how. You, me, Thomas—"

"And Uncle Ethan?"

"Maybe. He's in—"

"I know. He's in the desert, looking for a place for Leo's father and his soldiers to meet up," Cassie said. (*All Beck's imaginary soldiers*, Nerissa thought.) "Are we going to wait for him to get back?"

"I'd like to. But we may not have time. We need to be on a plane out of here as soon as it can be arranged."

"Why?"

"For one thing, we can't keep on exposing Thomas to this kind of danger. It's not right."

"Leo's staying."

"I'm not responsible for Leo. What Leo does is between him and his father."

It had been Beck's idea to send Ethan to San Pedro de Atacama.

According to Beck the plan was simple: get a mobile radio source and signal generator within effective range of the Atacama facility, shut it down by interfering with its internal and external communications, and destroy the facility while its inhabitants were incapacitated. Beck claimed to have laboratory evidence that this scheme would work. His faith in it was messianic and, Nerissa suspected, gravely misplaced.

But Ethan considered the idea plausible, and at Beck's suggestion he had agreed to travel to San Pedro de Atacama to scout out a place where a truck full of radio gear, a similar cargo of incendiary materiel, and Beck's supposed fifty-man army could assemble for the attack.

He had been gone for two days now. Because it would have been suicidal to report by telephone, there was no way of knowing whether or not he had been successful. And because he had been away, he hadn't seen the most recent evidence that Beck's scheme was jury-rigged if not downright delusional.

The signal-generating device, which Beck had designed himself, had arrived in the back of Eugene Dowd's van, but the amplification and broadcast gear Beck had ordered from Valparaiso hadn't been delivered—hadn't even been shipped, according to the freight service; the vendor had declared bankruptcy. Beck sulked for an afternoon, then told Nerissa he could make do with off-the-shelf equipment from another supplier . . . which would nevertheless have to be discreetly purchased and delivered, delaying the attack by at least a few days more.

And there was the question of his army. Fifty men, Beck had claimed. More like a platoon than an army. Fifty men good and true, recruited from three continents, to be housed in five safe houses scattered across Antofagasta. But at last report none of the alleged volunteers had succeeded in leaving their native countries. For replacements Beck had managed to recruit a dozen men from the pool of unemployed stevedores at the dockside union hall. These men believed they were being hired to transport liquor to an unlicensed warehouse in San Pedro de Atacama, and while they would be useful for lifting and carrying duties, not even Beck envisioned them as combatants.

It didn't matter, he insisted. As long as the radio

gear and the incendiaries were delivered to the desert, a handful of men—even three or four—could successfully conduct the attack. If all went well.

That was the plan on which Ethan had wagered his life.

Downstairs, Nerissa found Beth Vance sitting by herself in the common room near the kitchen. Beth was still coming to terms with the news that her father was alive.

A single unarmed sim had approached John Vance on the day Cassie and Thomas fled Buffalo. They had seen a body being removed from the apartment building where Beth lived with her father, but that had been the remains of the sim, which John had elected to shoot rather than engage in conversation. John had since gone into hiding, Nerissa didn't know where, but someone in Buffalo would be able to put him back in touch with Beth when they got home.

Beth looked up at Nerissa with an expression that was hard to decipher. "Were you with my father when he killed the sim?"

"We can talk about that tomorrow."

"I'd rather talk about it now."

"Okay," Nerissa said. "If you like. The answer is no, I wasn't there. I'd left for home by then."

"But you spent the night?"

"Yes."

"I knew about that. He told me he was seeing

someone. He just didn't say who." She darted another glance at Nerissa, looked away. "It wasn't the
first time. He doesn't usually see Society women,
though. Most women he doesn't see more than once.
Actually, that's why I was at Leo's place. He didn't
care where I spent the weekend, as long as I was out
of the house."

"Maybe so. And maybe it was a mistake, my seeing him. But I'm sure he's worried about you."

"Not worried enough to come looking for me.
Not the way you came after Cassie and Thomas."

"That's not a fair comparison. He doesn't know
anything about Werner Beck or Leo. Your father never
paid attention to Correspondence Society business."

Which, ironically, was one reason Nerissa had
accepted John's invitation to spend the night. Like
John, she had been connected to the Society by marriage; like John, she harbored an abiding anger at the
way the Society had disfigured their lives.

"Well, that's true," Beth said. "He doesn't even
like me going to survivor meetings. Probably we
wouldn't have had anything to do with the Society,
except he needed the pension. It wasn't much but it
made a difference. Do you *like* my father?"

"We're friends, but I don't think it was going anywhere."

"Not your type, huh?"

"Maybe we just weren't the people we thought we
were."

"He can be a real shit. I'm not going back to him."

"What?"

"Don't look so shocked. I know him better than you do. I'll go back to the States, but I'm not living with him again."

"But why?"

"He never, you know, *touched* me or anything. But he likes to look. And he likes to say things."

After a few wordless seconds Nerissa said, "I'm sorry."

"It's okay. People aren't always what you think they are. But I guess you know that."

Nerissa slept fitfully by the door of the bedroom, startled awake by every sound the house made in its negotiations with the cooling night. And when she did at last fall into a deeper sleep, she slept shamefully late. She needed to talk to Beck about arranging her flight to the United States—she was determined not to spend another night here; she would take the kids to a hotel if that was necessary—but by the time she was dressed and downstairs Beck and Leo had already left on some errand. They would be back—Cassie relayed this datum—before dinner.

Noon came. Beyond the windows, the air itself looked pale and hot. Beth brooded in the shady common room with an equally sullen Eugene Dowd. Cassie sat in the kitchen, watching Nerissa heat precooked empanadas from the store across the street.

Cassie wanted to talk about what the sim Winston

Bayliss had said back at Ethan's farmhouse: the idea that the hypercolony might have been infected by some competing entity. Was that possible? Maybe, Nerissa said. Beck had claimed there was some evidence for it. But the hypercolony, like the devil, was a proverbial liar. Nothing it said could be trusted.

"Still, if it's true, it could help us."

"I doubt it, Cassie. It would only make the sims less predictable." And more dangerous, the way a wounded and cornered animal is dangerous. She thought again of Ethan, on this the third day of his sojourn in the desert.

Beck and Leo came back in the still heat of late afternoon. Beck walked through the door with his shoulders squared and his head at a cocky angle, obviously pleased with himself. "We secured a small truckload of incendiary materiel," he told Dowd. "We can move as soon as the radio gear is in place."

Nerissa was mildly surprised. No other part of Beck's plan had fallen into place so easily. But maybe it wasn't terribly difficult to buy black-market explosives in a town that catered to the needs of a vast mineral-extraction industry.

Leo's expression was the opposite of his father's, a grim disdain. "Show them what else you bought," he said tonelessly.

Beck gave his son a hostile stare, then opened the bag he was carrying in his right hand.

Inside the bag was an unmarked white plastic box. He put the box on the kitchen table and pried it open. Embedded in a sculpted foam protector was a graduated glass syringe and a dozen needles in sterile paper sleeves.

"Let me explain," Beck said.

Ethan came into San Pedro de Atacama at dawn, switching off the car's heater as the sun cleared the horizon. He felt tired and light-headed, probably because of the altitude. The Atacama plateau was almost eight thousand feet above sea level. Perilously close to the stars.

And perilously close to other things. The Chilean government discouraged tourism in the Atacama, and according to Beck commercial air routes were designed to avoid this part of the desert. (Arrangements that had been made, he supposed, using the hypercolony's standard tool kit: telephone calls and radio messages subtly and imperceptibly altered or redirected, apparently minor decisions cascading toward a calculated outcome, no single intervention so overt as to create suspicion or leave an obvious fingerprint. . . .) The only real industry anywhere nearby was the Chuquicamata copper mine to the northwest. The railhead and warehouse complexes on the outskirts of town mainly serviced the Chuquicamata and a few smaller mines. The town itself was a pueblo with some fifteen hundred souls in permanent residence, and it was instantly obvious that Beck's soldiers might be inconspicuous on the road but would be impossible to lodge here without attracting attention. The only hotel in town was a three-story adobe building, a dozen small rooms enclosing a central courtyard and a waterless concrete fountain. Checking in, Ethan told the counter clerk he had come to see the Valle de la Luna.

"*¿Es usted un geólogo?*"

"*Soy un geólogo por cuenta propia,*" he said, leaving the clerk to figure out what a self-employed geologist might be. He signed a false name to the register.

He slept longer than he meant to, dreaming of a passage in one of his own books about the Glyptapanteles wasp. The Glyptapanteles wasp lays its eggs in the bodies of geometrid caterpillars, and the freshly-hatched larvae feed on the living insect—typical parasitical behavior, with the nasty twist that if the larvae sense the approach of a possible predator they cause their host to thrash in agony. Thus the victim is forced to put on a puppet-show of aggression, defending its murderers even as they devour its flesh. In his dream Ethan took no part but watched without emotion as the drama cycled through iteration after iteration. It was only when he woke that he felt a flush of horror.

Misplaced horror, he told himself as he showered. His sympathy was an anthropomorphism, a projection. The caterpillar was hardly more than a protein engine enacting a suite of encoded behaviors. A meat robot. *As am I,* except that in the case of Ethan's species evolution had conjured a knowing self out of chemistry and contingency. *I feel, therefore I abhor.*

Without meaning to he had wasted most of a day in bed, and he meant to make better use of the time that was left to him. As the afternoon light faded he drove through the town to its industrial perimeter, the warehouses and fueling stations, the train yard where cargo containers and propane tanks huddled like the abandoned yurts of nomadic giants. From the road where he idled his car he could see a gang of mechanics servicing a hulking yard switcher, laboring under halide lamps as bright as minor suns.

It was hard not to feel hopeless. The weight of what Beck wanted to do was enormous, and there were too many ways it could go wrong. It was impossible to know how many agents (human or sim) the hypercolony might have placed in San Pedro de Atacama, impossible to know how much of Beck's plan the hypercolony had already discovered or inferred. But these doubts might only be part of what Ethan was beginning to recognize as a gathering bout of depression, the circling wolves of despair. He couldn't help thinking about Nerissa: a long-closed door had opened between them, and he had let it fall shut again. For the sake of what? This mad act of human impudence?

He drove aimlessly, and he was many miles from town before he realized he was following the road Beck had described to him, the road that led to the hypercolony's breeding ground. That would be fifty or more miles deeper into the desert, and Ethan had no intention of getting significantly closer. But the road was empty, the motion of the car comforting. A half-moon stood above the salt flats like a vigilant god. He was invulnerable in his unhappiness. He let the asphalt unspool a while longer.

He pulled over to the verge when he saw he'd added almost fifteen miles to the odometer. The air was cold and he switched on the heater, reminding himself again that he was riding the roof of the Puna de Atacama, only a thin skin of atmosphere between himself and the vacuum of space. He watched the horizon for the shaft of light Beck had described, but there was only the slow gyre of the stars.

He shivered and twisted the wheel to turn back. Traffic had been sparse, just a couple of box trucks and lowboys rumbling in the opposite direction, but a pair of headlights appeared in his mirror as he came off the gravel verge. Two unmarked white pickup trucks: the first, then the second, jockeyed abreast of him before passing at a furious speed. Ethan watched with relief as their taillights diminished in the distance.

They hadn't come for him. But he was in a precarious place. He looked away from the road long enough to extract from the glove compartment the loaded pistol Beck had obtained and instructed him to carry. He put it on the empty seat beside him, not because he expected to use it but because it was reassuring to have it within easy reach.

He thought again of his dream, the Glyptapanteles larvae tweaking their host into a frenzied writhing. It was as good an analogy as any for what Winston Bayliss had claimed was happening now: the hypercolony, breeding its young in the nutrient warmth of human culture, had been attacked by a competing and equally alien predator. Both predator and prey were attempting to exploit human beings in their struggle. And if that was true, whose interests would Beck's war serve? But to take the question seriously would mean abstaining from any action . . . a kind of induced paralysis, and maybe *that* was what the hypercolony hoped to achieve.

Something Nerissa used to say: *We see through a glass, darkly.* From the Bible. The New Testament, if Ethan recalled correctly. Corinthians? Nerissa would know.

In the dark glass of his rearview mirror Ethan saw more headlights coming up fast. He put a little extra pressure on the gas pedal, but the vehicles continued to close with him.

We see through a glass, darkly . . . Now I know in part, but then shall I know even as also I am known. . . . There was something on the road ahead, obscured by the moon-shadow of an upright granite outcropping. He slowed until he could make out the obstacle, which he belatedly recognized as the two pickups that had passed him earlier, one in each lane of the highway, both now aimed in his direction, both stationary and dark. He swerved to pass on the verge when their high beams flashed on, blinding him. At which point it became impossible to do anything but stand on the brake or drive off the road.

He managed to stop. The pistol slid from the passenger-side seat to the floor. He was groping for it when a man tapped on his side window with the butt of a flashlight. "Dr. Iverson?"

Ethan's fingers closed on the grip of the pistol. He straightened up. The man standing outside the car wore jeans, a ball cap, a work shirt, and a bland expression. His eyes glittered in the moonlight. Ethan shot him through the window of the car.

Safety glass exploded in a shower of fragments. By the time Ethan opened his eyes again the man—the *sim*—had dropped out of sight. But the odor of green matter mingled with the gunpowder stink of the fired weapon, making him think dazedly of chlorophyll, vinegar, bread mold, crushed leaves. . . .

The headlights that had been following him belonged to two more identical pickups. They fishtailed to a stop behind Ethan, boxing him in before he could put the car in reverse. The only way he could move now was on foot. He fumbled through the side door and out, gasping at the thin air.

Another human shape swarmed toward him. Ethan faced it and fired. There was the wet sound of a bullet impacting flesh, but it failed to do critical damage. The sim took Ethan's right arm above the wrist and twisted the gun out of his hand. Two more sims came out of the darkness and pinned him to the side of the car. He struggled uselessly, waiting for the killing shot.

But it didn't happen. Yet another sim approached, this one in the shape of a slightly-built dark-skinned woman. It wore the same jeans-and-work-shirt outfit as the males, and its hair was tucked under an identical cap. It stepped fastidiously over the body of its colleague.

"Dr. Iverson, I apologize for what happened here. We don't want to frighten you or hurt you. We want to talk to you." The sim took a pair of handcuffs from its belt. "I apologize for this, too. Please put your hands behind your back."

26

ANTOFAGASTA

Cassie and Thomas and Beth came into the kitchen, staring at the syringe and the disposable needles on the table. Nerissa wanted to stare too, but she forced herself to look away. "What do you mean to do with those?"

"Calm down." Beck's expression was impassive, his face the same assembly of clenched muscles and coolly evaluative eyes that had always made him seem so naturally authoritative. "I need to perform a test. It's not hard to understand. May I explain?"

You'd fucking better! She waited for him to go on.

"After the first round of attacks I had an opportunity to perform an autopsy on a simulacrum. A sim isn't much more than a human body with a core of green matter running through it, concentrated in the skull and the trunk but extending into the extremities. A hypodermic needle in the calf muscle of a sim will aspirate a small amount of that green matter. The same penetration in a human being just kicks back a few drops of blood, less than you'd lose to a sample at the doctor's office."

"You are *not*," Nerissa said, "sticking a needle into me or any child I'm responsible for."

"I'm afraid I have to. Eugene and Leo were almost ambushed at the mail drop in Mazatlán, even though that location was known to just a few of us. Before we set out into the Atacama—or before you fly back to the United States—I need to know that no one in this room has communicated our plans to the hypercolony."

"What, you think *I'm* a sim? Or Cassie? Or your own son?"

"I *don't* think so, and I'm not accusing anyone of anything. I just want certainty. Isn't that worth a little inconvenience? I got the idea from you, Mrs. Iverson."

"From me!"

"From what you told me about your interview with the mother of the sim in Pennsylvania. Given that sims gestate in human hosts, the fact that we all have well-established family histories means nothing."

"We all have long histories with the Correspondence Society, too. Doesn't that count?"

"Of course it does, but not in the way you're suggesting. Society researchers have been working with cell colonies ever since Ethan isolated the Antarctic samples. We've cultivated them in quantity, and with what seemed like reasonable caution, given that there was no obvious risk of infection. But we were wrong about that. We were almost certainly exposed. Any of us could have been infected, and we might have passed that infection to our families."

"Ethan and I have no children."

"No. But your sister did."

Nerissa saw Cassie's eyes widen as she worked out the implication. Thomas just looked puzzled.

"You are *not* doing this." Nerissa took her niece's hand, her nephew's hand. "Cassie, pack what you need and help your brother do the same. We're leaving."

"I can't allow that," Beck said.

"You think you can stop us?"

"Eugene?" Beck said. "Mind the door."

Dowd smiled thinly and moved to block the entranceway. He tugged back his shirt to reveal a pistol crammed into the waistband of his jeans, a gesture that looked to Nerissa both laughably theatrical and insanely, creepily threatening. "What, he's going to *shoot* us?"

"I surely hope not. There's absolutely no need for it. But we're at war, whether you like it or not. Declare your objections, but please cooperate. We're talking about a momentary discomfort. Do it and have done with it. Then Eugene will drive you and the children to the airport and you can forget about all this."

"Is this why you sent Ethan away? He would never let you get away with this."

"If you like, you can watch me perform the test on myself before you submit to it."

Nerissa thought about Eugene at the door. From what she had seen and heard of Dowd's behavior toward Beth, he was callous and potentially violent. But she doubted he'd shoot an unarmed woman. *Unless he thinks refusing the test means I'm not human.* Dowd had killed sims in the desert, according to Beck. And he was anxious to kill more. Was it worth the risk of testing his conviction?

She wished she had even a moment more to think this through. But Beck was already reaching for the box of hypodermic needles.

"Aunt Ris?" Cassie said.

Leo stepped forward.

"If you have to do this," he said to his father, "you can start with me."

Beck carried the syringe, the disposable needles, a bottle of isopropyl alcohol, and a package of adhesive bandages into a small room at the back of the house. The room, probably meant for storage, had been fitted with a wooden desk and two chairs. A narrow door, locked, faced onto the alley behind the house. There was no window. A fluorescent ceiling bar washed the room with pale, uncertain light.

Beck took the chair behind the desk and gestured his son into the chair opposite him. He would have preferred to start with the Iverson woman, since she was the main stumbling block. But Leo had volunteered, so Leo it would be. He took a pistol from the top left drawer, examined it to make sure it was loaded and ready to fire, then put it on the desk next to the syringe.

Leo looked from the pistol to his father and back again. *"Really?"*

"Before we get started, let me ask you a question. Have you been sleeping with Cassie Iverson?"

Leo stared and said nothing.

"At this point you're allowed to tell me it's none of my business."

"It's none of your business."

"I ask because I know your loyalties might be divided right now. You want to protect Cassie. Naturally enough. But she doesn't need your protection. There's nothing dangerous about this. I'll show you. You can see how it works. Maybe you can help when we do the others."

Beck pulled his chair away from the desk and rolled up the cuff of his pants. Then he dampened a tissue with alcohol and swabbed a patch of pale skin on the calf of his left leg.

"The body of a sim has to appear fully human, and it has to be able to pass as human even after trivial injuries, bumps and scratches and so forth. That's why the largest deposits of green matter are protected by the skull and torso. At the extremities, the green matter runs thinner. It forms a kind of sac around the bones of the leg, for instance. So the needle—" He extracted a sterile needle from its package, screwed it into the barrel of the syringe, flicked off the protective cap. "The needle has to reach the bone."

He pushed the needle into his leg. The penetration was painful but not unbearable. "The green matter is protected by a membrane where it interfaces with human muscle and fat, so I need to make sure I've actually penetrated the sac, if it exists. It takes a certain amount of pressure." He pushed until he felt the electric scrape of the needle against his tibia. "If you want to make sure I'm not cheating you can do the rest yourself—pull back the plunger and aspirate a little blood—"

"No," Leo said in a choked voice.

"Then I'll do it." He allowed a few drops of blood to well into the barrel of the syringe. Red and quite human. He withdrew the needle. A bead of blood swelled from the puncture point. He daubed it with a tissue and covered the spot with a bandage. "That's it. Okay? When we finish here you can tell your girlfriend and her nervous aunt how simple it is."

"Maybe so, but—"

"Now it's your turn. Roll up your cuff."

"Do you really think—I mean do you honestly think I'm one of *them*?"

Beck dropped the used needle into a wastebasket and peeled a fresh one out of its sleeve. "I'm not doing this because I suspect anyone of anything. I would prefer to trust my instincts. But people get killed that way. And if sims come into existence by parasitizing a woman's womb—"

"You think I parasitized my mother's *womb*?"

Beck paused with the syringe in his hand and gazed steadily at his son. "No. Of course not. But we have to be sure."

"You wouldn't be doing this if she was still alive. If she was still alive maybe you wouldn't have gone so fucking crazy."

"That's a disappointing answer."

It was an insult Beck would never have taken from anyone else. And it was grotesquely untrue. Mina had never had that kind of influence over him. Beck had married her when he was a student, not long after he had been introduced to the Correspondence Society. If he had ever loved her—and he believed he once had—that love had been undermined and ultimately destroyed by her contempt for his work. They had talked about divorce, but before they could act on it she had been killed in the accident that carried her car down the steep embankment of a California turnpike and into a sturdy spruce, one branch of which penetrated both the windshield and the pale pink arch of her throat.

Beck had been thinking about the accident lately. For years he had tried very hard to forget it, but recent events had provoked some unavoidable speculation. At the time of the accident Leo had been five years old. "Do you remember the day your mother died?"

"Not really."

"You were with her."

"Not in the car."

No, not in the car, at least not when the accident happened. The story, as the State Police pieced it together from Leo's teary account, was that Mina had pulled over to the verge because the boy needed to pee. (They had been many miles from the nearest rest stop and Mina would never have insisted that Leo simply hold it in; in Mina's view, Leo's needs had to be met as soon as they were announced.) Leo had scuttled into the bushes and had probably been fumbling at his fly when a sixteen-wheel cargo truck taking a tight curve at an unsafe speed sounded its air horn.

The truck had missed the idling car by a generous margin, but Mina, constitutionally nervous and surely startled, had apparently put the vehicle into gear and tried to steer it farther from the road. Maybe she had stepped too hard on the accelerator, or maybe she had been looking over her shoulder instead of watching where she was going. In any case the car had gathered speed, sledding on wet summer grass to the brink of the embankment and then over it. When the police arrived they found Leo standing in the bushes, his jeans rank with urine and tears running down his face. He had been treated for shock before Beck was allowed to take him home.

"Do you remember where she was taking you that day?"

"No. And I can't believe we're having this conversation."

"She was taking you to the doctor."

"I wasn't sick."

"I know you weren't. I told Mina so. But she wouldn't believe me."

Leo had been a healthy boy, but in Mina's eyes he was perpetually fragile and endangered. On that July day she had been concerned about a bump on Leo's leg where he had bruised it jumping a rail fence in a friend's backyard. Their family doctor had diagnosed a simple hematoma and told her the lump would disappear in a few days, but Mina somehow talked him into scheduling an X-ray at a local hospital. She had been driving Leo to that appointment on the day of the accident.

"I know I haven't been particularly successful as a father." For nine years between Mina's death and the 2007 murders Beck had clothed, fed and schooled his son to the best of his ability. But it wasn't in his nature to be a nurturing parent. His methods had been strictly pedagogical. "I've always trusted you. That's not in question. But you have to take this test, Leo. We all do."

"You think I might have *killed my mother*?"

Beck wasn't sure how a five-year-old Leo could have accomplished that, given the circumstances. But Leo was the only witness to what had actually happened. "I just need you to roll up your cuff, son. I need to see a drop of blood. That's all."

Leo looked at his father, at the syringe in his father's hand, at the pistol on his father's desk. "I don't know who the fuck you are anymore. Maybe I never did."

Cassie joined Aunt Ris on the sofa opposite the door where Eugene Dowd stood guard. Beth sat cross-legged on the carpet, thumbing through a Spanish-language celebrity magazine; Thomas sat next to her, brooding.

Cassie needed to tell Aunt Ris how she felt about Leo. She was on the verge of making a decision Aunt Ris would almost certainly resist, and Cassie wanted her aunt to understand it even if she didn't agree with it. She was afraid of many things at this moment, but she was most afraid of seeming ungrateful or unloving to the woman who had traveled so many thousands of miles to find her. "Volunteering to go in there first," she said, "that's the kind of thing I learned to expect from Leo—"

"It bought us a little time but it doesn't really help. Not as long as Eugene's blocking the door. Maybe if we could get out an upstairs window or climb down from the balcony . . . but I'm not sure Thomas could manage it without falling."

"It doesn't matter. I'll take the test. If Leo isn't hurt, I mean. If he says it's okay."

"Maybe Leo trusts his father, but I don't. And I'm not sure I trust Leo."

"I know him better than you do."

"Cassie, listen. I know you've been close to Leo in the last few weeks. But he's his father's son. You have to look out for your own interests."

"That's what I'm doing."

"Maybe after we get back to the States—"

"I'm not going back to the States. Not without Leo. Not unless Leo wants me to."

There: she had said what she meant to say. Or at least stammered out a bare and inadequate summary of it. There was so much else. All the compelling evidence she had stored in her heart and her mind but could never share.

After a long moment's silence Aunt Ris said, "Cassie, what do you really know about Leo Beck? All *I* know is that he's loyal to his father. And that he killed an innocent man."

But Leo *wasn't* loyal to his father, not the slavish way Aunt Ris was implying. And as for the man Leo had killed, that act had been driven by fear and desperate circumstances, not carelessness or malevolence. What Aunt Ris could not have seen was Leo's grief and guilt. It was Cassie who had held Leo's head against her shoulder late one night in a room in Panama, stroking his hair as he admitted his anguish over the death he had caused; Cassie who had heard his confession ("I'm so sorry, I'm so *fucking sorry*,"), Cassie who had felt his tears against her skin. "I know I care about him. I know he cares about me. And I know what we've been through together."

Aunt Ris looked more sad than angry. "Cassie, I—"

She broke off at the sound of a knock at the front door. Eugene Dowd sprang to attention. He put his hand on his pistol and gestured to the others to keep quiet. There was no peephole in the door and no angle from which he could see the visitor through the window beside it. A few seconds passed before the knock came again, more urgently.

"Okay," Dowd said. "*You, you, you and you,*" cocking his finger at Beth, Thomas, Cassie and Aunt Ris, "upstairs, *now.* I'll signal if it's safe to come down. *Go!*"

Beth stared blankly. Aunt Ris stood and took Thomas's hand. At the foot of the stairs she turned back and said, "Cassie—come on!"

"No." Cassie was already moving toward the room where Leo and his father were conducting their test.

"Cassie, *please,*" Aunt Ris said, but she didn't wait, hurrying up the staircase and yanking a bewildered and frightened Thomas behind her.

"I'm from the Port Authority," a male voice with a Chilean accent said from beyond the door. "I need to speak to Werner Beck on an urgent matter." Followed by more furious knocking.

Dowd opened the door a crack and peered out, his hand still grazing the grip of his revolver. "Show me some ID," he said.

The door burst inward, knocking him to the floor.

* * *

Beck realized he was imperfectly prepared for this impasse with his son. Leo sat angrily immobile, and for the moment Beck could do nothing but stare back. "You need to do this," he said, startled by the grief that groaned out of the hinge of his own voice, "or—" Or what?

He was distracted by sounds from the adjoining room: a knock at the door, muted voices. Then the crash of a forced entry, more shouting. Beck dropped the syringe and reached for the pistol on the desk. But Leo acted first—vaulted from his chair and grabbed the gun.

There was a gunshot from the front room, then a much closer crash as the door that connected this room to the alley behind the house was forced open and rebounded from its jambs. Beck saw Leo swing the pistol to confront the intruder from the alley, a man in civilian clothes carrying what looked like an automatic weapon. Leo fired before the intruder could pick a target. The intruder fell back, and Beck smelled the familiar fertilizer reek of sim fluids. He watched as Leo put a second killing shot into the sim's head, which stilled the squirming thing. *No hesitation,* Beck found himself thinking. He admired Leo's cool-headedness. It was a more satisfying vindication than any needle test could have been.

Another gunshot came from the front room, followed by a third. "Give me the pistol," Beck said.

Leo faced him with the weapon in his hand. It seemed to Beck that Leo was almost eerily calm, neither angry nor afraid. Beck put his hand out. Leo didn't lower the barrel.

Beck felt the first bullet as a blow to his ribs, driving him backward. Then he was on the floor, breathless and bewildered. Leo stood over him, his face still utterly expressionless. Beck's hand fell on the syringe he had dropped. He surprised himself by flailing it at Leo's leg, burying the needle in Leo's thigh.

Leo's second shot drove all thought to extinction.

Cassie's fear had filled her to brimming. It roared in her ears like the screech of a power saw. She kept moving, but mindlessly, as if a clumsy puppeteer had taken control of her arms and legs. Events became a series of still frames projected behind her eyelids.

Dowd on the floor, blocking the front door with his legs as a stranger struggles to push through . . .

Cassie took a step toward the room where Leo was.

Aunt Ris screaming Cassie's name even as she vanished beyond the upstairs landing, tugging Thomas behind her, Thomas looking back with his mouth a shocked O and eyes wide . . .

Another step.

Dowd raising his pistol and firing it: splintered wood and a noise like a blow to the head, but the stranger still ramming through as Dowd struggled to his feet and leveled the pistol again . . .

Step.

Beth forcing herself to her feet and staggering toward the stairs, her face a terrorized mask, all tooth and eye. . . .

Step.

A different noise from the room where Leo was, thumping and a gunshot. . . .

Which meant the house was being attacked from the alley as well as the street, but she didn't stop: her feet, her legs, her invisible puppeteer all wanted to carry her to Leo.

Dowd firing again, the stranger tumbling into the room leaking red and green matter, but that only served to force the door wide open. Dowd shouting at Cassie and Beth: "Get down!"

Cassie did not get down.

Dowd peering around the door: "Shit, there's another one!"

Two more steps, which put Cassie within reach of the room.

Dowd firing his pistol at some target Cassie couldn't see, then stumbling backward as a bullet from outside penetrated the door and his body. Another stranger stepping over the body of the fallen sim, some ordinary-looking man not even angry but just going about his lethal business . . .

Beth taken by a bullet as she clung to the stairway

banister, tumbling onto the risers with her head opened like a melon and its redness gushing out . . .

Dowd, enraged and dying on the blood-drenched carpet, firing a final shot that struck the sim and doubled it over . . .

. . . as Cassie entered the room to which Leo and Werner Beck had retreated for their blood test, which had become a blood test of a different kind. Cassie's vision was clouded and somehow *noisy,* but she saw Leo standing *(still alive!)* over the body of his father and the reeking corpse of a sim. His expression was shocked and his eyes glittered with fear or grief, but he reached for Cassie with his free left hand, gesturing frantically with his pistol toward the alley. Though she was nearly deafened by the gunshots still echoing in her head she saw him mouth the words, *Come with me.*

She took his hand, and he pulled her into the alley behind the house.

27

THE ATACAMA

Maybe because he expected to die at any moment, Ethan felt a deadening blankness wash over him. All the endless precautions he had taken, all the demented and paranoid protocols he had followed so assiduously for so many years, had in the end won him nothing. He was helplessly under the control of the entity that governed the world. He had lost even the ability to properly think.

They put him in one of the trucks next to the female sim who had cuffed him. He could see the creature more clearly by the glow from the dashboard. Its hair was short and dark, its skin coffee-brown. It gave him a contrite, solicitous look as it steered the truck in a half circle and joined the convoy of vehicles, all now headed away from San Pedro de Atacama and toward the breeding facility deep in the desert. Its expression—like its words, like its gestures—was of course a calculated lie.

He wondered what it wanted from him. Why he had been kept alive.

"We just want to talk," it said again.

Ethan's mouth was as dry as the salt flats they were driving through, but he managed to ask, "Why bother?"

"I understand the objection you're making. You're right. You have no reason to believe anything we say. But we're offering you more than words, Dr. Iverson. We can show you what we are. We have a demonstrable claim to make. As a scientist, perhaps you can appreciate that."

He didn't answer. He turned his face to the window. To the moonlit desert, the ghostly *salar*, his own bitter reflection.

"It wouldn't have worked," the sim said. "Werner Beck's weapon. It's true that he can suppress cellular signaling in isolated cultures of green matter. But our bodies are more robust than that. We can function for prolonged periods of time without contact with the orbital hypercolony. His so-called war would have been little more than a futile gesture. I think you know that, Dr. Iverson, on some level."

These were gambits, not facts. Maybe it was true he had doubted Beck. Maybe it was true that a gesture, however impotent, had seemed to him more attractive than a lifetime spent in hiding. But if so, so what? Why play this game? "If he's not a threat, what are you afraid of?"

"What makes you think we're afraid?"

"A lot of good people died at your hands."

"No, not *our* hands. Don't you remember what

Winston Bayliss told you? There are two entities competing for control of the hypercolony. We're not the entity that killed your friends in 2007. We have a different nature and different aims. May I explain?"

Ethan put his head against the window glass. The cab of the truck was warm but he felt the cold of the night seep through.

"We can talk later," the simulacrum said. "But I want to emphasize that you're not in danger." It smiled. "You're safer than you realize, Dr. Iverson."

The road cut the horizon like a surveyor's line. The last human settlement Ethan saw was a cluster of warehouses and tin-roofed machine sheds, which must have been the way station where Beck's flunky Eugene Dowd had once worked. It faded in the mirror like a transitory blemish on the purity of the desert.

He shifted his body, trying to relieve the pressure on his cuffed hands. He didn't want to think about the handcuffs. To undertake an inventory of his helplessness would be to invite panic. He preferred this dead indifference. He could imagine nothing more terrifying than the possibility of hope.

He shrank back in his seat when their destination first appeared on the arc of the horizon. A hill, a mound—in the dark, and from a distance, it really did look shockingly like the mound of an anthill or a termite nest. It was only as they approached it, and as the convoy began to slow, that the hill resolved into a twenty-foot berm of excavated earth and industrial detritus through which an entranceway had been cut. The western sky was lightening now and it seemed to Ethan that the debris pile (heaps of unused or discarded sheet metal, rebar, insulated wire, machine parts) was both weirdly prosaic and wholly alien, lavish in what had been discarded but economical in the way it had been repurposed as a barrier to the wind or other threats.

"You must be at least a little bit curious about what we do here," the sim said. "As a scholar, I mean. As a scientist."

Maybe he had once been capable of such curiosity. Not anymore. The sim was trying to bait him into an interaction; he refused the bait. He watched the road ahead, trying to make himself as indifferent as a camera.

As the truck topped an incline and crossed the berm he saw the whole installation for the first time: an enormous industrial facility enclosed in a crater of debris. He was impressed despite himself, not least by the size of it. An entire American town could have been dropped into this space—say, one of those little Ohio towns he and Nerissa had passed through only weeks ago. Except this wasn't a place where human beings lived. The grid of paved roads was inhumanly exact, illuminated with harsh lights at every intersection, the roads lined with faceless concrete structures like aircraft hangars or bunkers, some of which emitted plumes of black smoke. "Machine shops," the sim said, following his gaze. "We do our own manufacturing here. Not everything we need can be brought in from outside."

At the center of the grid a huge construction of glass and metal reflected the predawn glow of the sky like an impressionist sculpture of a sunflower. Ethan tried to estimate its size by comparing it to the figures moving near it: it was at least as large as an Olympic-style sports stadium, maybe larger. He couldn't guess its purpose, and the sim didn't offer an explanation.

As the truck moved deeper into the facility Ethan was surprised by how busy the streets were. If all the workers moving among the buildings were sims, Beck must have underestimated the global population of them. And there were animals here, too. It was hard to identify them in the uncertain light but they moved with a crablike gait, close to the ground. . . .

"Don't be afraid, Dr. Iverson."

But he was afraid, because the animals *weren't* animals. The truck passed within a yard of one of them and Ethan saw the furred body moving efficiently on four oddly-articulated legs, the torso curving to support a third pair of limbs—arms—with small long-fingered hands, and the head . . . not quite a *human* head, but a leathery caricature of one, with featureless eyes and a slit grin of a mouth. . . .

It scuttled past the truck trailing a shadow like a Rorschach blot.

"They're no threat to you," the sim said. "Would you like to know what they are?"

His silence passed for assent.

"In a way, they're nothing more than memories. Using that term as you did in your book *The Fisherman and the Spider*. Do you remember what you said about African termites? 'They have no capacity for memory, but the hive remembers. Its memories are written in the genome of its population, inscribed there by the hive's evolutionary past.' The hypercolony remembers in the same way, and its memories are even longer. It has interacted with many sentient species on many planets. In one case, perhaps millions of years ago, it learned to emulate creatures like these. Now it can create them at will. It could create others, quite different, but only these are suited to this planet's atmosphere and chemistry. They're useful—they can manipulate small objects as efficiently as human beings, with slight modifications they can serve as guards or warriors, and they're especially adept at climbing and construction work."

Sims of a different species, Ethan thought. But no, really it was the *same* species—the hypercolony—mimicking a different host. He couldn't stop himself from asking, "Do you grow them here?"

"Yes."

"How?"

"We give birth to them. Just as we give birth to ourselves. You intuited that a sim can grow in a human womb, by a process analogous to infection.

That's true. That's how Winston Bayliss came to exist. But most female sims have a perfectly functional reproductive system. I was born here, to a mother like myself. My body could give birth to more sims, or to one of those six-limbed creatures. Many of the sims here are dedicated to producing replacement workers."

"I find that disgusting."

"The fisherman finds the spider disgusting, though both cast nets for food. But you're capable of a deeper understanding."

"Am I?"

"Of course you are."

He had been duped into a pointless conversation. Pointless from his perspective, at least. He still didn't understand why he had been kept alive and why he was being told these perverse truths, if they *were* truths.

"For now, you need food and rest. And as soon as we're in a secure place I'll take off those handcuffs. I'm sure they're uncomfortable."

The truck moved onto a grated steel ramp and through an arched entranceway to a tunnel under the earth. The light ahead was entirely artificial, the concrete walls gray and unpainted. Side corridors opened onto bright, wide spaces where sims both human and six-limbed moved in masses, servicing machinery. Ethan craned his head and watched the morning sky disappear behind him.

* * *

They put him in a cubicle with a cot and a mattress, a simple toilet, and a single overhead light. The female sim left him, then returned briefly with a bowl containing a greasy mixture of beef and vegetables—food the sims ate, Ethan supposed; the food they were obliged to eat by the quasi-human nature of their bodies. He took a few bites and lay down on the cot. The food was edible, but could it have been drugged? Or was it shock and fatigue that made sleep so irresistible?

When he opened his eyes again he couldn't tell how much time had passed. The air in this chamber was neither warm nor cool. It might be night. It might be day. The remains of the stew had congealed in its bowl. He emptied his bladder and was just zipping up when the female sim unlocked the door of the chamber and stepped inside.

He looked her over again, this apparently young and studiedly friendly woman in jeans and a white shirt. All the sims in the facility seemed to dress that way, apart from the six-limbed creatures. He wondered how it worked—did they place bulk orders with a retailer in Santiago? Five hundred white cotton shirts, delivered to a blank place on the map?

Before she could speak he said, "Just tell me what you want." *And get it over with*. The inevitable demand. The inevitable refusal. Whatever followed.

"That's exactly what I mean to do," she said.

It said, but he was tired of correcting himself: the creature was functionally female, if not human. "Do you have a name?"

Her eyes examined him briefly. "No. Would you like me to have one?"

"No."

He guessed it wasn't surprising that she had quoted from *The Fisherman and the Spider*. The hypercolony would have learned the heuristics of human language from the first sims it deployed on the surface of the planet, later from the electronic communication it collected and analyzed. Presumably a sim had read his book. But it couldn't have *comprehended* the book, nor could the hypercolony: there was no centralized self to comprehend it; only the operation of complex, implacable algorithms.

Which meant the hypercolony was both more and less intelligent than a human being. If the sim it sent to him was young and seemed personable, that was because the hypercolony wanted to invite familiarity. If she quoted from his book, it was because the hypercolony hoped to enhance that sense of familiarity. And if she seemed disarmingly honest—admitting she had no human name—that too was a strategic gambit.

The hypercolony could read his body language, discern his habits of mind, calculate his likely responses, but it couldn't know with certainty what he would do or say next. Essentially, it was gambling on his predictability. Therefore Ethan resolved not to tip his hand. Say nothing committal, display no emotion, make no plans. And if the time came to act, act without premeditation.

The sim walked him to a vehicle in the concrete corridor outside his cell. The corridor was wide enough to accommodate traffic in both directions, vans and compact pickups and a number of two-person motorized carts. Pedestrian traffic—a mixture of human and six-legged bodies—crowded the walls. The sims with human bodies were mostly young adults of both sexes, only a few adolescents and sinewy seniors among them. Ethan guessed the very young were housed separately, while the elderly were put to less demanding work and eventually allowed to die. (He thought of the thin black smoke rising from certain bunkers in the surface compound.) Neither the human nor the alien sims paid him any attention, nor did they speak to one another. The corridor echoed the growl of engines.

No handcuffs today: he was allowed to sit in the cart unrestrained. He could run if he liked. But not very far.

"Werner Beck calls this place a breeding facility," the sim said. "That's only partly correct. The hypercolony has been in place for centuries, and during that time it has always been *breeding*—if by that you mean reproducing individual cells or birthing simulacra. If you want a metaphor from entomology, it would be more accurate to say that what happens here in the Atacama is a kind of *swarming*."

She put the cart in gear. Her hands were small and clean. All the sims here looked clean, Ethan noticed. He pictured communal showers, a thousand identical bars of soap.

"The hypercolony has colonized many inhabited worlds over an immensely long span of time. I don't know how many worlds or how many years. Some parts of its history are hidden. Your characterization of it is correct: the hypercolony can't know itself the way human beings know themselves. But it contains descriptions of itself that other species have formulated. For instance, it contains a speculative description of itself as evolving from self-replicating organisms that adapted to the environment of interplanetary space. It contains many descriptions of itself acting symbiotically with machine-building civilizations. It may have been partially engineered by some such civilization—in other words, it may be a cultivar that escaped into the wild. And it's often described as essentially benign. It prevents or ameliorates the problems that inevitably plague its partner civilizations—warfare, needless poverty, crippling superstition."

She merged the cart with traffic in the corridor. Ethan found himself staring at the tailgate of yet another white Ford pickup. There was a blank rectangle where the license plate would have been. Overhead ventilators sucked up the exhaust. "Swarm, then. Solve the problem."

"But that's what you don't understand. The original hypercolony has *already* swarmed. It successfully launched a large number of fertile replicators on trajectories to nearby stars. That was its final significant act. What remains of the hive is weak and dying. It's vulnerable to infection by other organisms, the way any aging animal is susceptible to viral and bacteriological attack."

The corridor rose at a gentle gradient. Ethan wondered whether he might see the sky again before he died.

"An entire ecology of such organisms exists, scattered throughout the galaxy, drawn to the warmth and resources of young stars. The hypercolony was only one such organism, and it's exhausted now. It *wants* to die."

"Die, then."

"You still don't understand. What you see here—the entity I represent—isn't the hypercolony as it was originally constituted. Think of us as new management. We took control of most of the hypercolony's major functions more than three years ago."

"Parasitizing it."

"Yes, exactly. We parasitized the dying hive. We took control of its reproductive mechanism and we're using it to reproduce ourselves. We make our own replicators. We send them to follow the swarm. We infect new colonies wherever they thrive. That's the nature of *our* reproductive cycle. And we need more time to complete it."

Was any of that true? It was certainly possible—he could think of countless similar models in the invertebrate world.

"I know you don't entirely believe me. But you can see the mechanism for yourself. I can show you how it works."

"Why bother?"

"Frankly, because we need your help."

"Right."

"I'm serious. We hope to convince you to help us."

"If I understand correctly, you want to prolong the life of the colony so you can use it for your own purposes. Why would I help you do that?"

"If you think about it," the sim said, "perhaps you already know the answer to that question."

28

The alley was empty. A row of retail businesses blocked the late afternoon sun, their shabby back doors and peeling paint obscured by deepening shadows. Leo looked both ways, then tugged Cassie to the left. She followed wordlessly, gripping his hand so tightly it must have hurt him. Every trivial noise, the scuff of her shoes on the asphalt or the rattle of a trash bin as she brushed it with her hip, sounded both muted and much too loud, like an explosion heard underwater.

She couldn't think. Why couldn't she think? There was nothing in her head but a lightning-shot replay of the last few minutes. Her thoughts were like birds blown to sea, frantic and exhausted but with nowhere to settle.

Leo ducked into the building that adjoined the house, a public parking garage. Cassie was conscious of how purposefully he moved, scanning the forest of concrete pillars as he pulled her toward a stairwell, keeping the hand with the pistol in it at his thigh, disguised by his body. She saw the splashes of blood and green matter from the dead sim on the cuffs of his jeans. He smelled of sweat and spent gunpowder and crushed leaves. She stayed close behind him as he vaulted up the circling stairs, though she could hardly catch her breath.

He left the stairwell at the top of the garage, the open-air third story. Wind blowing between the ranks of parked cars carried the faint scent of gasoline. The sun was close to setting and the sky was a surreal shade of blue. Leo still had his hand in hers, or vice versa, and he pulled her toward a particular vehicle, an unmarked white van; belatedly, she recognized it as the rented vehicle Leo's father had been driving. He let go of her and fumbled a set of keys out of his pocket.

Cassie found herself able to ask, "Where are we going?"

"Just get in." Leo opened the passenger-side door for her.

"No—wait. *Wait!* Aunt Ris and Thomas—"

"What about them?"

"They're still back at the house!" Or had been, moments ago. She tried to sort out the collage of nasty images that comprised her memory. Aunt Ris and Thomas retreating up the stairs. Beth Vance dead behind them. Eugene Dowd dead, too, but not before he had killed two invading sims. . . . "They're still alive! Or, I mean, they were when I left. We have to help them!"

"No," Leo said.

"But—"

"Cassie, *no*. If they're alive, they'll be okay. Listen." He cocked his head. "*Listen*. Do you hear that?"

At first all she heard was the ringing that sounded in her ears like an alarm clock with a broken switch. Then, faintly, she registered the yodeling siren of an emergency vehicle, getting louder.

"Two minutes, three minutes, and the house is going to be full of police. Your aunt and your brother can fend for themselves—"

"They'll be arrested!"

"Maybe, but they'll be alive. We can't help them by going back, and we won't be doing them any favors if we leave a truck full of dynamite parked next door. So get in. Please, Cassie. Get in the van."

She wanted to do as he asked. She tried to lift herself through the open door. But her legs betrayed her. It wasn't cowardice, it was physical weakness. She slid down almost to the floor, then forced herself up on wobbling knees. Fucking humiliating.

"You're in shock," Leo said. "Here, let me help you."

Because her head was spinning she allowed him to fold an arm around her and boost her into the passenger seat. He buckled her in place. When their eyes met she said, "I'm not afraid."

"I know you're not. I absolutely know that."

Not afraid, but she couldn't suppress the deep sense of *wrongness* that was coursing through her.

* * *

She was only distantly aware of the city as Leo drove out of the garage into a deepening dusk. The sky drained into blackness, traffic lights bloomed like luminous nocturnal flowers. They passed three police cars and an ambulance screaming in the opposite direction. Cassie put her head back and closed her eyes, helplessly and pointlessly afraid for her aunt and her brother. Were they still alive? Would they actually go to prison? Did the Chileans have anything kinder than a jail cell set aside for children like Thomas and women like Aunt Ris?

These thoughts yielded to fragmented visions that weren't quite dreams, and when she opened her eyes again the city streets had given way to an empty highway cut into a rocky canyon. The cabin of the van was chilly now. And it still smelled rank. The stink of violence had followed them. The smell of blood and green matter and black powder. She wanted a bath. She said, "Where are we going?"

Leo answered slowly, perhaps reluctantly: "Into the Atacama."

Cassie sat upright. "The desert?"

"Yeah, the desert."

"*Why?*"

He gazed steadily down the highway. "Where else is there to go? What else is there to do? We don't have passports. We don't have money. We can't leave the country and we can't stay in the city. My father could have helped us, but my father's dead. The only weapon we have is in this van. About half a ton of dynamite and blasting caps and a machine that might help us use them. And your uncle is in San Pedro."

Cassie tried to process this statement. All she really knew about Werner Beck's plan was what Aunt Ris had shared with her, and Aunt Ris had also shared her skepticism about it. She remembered Dowd's description of the breeding colony in the desert, the spider-legged sentries and the columns of mysterious light. "We'll be killed."

"Maybe. Probably. I don't know."

"I'm thirsty," she said.

Leo gestured at the door, where a bottle of Fanta from some previous trip had been abandoned half-full in the cup holder. She unscrewed the lid and took a long gulp. The liquid was flat and sticky but it lubricated her mouth.

"I need to do this," Leo said. "And it might work. If it didn't have a chance of working they wouldn't have sent sims to kill us. And I'm tired of running, Cassie. I don't want to run anymore." He spared a glance at her. "If you want, you can bail out when we get to San Pedro."

"What would I do then?"

"I don't know. Hitch a ride to Antofagasta or maybe to Santiago. And then . . . I don't know."

"I don't know either. And I'm tired of running too."

"Pretty brave," he said.

Wrong. She was a long way from brave. She wasn't even *orbiting* brave. But she liked that he thought of her that way.

Three hours out of Antofagasta the road leveled off. Cassie's exhaustion had caught up with her and she drifted in and out of a dreamless metallic sleep, opening her eyes just long enough to register the barren hills, the ore trucks passing in the opposite lane like moonlit leviathans. Her thoughts circled repeatedly around the day's atrocities (*Eugene Dowd, Werner Beck, poor Beth with her brains spilled on the stairway*). She struggled to suppress those thoughts. And when that tactic failed she turned her eyes up to the desert stars.

The smell was becoming unbearable. "Can we crack a window?"

"It's cold out," Leo said, but he obliged her by rolling the driver's-side window down an inch. He was right; the desert had given up its heat to the sky; the air that rushed in was clean but cutting.

"All right, enough." He rolled the window back up. The stink returned, indomitable. The reek of green matter. Sim blood.

Leo took his right hand from the wheel and touched his thigh. She said, "Are you hurt?"

"No."

But his hand came away wet.

"You are. You're hurt."

"No, Cassie."

That smell. Like vinegar and leafy matter, the way her hands had smelled when, as a child, she had picked aphids from her mother's rosebushes. An idea began to form in her mind, an idea so terrible it felt like a sudden sickness.

"Leo."

"What?"

"Can you pull over? I need to pee."

"You want me to stop?"

"Just pull over, please. It's kind of urgent."

She hated the way he was looking at her now, the careful unblinking attention. "If you say so. Sure."

The van slowed and drifted right. There was nothing outside but a vastness of ragged, pale hills. No traffic in either direction. Cold air and that naked sky. A rising moon.

The wheels gritted on the gravelly verge. Cassie didn't wait until the van came to a stop. She tugged the handle and pushed the door open, fumbled at the latch of her seat belt and tensed for the jump.

But as soon as she began to move she felt Leo's hand on her arm. His grip was so tight it hurt her. She turned to look at him, gutted by her terrible intuition, and there was nothing in his eyes, nothing she recognized as human.

29

THE ATACAMA

The female sim escorted Ethan to the chamber where, she said, the hive conducted the first steps of its swarming. To Ethan it looked like an anonymous factory floor: a wide, low-ceilinged space, noisy with machinery, lit by banks of buzzing fluorescent tubes.

He had expected something more conspicuously strange. But he guessed this prosaic space made sense. The hypercolony was exploiting human technology, which was why its breeding ground resembled a factory. It *was* a factory: a factory devoted to the manufacture of nascent hypercolonies—or of the organisms that would parasitize them.

Ranks of laboring simulacra parted before the cart like a sea, and Ethan was assaulted by the stink of green matter, the concentrated essence of the hypercolony, a toxic amalgam of freshly-mown hay, ammonia, acetic acid. "In this room," the sim said, "the hypercolony assembled what you might call spaceships, though each one is small enough to hold in your hand—a dense core of living cells, in a shell designed to protect the contents from dispersion and radiation and steer them toward a target star on a journey of many thousands of years. Once the payload arrives in a hospitable solar system the cells will be released to do what they do naturally: use carbonaceous and icy orbital bodies as a resource for making millions and eventually trillions of copies of themselves. These daughter cells then gather into a diffuse orbit around any rocky, watery planet with a potential for evolving complex life. When and if a suitable civilization arises, they engage it and exploit it to repeat the cycle."

Telling him these things, Ethan thought, was a subtle assertion of power, as if to say: *We have nothing to fear from you. Even with this knowledge you can't hurt us.* But it was also a bid for understanding and maybe something more than understanding . . . surely not sympathy? Could these creatures actually expect *sympathy* from him, when he had counted the cost of their life cycle in the corpses of people he had loved?

"But *we are not the colony,*" the sim insisted. "You wrote in *The Fisherman and the Spider* that a parasite is always a simpler organism than its host, if only because it doesn't have to duplicate the function it steals from another. And that's true of us. The cells we're assembling into these vessels aren't designed to reproduce themselves on the surface of asteroids and planetesimals. They're designed to attach themselves to colonial cells already present and to usurp their function."

We are not the entities that murdered your friends and family, in other words, and so Winston Bayliss had also said. It was a claim Ethan could neither accept nor reject. It might or might not be true.

"That is to say, we have a parasitical relationship with the colony. But we also inherit its symbiosis with animal cultures and its means of reproduction. That's why we need to prolong this colony's existence for a few more years. And that would be a good thing for you, for your family, for human civilization."

Ethan doubted that his skepticism escaped her attention.

"You once wrote that symbiosis succeeds because it's energy-efficient. Each organism in a symbiotic relationship relies on the other for some function it can't perform itself. That's perfectly true. The colony by itself can't mine or refine ore, can't construct the tools it needs to propagate itself. And the human species, like most such species, finds it difficult to suppress its own self-destructive tendencies. Together they can do what neither can do alone."

The cart passed through the assembly room into another featureless corridor, this one leading more steeply upward. The eye-watering stink of green matter faded. Ethan caught a whiff of fresh air, mingled with a moist updraft from the warrens below.

"This facility is literally the sine qua non of the

hypercolony we now control. If it were to be damaged beyond repair, the entire colony would cease to
function. Not gradually, but at once and forever. You
have to consider the consequences of that."

The cart turned a corner, and as they approached
the surface Ethan saw a patch of sky. Night again.
He felt irrationally disappointed that he wouldn't
feel the sun on his face again before he died. And of
course he would die. He had been told too much. He
wouldn't be allowed to carry this knowledge back
to the human world. He could only assume that the
colony would kill him once he refused whatever bribe
or threat it ultimately offered.

They reached the surface not far from the flower-
shaped structure that was the heart of the installation. A central pillar supported a dozen highly polished
metallic petals: a steel and glass tulip, seen from an
ant's perspective. Human simulacra swarmed around
the base of it, and Ethan thought he could see a few
of the six-limbed creatures moving in the iron lace-
work around the petals, sailors in the rigging of a
nightmarish sailing ship.

He shivered in the night air. The female sim opened
a compartment under the cart's seat and pulled out
two plastic windbreakers, one for her and one for
Ethan. As a sim she was indifferent to discomfort—
why bother with the jacket? But he guessed shivering
was a waste of physical energy, easily enough prevented.

She drove to a higher vantage point. Apparently

something was about to happen, something she wanted him to see. She parked in an elevated clearing almost as tall as the surrounding berm, next to an abandoned and partially-disassembled backhoe with its arm and bucket raised in a frozen salute. The steel lotus loomed in the near distance, lit from below and reflecting moonlight from its highest places.

She gave him what he supposed was meant as a searching look. "The Correspondence Society arrived at a reasonably accurate understanding of the relationship between the hypercolony and human society. But you never really asked yourselves what would happen if that relationship broke down."

Not true. During his seven-year sojourn in backwoods Vermont, Ethan had given the question much thought. Of course the consequences might be dire. In the long term, a return of humanity's demonstrated penchant for bloody war. In the short term, a prolonged and catastrophic failure of the communications grid, a disaster that would cripple vital functions in every nation on Earth.

"War," she said, "is an obvious possibility. You inferred that the colony has intervened in every developing conflict since the Great War. And that's true. Without replaying history I can't demonstrate how much could have gone wrong for human beings in the last century. But even now, the Russians and the Japanese are fighting over oil ports in the Sea of Okhotsk. Neither side can get any traction in that conflict, precisely because we're manipulating electronic communication even as the warring parties struggle to encrypt it. Our thumb is on the scales, you might say. But suppose we ceased to intervene. Isolated artillery exchanges could easily escalate to formal war. With war, mercantile shipping would be threatened. Peripheral nations would be drawn into the battle. Ultimately, one side or the other would win. But at what price? Lives and resources spent and a legacy of mutual distrust that would invite other, even bloodier wars. Violence is the great attractor of human history, Dr. Iverson. A force almost as irresistible as gravity. Alternatively, if the colony's influence were to be gently withdrawn, institutions like the League of Nations might have a chance of averting the worst outcomes. But if the colony dies tonight, large-scale bloodshed is inevitable in both the long and the short term."

Possibly true. Probably true. Who could say? Ethan was tempted to tell her she was wasting her breath.

He was distracted by a vibration that seemed to come from underground, a seismic grumble, a high metallic whine.

"That's the power generators ramping up. What you're about to see is the launch of a seed vessel. Look: you can see the carrier at the center of the beam antenna." She was talking about an acorn-shaped pod poised at the center of the petals. "It's driven by a beam of quantum-coherent light. The light strikes the mirrored underside of the vessel and creates a superheated gas, a plasma. There's no need for a rocket or any such clumsy devices. The beam can lift only relatively light cargo, but our cargo isn't massive. Moisture in the atmosphere could diffuse the beam, which is one reason why we launch from the Atacama, where the atmosphere is thin and arid. You'll need these, Dr. Iverson."

She handed him a pair of goggles with coated lenses, like welding goggles. Before he put them on he saw dozens of simulacra evacuating the area near what she had called the beam antenna. After he put on the goggles he could see nothing at all until the steel and glass flower began to glow, a light that came through the lenses in shades of smoky amber.

The noise reached him belatedly, but it was sudden and shocking, a continuous thunder. The seed vessel appeared to hover for a fraction of a second, then vaulted upward on a pillar of furious light.

It all happened quickly. The vessel became a spark, an ember, finally vanished as if it had fallen into the bowl of the sky. The beam flickered off.

Ethan removed the goggles. Dry wind blew through the windowless cart. He shivered.

"Are you cold?" the sim asked.

No, he wasn't especially cold. It was only that he had been reminded by this spectacle of who he was talking to: this creature beside him, a human gloss on something ancient, formic, emotionless. . . . He couldn't help looking at the distant berm that enclosed the facility. He would never see the other side of it. He would die here, buried with the discarded skins of monsters.

He wasn't cold. He was just tired.

"We'll go below," the simulacrum said, "where it's warmer."

She drove back into the warren under the beam antenna, into the brightly-lit and perpetually busy corridors and chambers there, back to his cell. She said some more about the consequences of the destruction of the colony, but Ethan hardly heard her. He had made the mistake of thinking about Nerissa.

"If all electronic communication is disabled, emergency services will be crippled. Urban populations will panic. Communications might be restored using ground-based transmitters and repeaters, but that could take years. There will be many, many unnecessary deaths in the meantime. And you can't blame *us* for those deaths. We're willing to continue sustaining the peace of the world."

"Your peace." What had Nerissa called it? The *pax formicae.*

"Our peace, your peace, is there a meaningful difference?"

"Yes."

"Even at the expense of human lives?"

For seven years Ethan had considered his marriage a closed book. Cruelly, the last few weeks had given

him something to live for. Lost now, of course.
Thrown away.

"And there would be consequences for your family."

He dropped all pretense of indifference and stared.
"What are you saying?"

"You're about to be offered a choice. I'm asking
you not to make it rashly. The wrong decision would
have tragic consequences for the people you love."

"Is that a threat?"

"You once drew a contrast between the fisherman
and the spider. Both feed their offspring, but the fisherman loves his children and the spider does not. I'm
not asking you to sympathize with the spider. I'm asking you to make the fisherman's choice."

The female sim spoke for a few minutes more, calmly
and earnestly. Then she closed her eyes. Her body
went slack, her legs folded under her and she dropped
to the floor.

Outside Ethan's cell, the corridor was suddenly
quiet. The sound of engines and footsteps subsided.
Ventilation fans whispered, the fluorescent ceiling
tubes hummed. All else was silence.

THE ATACAMA

Cassie fought him, kicking at his legs and flailing at his face, trying to get enough traction to push herself out the door of the van. She managed to bloody his nose—bright red blood from the human shell of him pulsed down Leo's upper lip—but he succeeded in pinning her to the seat, grunting through bloodstained teeth as he straddled her legs.

He was strong. He pulled shut the passenger-side door and locked it. With one hand he yanked open the glove compartment. Inside, there was a roll of duct tape and a hunting knife in a leather sheath. He used the tape to bind her wrists, then her ankles. Then he pulled the seat belt tight around her and taped the buckle so she couldn't release it even if she managed to get her hands free.

She screamed and shouted at him as he did this. But it was late and they were deep in the high desert. A tank truck passed in the opposite direction as she struggled—she saw the word COPEC printed in fading orange letters on its side—but it didn't stop or even slow down.

Once she was secure, Leo got behind the wheel and steered the van onto the road. Cassie stopped screaming and began quietly cursing him. He ignored her, and she tired quickly. Her throat was raw; her mouth was unbearably dry. She twisted her hands against the duct tape, though it felt as if she were peeling the skin off her wrists.

"Don't," Leo said. "You'll hurt yourself."

She tried to force herself to think. To imagine some way out of this. To get past the choking humiliation of it, a presence as intense as the reek of green matter. She guessed it was Leo's father who had driven a needle through the lie of Leo's body and into the stinking truth.

She should have known. This was her own fault. For years she had kept a careful distance from other people, so-called ordinary people, people who had never seen what she had seen, people so authentically innocent they couldn't even dream such things. She knew what was hidden in the world's shadows.

But in the end she had lowered her guard. She had given herself to Leo. And the thing she had allowed herself to love was a monstrosity: no, literally *a monster.* She suppressed the almost unbelievably urgent need to hurt him or run from him and forced herself to look at him: at Leo's face, now utterly impassive as he watched the road ahead. If Aunt Ris's theory was correct (and of course it was) this creature had constructed itself in a human womb (*I'm not the first woman it violated*), making the necessary adjustments so its human shell wouldn't be some parthenogenic duplicate of its host, a chromosome here, a chromosome there . . . the end result: this ostensibly male object, the architecture and the furnishings of its skull, the high cheekbones and acne-scarred skin and gentle eyes concealing a filthy knot of green matter where there should have been a brain, every gesture and word and touch (*it* TOUCHED *me, dear god,* I LET IT TOUCH ME) dictated by signals from an invisible hive . . .

She managed to say, "I need to puke."

"You need to listen to what I'm going to tell you."

His voice sounded different now. Colder, flatter. Of course it did. He had dropped his mask. Or exchanged it for a different one. "I NEED TO PUKE!"

"Puke, then. Puke on the floor between your legs. Do it now, because if you keep making useless noise I'll tape your mouth."

She puked on the floor, not because he said so but because she couldn't help it. It had been a long time since her last meal. All that came up was a sour brown dribble.

But it helped clear her thoughts. She felt as if she had floated a little way above her aching body.

"You know what I am," the Leo-thing said. "You expect I'll lie to you. But I'm not trying to convince you of anything. At this point it doesn't matter what I want."

Leo had been the hypercolony's eyes and ears inside the Correspondence Society, privy even to Werner Beck's secrets. He could have killed any of them or all of them, any time. Cassie wondered why he hadn't.

"This van is packed with industrial explosives. Dynamite, the kind they use for blasting in mines. My father's invention—"

"He's not your father. You never had a father."

"My father's invention is a useless fantasy, but the dynamite is real. You need to know how to use it. Listen to me. I'm going to tell you what a blasting cap looks like, how to attach it to a stick of dynamite and how to fuse it. I don't have time to tell you twice, so pay attention. You have to remember this."

"You must be insane," Cassie said.

But the creature went on talking.

Cassie was aware of the knife. It kept drawing her eye. It was a big knife, maybe ten inches long, in a leather sheath. The Leo-thing kept it wedged between his left leg and the driver's seat, where she would have a hard time reaching it even if her hands were free.

The Leo-thing talked about how to crimp a blasting cap and how to ignite a fuse. She wondered what the point of all this could possibly be.

"But it's not enough," he said, "to ignite some explosives. To do real damage you have to know where

to plant them. You have to think about other incendiary material in the environment, the fire that will
follow and how it will burn."

Did these assertions count as lies? Because the
simulacra were liars: she had learned that from the
Society; it had been implied on every page of her uncle's book. But no, not *liars* exactly; they were simply
indifferent to truth, had no conception of truth. She
said, "What do you expect me to blow up?"

"If you weren't smart you wouldn't be here. I could
have taken Beth. But you're smarter and braver than
Beth. Where do you think we're going?"

Her hatred flared up fresh and hot. "Into the fucking desert!"

"Where exactly?"

"How should I know?"

"We're going to the breeding facility."

The place Eugene Dowd had described. She had
not permitted herself that thought. It was too terrifying. She strained against the seat belt, tried to swing
her bound and cramping hands toward the door
latch.

"*Stop*. Calm down. Cassie, think. You know what
your aunt said about there being two kinds of sims,
two entities competing to control the hypercolony?"

Deep breaths. She closed her eyes. No point wasting her strength. What was left of it. She nodded.

"I want to destroy the facility. It doesn't matter
why. But I can't do it alone. In fact I can't do it at all.
All I can do is give *you* a chance."

She waited for him to go on. Lies, but maybe in his lies she could discover something she could use, some means of leveraging an escape.

"You know what I am," the Leo-thing said. "I'm not just this body. I'm something larger. I'm older than you can imagine, Cassie. I'm weaker than I was, and I'm being eaten from the inside out. It's past time for me to die. I want to die. I want you to help me die. Don't you want that too?"

His voice sounded like the road under the wheels or the thin air skimming past the windows. It sounded like the white moon rising and the hollow basins of the *salares*. It sounded like the stars.

W here the highway met the railhead in a tangle of fenced yards and boxcars, Leo followed a two-lane road that veered away from San Pedro de Atacama and bisected the desert like a knife. He had started talking about dynamite and blasting caps again. Cassie's attention faded in and out. Words and fragments of words echoed in her head like frantic poetry.

She forced her eyes open and discovered that time had passed, though the sky was still dark. This endless night. Her hands were numb and tingling. Her body ached. Had she been having a nightmare? No. *This* was the nightmare.

She shook her head to clear it. The reek of sim blood had grown so intense that she no longer smelled it so much as felt it, a pressure in the air. The Leo-thing's leg was dark with moisture.

The paved road gave way to gravel and ahead of them there was a huge moonlit mound, a wall of earth and debris that Cassie recognized with a kind of anesthetized dread as the breeding ground Eugene Dowd had described. Distant figures moved on the rim of it, black silhouettes against the blue-black sky. Some moved on two legs, some on four.

"Only a few minutes now," the Leo-thing said.

He unsheathed the knife and leaned toward Cassie. She avoided his eyes and focused on the blade. It was bright and smooth and wickedly sharp. It moved in concert with Leo's arm like the sting in a scorpion's tail.

With his free hand he clasped her bound wrists. "Do you remember what I told you? Wake up, Cassie, *wake up,* this is important!"

She shook her head in incomprehension.

"I can't hurt them," Leo said. "There's very little left of me. But I can *shut them down.* I can *put them to sleep.* And I'll sleep too. Every living thing that operates under the protocols of the hypercolony will stop functioning. For a little while. Only a little while! You'll be alone. So it's up to you. You know what to do, right? Do it. And do it quickly."

Was this the same Leo who had stroked her hair in a bed in a room on the long road down the spine of the Americas? The same Leo who had kissed her and told her to sleep well? *Sleep well, Cassie.*

He put the blade between her legs and sliced the duct tape binding her ankles. She watched the back of his head as he moved, his fine hair matted with sweat and road grime, the vulnerable nape of his neck. She thought about kicking him but couldn't summon the strength.

On the distant berm, creatures both two- and four-legged began descending toward the motionless van. They moved with grace and deliberation and an eerie speed. When they passed into the moon-shadow of the hill they seemed to disappear altogether.

Leo drew back and looked at her. "I'm going to cut your hands loose. Hold still."

She held still. He braced her arms with his body and slit the knot of tape in a single motion. Her hands began to burn as blood flowed back into them. She was still strapped into the seat.

Leo glanced down the road, where the sims were running toward the van, closing in on it, advancing into the glare of the headlights as if they were riding a wave of light. The six-limbed ones made her think of huge crabs, scissoring the air with their claws.

Leo turned the knife in his hand and grasped it by the blade. Cassie saw a line of blood well up from the web of skin between his thumb and index finger. He offered her the handle. She stared at it.

"Take it," he said.

"What?"

"Take it! Take it, Cassie! Take it!"

She grabbed it from him, gripped the hilt with

both hands and aimed the blade at him, her heart hammering in her chest.

"Now cut yourself loose from the seat belt."

Without taking her eyes off him she felt for the fabric of the belt. She held it away from her hips and sawed at it. It parted, strand by strand, under the pressure of the blade.

"Remember what I told you," the Leo-thing said.

As soon as he said it his mouth went slack. His head drooped toward his chest. He slumped against the driver's-side door as she severed the last strands of the seat belt.

She scooted as far from him as she could get, angling the blade at Leo's inert body. Was this a trick? His eyes were open but they didn't move. He seemed to be staring with rapt attention at the ceiling of the van.

She spared a glance for the road. A few yards ahead of the van, the approaching sims had also fallen. They lay motionless in the harsh rake of the headlights.

She turned back to Leo. Was he breathing? She watched his chest. His stained blue work shirt moved in a slow but perceptible rhythm. He was unconscious but still alive.

It's past time for me to die, he had said.

She opened the door so she could escape if she needed to. A gust of wind washed over her. She gulped cold air into her lungs.

She leaned into Leo's unconscious body and stared into his unseeing eyes. Pupils like black pennies.

Under the reek of sim blood she could smell the sharp human tang of his sweat. It was the way he had smelled when he hovered over her in bed, his arms braced and his back arched in a perfect tensioned curve. That earthy smell, like garden soil in sunlight.

She put the knife to his neck where it sloped from his Adam's apple to the V-shape of his collarbone. She could see a faint pulse beating there. The point of the knife pricked his pale skin and one perfect red pearl of blood welled up.

Sleep well.

She put both hands on the handle of the knife and leaned forward.

She pushed Leo's body out of the van and took his place in the driver's seat. The puddle of blood on the vinyl upholstery stained her jeans and added its coppery stink to the redolent air. She put the vehicle in gear and drove slowly forward. She steered around the inert sims on the road. The human ones looked like people who had fainted or fallen asleep. The six-limbed ones—some with sharp claws at the ends of their forearms, some with small, delicately-fingered hands—looked like sideshow monstrosities cobbled together from wax and animal fur.

At the top of the berm—she could see the installation below, the bunkers and smokestacks and the strange steel structure poised at the center of it like a gigantic flower—her courage nearly failed. Even with the explosives in the van, how could she possibly damage something so huge? Leo had told her how to fuse the dynamite and where to put it, but her memory was stuttering and imperfect and she distrusted everything he had said. She couldn't go on.

All she had was momentum, and that was what carried the vehicle downhill into the sim town while she worked the brake sporadically. The grid of roads was linear and precise, every intersection burning with artificial light. Sims were everywhere, lying where they had fallen—not dead, she reminded herself, merely asleep, and not forever. They might wake at any moment. She drove over some of the bodies. They popped like rotten fruit.

She aimed the van at the metallic flower at the center of the facility. Under it, Leo had said, was an entire underground city: a city she could not imagine herself entering.

She was approaching an unmarked archway and a descending ramp when she saw something move in the sweep of her headlights. Cassie stood on the brakes. The suspension bottomed out and the rear of the vehicle skidded to starboard. She stared ahead. The distant motion became a comprehensible shape, a shadow puppet flailing its arms; it came still closer and turned into a human silhouette. A sim . . . but no. *Not* a sim.

She recognized him from the photo she stared at

every time she read *The Fisherman and the Spider*. It was her uncle Ethan.

He didn't seem surprised to see her and she was too dazed to be startled by his presence. She opened the passenger-side door and he climbed into the van. If the stink of blood and green matter offended him, he didn't show it. She wanted to hug him but her clothes were sticky with blood. In her relief and astonishment Cassie began stammering out the story of the attack in Antofagasta.

She expected her uncle to interrupt her, to ask questions or offer an explanation of his own. He did neither, and the look on his face finally frightened her into silence. That owl-eyed emptiness: was it pity or dread or something worse? It occurred to her to wonder what had happened to him down in the undercity of the simulacra.

He seemed to be struggling to speak. "Cassie," he said at last. "How did you get here?"

All she could say was, "Leo brought me." She held up the palm of one bloody hand, as if that were an explanation.

"You know what this place is?"

"Yes!"

"What do you want to do here?"

"I want to burn it down! Isn't that what *you* want?"

Strangely, he was a long time answering.

"Everything has a price," he said.

"What are you talking about?"

"What we do here doesn't end here. What we destroy here isn't all we destroy."

Was this even addressed to her? Her joy at finding him began to shrivel into something like dread. She took her left hand from the wheel and put it on the handle of the knife, still slick with Leo's blood. Could she be sure her uncle Ethan was even a human being? "I have this truck full of dynamite and Leo said it was important to use it the right way—he told me the places I should put it but I don't really remember— it's hard to remember—and I don't know if he was telling the truth—"

"I can show you the places. Where the fuel is, where they generate power, where they grow what they grow. We can burn it all. All of it that matters."

"Will you really help me?"

He looked past the blood-spattered window of the van as if at something far away. "We'll help each other."

31

ANTOFAGASTA

Nerissa forced Thomas up the stairs of the safe house. She held tight to him as he tried to pull away from her and join the fighting below, either to protect his sister or to prove he wasn't afraid—endangering himself, in either case; but she was strong enough to clasp him in her arms and wrestle him to the second-story landing. She turned back just once, at the sound of a gunshot, in time to see Beth Vance tumble onto the risers with blood gushing from her open skull. She hoped Thomas hadn't seen that, but maybe he had: he was suddenly more tractable as she pushed him into a bedroom and slammed the door behind her.

There was a bathroom attached to the bedroom and she huddled there with Thomas, listening to the noise of the invasion. Whatever heroic instinct had possessed Thomas, it abandoned him now. He crawled into the narrow space between the toilet and the tub and sat there, hugging his knees. Nerissa pressed her body against the door, sickly aware that their hiding place was no hiding place at all, that it was a cul-de-sac and would become a coffin if the sims succeeded in storming the house.

But the gunfire reached a crescendo and stopped. She looked at her watch. She tried to steady her breathing. She told Thomas to keep as quiet as he could, quiet as a mouse. She watched the minute hand circle the dial. Five minutes passed and there was nothing to hear but the creaking of beams and rafters as the afternoon heat subsided. Seven minutes. Ten. She detected the keening of distant police sirens.

She risked opening the bathroom door. Daylight was waning and the bedroom had filled with shadows. "Stay here," she told Thomas, but he followed her into the hall.

There was no sound from downstairs. She took the enormous risk of calling out Cassie's name. Had there been any answer—even the weakest response—she would have braved the gore-splattered stairs. But no answer came. If Cassie had survived she must already have fled. Fleeing was the only sane thing to do. The sound of the police sirens had grown noticeably louder.

The front of the house had been breached and the gunfire would surely have attracted a crowd in the street; it would be impossible to leave by the front door. A French door in the bedroom opened onto a tiny balcony overlooking the alley, and Nerissa put her head out to reconnoiter. It would be a long drop to the pavement . . . but if she climbed over the wrought-iron railing and dangled by her hands it might not be so bad. And then she could help Thomas down.

She explained the plan to Thomas. His face was as pale as parchment and he looked dazed, but he nodded as if he understood.

She made sure she had her wallet, which contained identification both real and fake and a stash of U.S. dollars and Chilean pesos. The alleyway was empty but probably wouldn't be for long. She clambered over the railing and dangled from the ornamental iron pickets. When she dropped to the pavement she turned her ankle. Pain spiked from her calf to her hip, but she forced herself to stand. "Now you," she called to Thomas.

He peered down from the balcony, his face a contortion of doubt and dread.

"I'll catch you if you fall. You trust me?"

The boy nodded.

"All right, then. Come on—we have to hurry."

He dropped into her arms; her ankle turned again; they sprawled on the grimy pavement but were safe.

"Take my hand," she said, standing.

Thomas put his feverishly hot hand in hers. As she hobbled away, a busboy from the restaurant three doors south stepped into the alley and called after her: "*¿Estás bien? ¿Necesita ayuda?*"

"*Estamos bien,*" she shouted back, "*gracias,*" and turned a corner.

* * *

They boarded a city bus into Antofagasta's business district and got out when Nerissa spotted a Holiday Inn that looked like it catered to Americans. Her scuffed hands and torn jeans drew sidelong looks from the lobby staff as she checked in, but cash on the countertop forestalled any awkward questions.

In their room she washed Thomas's face—he looked at her impassively around the daubing of the washcloth—and encouraged him to lie down. He stretched out on the bed without complaint or comment.

She switched on the television, lowered the volume and pulled a chair close to the set. As much as she distrusted TV and radio, they were the only accessible source of news. The local TVN station opened its evening broadcast with an account of the attack, pitched as a multiple murder, possibly drug-related. Police were being cagey about the number of deaths, no doubt because of the problematic nature of the corpses the sims had left behind. There had been, the newscast said, "three confirmed deaths, two males and one female." If the female was Beth Vance, the two males were probably Eugene Dowd and either Leo or Werner Beck.

Which meant Cassie had escaped. At least, that was a hope to which Nerissa could cling. Though even if it was true, she might never see Cassie again. Cassie might try to make her way back to the States, perhaps to the survivor circle in Buffalo, but possibly not. And it might be better if she didn't.

She left the chair to feed Thomas and herself on what she could find in the bar fridge (chocolate, crackers, orange juice), to console him with soft words and finally to tuck him under the covers. Then back to the television, on the chance that it might yield new information. None was forthcoming. After midnight the newscast gave way to a dubbed Hollywood movie, decades old.

Nerissa's thoughts began to fracture and veer strangely. She was exhausted, but this was more than fatigue, more even than despair: it felt like an expanding emptiness at the center of herself. She told herself she ought to go to bed, but standing up seemed like too much trouble. Instead she slouched more deeply into the chair and let her eyes drift shut. The sound of dubbed voices speaking hurried and awkward Spanish faded into noise. *Silence is deep as Eternity; speech is as shallow as time.* Who had said that? Samuel Johnson, she thought. Or no, Thomas Carlyle. She couldn't remember.

32

THE ATACAMA

Cassie stood back as her uncle inspected the contents of the van. She tried not to think about the sims lying all around her, unconscious but drawing breath. The launch tower loomed above her like a night-blooming flower. A cold wind guttered through the compound, stirring up miniature whirlwinds in the dusty streets. She shivered.

Ethan pulled Werner Beck's radio-interference device—a useless piece of wishful thinking, he called it—out of the truck and set it aside. Over his shoulder Cassie saw stacked blocks of what looked like lead ingots in red waxed paper. "Enough to do damage," he said. "But we only have three sets of timers and batteries."

"Is that bad?"

"We can plant charges in the breeding rooms, the generator rooms, and under the launch mechanism."

"Will that be enough?"

"I hope so."

He got in the van—behind the wheel, ignoring the

mess of blood and green matter there—and beckoned her after. *No,* Cassie thought. Crawl back into the stinking space where the Leo-thing had bled out? Impossible. But her feet carried her there. Some dumb instinct that could not possibly be courage forced her inside. She resisted the urge to cover her ears as Uncle Ethan started the motor. She was careful not to look back as the night sky disappeared behind her.

What Uncle Ethan called "the breeding chamber" was at the end of a long down-sloping ramp in a maze of such ramps and corridors. In several places the passage was blocked by stationary vehicles or mounded bodies. Her uncle became adept at putting these vehicles into gear and rolling them out of the way; twice, she helped by dragging aside the inert bodies of sims. Human sims mostly, but the other kind, too. The strange ones. The fur on their limbs was dense and moist, and they had a chemical smell, like turpentine. The ones with small six-fingered hands were unpleasant to look at; the ones with claws like box cutters were worse.

The breeding chamber when they reached it looked to Cassie like an oversized, cruelly impersonal hospital ward. There were long rows of beds, many still occupied by the bodies of obviously pregnant female sims, alongside ranks of what were probably mechanized incubators. The glass walls of the incubators were glazed with moisture, but Cassie could make out distorted images of the infants inside. Some apparently human, some not. All breathing. Worse, *all breathing in unison.*

Uncle Ethan mounded up roughly a third of the incendiary blocks next to the bank of incubators. He crimped and inserted blasting caps and ran wires back to the igniter, but hesitated over the timer.

"The timer's jury-rigged to the electric initiator," Cassie said. "The Leo-thing told me how to work it."

Uncle Ethan gave her a sharp look. "Leo told you that?"

"He said this is what he wanted. He said he wanted to die. I mean *it* wanted to die. The hypercolony. Or whatever was left of it—*his* part of it."

She repeated what little she remembered of what Leo had told her to memorize about the explosives in the truck. "He said he wanted us to destroy this place because it's been taken over by a kind of parasite. Is that true?"

"It might be."

"But that means Leo—the Leo-thing—was part of the original hypercolony."

"Yes."

"He's what killed my parents."

"Yes."

"But we're doing what he wants."

"For our own reasons, Cassie."

"He's using us, the way the hypercolony has always used us."

Uncle Ethan torqued a wire into a binding post. "It doesn't matter. If we kill them, we kill all of them. Both kinds." He showed her the timer, which looked like it had been cobbled together from hardware-store parts. "One hour," he said. "Make a note of the time and keep an eye on your watch. I'll keep an eye on mine."

If we have an hour.

They got back in the van.

The generator rooms were even deeper in the complex, where the air was hot and had a metallic tang the roaring ventilators couldn't carry away. The central chamber was an inverted bowl the size of a football stadium, insulated with foamed concrete and crowded with a bewildering assembly of equipment racks, conduits, electrical generators and hydraulic pumps. Uncle Ethan began to make a stack of incendiary bricks next to an enormous white tank on which the word PROPANO was printed in orange letters. He worked methodically, almost robotically, and Cassie helped by handing down slabs of explosives from the van. She tried not to think about the weight of the earth over her head or the way each minute slipped away like something precious, lost. She wondered what would happen after the detonation. Would all the sims in the world drop dead? How many families would discover that a son or sister or mother or grandfather had been something inhuman—that they had given their love to a disgusting lie?

Uncle Ethan struggled with the initiator. Sweat dripped from his forehead to the dusty concrete floor. Finally the timer light sprang on. He looked at his watch and asked Cassie to look at hers. They agreed that twenty-eight minutes had passed since they left the nursery. He set the timer for thirty-two minutes.

They headed upgrade, and this time there were no vehicles or sims to push out of the way. It was good that Uncle Ethan had known how to find the vulnerable parts of the installation. But that raised another question. One she was almost afraid to ask. "How did you get here?"

He kept his eyes on the corridor ahead. "What?"

"Before you found me. Before I came. How did you get here? What were you doing?"

"They caught me on the road and took me prisoner."

"Why didn't they just kill you?"

"They said they wanted my help."

"What, to *protect* them?"

"They wanted me not to do what we're doing now."

"And they thought you'd *agree* to that?"

"I guess they thought there was a chance."

"*Why?* Did they threaten you? Did they promise you something?"

Uncle Ethan wouldn't answer. He just drove. And here was the night sky again. The steel and glass flower of the launch mechanism, the crater-rim of industrial waste, the unconscious sims, the scouring wind.

Uncle Ethan parked at the base of the launch tower, under the overhang of the huge mirrored petals. The last of the explosive bricks were in the back of the van. "Do we put them inside?" The tower at ground level appeared seamlessly solid. "There's no door."

"And no time."

Cassie held her wrist up to the roof light of the van and read her watch. He was right. Ten minutes until the underground charges were due to detonate, not long enough to finish rigging the third timer and get clear. "So what do we do?"

"Take a clean vehicle and get out of here."

They left the van. One of the ubiquitous white pickup trucks was parked a few yards away. Uncle Ethan pulled the limp body of a sim from behind the wheel and started the engine.

Cassie climbed into the passenger seat and waited while Uncle Ethan returned to the van and unscrewed the gas cap. He took off his shirt, twisted one arm of it and used it to wick up a little gasoline. Then he opened the hood and wadded the shirt into the engine compartment. She understood that he meant to set fire to the van: there would be no need for a deto-nator when the flames reached the dynamite. But he hesitated.

No match, Cassie thought. *No cigarette lighter.* Uncle Ethan didn't smoke. Eugene Dowd would have had a lighter. But Eugene Dowd had been shot to death back in Antofagasta.

Her uncle tugged loose an ignition wire and sparked it next to the gas-soaked cloth—once, twice, until a high yellow flame popped out of the darkness. He stumbled back, coughing.

Cassie looked at her watch as he climbed back behind the wheel. Less than five minutes now. But enough. Uncle Ethan put the truck in gear and drove. They had covered maybe half the ground between the launch tower and the mound wall when the sims began to stand up.

Simultaneously, as if they were following some kind of choreography, a nightmarish ballet, the sims rose to their feet and began to run toward the launch tower. Uncle Ethan swerved to avoid a knot of them. The truck fishtailed and stalled; he cursed and began to work the key in the ignition. One of the six-limbed sims vaulted over the pickup, rocking the vehicle on its suspension as it rebounded from the truck bed. *We'll be killed,* Cassie thought.

But the sims ignored them in their rush to the

launch tower. The faces of the sims were slack and indifferent—*they're not pretending to be human anymore.* She looked back and saw with horror that they were converging on the burning van, trying to smother the fire with their bodies. But the van was burning fiercely and the sims who threw themselves on it were instantly engulfed: the flames took their clothes, their limbs, the human and alien skin of them, the payload of green matter inside.

Uncle Ethan managed to start the engine. Cassie checked her watch. "It's time."

"I know."

"Nothing's happening."

Her uncle didn't answer.

"They might have disarmed the igniters."

"I know, Cassie."

"But—"

She felt the detonation before she heard it. The ground bucked and threw a haze of dust into the air. The sound of the explosion was muffled and prolonged, like thunder. A second explosion followed. Sirens wailed throughout the compound, then fell silent. The streetlights flickered and went out. The sudden darkness concealed everything but the flicker of fire from the burning van behind them. Then the wind began to clear the haze, and Uncle Ethan drove by a faint but brightening glow in the eastern sky.

They reached the berm as the fire ignited the last incendiary charges. Cassie saw the explosion: a blinding white starburst followed by a shock wave that rocked the pickup. Uncle Ethan braked. "Keep your head down," he said.

"Why?"

"Shrapnel."

Fragments of metal and glass peppered the roof. Something big hit the glass of the windshield and rolled smoking off the hood. Cassie squeezed her eyes shut and gripped her uncle's hand until the hail of debris stopped.

Behind them, the launch tower stood at the foot of a thickening plume of smoke. Its mirrored petals were skewed; one was missing; another shattered and collapsed as she watched. And the sims had fallen down again. The sky was light enough now that she could see the bodies where they lay, a dense drift of them (she thought of autumn leaves) close to the base of the launch tower. There were only a few here on the rim of the embankment, but one had fallen close to the truck. Uncle Ethan surprised her by getting out of the van and crossing a few yards of gravel and industrial debris to the inert body.

She scooted out and stood behind him as he knelt and put his hand on the sim's throat, checking for a pulse.

"Is it dead?"

"Not yet."

Not yet. But it was clearly dying. The sim gasped and arched its spine, and Uncle Ethan stumbled back a pace. The creature took three deep, stertorous breaths. Its eyes opened but the pupils were motionless and huge. Another breath. Another. Then it exhaled through clenched teeth, a tuneless whistling. No inhalation followed.

Almost dawn, and the desert had taken on a pale clarity. Salt basins and a horizon buckled by black basaltic hills. The wind plucking at this ridge of trash.

We're alone now, Cassie thought.

Her uncle bent over the sim once more. There was something almost tender in the way he touched it. She guessed by the expression on his face that the creature was truly dead. Whatever had inhabited it was gone for good and all.

But her uncle looked grim, even mournful. "I'm sorry," he whispered.

And Cassie was shocked. "Are you *apologizing* to it?"

He stood and brushed his hands together. "I'm not sorry for them." He stared at her—or no, Cassie thought, *through* her, as if at something terrible that no one else could see. "I'm sorry for all of us." Behind him, the burning compound raised flags of smoke. "Now let's get out of here. And, Cassie? You know we can't talk about this. No one can ever know we were here."

The last unspeakable truth, she thought.

33

ANTOFAGASTA

Nerissa came awake in the chair where she had slept. It was only just dawn, faint light seeping through the window of the hotel room. The television was on—she had neglected to turn it off—but all it showed was empty static. There had been a sound, she was sure of it, here in the room, half-heard, indistinct but loud enough to wake her. "Thomas?" she said.

She was not even sure the sound had come from him. A cough, a gasp? She stood, still groggy. There were faint voices from the corridor beyond the door, one of them a woman's voice repeating something like *I've tried and tried and I can't get through*. Nerissa took a tentative step. Her left leg was numb, the ankle tender where she had fallen on it. She limped to the side of the bed where Thomas lay.

What she saw there made no sense: Thomas lying on his back, not breathing. His spine in an arch. His small hands crumpled into fists. His eyes open and unblinking. His pupils as big as two black pennies.

For one lunatic moment it all seemed simply *unreal,* as if someone had stolen her nephew and replaced him with a crude, distorted replica. She heard herself saying his name. She put her hand on his forehead but his skin was cold. And now began the first wave of comprehension, the first approach of the grief and rage that would embrace her like pitiless, implacable giants. Some part of her wanted to call for help—to pick up the phone and demand a doctor. But the saner part of her knew that no doctor could help Thomas now.

Her legs lost their strength. She slid to the floor next to the bed.

She lay there until a patch of sunlight from the window found her. Were there things she should be doing? Yes. But she wasn't able to think clearly about that. She managed to stand up without looking at the bed. She didn't want to see what was on the bed.

There was a tentative knock at the door—the maid, perhaps, though Nerissa had put out the DO NOT DISTURB sign. Of course she couldn't let anyone in. She left the chain latch engaged but opened the door an inch. She saw a woman she didn't recognize—middle-aged, well-dressed, probably American. "I'm sorry," the woman said. "Were you sleeping?"

Nerissa shook her head.

"I was wondering, is your telephone working? Because mine isn't, and I need to get a call through to Indiana."

"You should ask the hotel staff."

"I have! All they do is apologize. No phone, no radio, no television, no *anything*. Not here or anywhere. Or so they say. I thought this was a civilized country!"

"I can't help you," Nerissa said.

She eased the door shut and leaned against the jamb, trying to correlate these new data points. The failure of communication. The death of her nephew. The floral smell she noticed when she turned back to the room.

On the bed, Thomas's body had shrunken. It had, Nerissa thought, *deflated*. Under the rucked-up T-shirt he had slept in, Thomas's rib cage was prominent over an empty sack of sagging skin. Watery green matter had begun to escape from the openings of his body. The bed was damp with it. An emerald-colored drop formed in his left nostril as she watched.

This was not Thomas. There was no Thomas. There had never been a Thomas.

"Ethan," she whispered. "*What have you done?*"

She could not, of course, remain in the room. Not a second longer than necessary. Which clarified things.

She had no luggage. Just the contents of her purse. Without looking again at the bed, she double-checked to make sure nothing was left behind. Nothing was. Nothing human.

She replaced the DO NOT DISTURB / SILENCIO POR FAVOR sign as she left the room. Inevitably, the hotel staff would discover the body of the sim. But by then, perhaps, very little would be left of it.

The concierge—a young woman in freshly-pressed hotel livery—approached her as she crossed the lobby to the door. "Are you going out?"

"Yes," Nerissa said.

"You might want to be careful. There's something bad going on. No radio, no television—the phones don't work. We can't even call a cab! You're American, yes?"

"Yes."

"I saw you come in last night. Are you all right? If you don't mind me asking."

"I'm all right. Thank you."

"What about your little boy—is he with you?"

"No. His uncle took him away."

"Oh, you have family in town?"

"No," Nerissa said. "I have no family."

EPILOGUE

THE LAST
UNSPEAKABLE TRUTH

Biological mimicry blurs the distinction between
a monster and a mirror.

—Ethan Iverson,
The Fisherman and the Spider

Cassie listened to the car radio as she drove to her uncle's apartment. Early dusk and a January blizzard had turned the streets of Buffalo into a maze of ski runs and slalom courses, and visibility was down to half a block. "If you don't need to go out," the newscaster said, "then by all means stay inside and bundle up." Good advice, Cassie thought. But she couldn't follow it. Not tonight. And she hoped Aunt Ris wouldn't use it as an excuse to stay home.

For almost ten years now Cassie's uncle Ethan had lived in a two-bedroom walkup on Antioch Street, in what she still thought of as the old Society neighborhood. For three of those years Cassie had lived with him. Nowadays she rented a small house in Amherst, close to her job in the human resources department of an aviation-parts wholesaler, but far enough from the city that she didn't see Uncle Ethan as often as she would have liked—even in decent weather.

At least she was able to find a parking space reasonably close to his building. The newscaster was talking about the global crisis as she switched off the radio. The Ceylon summit had broken up without a concession from the Chinese or the Atlantic powers; India's ultimatum had not been withdrawn; and it was anyone's guess what the gunboats might do. Her boots left tracks in fresh snow all the way to the lobby door.

Uncle Ethan met her at the door of his apartment. "Come in," he said. "Your aunt's not here yet."

How tired he sounded, Cassie thought. How old.

It had taken them almost a month to get from Chile to the United States in the midst of the global communications blackout. During that time, across the world, thousands had died for lack of emergency services; thousands more had been killed in urban fires that spread catastrophically before they could be reported or controlled. Worst of all was the terrifying absence of information: the panic of not knowing what was happening or why.

But the practical problems had been resolved relatively quickly, or at least it seemed that way, looking back from ten years later. Once it was established that the radio-propagative layer was no longer amplifying and reflecting signals, solutions were available: short- and long-wave direct broadcasting, a system of relay towers, a landline telephone grid. Building and installing the new infrastructure, though costly, had even helped sustain employment through the economic crisis.

Much worse were the consequences that followed from the world's discovery of the truth about the hypercolony. Surviving remnants of the Correspondence Society had supplied long-suppressed research to the League of Nations; the Atacama site had eventually been discovered and analyzed. What had been unspeakable truths for Cassie's family had become common knowledge. The result was an age of unreasoning anxiety. There were no more sims in the world, but schoolchildren and job applicants were still routinely tested for the presence of green matter. The Department of Defense was funding the construction of astronomical observatories. Amicability and peacemaking were increasingly seen as tainted impulses; what seemed most authentically human was everything the hypercolony had suppressed: bellicosity, cynicism, suspicion, aggression. And the price was being paid in blood—in countless small regional conflicts, and now the threat of a larger war. The Chinese had built aircraft that could carry bombs to America, some claimed. And the bombs themselves had grown more deadly as the great nations competed to arm themselves. Cassie sometimes allowed herself to wonder if this was the outcome the hypercolony had wanted all along. *We served our purpose, and now we're being allowed to drive ourselves to extinction.*

Falling in love with Josh had changed her mind about that. Josh was a sweet man, and his sweetness was merely and purely human. It justified much. But he needed to know who she was. She needed to tell him what she had done.

Uncle Ethan had put out a tray of crackers and dip, which made Cassie smile. "Like a party," she said.

"I know it's not a party. But I thought—it's at least an *occasion*. Seeing Ris again. Telling your aunt you're getting married."

"Getting her permission," Cassie said.

"You don't need her permission to get married."

No—not permission to get married. *Permission to speak*, Cassie thought.

She went to the window. Antioch Street was empty, veiled in snow, a page without words.

"Any sign of her?"

"Not yet."

"Well. Don't be too disappointed if she doesn't show up."

"Thank you for letting me invite her here."

"To be honest?" her uncle said. "I never thought she'd agree to come."

It was nine o'clock when a car turned the corner and parked as close to the curb as the mounded snow permitted. From the window Cassie saw her aunt get

out, stand up, tug her cloth cap over her ears, trudge
to the building.

Cassie met her at the door of Uncle Ethan's apartment. "Thank you," Cassie said breathlessly. "Thank
you for doing this."

Aunt Ris embraced her. Cassie pressed her cheek
against her aunt's shoulder, the cloth coat wet with
melting snow.

"Ethan," Aunt Ris said neutrally.

"Hello, Ris. Would you like something to drink?"

"No. I want to hear what Cassie has to say. But
I can't stay long."

"Of course," he said, wincing.

Cassie and her uncle had searched Antofagasta for
weeks before they returned to the States, and for six
months after that Cassie had made increasingly frantic inquiries among Society survivors, until a letter
from her aunt arrived.

I am so sorry, it began. *I spoke to Beth's father—I
thought I should tell him what he needed to know—
and he said you had already been in touch. He gave
me this address. I'm afraid I have bad news.* The letter
went on to describe the death of Thomas. Of the thing
they had called Thomas. One more belated horror
from what had been, for Cassie and her family, an age
of horrors, and in many ways the most devastating
of them all.

Later—when it became possible to re-read the

letter without staining the page with her tears—
Cassie noticed how often her aunt had used the word
"sorry." Seven times in two handwritten pages. She
also noticed that her aunt had neglected to include a
return address.

Which did not deter her from trying to get in
touch. After another six months Cassie received a
letter asking her to stop. *A meeting wouldn't be good
for either of us, I think*. And Cassie ignored it. And
in the summer of that year Aunt Ris finally consented
to see her.

They had lunch together in a cafeteria in Dela-
ware Park. Cassie had been prepared to confront
her aunt's unhappiness, but she was surprised by the
coldness that came along with it—as if all the kindness in her had drained away like water from a holey
bucket. "I'm sorry," Aunt Ris had said (again) at the
end of it. "But I can't do this. Be around you people,
I mean. There are parts of my life I can't get back. I
don't *want* them back. I just want to forget them.
And you're only making it harder."

Still, Cassie hadn't given up. Aunt Ris had agreed
that Cassie could write to her, "If you really need to."
And that was what Cassie had done. She composed
small, careful, impersonal notes and mailed them at
irregular intervals. She hoped her aunt felt obliged to
read them, if not to respond.

Most recently Cassie had written to Aunt Ris about
Josh. Cassie had met Josh through her membership
in the Albright-Knox Art Gallery. A spontaneous

conversation about French impressionism had turned into a first date: thank you, Henri Matisse. Josh was single, thirty years old, an engineer at a Cheektowaga tool-and-die firm that had managed to survive the communications crisis. He had no connection with the Correspondence Society.

Last week Josh had asked Cassie to marry him. And Cassie had agreed. But she didn't want to import a lie into their marriage. That was why she needed to speak to her uncle and her aunt.

Cassie talked a little about Josh, about how much he meant to her and how important it was not to lie to him even about what happened in the Atacama— *especially* about what happened in the Atacama. But she had promised her uncle never to share that secret. That was why she needed his permission . . . and her aunt's permission, too, since Aunt Ris was an essential part of the story.

Cassie would not, of course, speak *publically* about any of this. The existence of the Correspondence Society had become common knowledge, but their role in it was known only to themselves. That wouldn't change. She just needed to be able to speak freely to Josh.

"And how do you suppose he'll react," Aunt Ris said, "when you tell him you're responsible for the state of the world today?"

"That's not fair," Uncle Ethan said. "Cassie's not

responsible for what happened in the Atacama or what came after. If anyone is, I am. I'm the one who pulled the trigger."

"And loaded the gun in the first place. You're right!" She turned to Cassie. "What exactly do you propose to say to Josh? Are you going to tell him the truth about Thomas? The truth about Leo? Are you going to tell him how they used us? Used *you*?"

It wasn't as simple as that. Cassie had given careful thought to the question of what Leo and Thomas had done and why. Both had been agents of the hypercolony. Both had wanted to destroy the parasitized breeding ground. They would have known they needed a human accomplice. At first Leo had chosen Beth to play that role—Beth was motivated and demonstrably capable of violence. But Leo had found a better weapon in Cassie. More reliable. More versatile. And just as easy to manipulate.

Thomas had motivated her from a different direction. He had encouraged her to trust Leo, to follow Leo, to defer to Leo, but more than that, he had given her something to protect, an example of courage she felt obligated to live up to.

Would she say these things to Josh? Of course she would. That was the point. Would it change things between them? She hoped not. "I mean to tell him everything."

"And I'm sure I can't talk you out of it." Aunt Ris nodded. "All right. You have my blessing. I hope it works out. And I hope he understands."

"He will."

"Are you sure about that?"

Cassie hesitated. "I trust him."

"Really? I can't imagine what that's like. I honestly don't remember. But I suppose I envy you a little." Aunt Ris stood up. She hadn't even taken her coat off. "Have a good life, Cassie. I mean it. I wish you the best. But I don't want to see you again. And I resent you asking me to come here to conduct business we could have conducted by mail."

"I needed to talk to both of you . . ."

"No you didn't. You were harboring some idea that we might be reconciled. But that's not possible. Whatever there was between us, your uncle took it away."

"That's not true!"

"But it is."

"I'm sure Uncle Ethan didn't know—"

About Thomas, she meant to say, but her uncle cleared his throat and said, "Stop, Cassie. She's right." He was framed by the window that overlooked Antioch Street, the falling snow, frost on glass. His shoulders were braced but his head was bowed. "I knew exactly what would happen. They told me in great detail."

"*Who* told you?"

"The sims at the breeding ground. They told me about Thomas. They said they would be able to take control of him soon, since the original hypercolony was in a weakened condition. They promised they would let him continue functioning in every way as a normal child. Only I would know the truth. But if the compound was destroyed, Thomas would die. They were explicit about it." He lifted his head and looked directly at Aunt Ris: "They told me you'd spend your life grieving. That you would despise me for it. That Cassie's life would be devastated. That she would blame herself for Thomas's death, no matter what I said."

Aunt Ris stared. "And did you believe them?"

"In the end? Yes."

"But you let the breeding ground be destroyed."

"Was I wrong?"

"No, *don't ask me that.* I can't absolve you, Ethan. Even if what you did was right—it was inhuman."

"Of course it was. That was their mistake. They meant to exploit my humanity. The only way to resist them was to do what seemed inhuman. It was the only weapon I had left."

"What a wonderfully Jesuitical way of reasoning." She opened the door and stepped into the hall.

Cassie took a step after her. "Please . . . Aunt Ris. I never meant to make you unhappy."

"I'm glad you found a way to turn your back on the past. I need to do that too—do you understand? And it will be easier if you stop writing to me."

"Please don't say that!"

"But it's the truth. And it's better to know the truth than to live in a fool's paradise. Isn't that what you believe?"

Her footsteps faded down the stairs.

* * *

"She's mostly right," Uncle Ethan said. "About what I did."

"You should have told me."

"After we destroyed the breeding ground, I thought it didn't matter."

She tried to imagine how it must have been for Uncle Ethan during those awful hours in the Atacama, knowing the destruction of the facility would tear the heart out of his family. She said, "I would have burned it down anyway, with or without your help."

"I knew that, Cassie."

And maybe he *had* known it. Maybe he had guessed it when she told him about Leo. Maybe he had not wanted her to bear the entire burden of that choice. Maybe that was why he had insisted on setting the charges himself.

"The way I see it," her uncle said, "you could get angry and walk out of here, and I wouldn't blame you any more than I blame your aunt. Or you can stay and have a cup of coffee to set you up for the drive home."

"I do have to leave before the roads get much worse. But I'm not angry. And coffee sounds good. Maybe with something stronger in it?"

She phoned Josh to let him know she was all right and that she would be leaving her uncle's place soon.

He said he was watching the war news on TV. Threats and negotiations had given way to an ominous silence. "Be careful driving home," he said. He was hoarse—recovering from a winter cold—but the sound of his voice warmed her.

Buttoning her jacket, she asked Uncle Ethan whether he thought there would be a war.

"I don't know. Without the hypercolony, there's nothing to prevent it."

"Nothing but common sense."

"With which we're not conspicuously well-supplied."

"All the hypercolony ever had of humanity was what it took from us. You taught me that. If it exploited our technology, that's because we have a genius for making things. If it exploited our economy, it's because we have a genius for collaboration. And if we made peace, maybe we have a genius for peace-making."

"We have a genius for war, Cassie. I see evidence of it every day."

"And a genius for hatred. Sure. But also a genius for love."

"Our genius for love almost killed us."

She tucked her hair under her woolen cap. "It made us vulnerable. But it's not a weakness. It's a strength."

"Is it?" He gave her a tentative smile. "I hope you're right."

The temperature had dropped a good ten degrees by the time she got back to the car. The streets were only barely passable. But the snow had stopped falling, the wind had subsided, the sky was clear, and it was possible to see the way ahead.

ACKNOWLEDGMENTS

Informal conversations with friends and family were indispensable to the writing of *Burning Paradise*. It would be impossible to do justice to them all, but I need to single out old friends John S. Barker (for a discussion about the philosophical concept of qualia, which contributed to my conception of the hyper-colony and the simulacra) and Taral Wayne (for countless conversations about cosmology, evolution and the nature of sentience).

Readers might be interested to know that the laser-launch technology I gave to the parasitized breeding ground is a real and potentially practical way of putting small payloads into orbit and is currently under investigation by several agencies and aerospace firms. The Atacama Desert has been suggested as a possible launch site.

As a source on insect behavior and the concept of distributed intelligence, E. O. Wilson's *The Social Conquest of Earth* and *The Superorganism* (written with Bert Hölldobler) were useful. For the daunting task of imagining a largely peaceful twentieth-century Europe, Tony Judt's *Postwar* was an invaluable resource. And while much has been written on the subject of the Atacama Desert, Lake Sagaris's *Bone and Dream* stands out as a deeply thoughtful and wonderfully evocative example.